# Hitts
## &
## Mrs.

# Hitts  & Mrs.

## Lori Bryant-Woolridge

AVON
TRADE

*An Imprint of* HarperCollins*Publishers*

HarperCollins books may be purchased for education, business, or sales promotional use. For information please write: Special Markets Department, Harper-Collins Publishers, Inc., 10 East 53rd Street, New York, NY 10022.

FIRST EDITION

*Designed by Elizabeth M. Glover*

Library of Congress Cataloging-in-Publication Data

Bryant-Woolridge, Lori.
  Hitts & Mrs. / Lori Bryant-Woolridge.—1st ed.
    p. cm.
  ISBN 0-06-054059-1 (alk. paper)
  1. Triangles (Interpersonal relations—Fiction. 2. Women interior decorators—Fiction. 3. New York (N.Y.)—Fiction. 4. Married people—Fiction. 5. Connecticut—Fiction. 6. Architects—Fiction. I. Title: Hitts and Mrs. II. Title: Hits and misses. III. Title.

PS3573.O6863H58 2004
813'.54—dc22

2003065090

04  05  06  07  08  WBC/RRD  10  9  8  7  6  5  4  3  2  1

*This book is dedicated to my parents,*
*General and Mrs. Albert Bryant, Sr.,*
*with all of my love and appreciation.*
*Mom and Dad, because I was so deeply loved,*
*I am able to love in return*
*and that priceless gift has made my life*
*full and rich of all the things that truly matter—*
*truth, love, and peace of soul.*

# Acknowledgments

God has allowed me the privilege of sharing my life with some amazing human beings. I love them and also love who I am when I'm with them. For this, my gratitude is boundless.

Craig, Austin, and Eva, thank you for loving me unconditionally through this life. Know that everything is possible for me because of the laughter and zest you bring to my daily existence.

To my brothers and sister, thanks for your support and for giving me such an exceptional brood of nieces and nephews: Christina, Brooke, Ashley, Michael, Benjamin, Gillian, Veronica, Kylle, Deja, and Alex. From each of you I know to expect good things. Paco, my pride overflows. I applaud all of your vigor and courage as you and your father dutifully serve our country in Iraq. And my terrific godchildren—Roya, Aubree, Tatiana, and Ryan— it is a pleasure watching you blossom.

Thank you Judi, Joyce, and Jonathan for all of your encouragement through the years.

I am also fortunate to have a second family of friends who touch my heart time and time again: Marie Dutton Brown, Patrik Henry Bass, Francesca Neilson, Beverly Hemmings, Cynthia Bagby, Dianna Clarkson, Benita Perkins, Cliff and Gina Strain, the always fabulous Mothers Off Duty and M.O.D. mentees, thank you for your unfailing support. Ameenah Poole, please know that though I have worn the title "mentor" these past ten years, you are the true teacher. I am so proud of you!

Thank you, Alisa Scott, for your medical guidance and Gilles Depardon for your friendship and architectural insight. Curb Gardner, you made my house beautiful and also gave my main character a career. Whitney LaRoche, thanks for your "vision" and love. Ted Bell, your talent touches my soul. Thanks for gracing my pages with your delicious poetry. Claire Wilson, thank you for always keeping the light on in the window. Patti Brown-Christenson, Cheryl Washington, Cheryl Crawford, Nina Cooper, and Gale Monk—the ladies lunch panel of experts—I appreciate your truthful insights. And many thanks to my legal eagles, Susan M. Bryant, Esq., and Francine Thornton Boone, Esq.

A huge thank you to Carrie Feron at Avon Books for picking up this ball and running with it and to Selina McLemore for her always cheerful assistance.

I am so grateful to the many book clubs that read my work and spread the word, as well as the independent booksellers who continue to support me, particularly Robin Green-Cary of Sibayne, Maleta McPherson of Heritage Books and More, Ruth Bridges of Atlantic Bookpost, and Blanche Richardson of Marcus Books.

And finally to you, the reader, may you enjoy this journey with peace in your heart and sunshine on your face.

# Purpose

*The sun's imagination of love*
*and the moon's fantasies*
*combine and entwine into*
*golden rays of light*
*so brilliant, so vivid*
*eclipsing darkness*
*serving only God's purpose*
*in that the moment our eyes*
*capture its luminescence*
*we conceive and breathe*
*visions of love directly*
*into our dreams*
*making us believe*
*in things we cannot see*
*making us believe*
*that if it's up to us*
*flowers will always bloom when*
*birds, butterflies, and bumblebees*
*dance to the rhythm of singing trees*
*that if it's up to us*
*children can walk to school*
*in a village that raises the child*
*that if it's up to us*

## Purpose

*welfare is cared for*
*hunger is fed*
*and greed is shared*
*that if it's up to us*
*homelessness finds a home while*
*domestic abuse becomes homeless*
*drugs are the cure not the cause*
*and peace and heroism*
*replace war and terrorism*
*that if it's up to us*
*Israelis play Twister with Palestinians*
*Crips break bread with the Bloods and*
*Tupac throws dominoes with Biggie*
*that if it's up to us*
*then it's . . . up to us*
*to allow God's light*
*to warm the imagination*
*of our hearts that will create*
*a river of love within our veins*
*so we can love ourselves*
*and then love each other.*

Teddy Bell

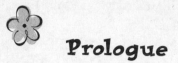

# Prologue

**M**elanie Lorraine Hitts nervously chewed her lower lip as she perused the ballroom of the Mayflower, an elegant, old-money hotel in the downtown section of the nation's capital. She felt strangely detached from the festivities taking place around her. She could smell the faint, fragile scent of gardenias, her favorite flower, scattered generously across the room. Like viewing Christmas tree lights through squinted eyes, she could see the blurry twinkle of candlelight dance gracefully above the tables and the festive and fashionable attire of this well-to-do, multi-generational crowd of African-American achievers. Off in the distance Mel could hear the deejay's current selection, Maxwell's hit song "Matrimony," and the vague but joyous sounds of laughter and fellowship as the people she loved and who loved her gathered to celebrate this important step in her life. Yes, her body was in the room but the sounds, smells, and colors scarcely penetrated the invisible bubble of detachment that separated her from this sparkling affair.

Melanie felt uncomfortably confused. Why now, on this beautiful June night, at a time when she should be blissfully happy and radiantly confident about her future, did she find herself second-guessing her decision to marry? Why, at this late date, did she feel so unsure and tentative about her future with her fiancé Will? Mel couldn't help thinking that her upcoming marriage, just like this engagement party, was a colossal mistake.

"Did I tell you how incredible you look tonight?" Will Freedman asked, his well-spoken baritone voice shaking Mel out of her solitary thoughts. Her short, sexy mop of corkscrew curls playfully framed a heart-shaped face, the perfect canvas for her diminutive pug nose, almond-shaped light brown eyes, and full sensual lips, which were stained in her trademark MAC lipstick, "O." At thirty-two, his fiancée's beauty was as accessible as it was enviable, and Will found the combination irresistible.

Melanie's gown, resembling spun gold, was scattered with one-inch metallic gold- and fuchsia-colored squares. The bright colors enhanced her flawless chestnut-brown skin, sparkling tonight with a thin layer of gold dust. The fitted, spaghetti-strapped gown could not keep secret the awesome curves of her petite body, revealing strong, muscular arms, the result of her rarely missed, three-times-a-week workouts. Skimpy gold sandals graced her pedicured bare feet and the thigh-high split revealed smooth shapely legs. Will loved the way Mel dressed, with a funky freshness that was elegant and at the same time cutting edge.

"Thank you."

"You also look a million miles away," Will said, taking her hand in his. "Whatcha thinking about?"

"That I am so incredibly blessed," Melanie replied wistfully, squeezing Will's hand as she watched her brother-in-law, Xavier, gently dip and twirl her very pregnant sister, Francesca, around the dance floor.

"I know I can't spend enough time on my knees in grateful prayer. I'm engaged to the most incredible woman on earth. My job here at America Online is working out beyond expectations—"

"I *do* love you. You know that, don't you?" Melanie abruptly interrupted in a tone that came very close to desperate.

"Of course I know that, baby. And I've loved you since the first moment we met."

"I would never do anything to intentionally hurt you. You do believe that, right?"

"What's up with you, Mel? The wedding is a month away. Don't tell me you have Popsicle toes already?"

"Will, I . . . It's just that . . . It's nothing, I'm just a little tired, that's all," Melanie said, fear preventing her from honestly expressing her concerns.

"Tired and a little scared, maybe?" Will said, as he pulled Melanie into a protective hug. "Baby, it will be okay. I know this is all happening so fast and you're bone-tired from going back and forth to New York, but it's almost over. Next month we'll be on our honeymoon, starting our perfect life together."

*Perfect. Without flaw or fault.* Melanie turned the word's definition over in her mind. Will's idealized view of their future frightened her. He was full of cotton candy dreams and Melanie was at the sticky center of each one of them. He wanted the two of them to be the perfect couple, create the perfect family, and live the perfect life. Will's confidence and clarity on the issue of their future was unsettling. How could he be so sure of himself—of them—as they embarked on this marriage? How could she possibly live up to all of his great expectations?

"Yo dog," interrupted a boisterous cry. The two turned in the

3

direction of the booming voice. Will's best friend Griffin approached and without warning put his arms around Melanie, dipping her low to the floor and delivering a loud, exaggerated kiss on her cheek. "For future reference, that is how you kiss the bride," he said as he set a laughing and slightly flustered Melanie upright.

"That's enough out of you, Dark Gable," Will said with a laugh as the two men embraced and exchanged their fraternity handshake. Griff's line name was truly fitting, as he had all of the same suave, manly, and handsome characteristics of the original movie star. Though with his tempting green eyes, copper-colored complexion, and sexy man-of-the-world accent, Melanie thought that Griffin was definitely more exotic and visually appealing than Clark.

"Hello, I'm Griff, and you, Melanie Hitts, don't even come close to the description given to me by my boy, here. You are far more lovely and charming than he ever let on."

"So finally I get to meet the *legendary* Griffin Bell—actor, poet, drummer extraordinare. A real throwback to the Harlem Renaissance. When did you get in from LA?" Melanie inquired.

"I came here straight from the airport," Griffin replied. "I almost didn't make it. The film went way over schedule. Let's just hope my small but vitally important part makes the final edit. But I got here as soon as I could. I had to be here for my boy as he announced to the world that he was officially off the market—and with good reason, I might add," Griffin said, winking at Melanie.

"I'm glad you're here for him too," Mel said, tentativeness creeping back in her voice.

"Always. I got to hand it to you, man. You did it, Big Willie style for sure. One day you're saying hello, three months later you're handing her a ring."

"Hey, man, when it's for real, you know," Will said, his voice full of love and excitement.

"I heard that. Now let me see the rock."

Melanie extended her hand to display the two-carat princess-cut solitaire set in platinum. The large stone caught the light and threw off flecks of rainbow-colored fire. Griff whistled appreciatively as Will proudly looked on. Mel glanced down at her ring as well, but couldn't seem to muster up the satisfaction she'd felt when Will had placed it on her finger six weeks ago. Her hand, like her heart, felt depressingly heavy.

"Excuse us, time to party," Will announced. "Grab yourself a honey, man. Mel's got plenty of single friends here." Will led his future wife to the dance floor and took her into his arms. Mel closed her eyes and tried to silence her concerns as they swayed to Bobby Caldwell's forever classic, "What You Won't Do For Love." She leaned into his six-foot-three, 230-pound body and attempted to relax. While in her early years she had preferred well-sculpted men with rock-hard bodies, Mel now loved Will's softer, more pliant torso. Experiencing a Will Freedman hug was one of life's little joys—like falling into a cozy rumpled bed at the end of a long hard day.

Griffin watched with the others as Will glided Melanie gracefully around the floor. After letting them dance two stanzas solo, Mel's father, Lawrence, gleefully cut in to dance with his daughter, while Elizabeth Hitts stepped into the arms of her soon-to-be son-in-law. After a quick glance around the room, Griff sauntered over to a feminine spectacle of well-placed curves standing alone near the bar.

"Hello there. Care to dance?"

His low alluring voice captured the attention of Melanie's best friend, Candace Bennett, forcing her to turn around. Her smile, however, stopped short of genuine as she gave its owner the once-over. Her experienced eye immediately took inventory—Timex watch, poly/wool blend suit, inexpensive leather shoes—and within seconds earmarked him as a Filene's Basement dweller. This brother represented the male economy model, which like cheap champagne could be found overflowing the bar at any chickashay downtown nightclub. Thanks, but no thanks. When it came to men, Candace Bennett was interested strictly in the luxury edition.

"I don't think so," Candace responded in a tone that, despite the slight upward turn of her lips, translated into, *I can't believe you even had the audacity to approach me.* She really wished her lover, Frank, had come down from New York with her, but he was too much of a coward when it came to public displays of their relationship. He claimed that as a prominent lawyer he had to guard his professional and media reputation, but Candace knew that he was simply too afraid that someone might see them together and run back and tell his wicked witch of a wife.

"Hey, it's just a dance. I ain't askin' you to be my babymama," Mr. Economy said, breaking into street vernacular, no doubt to further irritate her. "And you got ashy ankles anyway. Girl, a little dab will do ya."

"Negro, please," Candace said, sucking her teeth and rolling her eyes before turning her back to him. She could feel her face warm with the glow of embarrassment. Candace waited for him to leave before glancing down at her feet. *Damn,* she thought as she hurried off to the ladies' room in desperate search of some Jergens.

Griff could only laugh. Typical uppity sister. Always steppin' over Mr. Wrong Pedigree in search of Mr. Right Bank Account. When will they learn that the most expensive and visually appealing dessert ain't always the sweetest?

Their caustic encounter was replaced by the distinctive clink of sterling silver on fine crystal. Griff looked up to see Melanie's parents standing at the microphone with champagne flutes in their hands. The room began to settle down as guests drifted toward the bandstand.

"May I have your attention?" Lawrence's request boomed through the speakers. "As father of the bride-to-be, it is my *honor* to propose the first official toast to the future bride and groom. It is also my *duty* to warn this young man that if he does anything to hurt my baby, he'd best head for the hills." He paused as the crowd chuckled. "Seriously, I know we're well past the day of arranged marriages, but I could not have picked a better man for my Melanie.

"Let me brag a little bit here. Will graduated magna cum laude from Morehouse College, went on and got his MBA from Wharton School of Business, and is now a vice president for one of those big Internet companies. Even more important than all those important credentials, he is a man of integrity and I respect him. God bless you kids, Elizabeth and I are proud of you both. We wish you a lifetime of love and happiness," he concluded, raising his glass.

"Love and happiness," the guests chimed in unison.

"And laughter," Candace called out as she slinked to the stage in her cleavage-popping, butt-hugging, waist-clinching ensemble. It wasn't just the bright red color that set her dress off from the others, it was the way it embraced every curve and sway of her body with an over-the-top, hot-on-the-verge-of-vulgar familiarity. Candace Bennett put the "sin" in sensual. A solid size ten cruising toward twelve, she had squeezed every inch of her voluptous, brickhouse body into a size eight, making the rest of Mel's friends appear modestly attired in the formal equivalent of housedresses.

Candace reached for the microphone, lightly brushing Lawrence's hand while serving him her killer half smile, half smirk. Lawrence, wearing the dumbfounded look of cornered prey, grinned broadly as he released the microphone, while Melanie's mother frowned. This was vintage Candace. She could strip the cool off any man in the room while simultaneously working the last nerve of every female. To look at her you'd never guess that she had such an ambitious and cunning legal mind. She was a top litigator at the small but prestigious law firm of Margent, Katz, Crawford and Thames, and had been Melanie's best friend and closest confidante for nearly ten years.

"Laughter and lots of it is something that makes my girl here happy. I've known Melo, as I like to call her, since our junior year at Hampton University, and she has always had a zest for life that keeps her curious and open to new challenges. I don't think she could have picked a better partner than Will. All the best to you both. Keep the laughter flowing. And most of all, *stay* Melo."

Candace finished as another glass clinked, signaling the couple to kiss. She looked out at the two of them, genuinely happy for her best friend, but unable to stop the twinge of envy that was tickling her ego. Once again, Melo had it all, and here she was, alone and unescorted at yet another important affair.

Will gathered Candace in a grateful hug before stepping to the mike and gesturing Mel to join him. She looked out into the crowd of friends and family and silently began to question herself.

*What is wrong with me?* Will was the kind of man most women dreamed of and few were lucky enough to find. He was intelligent, compassionate, and responsible. Most importantly, he loved her with a quiet gentleness that made her feel treasured and secure. Why wasn't that enough?

*Because, all romantic poems and flowers aside, the truth is, we barely know each other,* Mel admitted to herself. She felt her heart begin to crumble as she stood viewing what could only be described as a human collage of gentle dignity. Romare Bearden could not have pieced together a more handsome work of art detailing the simple perfection of imperfection. From a slightly gap-toothed but sincere grin that penetrated his friendly brown eyes to his smooth bald head, everything about this man whispered quiet strength and genuine warmth. His robust body, dipped in creamy dark chocolate and wrapped in a navy blue Armani suit, crisp white shirt, and silk tie, stood erect with pride and integrity as he addressed the crowd.

"Thank you all so much for being here," Will said. "I wish my parents had lived to see this blessed day. It's times like these when being an only child is tough, but I've come to love Melanie's family as my own. . . ." Consumed with emotion, he paused as tears of both sadness and joy rolled down his cheeks.

"It is true that Melanie and I haven't known each other long, but it doesn't take years to realize when you've found the missing piece of your soul. Our minds and bodies have a lifetime to get to know each other, but our hearts have already been friends and lovers for years," Will said, turning to face Melanie, taking her hands into his.

"Baby, I look at you and know why I was put on this earth. You have me locked in a place where I am grateful to be," he said, reaching in his pocket and pulling out a key tied to a white satin ribbon. "This is the key that unlocks the place where my heart is home—our new house in Mitchellville, Maryland."

Will's extravagant surprise stunned Melanie into paralysis. Overcome by emotion, she could only stare blankly at him as the tears ran down her cheeks. Every sweet word Will spoke, every loving look he sent her way simply made the situation more intolerable. She had to do this here and she had to do it now.

His announcement clinched her decision. She was certain that Will deeply loved her, but how well did he really know her? If he truly understood her, he wouldn't have bought a house without her knowledge, even if it was located in the upscale, predominately black suburb. He'd know that she had not labored to earn her master's degree from the New York School of Interior Design or paid her dues apprenticing in upscale furniture stores to make a career of choosing tile and curtains for suburban housewives.

Melanie knew that if she really was to become a world-class interior decorator, Washington, D.C., was not the place to work. She needed to return to New York, the internationally recognized breeding ground for trend-setting ideas. She'd loved being back in Manhattan this spring and had high hopes that the recent collaboration with her architect friends to design and decorate an entertainment lounge for the prestigious Kips Bay Decorator Show House would pay off.

Melanie had no intention of staying in D.C. She'd only come back following her father's heart attack last year. Even though she'd met and fallen in love with Will during her prolonged visit, the move was always meant to be temporary. If Will didn't realize this about her, what else didn't he know? And what important things about him did she not understand?

Melanie found herself reaching not for the ribbon dangling in Will's hand, but for the microphone. She cleared the tears from her throat and turned to face the crowd. Feeling nauseous and dizzy, Mel prayed not to faint or do anything to embarrass herself.

"Will Freedman is a truly wonderful human being," she began. "And any woman would be lucky to have him," she said, her eyes pleading with him to believe her.

Will merely smiled, seeming confused by Melanie's anxious demeanor. Mel forced herself to look directly into his eyes as she delivered her crushing news.

"I do love you, but I . . . I . . . can't marry you."

Will stood there, clearly consumed by confusion and dread. The collective gasp and shocked reaction to Melanie's announcement slowly rumbled around the room before settling into a muffled silence much like the eerie aftermath of an avalanche. Everyone, including Candace, the woman Mel confided everything to, was shocked by this totally unexpected turn of events.

"My decision not to get married has nothing to do with Will. It's *me*. I'm just not ready for this. I thought I was, but . . ." Melanie's voice trailed off as she tried unsuccessfully to keep her tears under control. She kept her focus on the crowd, unable to stomach the anguish in Will's eyes.

"I only want what's best for Will. He is entitled to someone who can love him like he deserves to be loved."

Melanie sobbed while quickly removing her engagement ring. She took Will's hand, placed the diamond in his palm, and gently closed his fingers around the ring. "I'm so sorry," she whispered.

She took one last look and then swiftly vacated the room, with Candace, Francesca, and her mother following closely behind.

*Don't look back,* Melanie commanded herself. There was no thrill to be found in watching this particular bridge burn.

# Chapter 1

**M**el lit the candle, settled back onto the couch, and assumed the position. Slowly she dipped her chin to her chest, inhaled deeply, and then exhaled as her head rolled back. She repeated this action five times to regulate her breathing before settling into her daily meditation. Repeating her mantra, "I am," Mel waited expectantly to be overtaken by the deliciously serene feeling of melting within herself.

Just as she began to feel herself slipping deeper into the comforting and familiar void, the shrill ring of the telephone shocked her back into the room. Melanie tried to ignore the interruption, concentrating on her breath and chanting her mantra with added determination.

The phone continued to ring and, surrendering in frustration, Melanie bounded from her seat and pounced on the offensive distraction. By the time she reached the handset, the caller had disconnected. She glanced down at the caller ID. It was a name and number she recognized. It was the same name and number she'd been trying to avoid for weeks.

The six weeks she'd been back in New York, living with Candace on Manhattan's Lower East Side, Melanie had successfully, though painfully, evaded any prolonged communication with Will. When she'd first left D.C., just a week following the disastrous engagement party, he had called or e-mailed at least twice a week, begging for some kind of rationale for her unexplained decision and hasty departure. Mel had put off his requests for clarification with a lame plea for time and space. She wasn't ignoring his outreach to be cruel. Melanie simply didn't know what to say to the man whose dreams she'd shattered.

"I left some clothes on your bed for you to send to your Mississippi 'kinfolk,'" Candace said, walking into the room dressed in her Saturday workout clothes and carrying a spoon and a pint of coffee Häagen-Dazs ice cream.

"Thanks. I'm sending their box down this week," Mel said, speaking of the rural family she'd "adopted" through the Box Project, an organization established in 1962 to help fight poverty in America.

"Who was on the phone?"

"Take a wild guess."

"Eventually you're going to have to talk to the boy. You can't go on dodging Will like he's some annoying bill collector."

"I don't know what to say to him, Candy. He wants answers and I don't have any to give him. I really can't talk about this now. I was just getting ready to meditate."

"Not this time, Melo. You've been holed up in my apartment for weeks refusing to talk to me or your parents and hiding from the one person you really owe an explanation to. I don't get you, Melanie Hitts. You've snagged a successful, handsome man and you're willing to throw it all away because he had the *audacity* to buy you a house? What the hell kind of sense does that make?" Candace asked in a tone underscored with irritation.

"The issue is not buying the house, it's the fact that he didn't tell me."

"Correct me if I'm wrong, but isn't a surprise *supposed* to be kept secret?"

"This isn't as simple as being disappointed with some gift. Look at the reality of the situation, Candace. Will and I met in February, got engaged after three months, and were supposed to get married two weeks ago just five months after our first hello. Everything happened so fast—too fast. Will insisted on a July wedding, my mother was intent on throwing that stupid engagement party, which was more about her than me, and I was coming back and forth to New York working my butt off on the show house and worrying about my dad the entire time. I didn't have time to really think about all of the ramifications of my decision. It was like I was caught up in the eye of this monster hurricane and the next thing I know I'm standing up in front of a hundred people engaged to a man I barely know," Melanie tried to explain.

"So why call off the engagement—in public, no less? Why not just postpone the wedding?" Candace continued to probe.

"Because it just felt like the right thing to do. Do you know what I was thinking about the entire time I was standing up there? Divorce. In five generations of the Hitts family, there has never been a failed marriage, and all I kept thinking was that mine would be the first."

"I'm your best friend and you never once mentioned to me that you were having second thoughts," Candace pointed out.

"I thought they were just normal jitters. I knew that I loved Will. I thought things would be okay."

"You love him and it's been damn obvious that he worships your dirty draws. That's not enough?"

"It's not that simple," Melanie repeated slowly, her frustration apparent. How could she make her parents and friends understand how she felt? It wasn't that she didn't *want* to be married to Will. Until William Freedman, Melanie had met no other man with whom she'd even considered sharing her life. It was simply that she didn't know *how* to be married to him, or to anyone, for that matter. While her kinfolk held up traditional beliefs and customs as the glue that kept family together, to Melanie they represented just the opposite. In Mel's mind, the conventions of married life symbolized the strangulation of her independence and individuality—two vitally important characteristics in the makeup and survival of any creative person's soul.

"If you ask me, you're being a real chickenshit about this whole marriage thing."

"But I didn't ask you, Candace. You know, *dating* married men doesn't make you an authority on marriage," Mel snapped angrily.

"I may not know a lot about being married, but I can tell you this: Black men like Will Freedman come few and far between. You have no idea how lucky you are. Do you know how many women dream about that whole love at first sight thing? Women who would love being in your situation," Candace stated, dramatically waving her spoon in the air for emphasis.

"Candy, my situation isn't one to be envied at this point," Melanie said, her voice tainted with distress. "But you're right, I really screwed up. I should have never gone through with the party if I had doubts and maybe I shouldn't have broken up with Will in public, but I did. And it's over, and now I have to move on with my life." Her thoughts were once again interrupted by the telephone. She felt herself bristle with apprehension. "If it's Will or my parents, I'm not home," she said.

"Sorry, you're on your own," Candace said before heading toward the kitchen.

"Hello," Melanie said, checking the caller ID before picking up the handset.

"Melanie Hitts? Paco Benjamin from the BenAlex Design Group."

"Yes. I know your work. I love your bar in the Tribeca Royal," she commented, speaking of the city's latest rage in trendy hotel watering holes. "Definitely an inspiring use of color."

"Thank you. I'm calling because I was really inspired by *your* work in the Kips Bay Show House. You've been all the buzz since the opening night gala, though you disappeared right after the party. Look, we're looking to expand and bring on a new designer and I think you fit the bill nicely. Would you be interested in getting together next Tuesday afternoon at one to discuss it?"

Melanie bit her lip while writing down the directions in an effort to keep her excitement from spilling into the receiver. "That would be great. Thank you. How did you find me?"

"When the advance copy of September's issue of *Interior Design* hit my drafting table, I took it as a sign that I *had* to talk with you, so I called the architects you worked with and they gave me this number. Having your entertainment room so prominently featured was quite a coup. Congratulations."

"Thanks," Mel replied. She had absolutely no idea what he was talking about, but she intended to call her design partners to find out. "I'll see you Tuesday."

She quickly got Jacques Augustan on the phone and pumped him for information about the magazine and Paco Benjamin. The news about both was encouraging. According to Jacques, the influential *Interior Design* had not only showcased her work, but called her "a young designer worth keeping an eye on." Paco was one of two partners at the BenAlex Design Group, also a firm with a "must watch" alert. Jacques informed her that they were small— two partners, two designers, and a couple of young assistants—but growing fast. At the moment they were the best-kept secret in the hospitality market, but in his informed opinion, were about to catch fire. Her friend's bottom-line advice was that for Mel, BenAlex was the way to go. The firm was small enough to groom her, but high-profile enough to get her noticed.

Melanie hung up the phone feeling like she'd just done a swan dive from pity's platform with an elastic tether tied to her waist. Just moments ago, while discussing her painfully aborted romance, she'd been free-falling toward the emotional ground with her heart in hand. Now, fifteen minutes later, she was bouncing skyward, riding a momentary adrenaline rush and clinging to her professional bungee cord.

Melanie took a deep breath as she walked over to the couch and resumed her meditation position. She gazed into the candle's flickering flame, feeling a desperate need to slip into the gap, center herself, and balance this agonizing sentimental seesaw.

# Chapter 2

**M**elanie wasn't sure if it was the bright August sun pouring through her bedroom window or NYC's unrelenting triple-H weather—hazy, hot, and humid—already in full scald that woke her. It was minutes past six o'clock, still a half an hour away from her radio wake-up, courtesy of the local smooth jazz station. She yawned and considered going back to sleep, but with the ceiling fan providing little relief from the sticky heat, a cool shower proved a far more powerful temptation. Damn Candace and her unwavering aversion to air-conditioning.

Mel stood under the invigorating spray and let the brisk water wash away the sleepy cobwebs, allowing her to concentrate on the tasks that lay ahead. First up on her To Do list was to stop by the post office and mail the package to the Hawkinses, her Box Project relatives. She'd learned about the organization in college when her sorority, Alpha Kappa Alpha, adopted a family in Louisiana as a community service project. After graduating, she decided to take on her own family and each month Melanie sent Mamie Hawkins much-needed supplies to help feed and clothe her seven children in Greenville,

Mississippi. It was a simple task that took very little effort but made Melanie feel good about making a difference in somebody else's life.

Following her detour, she would head straight to the office. Today, like all the rest of these past four weeks, would be grueling and nonstop—more eight-to-ten than nine-to-five—and Mel loved every minute.

Now a full-fledged designer, Mel had been hired to work with BenAlex Design Group's residential clients. Initially she was disappointed, feeling like she'd been once again relegated to homeowners' hell, but with subsequent reflection Melanie decided that this was definitely a one step back, two steps forward opportunity. The reputation of the BenAlex Design Group was growing steadily among the coveted chain of wealthy clientele, particularly among New York's young new millionaires with adventurous attitudes and disposable income. By working with the Wall Street princes and enterprising dot.com kings, the funky fashion divas and heroes of hip hop, Melanie realized that she would have greater opportunities to unleash her design savvy and creative risk-taking. These jobs would become her stepping-stones to resorts, museums, and the larger, more important projects she intended to become known for.

After years of visualizing success, Melanie was finally on the path to achieving her dream of becoming a world-class interior designer. She kept reminding herself to stay focused, have faith, and patiently allow God's plan for her to unfold, a plan which was infinitely more magnificent than she could ever imagine for herself. In her heart she knew that it was only a matter of time before she would progress to the hospitality side of the firm.

Already she had her finger in the mix, assigned the task of helping to pull together ideas and materials for this week's presentation to the highly regarded firm of Carlson and Tuck. Even though she'd begun work on her first solo project—a costly makeover for a summer home in East Hampton—Melanie was most excited about the potential Vogue Belize job. While she was simply coordinating the furniture and accessories for the private balconies of this luxury resort, it kept her in the loop and gave her direct exposure not only to her firm's partners but to the decision-making employees of one of the most prestigious architectural companies in the business.

Melanie finished her shower and decided to air dry, enjoying the cool clash of damp skin and artificial wind. She pulled on a light cotton kimono robe and turned on her laptop. It had become part of her morning ritual to check her e-mail as her bosses, Paco Benjamin and Whitney Alexander, sent daily morning messages with project updates to each of the firm's designers. While her computer booted up, Melanie laid out her work attire. She always wore stylish but comfortable clothes, as her day often sent her traipsing all over the city in search of the perfect "whatever."

When she heard the you've-got-mail signal, Melanie turned her attention from the closet to her computer. She read down the list of e-mails, noting her daily communication from work and happily recognizing several of the e-mail addresses as contacts from the East Hampton house renovation. There was also a message from COCOMOM, a.k.a. her sister, Francesca, and one screen name that caused her heart to drop. Melanie read all the others, taking notes and writing down dates in her day planner.

Upon completion, she paused, took a deep breath, and double clicked on STILLWILL.

Subj: Hello
From: STILLWILL
To: VINTAGEJEWEL

Hello Melanie,

I saw you on-line yesterday. It took me five minutes to compose a witty opening line to instant message you, but I couldn't drum up enough courage to click SEND. I guess I was afraid that like my phone calls and other messages, I'd be left hanging. I just sat there staring at your name on my AOL buddy list, feeling strangely comforted by the knowledge that you and I were in the same space for those few minutes.

As I sat there, I came to the sad realization that in all this deafening silence between us these past months, I can no longer hear the sweet sound of your voice. I've been trying to let go and get on with my life, but baby, I have to tell you that the void I feel without you is unbearable. Knowing you are a part of my life is what makes me feel complete and whole. I desperately want and need to feel connected to you again.

Please, Melanie, we have to talk. Tell me what I can do to fix this for you so we can get on with our life together. We are meant to be, Mel. I truly believe this. You said you love me and God knows that I still love you. I won't give up on us. I can't.

Today and forever,
Will

Melanie felt the pain and guilt over her failed engagement bubble its way to the surface. She had deceived herself into believing that by throwing herself into work, she could successfully ignore the responsibility for her actions. Will's ardent plea for communication was a melancholy reminder of the popular maxim: You can run but you can't hide.

Melanie sat back, closed her eyes, and heard the rhythmic drip of the shower faucet. She felt her face grimace in strained concentration as she listened for the voice she desperately needed to hear, but only the quiet whir of blades cutting through air breezed through her ears. Melanie felt tears pooling around the lower lids of her eyes. She could no longer hear Will's distinct sound and took this to be a definitive sign that their short and bittersweet stay in coupledom was over.

With doleful determination, she maneuvered the arrow to the right of the screen and pushed the REPLY button. Through teary eyes Mel watched as a fresh "write mail" template appeared. After thirty-five minutes of composing and editing her reasons why, of documenting and deleting her excuses for why not, Melanie gave up and erased it all. Finally she bit her lower lip and proceeded to tap out the most difficult and unavoidably hurtful words she'd ever written:

Dear Will,

There's nothing to fix and no one to blame. Sometimes love is simply not enough. Please don't contact me again.

To soften the blow, she signed her note *Love, Melanie.* Mel quickly reconsidered and then deleted the affectionate expression, asking the same question Tina Turner had turned to gold: What's love got to do with it?

After a long and laborious morning meeting, Will was anxious to return to the privacy of his office cubicle. He tossed his yellow legal pad on the desk and sat down to decipher his notes. His concentration held for approximately three minutes before he found himself leaning back in his chair, hands behind his head, searching out the white noise the company piped in to filter out extraneous hubbub. After one grew accustomed to it, the light humming disappeared unnoticed into the atmosphere, but there were times when Will actively listened for it, finding the monotonous sound soothing.

As usual, thoughts of Melanie clogged his mind, usurping all available space for anything work-related. He knew that if he could just see her face again he'd be all right. And while Mel's brutally direct response to his e-mail this morning dismayed him, its brevity also breathed hope into his sagging heart.

*I am losing it. She tells me not to contact her again and I read hopefulness into the situation? This is the same woman who broke up with me in front of a room full of people, left me and the life we were planning together, and two months later has yet to give me any reasonable explanation for her actions. What kind of chump am I?*

*A chump still in love with a woman I'm certain still loves me,* he answered himself, feeling his anger dissipate as quickly as it had erupted. While Will fully acknowledged his feelings of hurt and confusion, he would not allow himself to give life to his anger, knowing it would only eat away at his soul, leaving him as emotionally barren as his empty house for sale in Mitchellville.

Will knew full well that most men, and some women, would

call him soft for his willingness to cling to any scrap of hope Melanie threw his way. But they couldn't know how important she was to his ability to *live* life, not just plod through it. A huge part of him died nearly ten years ago—a plane crash taking from him not only his beloved parents but also his sense of security and belonging. Yet in Mel's arms he felt reborn. No woman prior or since had made him feel that way. Life with Melanie Hitts meant escape from the prison of his solitude and he refused to give up on his heavenly stay of execution.

Understanding Melanie as well as he did, Will was certain that the short and impersonal communiqué was her way of running from a situation that continued to perplex and frighten her. A patient and empathetic man, Will decided that if Melanie needed more time to work out her issues, he would give it to her. He would honor her request and not contact her, at least for the moment. But he was also self-respecting and tenacious, and as far as he was concerned, Melanie Hitts was living on borrowed time. Will fully intended to make good on his pledge to not give up on the two of them. They were meant to be together and he was capable and damn sure willing to do any- and everything necessary to reclaim the woman he loved.

# Chapter 3

"**I** definitely think it's the right thing to do, honey. And now is the right time. Look at this," John Carlson said as he handed his wife the real estate section of the *New York Times*. "It's a seller's market. Real estate around Connecticut is booming. We can more than double what we paid for this house."

"This is not just a house, John, and it's certainly more than just an investment. This is our *home*," Sharon Carlson replied, emotion causing her voice to waver.

"Home is where you make it, not the bricks and mortar you make it with. We bought the apartment on Central Park West over three years ago. It's time we moved in. Let's start taking advantage of New York City's good life before it's too late."

Sharon looked out over the deck and onto their lakefront property. Immediately she was transported to a peaceful, relaxing Louisiana bayou. The hydrangeas, daylilies, and mountain laurels were in magnificent bloom, peeking colorfully over the split-rail fence. A gaggle of geese floated aimlessly under the feathery foliage of two large weeping willows, while the empty hammock tied to their trunks rocked in the gentle breeze. Her hazel-green eyes became fixated on the rowboat tied to the small dock and floating on the watery edge of their grounds. What could Central Park offer her that she didn't already have in her own backyard? The Carlsons' five-bedroom, saltbox-style farmhouse was built on over an acre and a half of prime wooded real estate in the lush community of northern Stamford, Connecticut. How could John even imagine leaving this serene splendor of nature for the cement thicket of New York City?

"I thought we were already living a good life."

"Sweetheart, we are, but we've lived here for almost fifteen years and we certainly don't need this big house for just the two of us. It's time for an exciting change of venue. Think about it. Broadway, Times Square, Lincoln Center, museums, art galleries, and some of the finest restaurants in the world—right at our front doorstep."

At forty-four years old, Sharon rarely craved the kind of excitement New York's social scene had to offer. And on the rare occasions she did, she was a mere fifty-minute train ride from the city. She loved this place. Summering in Nantucket or accompanying John on his business trips around the world always left her eager to return to the familiar sanctity of her home. She had all the thrills she needed right here in Stamford. Sharon was a member of the local tennis team, competing twice a week during the season, was a volunteer for various charities, and helped organize the annual fundraisers for the community's literacy program and the Stamford Museum and Nature Center. A self-imposed loner, she didn't have many close friends in town, but those she had, like Joe and Myrtle Nunn, whom she and John played golf with once a month, and her doubles partner, Cathy Callahan, would be missed terribly.

"Why is moving such a priority for you all of a sudden?"

"It's not so sudden. I've been thinking about this for a while now. After nearly twenty years of designing buildings around the world, I'm burned out. I feel like I'm losing my edge—the punch that makes my work unique. I need to infuse myself with New York's energy and get my creative spark back," John admitted to his wife with more honest emotion than he'd shared in years.

"You're in New York all the time. You stay in the company apartment at least twice a week. Why do we have to move?" Sharon asked.

"I stay because work keeps me in the city late and constantly commuting back and forth wears me out. Honey, the truth of the matter is that I'm fifty years old and living out here is beginning to make me feel ancient. I'm not ready to be put out to pasture, Sharon. I really want this. I *need* this change," John said softly as he gently massaged his wife's slender neck and ran his fingers through her ash-blond hair.

Sharon turned and gazed intently into the face of her husband. Staring back at her was the rugged sex appeal and sophistication of Harrison Ford, Richard Gere's smooth boyish charm and thick can't-wait-to-get-my-fingers-tangled-up-in-those-salt-and-pepper curls, and the mischievous eyes and creative intellect of Warren Beatty. My God, how she loved this man! If this was what John felt he needed, how could she deny him?

"I'll call the real estate agent on Monday," she conceded with a sigh.

"Thank you, sweetheart." John stood up from the table and tightly hugged his wife. "This move will be a brand-new start for us. It will be great, honey. I promise," John said as he kissed her on the lips before heading down to the pool house to change for his daily swim.

*Great for whom?* Sharon wondered as she cleared the breakfast dishes and stepped back into the house. She stacked the dishes into the dishwasher and mechanically cleaned off the counters as she mulled over her decision. With less than half an hour of discussion, she had once again acquiesced to the wishes of her spouse, this time agreeing to sell the home and life she loved.

*But John says he really needs this*, she told herself as she swallowed her disappointment and tears. *And how much of a sacrifice is it really if we'll be able to spend more time together?*

As she finished straightening the kitchen, Sharon continued to rationalize the situation and sweep her pain and anger into the corner of her heart that stored the countless other sacrifices she'd made throughout their marriage. Over the past two decades she had willingly given up her life to meet the needs of John's reputation as internationally renowned architect. Yes, she had made personal forfeits that sometimes pained and saddened her, but they'd certainly been worth it. In retrospect only one had been truly traumatic. The others had been relatively small when compared to the rich and joyful life John had afforded her.

Sharon watched from the window as John's toned and tanned body sliced through the icy water of their lagoon-shaped pool. John liked to do his laps in near-frigid water, claiming it invigorated him. Even though she was a good swimmer, Sharon rarely used the pool, opting instead to sunbathe in the surrounding natural rock garden. She observed his smooth, even stroke take him from one end of the pool to the other and then watched as he climbed out and dried himself. Surely he'd miss his daily laps if they moved or the lazy summer afternoons he spent floating in the rowboat while she read aloud to him.

*Let's talk about the real reason you don't want to move,* directed a small but forceful voice inside her. Sharon tried to push the thoughts back into the Pandora's box from which they came, but like a prankster's can of snakes, they kept popping up, bringing with them a fresh onslaught of the tears.

*Okay. Okay,* Sharon silently yelled back. The truth was that yes, she did love this home dearly, but it wasn't leaving this particular house that pained her so, it was leaving what it had come to represent. When she and John moved to northern Stamford, Sharon brought high hopes of fulfilling her longtime dream. She held on to and fostered her desire for twenty years, refusing to let it wane, allowing it to sustain her during all the lonely stretches of time when John was away on business. In her mind, as long as they continued to live in this house, her wish and the possibility of it being realized lived on as well. How could she ever explain to John that moving into Manhattan was not about giving up her home? It was about giving up the one dream that had made all her sacrifice tolerable.

"Make it the diamond watch. I don't care which one. You pick something out and send it directly to the house," John instructed his jeweler. "The card? Say, 'You'll always be my girl. I love you, John.'"

He hung up his cell phone, feeling uncomfortably conflicted. While a six-thousand-dollar diamond timepiece was a small token for the woman who had unselfishly given him the life he'd always wanted, John knew that his gift came just as much from a guilty conscious as a grateful heart. He leaned back into his poolside chaise, unable to curb the renegade twinge of guilt rising within him. John had long since eliminated that particular sentiment from his repertoire of emotions. Guilt was wasted energy, sapping valuable concentration that could go into his work. But every now and then the feeling defied him and bobbed to the surface, riding his emotional tide like a message in a bottle.

He knew that Sharon didn't want to leave Stamford, just as he knew that she wouldn't fight his decision. She never did. In twenty-three years of marriage, his wife had always been predictably compliant. There was an inherent fragility about Sharon that often left John feeling and acting overly protective. Sometimes he felt more like a parent than a spouse. And even though he had gotten used to being in total control of their life together, there were times when John wished Sharon would display more backbone and fight for her desires. Yet John also realized that this freedom to act unilaterally in both his personal and professional life had been the number one factor in his meteoric rise to the top of the architectural tower.

John Remington Carlson was a talented man of creative vision. His lifelong professional desire to erect standing monuments of functional art was second only to his wish to live the solid, stable personal life he'd never known as a child. Even as a teenager, John had been determined to prove that the Carlson family legacy of alcoholism and divorce ended at his threshold. He vowed to never repeat the selfish and hurtful mistakes of his womanizing father. In all their years together, out of respect for his wife and dread for his past, John had successfully curbed any attraction he felt toward other women.

Together they had built a gratifying existence, and while Sharon frequently credited him for saving her from a lifetime of being ignored, in many ways John felt that she was the legitimate hero. He was so fortunate to have found such an understanding and unselfish mate and was conscientious about not taking her unfailing support for granted. Through the years John had been a responsible and loving spouse, working hard to provide her with the best that life had to offer. He'd bought her jewelry, exotic vacations, luxury cars, and even had a suite in a hotel he'd built in Dubai named after her.

*You've given her everything except the one thing she really wanted,* he thought, unable to will away his annoying guilt pangs. John looked up into the kitchen window and saw Sharon staring down on him. He blew her a kiss and smiled. Grateful love was a heavy burden to bear for both giver and receiver.


"You've been going back and forth on choosing a Realtor for three weeks now. If we want to be living in Manhattan by the holidays, Sharon, we have to get moving on this. Now I have to get to the office. We'll finish discussing this at dinner," John said, ending their breakfast discussion as he grabbed his Coach briefcase and headed toward the garage door.

Sharon heard the electric door rise and John's Lexus slowly back down the gravel drive. She poured herself another cup of Earl Grey, tore open a packet of Equal, and watched the white powder slowly descend into her cup and dissolve into the hot liquid. She picked up the lemon wedge and squeezed so hard that a lone seed popped loose from the pulp and flew across the table. This morning's discussion with her husband, like every other conversation they'd had about moving, had left her feeling as steamed as her morning cup of tea.

She had agreed to sell the house and move, but Sharon refused to let John rush her. She fully intended to spend one last Christmas in her home. If that meant postponing Realtors and contractors or taking her time to find the perfect decorator, so be it. In Sharon's view, the longer it took to move, the greater the chance that John might change his mind.

The phone rang and before answering Sharon waited long enough to send a wish that it not be John calling from his car. Relief came when she heard Gwen Robinson's perpetually cheerful and soothing voice over the receiver.

"I was about to hang up. I just called to see if we were still on for lunch in New York tomorrow."

"Of course. Let's meet at Restaurant Aquavit on West Fifty-fourth Street. We can eat lunch, and then head over and hit the sale racks at Bloomie's," Sharon said, attempting to replace the exasperation in her voice with cheer.

"Sounds like the perfect day. *Veni. Vedi. Visa.* I came. I saw. I did a little shopping."

"Gwen, you and your greeting card philosophies."

"That should have at least evoked a chuckle. You okay? You sound upset," Gwen remarked, concern coloring her voice.

Sharon was once again amazed by her friend's ability to read her emotions so well. It was a knack she'd had since the two had met nearly twenty years ago when they both worked for John's fledgling architectural firm. She could picture Gwen now standing in her home office in Montclair, New Jersey, her face painted with genuine worry.

"John and I were just talking about the apartment. He wants to move in by Christmas."

"How do *you* feel about it?"

"I want to spend the holidays here in my home."

"Did you tell John?"

"Not in so many words."

"You know, my friend, you'd be a lot happier if you'd simply say what you mean and mean what you say."

John sat back in his chair and thought about his earlier conversation with his wife. On the drive into his office he'd realized that he'd been wrong to try and push her into moving before the holidays. Sharon adored Christmas in Stamford. It was selfish of him to ask her to give up her Yuletide pleasure, especially when she was still so lukewarm about moving at all. He would agree to wait until the renovations and decorating were finished before they moved in, but John had every intention of spending springtime in Manhattan.

John hated the idea of taking Sharon away from the home she loved, but he was desperately hoping that this major reorganization in his life would somehow shake loose the growing malaise he was experiencing. He had been honest about feeling burned out, but, wanting to protect his wife from worry, John did not mention that his fears were compounded by the recent loss of two major projects, a new theme hotel in Las Vegas and a hotel/spa in Singapore. Both had been awarded to lesser-known firms with fresher ideas. Additionally causing concern was the company's slippage from number three to number ten on the list of the top fifty firms, and the fact that heading toward the fourth quarter the firm's projected yearly revenue was down by approximately one-third.

John's mental monologue was interrupted when his secretary buzzed, reminding him of his next meeting. His domestic life was pushed to the back of his mind as he strolled the opulent office space that housed the international headquarters of Carlson and Tuck. When he and Milton Tuck merged companies, neither had any idea in a short fifteen years they would carry a global employee roster topping two hundred and be among the two most sought-after architectural visionaries in the world. The award-winning partners specialized in the hospitality market, designing and overseeing the construction of some of the most luxurious and talked-about hotels, resorts, and restaurants frequented by the world's rich and famous.

When Milton insisted on retiring two years ago, it was this impressive reputation that brought on a flurry of offers from other companies to buy or merge with Carlson and Tuck. Instead, John bought Milton out, leaving the company name intact. It was now up to him to make all the important decisions that would ensure that their legacy would grow and flourish. But lately John was feeling the pressure of running Carlson and Tuck solo. He just didn't seem to care as much as he knew he should. Maybe Milton had had the right idea after all. Perhaps it was time to sell the company and retire.

*And do what?* he queried as he entered the boardroom and greeted the group of ten employees assigned to the Vogue Belize hotel. With a price tag of $85.8 million, including the firm's ten percent fee, it was the largest and most pressing project presently on the firm's drawing board. John took his usual seat at the head of the large conference table. Before beginning the weekly Tuesday staff meeting, he took a moment to view the scale model of the impressive hotel. John usually loved seeing his projects in this three-dimensional state. But now all the models were based on other people's ideas—mostly his young staff. Downstairs, in the design shop on the fifth floor, each basswood-and-chipboard mock-up was preserved as a diminutive representation of his life's work. Lately John found himself sitting among them and reminiscing about easier times when all he had to worry about was translating his blueprint conceptions into concrete realities.

"Morning, folks, how is everyone? Good," he said, acknowledging the group's affirmative nods and smiles. "Let's get down to business. What's doing with the Vogue? Have we resolved the zoning issue?"

"City officials and the client seem to be pleased with our compromise and I'm anticipating the final go-ahead this week," Austin Riley, the project manager, reported.

"Great. Now, with approval pending, let's move ahead with interior design. Where do we stand on finding a replacement for Total Image Design?"

"The response to the pitch requests has been damn near one hundred percent. Not many firms are willing to turn down an opportunity to attach their names to Carlson and Tuck, even if it does mean coming in after the project is well under way," Austin reported. "We've narrowed it down to four firms and we're scheduled to hear presentations beginning next week," he said, handing John a list of names.

"Whose this BenAlex Group? I'm not familiar with their work," John admitted.

"They're the outfit who designed the lobby bar at Tribeca Royal," architect Dianna Powell said.

"Trendy bars are a world away from a huge resort hotel. I think size and experience matter here," John commented.

"They have a real freshness to their work. I think it's worth listening to what they've got to say," Austin said.

"My instincts tell me otherwise, but since you've already

extended the invitation, we have no choice. What's next?" John asked.

"The owners have boosted the budget up to twenty-eight million on the Hotel Rico in South Beach. They really want us to take on the project and would like an answer by month's end," Austin informed the group.

"Pass. Carlson and Tuck stopped doing boutique-sized hotels years ago."

"It could be fun," Dianna suggested. "A chance to get really creative."

"Not interested," John insisted. "Anything else?"

The group spent the next forty minutes going over additional firm business before adjourning. While his team dispersed and cleared the room, John lingered behind, staring at his reflection in the window. He had just turned down almost three million dollars in revenue for Carlson and Tuck. Three million dollars. A huge price to pay for being bored.

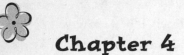

# Chapter 4

**M**elanie sat in the lobby area of Carlson and Tuck, nervously twisting the silver chain around her neck and trying to retain the serene and positive feelings from her morning meditation. She still couldn't believe her good fortune at being asked to sit in on this major presentation. Even though she wouldn't be speaking, she'd gone over each detail of every room, just in case anyone asked her a question. She'd dressed sharply too, figuring even if she just flipped presentation boards, she'd make a good impression. Her boss had told her that the BenAlex Group was up against some stiff competition and their firm's experience was not what it should be for a job of this size. It was a coup that Carlson and Tuck had even given them the chance to present their ideas. Melanie was thrilled to have the experience of presenting to such an important client.

She crossed her legs and accidentally kicked over her large black portfolio case containing the presentation boards. It fell to the floor with a dead thud. According to plan, she'd brought all the necessary materials from the office and was to convene with her boss Paco and his assistant, Alisa Scott, at the meeting site. As she reached down to retrieve the case, Melanie checked her watch for the sixth time in ten minutes. It was 2:56. Four minutes before they were scheduled to begin the firm's most important presentation to date, and the senior partner was nowhere to be found.

She heard the ding of the elevator and anxiously turned around, hoping to see Paco Benjamin walk through the glass doors. Instead, a young woman exited the elevator and treaded in the opposite direction.

"Excuse me, Ms. Hitts, there's a call for you," the receptionist informed her. Melanie reached over to the table at the end of the leather couch and picked up the phone. She said hello and in return heard the frantic voice of Paco's design assistant.

"Melanie, it's Alisa."

"Do you know what time it is?" Mel asked, trying to remain calm and keep the volume down on her voice. "Where are you guys?"

"At the hospital. Our cab was in an accident."

"Are you hurt?"

"I'm okay, just banged up my knee pretty bad. Paco hit his head on the Plexiglas divider. He's seems to be okay. The doctor is in with him now, so I guess we'll know for sure soon."

"Ms. Hitts, they're ready for you," the receptionist interrupted. Melanie smiled, held up her index finger in acknowledgment, and continued talking. She hoped that the stress she was feeling within was not displayed on her face.

"They're calling me," Mel informed Alisa. "Maybe we should just postpone this until Paco or Whitney can be here. Or how about Jude?" she asked, referring to the firm's other designer.

"Can't. It's now or never. Carlson and Tuck made it very clear that they are in a hurry to hire someone, so all presentations must be made this week. Paco says just to wing it the best you can."

"Tell him to feel better. You too. And Alisa . . ."

"Yeah?"

"Say a prayer. I could use a little help." Melanie hung up the phone, stood, and nervously smoothed out the front of her gray silk shantung dress. She picked up the portfolio, her tote bag full of tile, fabric, and paint samples, took a deep breath, and steadied herself on her favorite shoes—burgundy patent-leather pumps with stiletto heels. No comfortable kicks today. She always wore high heels to important events. Physically they lifted her diminutive five-foot-one frame up to a more womanly elevation, while psychologically they quieted her lifelong short person complex, making her feel confident and powerful. Cinderella knew the deal. Never underestimate a great pair of shoes.

Mel followed the receptionist down the hall into an empty room dominated by a large conference table. At this moment Mel felt like a walking Calvin Klein ad for Contradiction perfume— apprehensive yet excited, confident yet petrified. While thankful she'd boned up on the material last night, she hadn't anticipated carrying the entire presentation on her own. But opportunity was knocking and Mel refused to deny it entry. *You can do this,* she assured herself.

Alone and uncertain where to sit, Melanie walked toward the empty easel standing near the head of the table and began preparing for her demonstration. She opened her tote bag and neatly created several small heaps of stone tile, metal fasteners, and other materials chosen by Paco and Whitney. Next she unzipped the portfolio case and sat the boards on the easel's shallow ledge, only to have them slide off and scatter all over the floor.

Mel quickly gathered them up, checking to see that the carefully attached fabric swatches, sketches, and photos were still firmly in place. She had just managed to restock the easel and temporarily settle her nerves when the members of the Carlson and Tuck team entered the room.

"Hi, I'm Austin Riley, and these are my colleagues, Dianna Powell and Trevor Kensington."

"Melanie Hitts," Mel responded, enthusiastically shaking hands and hiding her uneasiness behind a vivacious smile. "It's nice to meet you."

"We were expecting three people. Is the rest of your team here?" Austin inquired.

"I'm afraid not. Unfortunately, Paco Benjamin and Alisa Scott were in a traffic accident on their way over. It was fairly minor, just a few bumps and bruises, but they are both still at the hospital being checked out. We understand and appreciate your time constraints on this project, and thought it best that I go ahead with our presentation."

"Great. John Carlson will be joining us in a minute, so why don't you get comfortable?" Austin suggested.

*Keep it together,* Mel commanded herself as she took a seat. Mel had been prepared to speak to the Carlson and Tuck team, but not the legendary John Carlson. She settled into the cushy leather chair and glanced across the table, only to find a distressed look on Dianna Powell's face.

"Perhaps you'd like to sit—" Dianna began. Before she could finish her sentence, John Carlson, preceded by the strong exhilarating scent of Cerruti 1881 cologne, sauntered into the room. His displeasure at having to attend this meeting was only slightly masked. Thank goodness this was the last presentation. He had a throbbing headache and the thought of having to listen to one more perky interior decorator wax on and on about the magnificence of minimalism or the triumphant return of opulence repulsed him.

John greeted his employees with a brusque nod before walking toward the head of the table. Immediately Melanie understood the disturbed look on Dianna's face. She was sitting in the boss's chair.

"John Carlson," he said, stopping in front of her.

"Melanie Hitts," she replied nervously as she vacated his seat.

John sat with uncommitted intent. Melanie couldn't read his face for any clues. Was he amused or irritated by her error?

"I was just explaining to the others, Mr. Carlson, that due to an unforeseen emergency, my colleagues are unable to join us. Well, I guess that's a bit redundant, as what is an emergency but an unexpected event?" Mel said, nervousness causing her voice to break slightly. *Shut up, you idiot. You're rambling on like a fool.*

"So your firm sent, who . . . a design assistant?" John asked in a tone that straddled the line between amazement and appall.

"No, Mr. Carlson, I am a fully accredited interior design *professional*," Melanie informed him, unable to keep the annoyance out of her voice. "Perhaps you saw my work featured in the latest *Interior Design* magazine?"

Granted, she'd only left the ranks of design assistants two months ago, but who did this man think he was to question her credentials and the appropriateness of her presence? Was it because she was black? Mel was well aware that being African-American made her an unfortunate anomaly at this enormously lucrative level, but wasn't Carlson savvy enough to realize that underexposed did not mean underqualified? Melanie hated to go to that nasty, negative racial divide, but sometimes, with some people, you simply had to wonder.

"I knew your name sounded familiar," Dianna piped in. "John, Melanie's room for Kips Bay was the talk of the industry."

"I stand corrected. Please continue, Ms. Hitts," John said dryly as he sat in his chair, massaging his temples.

"Thank you," Melanie began, forcing away the thought of going upside this rude man's head with her shoe. "On behalf of the BenAlex Design Group, I'd like to thank you for inviting us to present. We're honored that such a well-known and universally respected company as Carlson and Tuck is interested in the ideas of a relatively new firm such as ours."

"Exactly how long has your firm been in business?" John queried.

Melanie searched her memory for the answer, only to come up blank. She didn't want to lie, as this information was far too easy to confirm. "Close to four years," she fudged.

"Hmm," John murmured impassively. "And how many design *professionals* are employed at your firm?"

"There are two partners and two designers, myself included."

"I see. Do you have any idea how large a job this is, Ms. Hitts? We're talking about a three-hundred-and-ten-room hotel, plus twenty-three suites and dozens of other public rooms. What makes you think that a company of your size could handle such a job?" John's challenge came to the amazement of the others in the room. Lately he'd been irritable and distant around the office, but they'd never seen him quite so combative and discourteous to an undeserving stranger.

"Frankly, Mr. Carlson, though there may indeed be three hundred and ten rooms, the fact is that you're really only conceptualizing a single design schematic. The other three hundred and nine rooms will be identical. A talented design firm of *one* could handle, that," Melanie retorted, all the while wondering why this man was riding her so obnoxiously.

"And if I might also add, it seems obvious that the caliber of work we've become known for, despite our relatively small size, has caught *your* discriminating eye. After all, your company did invite us to present our ideas." Melanie punctuated her last statement by pressing her lips together in a defiant and challenging smile.

The Carlson and Tuck team sat in stunned silence. They'd never seen anything like this. Melanie Hitts, a relatively unknown design ingenue, was going toe-to-toe with one of the industry's architectural giants. Was she simply too green and naive to understand that John Carlson, by sheer reputation alone, had it within his power to squelch any inkling of a chance she had to make it in this highly competitive industry?

"The BenAlex Design Group's philosophy is simple," Mel continued, anger fueling her boldness. "A well-designed space can and should inspire the human spirit. So, if there are no further questions regarding the personnel roster, I'd like to show you how we've taken this fundamental philosophy and incorporated it into a design concept that we feel will not only greatly enhance your architectural vision but the customer appeal of the Vogue Belize Hotel." As she paused to take a sip of water, Mel noticed the tight-lipped grins and polite nods. She sensed that the account was already lost, but she'd come here to give a presentation, and give it she would. She'd be damned if she'd let some impolite old man with bug up his butt keep her from finishing.

"Let's begin with the main lobby," Melanie continued, acknowledging Austin, Trevor, and Dianna, while purposely avoiding direct eye contact with John Carlson.

When Melanie turned her back, directing their attention to her sample boards, John bent over, whispered something in Austin Riley's ear, and quietly vacated the room.

*Why would John Carlson want to see me?* Melanie wondered as she stepped off the elevator and followed Austin Riley down the hall. What could they possibly have to discuss? Her stellar performance that he'd ungraciously chosen to ignore? Or maybe, if he had any sense of decency at all, John wanted to apologize for rudely stepping out on her presentation.

They walked into the outer office of the Carlson and Tuck executive suite. John's secretary, Gale, was not at her desk, so Austin gently tapped to announce their arrival. Receiving no reply, he opened the door and led Mel into the large inner sanctum of John Carlson's professional domain.

"John should be with you in just a moment," he informed her, shaking her hand.

Melanie stood looking around John's office, her decorator's eye intrigued by the room's ambience. With its dark wood paneling, stately brass lamps, plush Oriental rug, and the faint scent of Cuban cigar smoke, it resembled an English gentleman's social club.

The space reeked of distinction and prestige, but it also spoke of staid boredom. Not at all like the glimpse of the man she'd just met. Judging by reputation and their brief encounter, John Carlson seemed much more dynamic and bold. This was the office of a successful but stuffy banker, not a highly creative, albeit ill-mannered, architectural visionary. The only clue to the artistic side of the man was the gallery of paintings that hung on the wall opposite his desk.

Melanie walked over and began to inspect each of the four large canvases. Obviously a series, each painting featured a different pose of the same mysterious femme fatale, her face veiled in the shadows by a large hat. The artist had captured her essence layer by layer—stopping short of full disclosure, a technique that left Melanie intrigued and anxious to peel back the layers and learn what relationship lay between artist and subject. Just as Mel leaned in close to inspect the illegible signature, John's voice sent a startled jolt through her body, causing her to quickly stand upright and turn around.

"Art lover, Ms. Hitts?"

"I appreciate talent in any form. These are very nice. I like the rich, earthy color palate against the cool backgrounds. It creates context without distraction," Mel remarked authoritatively, grateful for her undergraduate degree in art history. It irritated her that she felt compelled to prove herself with this man.

"Are you the fan of any particular artist, Mr. Carlson?"

"Many, though I share the same philosophy about my work as Henri Matisse."

"Meaning his reverence for the fusion of intellect and sensuality?" Mel asked, enjoying his surprise at her obvious expertise.

"That too. Matisse preferred to be judged by the total expressiveness of his work, feeling that it was the vision and handling of the materials that was most important, rather than the reality of the subject itself."

"So for you it's the design process that's most intriguing? Not the finished product?"

"You could say that," John revealed. "So do you like the paintings?"

"They're very good, but . . ." Melanie let her voice trail off as she rethought her unspoken remark.

"But what?" John probed.

"But they don't really fit into the office décor. Then again, Mr. Carlson, neither do you," she replied, honestly speaking her mind.

"Meaning?"

"Meaning that this office doesn't seem to match your personality," she said, bracing herself for more of this afternoon's gruffness.

To Melanie's surprise, laughter erupted from John's mouth, melting away the hard unpleasant lines of his earlier face, replacing them with more youthful, character-enhancing ones. The transformation was remarkable. Along with John's hearty laughter, the terse, impatient tone he'd used earlier also came tumbling out, leaving a lighter and much more acceptable resonance.

"I'd be interested in knowing what kind of décor you think would fit me, though based on my behavior in the meeting, I suppose a cave would seem more appropriate."

Melanie found herself chuckling in agreement. Not only did she find the visual depiction of his words apropos, she appreciated John's self-depreciating attempt at an apology.

"Maybe not quite *that* retro, but I definitely see you working in a lighter and less formal atmosphere. One not quite so Wall Street Willie," Mel said with a laugh, gracefully sweeping the room with her arms. "I would think that you'd find it difficult to be creative in this space."

"I'm impressed," John said, surprised that this young woman's insight was not only bull's-eye accurate, but thoroughly welcomed.

"Are you saying that I'm right about the mismatch between you and your work space?"

"Totally. Except for the artwork and photos, nothing in here is mine. This was actually my former partner's office. I moved in here when he retired and, frankly, haven't had the time or energy to have it redone. I have to say that you seem to have an uncanny ability to deduce personality and apply it to your design strategy."

"Had you stayed for my entire presentation, you'd have already discovered that," Mel jabbed lightly.

"I walked in that room with a major headache both figuratively and literally. You had nothing to do with my abrupt departure."

"I'm glad to hear that," Melanie replied, not sure if he was actually apologizing.

"Good. Now, have a seat and tell me about yourself. How did you get into this crazy business?" John asked, enjoying the vision of Mel crossing her shapely legs.

"As far back as I can remember, I was always rearranging the furniture in the house. My mom and dad pretty much humored me, until I discovered Feng Shui and reorganized all the living room furniture, making it more spiritually in tune with the Universe. Unfortunately, when my father came home from work late that night, he tripped over the newly placed rug and broke his collarbone. After that, I could do whatever I wanted with my room, but the rest of the house was off-limits."

"As a kid I would sit for hours building houses out of anything I could get my hands on—playing cards, sugar cubes, matchboxes, you name it," John revealed, smiling at memories that hadn't surfaced in years.

"I guess Legos just weren't good enough for you?" Mel teased.

"Your young age is telling, Ms. Hitts. I am part of the Lincoln Logs generation. My building material of choice, however, was cardboard boxes, especially the big refrigerator ones. My father owned an appliance store and would bring them home from work, and using scraps of carpet and various odds and ends laying around the garage, I would build my own little world. The best part was that I could actually live in my creation. It made a great place to hide," John added unconsciously.

Melanie saw the faraway look in his eyes and let the last comment go. "Is that what you love about being an architect? That your art is functional?"

John paused for a moment, contemplating her question. It had been so long since he'd thought of himself as an artist. When and where had that side of him disappeared?

"I guess in a way it is," he answered. "I like the idea of civic art . . . that what I create can be utilized and enjoyed by the public as well as add beauty to the environment."

"I totally know what you mean," Melanie said, leaning forward, the excitement of mutual understanding apparent in her body language. "I love being an interior designer because each client provides a new challenge to produce something beautiful and individual. Most people think that architecture and design are simply about building and decorating, they don't understand that in the theater of life, we create the backdrops that set the mood for people's daily existence."

"You're absolutely right." He nodded, enjoying the obvious delight she felt toward her work. How long had it been since he'd felt that joy? Their conversation was halted by the grating buzz of John's intercom. "Yes, Gale? Thanks for the reminder," he said into the phone before hanging up and standing. "Unfortunately, as much as I'm enjoying our conversation, I have an important meeting in a few minutes."

"And I really should get back to my office," Melanie said,

knowing it was true, but wanting to stay and talk more. Since encountering John Carlson two hours ago, she'd gone through the full Monty of emotions—fear, anger, and now respect. It was gratifying to finally speak with someone who understood the deeper reasons why she loved what she did.

"I'd like us to sit down again to discuss how our two firms can work together. I still believe that BenAlex is too small for a job of this size, but I'm sure there will be other opportunities," John remarked, smiling broadly, surprised by his comment. He was perplexed by his potent desire to see this young woman again.

"I'll let Paco and Whitney know. They'll be thrilled to talk with you personally."

"Great." At the risk of sounding flirtatious, John didn't verbalize that he had no intention of convening with her firm's partners if Melanie was not part of the conference.

"Despite our rocky start, it was a real pleasure to meet you, Mr. Carlson."

"Please call me John. May I call you Melanie?"

"Of course."

"It was delightful talking with you, Melanie. We seem to be of like mind when it comes to our work, so I'm sure we'll be speaking again soon. And hold on to that feeling of exhilaration for what you do. I'm afraid that after you've been around as long as I have, it's easy to get burned out and forget why you come to work every day," John advised.

"But it must be hard to keep that excitement going when you're simply overseeing someone else's inspiration. No true artist can be happy merely being an administrator."

Like a gentle breeze clearing the morning mist, Melanie's comment brought instant clarity to his mottled emotions. This young woman who was blessed with the face of cherub, the soul of an artist, and the intelligence of a scholar, had tapped into the root cause of his long-running ennui. In the short span of time they had spent together, John had recalled moments and feelings about his life and his work that he hadn't thought about in years. Melanie's intuitive knowledge of him and who he was as a man amazed and frightened him. It was a dichotomy of feelings John Carlson neither wanted nor intended to ignore.

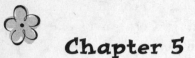

# Chapter 5

**D**uring the forty-minute conference call with the Vogue Belize representatives, John paid only minimal attention, instead concentrating on compiling a list of tasks necessary to get rolling on his newest pet project. Immediately after concluding his phone meeting, he buzzed his secretary into the office. While he waited for Gale, he rang downstairs.

"Dianna, call the folks in Miami and set up a meeting as soon as possible. And then bring me the files on the Hotel Rico."

"I thought you weren't interested in doing a boutique hotel."

"I've change my mind."

"Okay. My team is pretty tied up with the Vogue, but I'm sure we could get some preliminary ideas to you in the next couple of weeks."

"Not necessary, I'm going to take care of this myself," John said as he excitedly waved Gale into the room.

"*You're* going to do this? By yourself?"

"Last I looked, I was still a licensed architect. I think I can handle it," John replied with a chuckle.

"All righty, then, I'll get that file up to you pronto," Dianna said.

"Thank you," John said before hanging up and turning to his secretary. "Gale, would you please call the BenAlex Design Group and set up a meeting? Check my calendar and juggle any appointments necessary so it can happen *yesterday*."

"What shall I tell them the meeting is regarding?"

"Tell them we've decided to use Melanie Hitts for the Hotel Rico."

"Will Dianna and Austin be taking the meeting?"

"No, I'll be taking the lead myself. Oh, I've decided to move down to the fifth floor while I'm on this project. I can't work in here. Get someone to clean up that vacant office next to the model shop. . . . What? Why are you standing there staring at me?"

"It's just that I haven't seen you this inspired over a new project in a long time."

"Is that bad?" John laughed.

"Not at all," Gale said. "As Martha Stewart would say, it's a good thing."

*Too good a thing to ignore,* John thought, happily recognizing a twinge of professional thrill tiptoeing through his body.


Melanie dropped her keys twice before successfully negotiating the locks and stumbling into the apartment. She leaned against the front door and immediately freed her tired, aching feet by kicking off her heels. They landed across the room with a loud thud.

"Shhh. Shhh, you'll wake Candy," she reminded herself before remembering that Candace was spending the weekend with her married lover, Frank. With no need to be a considerate roommate, Melanie turned on the stereo and pumped up the volume on her favorite Macy Gray CD. Attempting to keep her buzz on, she poured herself a glass of Merlot.

She'd been out with Whitney, Paco, Alisa, Jude, and the rest of the firm celebrating the acquisition of not only one, but two jobs from the almighty Carlson and Tuck. This meant huge revenues for BenAlex and personal kudos for Melanie. At first she'd been disappointed to learn that Jude had been selected for the Carlson residence account, but when Whitney broke the news that she would be the lead designer on the Hotel Rico, Mel could not believe her incredible fortune. To make the announcement even more special, her colleagues seemed genuinely happy for her. Melanie felt doubly blessed to have landed in such a warm and supportive working environment.

"A toast to Melo. Job well done," she mumbled, turning to refill her wineglass and noticing the blinking light on the telephone. She picked up the receiver, dialed her code, and listened to the messages. There was a request from Candace asking Mel to water her orchids and a second, more instantly sobering report from her sister:

"Hi, sis. I know it's after midnight, but this news couldn't wait. Actually I'm glad you aren't home. Hopefully it means you're out somewhere having a good time. I have some juicy information for you. Xavier and I were at the reception tonight at the Kennedy Center, you know, the fundraiser for the 100 Black Men's mentoring program, the one I tried to get you to come down for? Anyway, guess who we ran into? Will. And guess whose name he managed to slip into our conversation at least ten times? The man definitely still has the hots for you—BIG TIME. He wanted a complete update on your life and was anxious to give me his. I'm sure he's hoping that I'll pass his success story on to you, so here goes. Your ex-fiancé just got a huge promotion at his job. Looks like America Online has big plans for his future. Now, don't be upset, sister dear, but I invited him to the christening this weekend. You used to be pretty crazy about the brother, and as far as I can tell, you haven't hooked up with anyone since you've been up in the Big Apple. I figure that must mean something. Like maybe you still have feelings for Will too? Call me."

Melanie returned to the main menu, followed the recorded instructions and left an angry voice message in her sister's mailbox:

"Francesca, have you lost your mind? What are you thinking? Will and I are over. I thought I'd made that clear to him and everyone else. We haven't spoken in months and that's exactly the way I plan to leave it. And while you were busy minding my business, did you ever stop to think about what this is going to do to Mom and Dad? They were more upset when we broke up than I was. Getting their hopes up is just plain cruel. I suggest you explain the realities of the situation before I get down there. I know it's your party and you can invite who you want to, but in the future, sister *dear*, keep your nose out of my love life."

Melanie slammed the phone into its cradle, mentally cursing Francesca not only for ruining her good mood, but for putting her in such an untenable situation. There was no way she could or even wanted to skip the christening of her niece, just as there was no way that Will would pass up an opportunity to see her. Thanks to Franti's meddling, what should be a wonderful family occasion now had the potential of turning into emotionally charged chaos.

Mel walked back into her room to get ready for bed. As she removed her clothes, she also stripped away the anger, forcing herself to acknowledge the truth in Francesca's comments. There wasn't a day that she didn't wake up thinking about Will Freedman or fall asleep without his name being the last thing on her mind. In fact, he had been the first person she'd wanted to call and share the good news with about her new client. It was true that her love for Will remained, but so did all the nagging questions and doubts.

*AOL has big plans for his future.* Francesca's words slithered through Mel's mind like a king cobra. Will's job was also taking an upward turn toward the stars. So even if they did get back together, how could it possibly work? He couldn't leave Washington and she certainly wasn't about to return. Not when her career was taxiing down the runway of success.

The Hotel Rico was going to be Mel's launching pad into the stratosphere of big-time decorators. The research, travel, and creative time involved would leave no time for working out romantic relationships. Melanie could not afford to squander this opportunity by letting anything or anyone get in the way. Nor could she ask Will to do the same.

She sat down at her computer and signed on to America Online. There was absolutely no point in trying to rekindle a relationship that could never work. She proceeded to compose and send her message to Will, uninviting him to the christening and asking him to understand.

Mel crawled into bed, her earlier euphoria evaporated and gone, replaced by a heavy and lonesome melancholy. As the tears snuck down her cheeks, Melanie pulled the sheet tight around her chin, swaddling herself like a newborn. Maybe, once her professional dreams came true, her personal ones would follow.

As Melanie strolled through Carlson and Tuck's model shop, her thirty-inch strand of vintage black pearls swung from side to side, keeping time with her heart, which was pounding with nerve-racking intensity. Mel glanced around with admiration at the dollhouse-sized trophies of John's work. There were buildings and hotels she recognized and some she'd actually stayed in. She sighed, feeling a mixture of respect, pride, and nagging anxiety weighing on her.

The thought of working so closely with John Carlson concerned her. Although she was no longer fearful of the man, the pressure to produce for this architectural demigod was tremendous. John had handpicked her for this coveted assignment and Melanie was eager to please him and prove herself worthy of his demonstrated faith in her abilities. The time had come for Mel to live up to the incredible potential that people, including herself, always claimed she possessed.

Melanie knocked softly on the open door. Talking into his telephone headset, John looked up from his drafting table and smiled broadly, gesturing her into the room. While he finished up his phone call, Mel took the opportunity to inspect his new work space. Unlike the stuffy conservative décor upstairs, this space was light, airy, and sparsely appointed. Next to his wooden drafting table stood a desk topped with a computer and a pile of art and architectural books fringed with fluorescent Post-its marking items of interest. On the opposite side of the room was a sand-colored leather couch and glass coffee table topped with two large silver jacks. Above the sofa hung a large canvas of female faces, displaying the same unique style and earthy color palette of the work hanging in John's upstairs office.

"Melanie, welcome," John said, stepping down from his stool to greet her. "You certainly look nice," he said admiring her slim, pink wool skirt, brown leather jacket and high-heeled boots.

"Thank you."

"So how do you like my new office? Does it pass muster?" John asked, feeling boyishly awkward.

"It's definitely an improvement, and you get extra points for the jacks."

"You like jacks?"

"I don't just *like* jacks. I *rule* at jacks. Mr. Carlson, you're looking at the jacks champion of Page Elementary School," Melanie revealed with a chuckle.

"Come sit," he said, laughing and pointing her toward the sofa. "Can I get you something?"

"No, thank you, I'm fine, and thrilled to be working with *you* on this hotel. You're making my dreams come true."

"Then I guess we should get down to work," John said, trying to hide the fact that her comment pleased him immensely. "I've got to warn you that this might get pretty intense. We only have a few months before we make our presentation to the clients."

"Not a problem. One question, though. Why are you bringing me in so early on in the project? Aren't the building plans usually further along before you bring in the interior designer?"

"Usually, but this project is a bit different. Unlike the large resorts we usually build, this is a boutique hotel in South Beach, Miami. There will be only twelve rooms and two penthouse suites. I want to go to the owners with a unique concept that is unlike anything else they've seen down there," John told her. He was satisfied that his explanation sounded totally plausible. There was no reason for Melanie to suspect that he'd taken this job hoping that by stepping away from simply overseeing company projects and concentrating on actually producing something himself, he could jump-start his own creative batteries.

"Why are we deciding this? Don't the owners already have a concept?"

"The only way I would agree to take on the project was if I had total control from concept to finish," John explained.

Melanie's eyes grew wide with complete awe. What power this man commanded. By reputation alone he could inform savvy businessmen how *he* intended to spend their millions, and they acquiesced, knowing that an investment in John Carlson's genius was well worthwhile.

"Then I guess we'd better get down to some serious brainstorming," Mel said, standing up to remove her jacket, revealing a pink, body conscious silk T-shirt. John was struck by the graceful sensuality of her innocent movement.

"So I suppose we start with exactly who is the preferred clientele. With a name like the Hotel Rico, or Rich Hotel, I'm assuming we're not talking Holiday Inn crowd."

"No, we're talking wealthy businessmen, celebrities, rock stars, models, each spending eight hundred to fifteen hundred a night."

"Well, for that kind of money they'll be expecting luxurious accommodations."

"One would think, but not necessarily. South Beach is all about trendsetting gimmicks."

"And art deco," Melanie remarked.

"We need something different." John had done his homework on the area, carefully checking out the competition, measuring their strengths and weaknesses. Unbeknownst to Melanie, he had unsuccessfully been racking his brain trying to come up with something special to wow his clients. But he'd quickly shot down every concept conceived for being too contrived, too hokey, or too unoriginal.

Melanie began to pace the room and John studied her. She glided across the floor like a dancer, gracefulness in her stride, intensity in her face, as she processed her ideas. "We're going about this all wrong. It's not about the hotel, it's about the guests," she decided aloud. "John, you've built and stayed in some of the finest hotels in the world. What do you look for?"

"Comfort, elegance, something that feels familiar but different."

"Doesn't sound hip and trendy to me."

"I guess I'm too old for neon-lit elevators and communal dining tables."

"My point is hip and trendy has already been done over and over down there. So why not provide guests something elegant but modern, artsy but . . ." Melanie stopped in midsentence as her eyes fell upon the canvas of painted faces above the couch.

"Artsy but . . . ?"

"Pablo Picasso once said, 'Art washes away from the soul the dust of everyday life.'"

"And?"

"And outside of business, why do folks check into hotels? To escape everyday life."

"I'm not sure I'm following you."

"Why not build a hotel-cum-gallery that showcases the amazing array of international art?" Mel suggested.

"It's too subjective. One man's work of art is another man's garbage. It would be too difficult to get a consensus," he stated, playing devil's advocate.

"Which is exactly why we mix it up with African-American, Haitian, and Hispanic art, abstract, modern, classic—span the entire spectrum!"

"Go on," John prompted. He could see the spark behind her eyes that fueled her creative process, and it intrigued him.

"Maybe the public spaces exhibit the classic reprints of the masters like Picasso, Renoir, and Monet, while each room could be a miniature gallery displaying the work of world renowned contemporary artists. You know—the Diego Rivera/Frida Kahlo Bridal Suite, the Lois Mailou Jones Suite, the Andy Warhol Suite. The décor for each room would be designed around the artwork, but it wouldn't be cold and sterile like a museum. Each room would be warm and full of texture—exuding the sensuality of the art."

"The building could also carry out that sensual theme—lots of curved, soft lines, materials that beg to be touched," John thought aloud, his wheels beginning to turn at full speed.

"Original pieces by local artists could be displayed in the restaurant. And we'd have a sculpture garden on the roof and an outdoor studio adjacent to the pool. The hotel could hire someone to teach art lessons," Mel continued to brainstorm.

"Even the bottom of the pool could be a print," John suggested, getting caught up in Mel's contagious enthusiasm.

"*The Swimming Pool,*" they both cried out in unison, recalling the paper cutout masterpiece by Henri Matisse.

"Melanie, this is a *great* idea. Better than great, ingenious."

"We'll call it the Casa de Arte," she suggested, her grin broad and unrelenting.

"Perfect. This is going to be a world-class hotel when we're done, and you, Ms. Jax, are going to be a highly sought-after designer."

She could only smile and try to contain the excitement bubbling up inside of her. Melanie's instinctive reflex was to give John a big, grateful hug, but concluding it would be unprofessional, she opted for a handshake.

They both smiled as their eyes and hands touched. For the brief moment, he and Melanie stood, connected by sight and touch. The energy exchange was palpable. It shot around the room like a lit fuse, igniting the vulnerable edges of their mutual admiration. John's grin narrowed as his eyes took in her appealing bronzed loveliness. The woman was truly talented, and with him as her mentor and her as his muse, who knew what professional heights they could reach together?

Melanie nervously bit her lower lip before gulping slightly and willing herself to break their powerful magnetic gaze.

"Well, I . . . uh," she managed to stutter. Her words were halted by the unprovoked flow of black pearls dropping from her neck and spraying across the sisal rug. "How bizarre. I wasn't even touching them. Oh, well, what can you expect from fifty-year-old beads?" she remarked nervously after reclaiming her hand.

"Kinetic energy," was John's simple explanation as he got down on all fours to help Melanie pick up her beads. "The power of positive energy is a force to be reckoned with."

They scurried around the floor in silence, both picking up pearls while contemplating what had just occurred between them. Deep in their individual thoughts, neither heard the tap on the door, nor focused on the presence of John's secretary until she let out a surprised and bewildered gasp, followed by uncontainable laughter.

"You two look like a couple of preschoolers on an Easter egg hunt," Gale said with a chuckle.

John smiled as he looked up from the floor, his shirt pocket full of pearls, his heart full of wonder. The exchange of energy between them was indeed real and John could not help pondering the question: If investigated further, could this force between them be harnessed into a positive flow that would enrich and benefit both their lives?

# Chapter 6

**Send Instant Message**

**STILLWILL:** Hey, where have you been hiding? I've been watching my buddy list like a hawk waiting for you to sign on.

**LOLLIEPOP:** Hi Will. So AOL is really an alias for "Big Brother"?

**STILLWILL:** Very funny. How are you, Candace. How's life in the Big Apple?

**LOLLIEPOP:** Great. The case I'm working on is a bear, but I'm handling it. But why waste time on me when you're really interested in how my roommate is doing?

**STILLWILL:** For the record, Counselor, I am interested in how you're doing too. I really appreciate you helping me out like this.

**LOLLIEPOP:** What are friends for?

**STILLWILL:** You've been Mel's friend much longer than you've been mine. It's got to be hard for you to spy on her like this.

**LOLLIEPOP:** I like talking with you. Secondly, I don't consider myself spying on Melo. I'm just keeping you in the loop while she's getting herself together. She'll thank me for it later when you two are back together.

**STILLWILL:** So how is she?

**LOLLIEPOP:** Up to her silver hoops in work and loving every minute.

**STILLWILL:** Sounds like she's working a lot of late nights.

**LOLLIEPOP:** To answer the question you're *not* asking: Yes, she's too busy with work to have much of a social life. The little she does have revolves around me.

**STILLWILL:** So, no new boyfriend on the horizon?

**LOLLIEPOP:** I was wondering how long it was going to take for you to ask outright :-). Don't worry, your girl seems to have neither the time nor the interest in anything remotely related to a love life. I think she's just scared and confused right now. Give her some more time. I'm sure she still loves you.

**STILLWILL:** My girl. Thanks for that little piece of hope. By the way, do you remember my friend Griffin Bell? You met him at the engagement party.

**LOLLIEPOP:** Vaguely. Why?

**STILLWILL:** He's scheduled to be up your way soon.

**LOLLIEPOP:** And I should care because?

**STILLWILL:** Because I was going to suggest to him that he give you and Mel a call when he gets in town, but given your reaction . . . maybe not.

**LOLLIEPOP:** I'm sure Melanie can entertain him by her lonesome.

**STILLWILL:** Give him a chance. He's a cool brother. I have to run to a meeting. Thanks again, Candace. You're a special friend.

**LOLLIEPOP:** I feel the same about you. Talk soon.

**STILLWILL:** 'Bye.

*"The wings*
*of a butterfly*
*create the wind*

*and the movements*
*of a starfish*
*make mighty waves*
*as I glance*
*at your lips*
*I can only imagine*
*the aftermath*
*of a single kiss."*

As the words softly tumbled from his lips and were swept up by the enthusiastic ears of the crowd below him, Griffin Bell smiled. As if donning a luxurious Russian sable, Griff wrapped himself in the cheers and whistles, the applause and admiration of his appreciative audience. He loved this moment when the show was over and he stood onstage holding the imagination and desires of his listeners. It thrilled him to know that for whatever brief period of time he commanded the rapt attention of the audience, he was providing them a welcomed diversion from life's realities.

This was why he performed. It wasn't about the money. God knows when it came to his bank account, the demands of others far outweighed his supply. No, Griffin performed for the love, both given and received. While up on that stage he had the power to fill their heads and hearts with fancy or fury, whatever the role required. And when it was all over, the rush of love that came his way was addictive. It was a rush he had yet to find in the arms of any woman or in the promise of any illicit pharmaceutical.

"Thank you," Griff mouthed to the throng of female patrons

as he stepped offstage. He wound his way through the crowd toward Melanie and Candace, his progress slowed by the constant clamor of delighted women, mesmerized by his magic and pushing for more personal attention.

Candace, dressed in a tight black leather dress and high-heel pumps, sat at the table with the aloof confidence of a dominatrix. The only contradictory clue to her agitated emotional state was the constant swing of her foot as she watched the attention being doled out to Griffin. Instant reflex caused Candace to suck her teeth and roll her eyes.

"Can you believe how desperate these heifers are?" Candace remarked to Melanie. "This is a ladies-only *poetry* night, not an evening with the damn Chippendale dancers."

"Can you blame them? He's got that DiAngelo meets Seal thing going for him. Plus he's smart *and* talented. That combo package doesn't come around every day."

"Whatever." Despite her nonchalance, Candace was impressed. Ghetto-fabulous or not, the boy obviously had skills.

"Don't tell me he didn't get to you too. Look at you bouncing that foot up and down, dangling that CFM pump like fish bait. You do that whenever some man gets you fired up."

"Yeah, well, if I am fired up it's not because of Rhyming Raymond up there, but because Frank was supposed to pick me up an hour and a half ago. This shit is going to cost him. In fact, just this afternoon I saw this gorgeous David Yurman ring. It will go perfectly with my bracelet," she said, admiring Frank's last apology wrapped around her wrist—links of heavy silver cable ovals with an eighteen-karat gold clasp.

"So you're telling me you don't find Griffin attractive at all?"

Melanie asked, choosing to ignore the unending saga of Candy's floundering relationship.

"I'll admit the brother is fine and he's got game, just not in my league," Candy concluded. "Like the song says: 'You gotta have a J-O-B, if you wanna be with me.'"

*More like a W-I-F-E,* Melanie thought but didn't repeat. After all these years, she still couldn't understand Candace's penchant for dating married men. Couldn't understand it and certainly didn't condone it. While Candy claimed it kept life simple and allowed her to enjoy the benefits of intimacy without the hassles of marriage, from Mel's point of view it brought her friend nothing but certain grief and loneliness.

"What about potential?" Mel asked.

"What about it? If a man over thirty doesn't have it now, he's never getting it. At least not here. I'm thirty-four years old. Life's too short for me to wait for some broke-ass scrub to play catch-up."

"Griffin," Melanie greeted the poet, abruptly putting an end to their girl talk.

"So this is where all the superstars sit."

"If it is, then you'd better come join us. Congratulations. You were amazing up there. You've got all these women in a tizzy," Melanie said as she stood up to hug him.

"I aim to please. Girl, let me look at you," he said, holding Melanie at arm's length. "Still superfine as ever! It's no wonder my boy's nose is still wide open."

"How is Will?" Mel asked with cool but undeniable curiosity. Despite her renewed resolve to stay apart, it pleased her that Will's feelings were still intact.

"He's making it. He was pretty bummed that he didn't have the chance to see your family at the christening, but I think he respected your reason. Didn't like it, but respected it."

"It just would have been too uncomfortable . . . for everybody," Mel tried to explain while pushing the guilt away.

"You've got to know how tough this 'no contact' rule is on him. Can't you bend the rules at all? I mean, I'm not trying to be his mouthpiece, but at this point, Melanie, if all you can give is friendship, he'll take it," Griff told her.

"Maybe in time. But speaking of friends, this is Candace," she said smoothly, changing the subject.

"Hi there," Griff drawled, giving no indication if he recalled their turbulent meeting at the infamous engagement party. Candace accepted Griffin's European-style kiss on each cheek, while breathing in his sexy, musky scent. Gleefully noticing the resentful eyes of several women focused on them, she pressed a little closer, lightly brushing his muscular biceps with her fingertips. Pissed off at Frank for standing her up again and enjoying all the feathers ruffling around her, Candy decided that Griffin Bell was the perfect salve for her bruised ego.

"It's good to see you too. I had no idea you were so talented," Candy flirted.

"If I recall correctly, the last time we met you had absolutely no interest in finding out," Griff challenged with a teasing twinkle in his dark eyes.

"Funny, I don't remember being anything but thoroughly impressed," Candace said completely straight-faced. The total inaccuracy of her statement caused them all to burst into laughter, their chortles hitting the atmosphere with a mixture of amusement, coquetry, and curiosity.

"So how long are you in town?" Melanie inquired.

"I'm not quite sure. I'm here to audition for Lexis Richards's new movie. And my agent also set me up to read for an off-Broadway play."

"How did you get hooked up with Lexis?" Candace asked, curious about his apparent networking capabilities.

"My agent, Lois Jourdan. She and Felicia Wilcot are partners and Lexis is her client—"

"And fiancé," Candace interrupted, impressed with his connections. She'd read about the power couple in a spread about their New York penthouse in *InStyle* magazine. Along with Russell and Kimora, Will and Jada, Denzel and Paulette, Lexis and Felicia were part of celebritydom's glittering black gold set. *Maybe he could introduce me to Lexis,* she thought, smiling at Griff while visions of star-studded movie premieres flashed through her head.

"Six degrees of separation, baby," Griffin remarked. "So, to answer your question, Mel, if I get both parts I'll probably be here a good while."

"Not *if* you get it. *When* you get it. Always think positive. Where your mind goes, your butt follows," Melanie encouraged.

*And what a fine ass butt it is,* Candace thought, pursing her lips. *Oh, snap the hell out of it. So what the boy has a body and voice that make you wanna drop your draws? So what every ho in this room wants to be sitting in my seat? And so damn what he has a chance to be in a major movie? Underneath it all, he's ultimately a waste of time.*

In her book, Griff was unsuitable, as evidenced by his Latrell Sprewell cornrows and unconventional dress. She could never bring him around her conservative legal partners and be taken seriously. He was talented, yes, connected, maybe, but without a steady income, how much of a catch could he be? Plus, he fancied himself an artist, and everyone knew how unreliable creative types could be. So, bottom line: Griffin Bell was fine, sexy, and talented, but a total UN-C.O.L.A—UN-CIVILIZED, UN-OCCUPIED by full-time employment, UN-LIKELY to get his act together soon, and UN-ACCEPTABLE for anything more than a quick, curiosity fuck.

*And there ain't nothing wrong with a little hit and run,* she decided, already fantasizing about the possibilities.

"So what do you want, Candace?" Melanie asked, gesturing toward the waiter.

"What?" Candace responded, forcing herself to snap back into the moment.

"What would you like to drink?" Griff asked.

"What are you having?"

"An Absolut martini, straight up with olives," Griffin replied.

"Hmm . . . a sexy and bold choice. Just like the man, I presume?" Candace commented coyly.

"Don't forget potent," Griffin lightly tossed back, lusty interest shining in his eyes.

"I'll have a Cosmopolitan," Candace told the waiter.

"Sophisticated, sexy, and sweet. Just like the woman?" Griff echoed.

"Good God, you two, get a room," Melanie teased.

Mel's comment and the nervous laughter that followed temporarily broke through the sexual tension that had descended on their table. The three of them drank and made small talk while catching up on each other's lives. Melanie shared the excitement of her professional progress but was careful not to reveal too much personal information, knowing it would go straight back to Will. She watched Candace with amusement as her professed disinterest in Griffin turned into one of the greatest seduction scenes since Scarlett O'Hara tried her Southern belle best to snag Rhett Butler. And although Griff was busy giving as well as he was getting, Melanie was sure that the poor boy had no idea what grief he was ultimately in for.

Mel checked her watch and quickly drained her glass of Merlot. It was already after eleven and she had an early morning appointment at Carlson and Tuck. Besides, all the lusty eye contact and barely concealed come-ons between Candace and Griff were making her feel like the fourth wheel on a tricycle. "Sorry, kids. I've got to call it a night. Big meeting tomorrow. Candace, you coming?"

After a quick inquiring glance over at Griffin, Candace declined to accompany her roommate home, opting instead to stay and have a nightcap. After making Griff promise to keep her abreast of his progress, Melanie said her good nights and then requested that Candace walk her out.

"Damn, that man is sexy," Candy exclaimed as they strolled to the front door. "I think I'm going to give him some."

"What happened to no romance without finance?"

"Please. This is no 'ever after' kind of thing."

"You don't even know Griffin and an hour ago his 'broke ass' was out of your league. If you're not interested, why sleep with him?"

"Because I'm horny, Frank's a fucking no-show, and Griffin is turning me the hell on."

"And so you're going to turn him out?"

"I'm gonna try my best, so don't wait up." Candace laughed.

"I may have to. I still have a ton of work to do before my meeting tomorrow."

"You know what your problem is, Melo? You're overworked and underlaid. You need to play as hard as you slave. Whoa! I guess Griff's poetic side is rubbing off."

Melanie opened the door, took one step out into the cool night, and turned to face her roommate. "And you know what your problem is, Candy? You don't seem to understand that eventually, even the player gets played," she said with the heartfelt honesty that only a true friend can impart.

It took all the self-control Candace could muster not to mount Griff right there in the taxicab. By the time they reached his hotel, his deep kisses and naughty whispers had fueled her imagination and were unmercifully teasing her body. As the two walked arm-in-arm through the hotel lobby, Candy leaned into his muscular body, not only because her body demanded contact with his, but also because she felt too weak to stand on her own.

They stepped into the elevator and as soon as the doors closed, melted into each other. In the private space they explored each other's bodies for as long and as much as their ride up to the fourteenth floor would allow. Griffin was totally turned on by her shapely curves and adventurous nature, and Candace by his well-built torso and tight buttocks.

"Easy access. I love it," Griff observed as he popped the snaps on her leather dress down to her waist. By the time they exited the elevator, her bra and libido were in his capable hands.

The two quickly walked down the empty hallway until they reached room 1420. As Candace's lips hungrily searched for his,

Griff searched his trousers for the thin plastic card that would swing open the door to paradise. Abruptly he disengaged himself from her mouth and frantically rummaged in his pants pockets.

"Shit. I left my key in the room. Stay here while I run down to the front desk."

"I don't think so," Candace said, feeling the familiar tug of a turned-on clitoris. "Follow me." She was curious and horny—a combustible combination that left her unwilling to wait.

"Where are we going?"

"To fulfill a fantasy." As Candace continued down the hall, Griff waited, grinning hard as he treated himself to the splendor of her voluptuous form in motion. Fully aware that she was being watched, Candace swayed enticingly until she reached the exit leading to the stairwell and turned toward him. "Are you coming?"

"Not yet, but I damn sure plan to," he cracked, and jettisoned down the hall to meet her. "You don't care if someone sees us?" he asked as they walked through the door and onto the landing.

"All the better."

"Works for me, baby," Griffin said as he locked his gaze onto hers. Candace Bennett had the unmistakable look of a woman who wanted to get fucked. Without another word. Griff introduced his hungry mouth to her silky skin, detailing every hollow and bend of her face and neck with his tongue as they fell back against the wall. "Ohh, girl, you are sexy as hell," he whispered in her ear before unsnapping the rest of her dress and making a happy meal of her full and bubblelicious breasts.

Standing up against the wall with this man so expertly fondling and sucking her breasts, Candy could only moan in response. Griffin's kisses were igniting fireworks that erupted beneath her skin and caused her entire body to shake and shiver in response.

She felt the faucets of her vagina open up and release her juices into her panties. Candace could smell the moist scent of her sex and wondered if it made Griffin as hot as it made her. His erect penis against her thigh told her what she wanted to know.

Candace drew his tongue in her mouth and sucked in a gentle pulsating manner, making Griffin groan and grind his pelvis into hers. She backed off slightly, for as much as she was enjoying this delicious appetizer, her body was ready to move on to the next, more filling course.

"I want to taste me some Candy," Griffin moaned, as if reading her mind.

They moved away from the wall to the staircase and Griff sat down on the top riser. Candace positioned herself on the step below him and put her right foot on the tread above him, placing her pleasure zone directly in his face. With his index finger he pulled aside her thong panties to reveal a fresh Brazilian wax. Griff felt his penis jump and swell in response to this enticing visual.

Gently pulling the lips of her vagina open, he swiped at the creamy middle with his tongue. "Baby, your mama sure did name you right," he said, slowly licking his lips as he gazed into her face. Candace smiled slightly and winked before gently pushing his face back between her legs. Griffin blasted her clitoris with a gentle but concentrated stream of warm breath before tickling it with first the tip and then the whole of his tongue.

Candace, feeling momentarily weak with pleasure, grabbed tightly on to the handrail. Griffin inserted two fingers inside her and she felt herself instinctively begin to pump his face as she clenched her inner muscles around his fingers. Several floors down, they could hear the faint squeak of an opening door and the slow heavy thud of feet ascending the stairs. The intruding sounds pushed Candace to the point of no return and she exploded in his mouth, climaxing in pleasurable and powerful rhythmic spasms. Her lusty wails echoed up and down the stairs, stopping the intruder, and causing Griffin and Candace to burst into muffled laughter. They stood still for several seconds and after hearing the steps disappear through another door, he pulled her to him. "I want to fuck you," Griff declared.

"You do have a condom?" Candace inquired.

"In my room."

"Not to worry, I was a Girl Scout way back when." She reached for her purse and pulled out a rubber from her cosmetics bag.

Griffin stood in anticipation while Candace untied the draw-string on his pants and watched them fall over his meaty thighs and puddle around his feet. She slowly coaxed his boxers down to the floor to join them. Candace smiled and pursed her lips, pleased by her plentiful discovery. At that moment in time she wanted nothing more than to feel that beautiful, brown, rock-hard shaft inside her.

After wrapping him in latex, they moved in unison back onto the landing and against the wall. Candace raised her leg and placed it around his thigh as Griffin entered her. Both her mind and body sighed as he penetrated her and began gliding in and out. To keep his balance, Griff placed both his hands on the wall beside her head, and began to thrust and grind with mounting intensity.

"Oh, girl, you feel so good," he sputtered, getting lost in the pool of pleasure that was spreading through his body and threatening to overcome his senses. With each thrust she could feel him grow longer and harder, massaging the walls of her aroused vagina and teasing her engorged bud. Candace began to moan, and each sound signaled another burst of gratification for Griff. His penis was begging to explode, but Griff concentrated hard on holding back, forcing himself to enjoy the agonizingly pleasurable ride for as long as he possibly could.

Candace felt herself climax again and the powerful contractions around his shaft signaled the end of his self-control. Griff thrust hard, releasing his fluid. His moans mingled with hers, covering them both in a cloud of euphoric eroticism.

"So, baby, do you think that will hold you until I can run downstairs and get my key?" Griffin asked as he pulled on his pants.

"I think so, but hurry," she purred. "I've got a long list of fantasies to fulfill."

"Girl, you are too much. Wait here and catch your breath, cuz I got a few of my own."

With her curiosity piqued and her desire momentarily sated, Candace buttoned up her dress and leaned against the wall. Forget Jamaica. One night with Griffin Bell would have definitely given Stella her groove back, causing the girl not only to exhale, but also to scream out loud with primal gusto.

Griffin may be socially undesirable, but he was also erotically appealing. He was an uninhibited, unselfish lover whose moves were as lyrical as his poems. And with Frank acting like a total ass, Griff was exactly what Candy needed to get her through the long cold winter looming ahead. Candace Bennett had no long-range interest in Griffin Bell. He could give her nothing but a fuck and a smile, and that was plenty for her.

By the time Griff returned and the two hit the sheets, it was clear in Candace's mind that for however long this UN-C.O.L.A. was in New York, she had every intention of obeying her thirst.

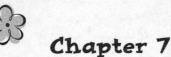

# Chapter 7

"**H**ow's the apartment coming?" Gwen asked before helping herself to generous forkful of amaretto cheesecake. "Have you found a decorator yet?"

"John hired someone. I have an appointment with him next week," Sharon replied. "We've agreed to be in by June, so that gives me eight more months in Stamford, including the holidays. I know it's months away, but you're coming for Christmas Eve, aren't you? After all, it will be the last at the house."

"Of course we'll be there," Gwendolyn confirmed before finishing her dessert, "After all these years, I don't think the boys would know what to do if we broke with tradition."

"So how are my handsome godsons?" Sharon asked.

"Terrific. They send their love and thanks for your latest extravagant care package. You spoil them terribly, Sharon."

"It's my job to spoil them."

"If you had your own kids, you'd think otherwise," Gwen commented.

Sharon let the remark slide down the prickles on her back without comment. No matter how long ago she thought she'd made peace with that touchy subject, Gwen's comment made her cringe.

The gurgle of water cascading down the restaurant's back wall filled the hushed gap created by the waiter's appearance with the check. Gwen withheld any comment until Sharon signed the bill, took her copy, and sent him off to his next station.

"I'm sorry. That was really an asinine remark."

"No need to apologize, so let's just drop the subject," Sharon replied, as they gathered their belongings and walked through the restaurant into brisk fall air.

"You know what you need right now?" Gwen asked, anxious to get their afternoon back on a happy track. "A chance to P.M.S."

"What are you talking about?"

"Purchase. More. Shoes," Gwen revealed, causing her friend to chuckle lightly.

"I can't believe you get paid for coming up with this stuff. Card Craze really did hire the perfect part-time copywriter."

"That one came to me this morning when I tried to take Bob's head off with my slipper while eating a bag of chocolate-covered pretzels. I would've hit him if I wasn't so damn bloated."

"What did the poor man do to deserve a breakfast beheading?"

"Bob *claims* he said 'Morning, sweetheart,' but I swear it sounded like 'Move it, old fart.'"

Sharon burst into laughter and Gwen continued to entertain them with silly copy ideas for future greeting cards until the cab dropped them at Bloomingdale's. After thoroughly inspecting the shoe department, they wandered aimlessly through the famous department store, taking time to explore each level, try on and purchase various sundries. Two hours later, standing on tired feet and laden with shopping bags, Gwen and Sharon sauntered over to the juniors department in search of a birthday gift for Gwen's fourteen-year-old niece.

"I don't understand why the sleeves of a sweater cost more than the whole thing," Sharon remarked, holding up a beaded knit shrug.

"Apparently, when it comes to fashion, less really is more."

"How about this?" Sharon asked, holding a pink, button-down shirt proportioned for a toddler, despite the size-nine hangtag. "Do you think she'll like it?"

"I have no idea what a fourteen-year-old likes."

"Then let's ask an expert," Sharon suggested after spotting a head of dark hair bobbing behind a hanging row of denim jeans. They walked over to the clothing rack in search of enlightenment.

"I was hoping you could help me," Gwen said, before noticing that the girl was busy stuffing a pair of jeans into a black Prada backpack.

The startled young woman abruptly turned around, her blue-gray eyes and plum-lipped mouth opened wide in surprise. Paralyzed by fear, she stood motionless like a guilty inmate caught in the prison yard floodlights. Immediately the girl dropped her bag and tried to dash, but Gwen quickly grabbed the unhooked strap of her Phat Farm overalls.

"Hey, let go of me," the teenager demanded, keeping her voice low as she tried to pull away.

"What are you doing?" Sharon asked, picking up the backpack.

"Minding my own business."

"Are you trying to steal those jeans?" Gwen queried.

"If you ask a little louder, maybe security will hear you. Now get off me, goddamn it, and give me my bag," the teen demanded, glaring at both of them.

"Young lady, don't you curse at me," Gwen snapped. An experienced mother, Gwen was not put off by the girl's defiant scowl and rude mouth and, instead of releasing her grip, hung on tighter.

Sharon stood by, studying the teenager with bewildered curiosity. While she was not a conventional beauty, her appeal was in her uniqueness. There was a dark and mysterious allure about her. Her hair was pulled back off her oval-shaped face, parted and plaited to her scalp, leaving the remainder of her auburn mane to fall straight to her narrow shoulders. She was wearing a small diamond stud in her left nostril and two gold hoops in each earlobe. A gold necklace encircled her neck, spelling out the name "Amanda." Despite her urban edginess, the girl exhibited the telltale signs of a teenager well acquainted with the mighty D.O.D.s of privileged youth—dermatology, orthodontia, and designer clothes. Her soft ivory complexion was smooth and clear; her teeth, white and perfectly aligned; her posture, aristocratic in stature. Even the well-crafted dishevelment of her casual clothes and accessories screamed of expensive nonchalance. It was obvious that the girl didn't *need* to steal, making Sharon all the more interested in knowing why she would want to.

"Is your mother with you, Amanda?" Sharon asked in a calming tone.

"How do you know my name?"

"It's on your necklace. Is your mother here in the store?" Sharon repeated.

"I'm fifteen years old. I don't need my mother tagging along if I want to go shopping."

"Judging by your unlawful 'shopping' habits, it appears you do," Gwen remarked impatiently. "Why aren't you in school? And don't tell me it's a holiday."

"I don't have to explain anything to you," the girl said, insurgence underscoring every word.

"Well, then perhaps you'd like to explain things to *her*," Gwen said, waving to get the sales associate's attention. "And then she can return the favor by explaining it to the police."

"So call her," Amanda said, her defiance strong. "It's after four o'clock. School's been out for hours."

A twentysomething salesgirl dressed in all black sauntered over to them, donning the standard-issue may-I-help-you grin on the way. Sharon quickly pulled the jeans out of the Amanda's nylon backpack and tossed them over her arm.

"Don't you dare go anywhere," Gwen warned under her breath as she released her grip.

"How can I help you?" the salesgirl inquired.

"Yes, this young lady here was trying to—" Gwen began before being cut off by Sharon.

"Trying to convince me that she couldn't live without these," Sharon said smoothly, holding up the patched and faded jeans.

"Well, I don't want to cause any family problems, but I have to agree with your daughter. These low-rise jeans are to die for. They're from Maynard Scarborough's debut denim line. The best thing, they're under four hundred dollars."

"Four hundred dollars to look like a bum?" Gwen asked in disbelief. "Who's stealing from whom?"

"They are *very* fashion-forward," the salesgirl tried to explain.

"Even so, I don't think she'll be bringing them home today," Sharon replied, handing her the jeans.

"Maybe next time," she said before strolling off to help another customer.

"I'm assuming there won't be a next time. Right, Amanda?" Sharon asked.

"Whatever," the young woman answered before taking the opportunity to make her getaway. Like the angry and misunderstood teenager she was, Amanda stormed away from her captors and immediately began running toward the escalator.

"Why did you let her get away like that?" Gwen asked her friend.

"I don't know. Even though she came off so brash and cocky, she had this lost and vulnerable look in her eyes. I guess I felt sorry for her."

"That little brat needs some serious home training. A couple of hours with the NYPD might do her good."

"Come on, let's get your niece's gift and get out of here," Sharon suggested, attempting to put the young girl out of her mind.

Convinced she wasn't being followed, Amanda paused on the down escalator long enough to catch her breath and sort out her emotions. She could feel the tears welling up behind her eyes, threatening to fall. They were tears of relief and regret that she hadn't gotten into serious trouble. On one hand, she was grateful that the blond lady, and not her bitchy friend, had interceded on her behalf. Still, while the situation would have been much more difficult if store security had alerted her mother, Catherine, perhaps the disappointing news would have been enough to keep her from moving to Japan and abandoning her.

Amanda discreetly wiped away her tears. Why was it that every mother in the world was ready and willing to come to her rescue? Every mother except her own.

*   *   *

While her decorator and contractor remained in the apartment to work out the details, Sharon walked out into the cool November afternoon to hail a taxi. She left the place feeling satisfied that the design decisions made today were on point and that she and Jude could indeed work well together.

As the yellow cab traveled across town toward Grand Central Station, the muffled notes of the minuet sent Sharon searching through her pocketbook for her cell phone.

"Hi, it's me. Did I catch you in the middle of anything?" John asked.

"No. What's doing?"

"Do we have any plans for Saturday?"

"Not that I know of. Why?"

"I need to do some research for the new art hotel and I thought we could spend the afternoon together at the Museum of Modern Art and then grab some lunch," he suggested.

"You know museums bore me to death. I get nothing out of that kind of 'artistic expression.' It all looks like scribbles on the wall to me. You don't mind if I pass, do you?"

"No, it's okay," John said, disappointed but certainly not surprised. "It was just a thought." They chatted until the cab turned the corner of Forty-second Street and stopped in front of Grand Central Station. "Thank you," she told her driver, pushing the fare and a healthy tip through the divider. She strolled into the station, and checked the schedule board for her train to Stamford. Seeing she still had another twenty-five minutes before departure, Sharon began walking to the nearest store for a bottle of water.

She noticed two black teenage boys approaching. They were dressed in Sean John T-shirts, low-riding baggy jeans, Timberline boots, and thick silver chains. Pressing her shoulder bag tight to her body, Sharon immediately crossed to the other side, taking her past a bank of public telephones. Several businessmen were engaged in conversation, but it was the teenager at the end or the row that caught her attention.

The silent body language of the young girl spoke loudly of depression and unhappiness. She stood, slumped forward into the cocoon of the Verizon pay phone, her ear pressed to the receiver, sniffling and wiping away tears with the back of her shirtsleeves.

Sharon went into the shop and made her purchase. On the way out she heard a loud angry voice that she vaguely recognized. She looked over in the direction of the sharp words and saw Amanda, the would-be shoplifter she'd met two weeks ago, red-faced and teary-eyed, screaming into the phone.

"I told you already, I'm not coming, so don't worry. You and that skank rah-rah have a good time," Amanda yelled before hanging up.

Sharon approached the girl just as she made an angry swipe with her arm, knocking her backpack off the shelf and sending it flying across the floor. "Amanda?"

"Oh, no, not you again," Amanda whined, recognizing Sharon. "Can my day get any worse? First Kevin, now you," she said, and broke down in tears. "Why do you keep popping up to hassle me?"

"Honey, are you okay?" Sharon asked, ignoring the girl's rancor as she searched her mascara-streaked face.

"What? Did my parents hire you to follow me?"

"I don't even know who your parents are. Why don't you tell me, so I can call them for you?"

Amanda's face donned an ironic smirk as she listened to Sharon's suggestion. "That's a funny one. Look, Mrs. . . . what *is* your name?"

"Sharon Carlson."

"Look, Mrs. Carlson, thanks but no thanks. I can get myself home all right."

"Shouldn't you still be in school?"

"Nah, we had early dismissal," Amanda said, avoiding Sharon's eyes.

"Is that the truth?"

Amanda took a deep breath and shook her head no. Her exhale brought with it a fresh onslaught of tears.

"Why don't we go sit down and talk?" Sharon suggested, eyeing a small gourmet shop across the terminal. Instinctively, she put her arm around the troubled girl and the two of them crossed the floor, stopping to pick up her backpack, and walked into the restaurant. Sharon went straight to the front counter, while Amanda headed toward the back in search of the bathroom.

"Sorry, miss, bathrooms are for paying customers only," the guy behind the counter called out to Amanda, clearly misunderstanding the makeup that had exploded on her face.

"Excuse me, but we are paying customers," Sharon intervened. "Go on, honey. I'll get a table while you're gone."

Amanda smiled slightly, once again surprised by the protective nature of Sharon Carlson. First in Bloomingdale's, now here, the woman was always coming to her rescue.

"We've never really been properly introduced," Sharon stated when Amanda returned and settled into the chair across from her. "I'm Sharon Carlson," extending her hand.

"Amanda Weiss."

"Nice to meet you, Amanda. So would you like to tell me what's wrong?"

"My boyfriend . . . my *ex*-boyfriend . . ." Amanda corrected herself as her voice wavered. "He dumped me," the teenager revealed, bringing on a fresh onslaught of tears.

"I'm sorry, honey," Sharon said, pulling a Kleenex from her purse and handing it to Amanda. "Losing someone you care for is never easy. Do you want to talk about it?"

Amanda stared blankly at Sharon as if she were speaking a foreign language. Few adults, particularly her parents, ever asked if she wanted to discuss *anything*, let alone something as painful and personal as breaking up with her boyfriend. Hell, Catherine and Nelson Sarbain didn't even know that she had a boyfriend.

"If you don't want to, I understand," Sharon said. Silence permeated the table. Sharon sipped her coffee while she waited for Amanda to make up her mind whether she wanted to talk or not. She watched as the girl, eyes cast downward, picked apart the tissue, leaving a snowy pile of paper on the table. Sharon sensed the internal struggle going on inside Amanda as she tried to determine whether she could or should be trusted.

"He met someone else. Someone he likes better. A stupid cheerleader," Amanda said softly, the hurt in her voice apparent. *Someone who will keep having sex with him. A girl who won't do it just once and quit,* she thought but didn't say.

"Tell me about him."

"Kevin is seventeen, a senior, and captain of the soccer team. He plays goalie and even made All-American. He's that awesome," Amanda announced with pride. "He's also smart, especially in math, and already has a scholarship to M.I.T. He loves music and basketball and is really fine—all the girls think so."

"Sounds like a catch."

"I thought we'd always be together. I mean . . . I love him. . . ."

"I'm sure you do, Amanda, but . . ."

"But what? I'm only fifteen and too young to know what it's like to really be in love?" the girl retorted angrily.

"I wasn't going to say that at all, honey. I think love is too powerful a feeling not to know when you're head over heels—at any age."

"When he broke up with me, he said he still loved me but didn't want to be tied down right now," Amanda revealed, grateful for Sharon's gentle understanding.

"I'm sure he does in his own way, but boys are kind of fickle at this age. They seem much more interested in quantity than quality."

"Do you have teenage sons?"

"No, I don't have any children of my own, but I do have two godsons in college, so I know a little bit about young affairs of the heart. Enough to tell you that with a little time and TLC you'll get over Kevin and happily move on to your next relationship."

"You seem like you have kids. You're really, you know—motherly," Amanda observed.

"Unfortunately, my husband and I aren't able to have children," Sharon explained.

"Figures. Those who should be parents can't be, and those who can—like mine—don't give a damn about the ones they have," the teenager said bitterly.

"I'm sure that's not true, Amanda. I'm sure your parents must love you very much," Sharon said reflexively, really not knowing if they did or not.

"Maybe they do love me, but they certainly don't like me."

"I don't understand."

"My newest stepfather, Nelson, is the head of one of the world's most successful law firms in New York, and Catherine prides herself on being an international socialite and snob. I am the ungrateful daughter my mother and my AWOL father spawned, and Nelson puts up with. The one who let them down by not buying into their bullshit lifestyle."

"I have to be honest, Amanda, I'd feel let down too if I knew my daughter was stealing from stores and doing who knows what else," Sharon said, noting Amanda's first name reference to her parents.

"I didn't want those jeans. I know this sounds stupid, but I was trying to get them to stay in the States instead of spending the next year in Tokyo while Nelson works on some big lawsuit. I figured if I got into a little trouble, they'd have to pay attention to me. But of course you came along and wrecked my plan," Amanda said, smiling for the first time since they sat down. "I guess I should thank you. They still would have gone anyway and I would have just gotten into more trouble and been a bigger disappointment to them."

"Why do you keep saying you're a disappointment to your parents?"

"I just don't seem to do anything right," Amanda replied without telling the entire story. How could she explain that Catherine wanted the perfect debutante? The ideal daughter who adored all the really shallow things in life, just like her mommy? Amanda had tried to be that girl. She had played along up until last year, when they tried to keep her in that stuck-up Cameron School for Girls, one of the most prestigious private high schools in New York City.

Her parents had claimed they wanted her to get a good education. A good education while mingling with the *right* kind of kids, was the way Amanda saw it. She hated it there—all the pretense and who's-got-what crap. It was full of girls who dot their *i*'s with hearts, and whose biggest worry was if the cafeteria served sugar-free Jell-O. Nobody there was real or interested in anything that mattered. Amanda felt isolated and alone, so she stopped going. When she threatened to drop out of high school altogether if they didn't send her to public school, the Sarbains let her transfer to Stuyvesant High School for her sophmore year. It was one of the top-rated high schools in the city. It just didn't have the snob quotient her mother found so desirable. It didn't seem to matter to Catherine that Amanda's grades were excellent or that her daughter was happy and loved her new friends. From Amanda's point of view, Catherine's focus was on the fact that she was hanging out with the wrong kind of people. It was probably a good thing Kevin and she broke up. Her parents would have *never* approved.

"Even though you can't see it now, I'm sure your parents only want the best for you," Sharon said, sadly repeating the words she'd heard all her childhood.

"How do you tell what's best for someone when you don't even know who they are?" Amanda asked. "Maria, our housekeeper, knows me better than my own parents do."

Sharon looked into the girl's sad blue-gray eyes and her heart melted. Sharon knew all too well the hurt this young woman was going through. Having been raised in the austere and cold household of her paternal grandparents, she knew from firsthand experience that no matter how grand the accommodations, a house without love that flowed freely and unconditionally was nothing more than a fancy prison.

With her parents, both medical doctors, continuously away administering to the needs of others in some third-world or war-torn country, their only child was left to grow up under the strict and confining supervision of her grandparents. Each time Ernest and Terry Parker returned home to visit, laden with exotic toys and exciting stories from around the world, Sharon would ask God to make her sick, so they would stay home and take care of her. But despite her fervent prayers, Sharon's body thrived and the Drs. Parker would once again leave their own child to take care of someone else's.

She was orphaned at age eleven, when her mom and dad died in a minefield accident. Sharon grew up feeling abandoned by her parents and unwelcome by her aging grandparents. The constant tug of guilty abhorrence for those responsible for her unhappy upbringing nagged at her. It stunted her emotional growth and left a cold spot on her heart along with a lifelong fear of exposing herself to the joys and pains of true intimacy.

Sharon pulled herself out of her memories and back into the room with this teenager whose life in so many ways mirrored hers. It was just like Kevin had told Amanda. People who were meant to be together eventually found each other. Fate was pushing her and Amanda together and Sharon felt compelled to find out the reason why.

"Amanda, I have to get going, but here's my telephone number," she said as she wrote her number down on a napkin. "You call me anytime you want to talk. Believe it or not, I understand what you're going through a lot more than you think. My parents weren't around much either when I was growing up."

"Thanks, Mrs. Carlson. If you really don't mind, maybe I will."

"Call me Sharon, and I really don't mind."

The two stood up from the table with genuine smiles for each other. As Sharon gathered her things and stepped away from the table, Amanda stepped toward her and delivered a shy embrace.

"It really is a shame that you aren't somebody's mom," she remarked sincerely.

Sharon tried to respond but was too overcome by emotion to speak. She merely smiled, silently conveying to Amanda that she couldn't agree more.

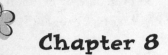

# Chapter 8

As Friday's sunlight slipped away, John was forced to turn on the lamp clipped to the side of his drafting table. He'd left his office at five-thirty, finished for the week with the massive projects under Carlson and Tuck's banner, and happily escaped to the place he now considered his creative haven. Upstairs he was John Carlson businessman and administrator; five floors down he became John Carlson architect and artist. It was amazing what a positive impact one short elevator ride could have on his psyche.

It was now seven-thirty and John worked in the hushed silence of a floor abandoned for the weekend. He really should be heading home himself, but he was too jazzed by the imaginative flow of possibilities now pouring from his head. His tabletop was buried with sheets torn from his sketchpad—all additional renderings for the interior of the Casa de Arte. All but this last drawing.

He sat back and took a long look at his work. He was supposed to be refining his sketches for the façade of the new hotel; instead he was holding a highly favorable and accurate portrait of Melanie Hitts's exquisite face.

*Oh, it's a façade, all right,* his inner male called out. *You keep pretending that your interest in this woman is strictly professional. Isn't it time to admit the truth?*

*What truth?* he silently shot back. *That I, John Remington Carlson, a fifty-year-old married white man, am attracted to a much younger, multitalented black woman whose creative juices I am unabashedly vampiring?*

Unwilling to have this telling and uncomfortable conversation with himself, John attempted to end his internal discourse by relocating to his office couch and concentrating on the quality of his work before him. It had been a long time since he'd sketched anything that wasn't meant to house, feed, or entertain people. He took this as yet another example of how this bright beauty inspired him. It meant more to John than he was willing to admit that Melanie had admired his paintings, though he was still too self-conscious to reveal that he was the artist.

John shifted positions and went back to work on his sketch. He took care to detail Melanie's high cheekbones and the springy mop of spiral curls that haloed her face, loving the captivating, wild-child look it gave her.

*But she's definitely no child,* he reminded himself, picturing her petite but shapely form. Closing his eyes, he could visualize the graceful sweep of her neck and back, and the enticing curves of her small but well-proportioned body. He could smell the sweet, floral essence of her signature fragrance—the classic Chanel No. 19, he was pretty sure—and for an instant he swore he could feel the soft pressure of her luscious full lips pressed up against his.

John forced his eyes open, feeling both ashamed and aroused. Since their initial meeting nearly two months ago, he'd been hiding his attraction to her behind his professional interest. It was true that Melanie Hitts was the first real source of inspiration he'd found in years and it felt good to be working with her. It was also true that she captured his imagination as no other female, including his wife, had managed to do in a very long time. John found himself irresistibly drawn to this young woman like a magnet to metal.

John put his drawing materials down, reached into his trouser pocket, and retrieved the single black pearl he always kept with him. He stretched open his palm and watched the small dark sphere roll around his hand, thinking it to be the perfect metaphor for Melanie Hitts—exotic, unique, precious, and highly sought after.

He returned to work on the portrait, further defining Mel's almond-shaped eyes, taking special care to include the tiny sparkle that appeared each time she smiled. As he sketched, it dawned on him that his interest in Melanie went far beyond the surface physical attraction. He very much wanted to see her again and find out what was hiding behind those incredible eyes and that enchanting smile.

This nagging desire dragged him over to the phone and prompted him to dial Melanie's number. As it rang, John rehearsed the reason for his call, wanting to sound convincing, though he was fearful that she would see right through his flimsy excuse. He took a deep breath when she answered the phone.

"Jax. It's John. I'm sure you're on your way out, being this is Friday night . . ." he quickly and rather awkwardly blurted out.

Melanie felt herself smile. She liked when he called her by this special nickname.

"Actually, I just got in from the office and plan to spend an exciting evening going through some art books."

"I admire your work ethic," John told her, feeling silly and grateful that she was staying home. "In fact, that's why I'm calling. I was hoping we might be able to meet tomorrow. I'm planning to go over to the Museum of Modern Art for a little inspiration and it occurred to me that you should join me. You know, to help narrow down our twelve artists," John added, not wanting Mel to think he was asking for a date.

"I love MoMA, but . . ."

"I know it's Saturday, but it's impossible for me to get away during the week and we should get this nailed down. Plus, we really need to discuss the rooftop sculpture garden," John added, attempting to use her penchant for hard work to his advantage.

"Any other Saturday would be fine, but . . . well . . ."

"You have plans," John finished, embarrassed by his disappointment. *You're behaving like a ridiculous teenager,* he scolded himself.

"I was going to do some antique shopping tomorrow."

"For a client?" John asked, knowing interior decorators often scoured vintage stores and flea markets on behalf of their customers.

"No, for me. I guess it's time to come clean and admit that I am a flea market hag with a *serious* addiction to vintage jewelry."

"A jewelry addict maybe, but certainly no hag," John joked, as he quickly plotted his next move. "Look, I'm on a roll right now and I hate the idea of losing my momentum, but to go any further we really need to make some decisions and we have to make them before the Thanksgiving break next week. So, at the risk of being pushy, how about I invite myself along? We can talk shop while you . . . well, shop."

"You're sure you don't mind?" she asked with slight trepidation. Usually Mel liked to go alone so she could browse at her leisure, but how could she refuse him?

"Not if you don't."

"Okay, then, let's meet at 112 West Twenty-fifth Street. Nine o'clock?"

"Perfect." John smiled at the idea of seeing her again. The museum could certainly wait until next week.

"John, please don't be late. The early bird gets all the tasty worms."

"I'll be there," John assured her, looking down at her sketch. He had no intention of making himself wait any longer than necessary to see her.

By 8:40 A.M. John was waiting for Melanie to arrive. He distanced himself from the small crowd beginning to assemble, all eagerly waiting to see what treasures the past held for them. John peered across the street and, abandoning his usual habit of studying the architectural details of the surrounding buildings, allowed himself to get lost in his thoughts of Melanie. All last night, he had tried to block their meeting from his mind—knowing that such romantic reveries were inappropriate for a man in his situation. But the harder he tried not to, the more his mind and imagination insisted, and John felt himself being overtaken by a sensation he hadn't experienced in decades—giddy nervousness brought on by sweet anticipation.

These sophomoric feelings were as delightful as they were outrageous. John had lived half a century and been married nearly a quarter of one. At his age, with his abundance of worldly life experience, he should be well past the time of sweaty palms and schoolboy crushes. But here he was, standing on the corner, feeling his heart go pitter-patter at the sight Melanie Hitts, and loving every minute. John watched as her denim-clad body approached, enjoying the slight sway of her hips caused by the three-inch heels on her boots.

"Been waiting long?" Mel asked, looking up at him. Even in high heels Mel was such a tiny thing, but in their brief acquaintance John had learned that her diminutive size in no way detracted from her dynamic strength.

"Not really. Shall we go inside?" he suggested as they blended into the rest of the shoppers and shuffled their way up and into the building. "This is a first for me," he admitted.

"Then today I dub you an honorary lord of the fleas," Mel joked, playfully tapping his shoulder. "Now let me give you the short list of rules."

"Should I take notes?"

"Nah. The two most important things you should know are: Don't be overenthusiastic about something or the price will go up, and don't pay more than fifty bucks for anything unless you really know it's a score. Bottom line: If it makes your heart sing and the price is right, buy it."

"Sounds a lot like dealing with building suppliers," John said.

"Exactly. Today, we are searching for charms," Mel announced, holding up a heavy gold-bearing bracelet. "Now try to keep up," she added playfully as she headed for a table laden with tempting trinkets and brilliant baubles. Gone from her eyes was the warm and seductive twinkle that brought John's forgotten emotions alive. In its stead was the steely-eyed coldness of a ruthless, experienced shopper.

Melanie quickly cast her knowing glance over the shiny offerings, but nothing captured her attention so she didn't linger. With John following, Melanie hurried to the next aisle of tables set up in the converted garage. "This is the good stuff," she whispered before stopping at a table covered with black velveteen trays stuffed with rings, charms, bracelets, and pins—each piece of estate jewelry posing the difficult question: to buy or not to buy?

John watched as a poker-faced Melanie quickly perused the table, stopping several times to pick up and inspect the merchandise. As his eyes followed Mel's hand reaching for an art deco diamond ring, he saw a glittery pin that caught his attention. It was a combination of baguette rubies and round diamonds wrapped around what resembled a scepter encrusted with tiny pearls. He had no idea if the stones were genuine or faux, but it didn't matter. His interest was in the architectural flow of its design. Through his professional eyes he saw an alluring and uniquely curved staircase flanked by glistening banisters. Automatically his professional mind replaced the fiery rubies with glass blocks lit by fiber optics for sparkle and anchored by expanded steel. He then picked up an antique sapphire ring whose intricate carvings on its shank and gallery immediately conjured up visions of dramatic ceiling details and other decorative possibilities.

On impulse John purchased the ruby pin and then continued to browse with a renewed interest. Though he'd given Sharon a pirate's bounty in gems over the years, he'd always had his jeweler pick things out, never really paying attention to his choices. Never before had he noticed how much the design of jewelry and architecture had in common. Both utilized line, form, and function to create beautiful, livable art. He smiled as he realized how this simple shopping expedition had turned into an inspired adventure. And he knew just whom to give credit to.

John caught up with Melanie at a table teeming with exquisite antique evening bags. He watched her inspect a small beaded purse and gently finger the stones embedded in the frame. "I'll give you seventy-five dollars," she announced nonchalantly.

"This bag is circa 1930. Three hundred," the man behind the table replied.

"One hundred," Mel countered. The two continued to haggle, but could not come to a financial meeting of the minds.

"Too much," Mel announced, declining the man's best price of $225. She handed back the purse and walked away. John could see that she was disappointed, but intent on sticking to her budget.

"I'll give you two hundred," John said once Mel was out of earshot. It was the least he could do to thank her for bringing him here to help replenish his creative well. "I'll take this one too," he announced, pointing to the small mother-of-pearl clutch with a turquoise-encrusted clasp that had called out to him, proclaiming itself to be the perfect Christmas gift for Sharon.

After nearly three hours of browsing and bartering, John and Melanie walked through the exit doors as satisfied customers and headed for the closest restaurant to have lunch.

"I can't believe I found a complete set of milk-glass dishes for twelve. The Hawkinses are going to love them," Mel said.

"Relatives?"

"No, though they feel like they are. They're a family I try to help out whenever I can. It makes me feel good—you know, spread the wealth a bit. Speaking of which, your wife is going to love that clutch. Lucky girl. I can't believe that guy sold my purse before I could get back around to him. So much for my haughty take-it-or-leave-it attitude."

"You know the rules. If it makes your heart sing, buy it," John repeated Mel's words with secret pleasure. Feeling awkward about giving her a gift for no apparent reason, he'd decided to surprise her with it for Christmas.

"Which is exactly why I snatched up this lovely," she proclaimed, holding up a tiny gold tube of lipstick that actually retracted like the real thing. "They don't make intricate charms like this anymore. That's why I love the old stuff."

"As a man some might describe as 'old stuff,' I thank you for the compliment." John smiled, flashing his dimples.

"You're not old. You're seasoned," Melanie replied, returning his grin. John Carlson was definitely no senior citizen. Mel estimated him to be at least fifteen years older than her, yet he was more energetic, curious, and fit than many men she knew her own age.

"So, what got you interested in vintage jewelry?" he asked after they ordered lunch.

"I always loved rummaging around in Grandy's jewelry box when I was a little girl. She was quite the socialite and for each piece she owned there was always some fascinating story behind it. Now I look at every antique and wonder what kind of life it led before it landed in my hands," Melanie explained.

"I have to admit that I was inspired by some of the designs I saw today—particularly the estate pieces."

"I know what you mean. The rings and bracelets, especially from the twenties and thirties, are amazing works of craftsmanship."

"I saw you examining the diamond rings," John said, setting himself up to take the plunge. "Tell me why an attractive woman like you isn't showing off your own engagement ring."

"Long story."

"Well, I've got all afternoon and an entire cheeseburger to go," John prompted in a blatant attempt to satisfy his curiosity.

"I was engaged but broke it off earlier this year," Mel conceded softly.

"I can see by your expression that it must have been a difficult decision."

"It was . . . in many ways. Will is really a terrific man, but we hadn't dated very long, and as it turned out, there was a lot he didn't understand about me," Melanie admitted. "I can't really blame him. Most days *I* don't even know myself."

"Getting to know yourself is a lot like building a skyscraper— with each new floor you add, the view changes."

"Yeah, but from my vista, I still feel like a bungalow on a block of high-rises."

"Sometimes when you're on the inside looking out, it's hard to remember what an impressive addition you are to the landscape," John offered as both advice and a compliment.

"Maybe, but I think I've always felt out of place."

"Where did you grow up?"

"In Richmond, Virginia, until I started high school and my parents moved to the Washington, D.C., area."

"What made you feel so out of place?" John inquired with genuine interest.

"Just about everything—school, religion, clothes, family values."

"That's sounds heavy."

Mel proceeded to reveal to John how she found little inspiration in the traditional family values that had obviously worked well for over five generations of her people. But then again, none of the Hitts women had aspirations of being anything more than happy homemakers. While some had dabbled in the workforce, they'd all gladly given up their jobs once married, proudly excelling in their roles as wives and mothers. Old-fashioned as it might seem, even her sister Francesca had bought into the family legacy. Only Melanie had postponed marriage for the sake of her career.

"That almost killed my mother," Mel revealed, surprised by how comfortable she felt discussing this very private part of her life with John. "I think she could accept the idea of a 'spinster' daughter who gave up marriage and children to be something important like a doctor or lawyer, but to buck the family legacy for a career decorating office buildings and hotels is troubling. She doesn't seem to grasp that the opportunity to be creative and work at my passion is very fulfilling—at least for now."

"You're lucky. Very few people love what they do. Most work simply to pay the bills. It's also a shame that most people see artistic endeavors as egotistical and unproductive, when really the opposite is true. They have no idea of the time, commitment, and perseverance it takes to realize one's dream," John stated with aged impatience cracking his voice.

"Well, enough about me. Shouldn't we discuss the hotel?" Melanie asked, veering the conversation onto safer, less personal ground.

For the next hour they reviewed various aspects of the project, concluding with satisfaction that their concept was fresh and strong.

"One more thing," Mel said after discussing the lobby. "I think *your* artwork should also be displayed," she suggested.

"Mine?" John paused before admitting the truth. "How did you know?"

"Just a gut feeling. When we talked about it, you had the look of the embarrassed but proud artist. You're very good. Why didn't you pursue it professionally?"

"Long story."

"Well, I've got time and half a cup of coffee left," Melanie replied impishly.

"Fair enough. I know very well how it feels to be 'different.' As much as I always loved building things as a kid, I loved painting more."

With the annoying jabs of childhood pain punching at his gut, John explained how his announced intention to move to Paris to paint and study art was answered with an unscheduled trip to the state fair the day after his high school graduation. Instead of viewing the prize cows and pie-eating contests, his father proceeded to point out all the folks trying to eke out a living drawing caricatures of people for two dollars a pop—making it clear that no son of his was going to sit around all day painting pictures like a child because he was too lazy to get a real job.

"Did you ever make it to Paris?" she asked, fighting the urge to wrap her arms around him in a comforting hug. Melanie could hear his bitterness in each word and feel the hurt in each breath.

"No. I stopped painting that very day and haven't picked up a brush since. I still sketch every now and again, but those paintings you saw in my office were my last."

"Only the last of that era," Melanie encouraged. "Every great artist, from Matisse to Warhol, went through some sort of tough transitional period. Maybe our hotel will mark your reentry into the art world."

John said nothing. He simply smiled slightly and shrugged his shoulders before reaching for her hand across the table. This day spent shopping and sharing everything from their views on jewelry to the painful and intimate secrets of their pasts had caused a shift in the tide between them. No longer simply bound by work, Melanie and John had fused a undefined connection to each other that teetered precariously on the border between friendship and something deeper and far more complicated.

"Thank you for spending this day with me, for listening, for everything," John said tenderly.

"No, thank *you*," Melanie murmured as she leaned forward and delivered a lingering whisper of a kiss to John's cheek. She pulled away, but their gazes held and Mel witnessed a tender meltdown take place behind his eyes. For a brief moment, they each sat studying the other's face for a clue to what was happening between them. The same bewitching pull they'd felt between them the day her beads burst was back, once again playing tug-of-war with their hearts and minds.

The earlier comfort Melanie had felt was gone, replaced by the immediate need to remove herself from this perplexing situation. "John, I really have to go. I didn't realize it was so late," she said abruptly, looking at her watch for added emphasis. She quickly gathered her things, extended a brief farewell, and hurried toward the exit.

John sighed as he gently stroked the place where Melanie's soft lips had touched his skin. It was the most innocent yet powerful kiss he'd ever received. Its residue lingered, propagating disturbing questions in his mind. Was he falling in love with this woman? And why did she run off so suddenly? Did she feel it too?

*Be serious*, John thought, quickly pulling back the notion and discarding it from his mind. *She ran off because you probably scared the hell out of her. The reality is that the idea of a taboo love affair excites you. With Melanie you feel young, adventurous, and a bit dangerous. So chalk this up to a simple midlife crisis and get over it.*

Be it midlife crisis or true love, John knew one thing for sure. This five-foot-one dynamo who reeked of mystery, undeniable sensuality, and talent with a capital *T* had gotten firmly under his skin.

# Chapter 9

"I'm not sure that 'only twenty-three shopping days left until Christmas' qualifies as a legit reason for skipping work," Melanie told Candace as the manicurist filed her nails. Mel was still feeling guilty for letting Candy talk her into calling in sick today. Celebrating Thanksgiving down in Richmond with her extended family last week had afforded Melanie little time to whittle down her lengthy To Do list for work, and she still had at least five major tasks to complete before her meeting next week with John.

"Consider this a mental health day. You've been working so hard and I never see you anymore. How can I be your nosy best friend if we never talk? Now, what's been bugging you?"

"It's really nothing," Melanie insisted. "I met this guy through work—"

"You met a man?" Candace shrieked in disbelief. "How can you hold out on me like this?"

"I meet men all the time. Don't make this into something bigger than it is."

"Then why don't you tell me exactly what *it* is?"

"Do you want your cuticles clipped or pushed back?" the manicurist asked.

"Pushed, please," Mel replied, grateful for the interruption. She was reluctant to answer her friend. Melanie was too confused by what was going on between her and John to even attempt to explain it to anyone else, particularly Candace, whose understanding of men and the complicated relationships often associated with them was based solely on the notion of "What have you done for me lately?"

Melanie knew that Candy would have a hard time understanding her attraction to John Carlson. First of all, John wasn't Will Freedman and Candace still championed Will's cause, seizing every opportunity to remind Mel what a great catch she'd given up. Second, he was white, and for reasons unknown to Mel, Candace abhorred the idea of dating "Europeans." When it came to men, she didn't care if he was older, younger, single, married, with kids, or without, as long as he had a big johnson, an even bigger bank account, and was a man of color—*any* color but white.

"What it is is friendship. He's a colleague whose work I admire very much and whom I find really inspiring," Melanie replied, concentrating on her half-finished French manicure.

"Friendship?"

"Friendship," Mel reiterated.

"Between a man and a woman? I don't think so."

"You want to join us in the new millennium? That attitude is as old as Jesus."

"I'm sorry, but men and women are not meant to be friends," Candace refuted, while signaling the manicurist to clip her acrylic tips a tad shorter.

"And why not?"

"A little thing called s-e-x. I don't know one man who is satisfied with talking and swapping secrets without hitting the sheets—unless he's gay. Besides, almost every pain-in-the-ass ailment that inflicts women starts with men."

"Like?" Melanie asked, knowing she was venturing into dangerous territory. For as much as Candace loved men, there was also a rancid bitterness that ran through her heart.

"Like MENstrual cramps. MENtal illness. MENopause. With that kind of track record, why would you want one as a friend?"

"Yeah, but there's also MENtor, which is a very positive thing. We all need one and should be one. And what about MENage à trois? I know that's a fantasy that's kept you up more than a few nights," Melanie joked.

"True, that," Candace replied, "but don't try to change the subject. Let's get back to this new colleague who is talented, insightful, and inspirational. All admirable attributes, but the question remains: Is he fine?"

"I think so."

"And you're not drawn to him at all? Not one little iota of a I'd-like-to-break-me-off-a-piece-of-that buzzing around your head or other, more pertinent parts?"

Melanie took a moment to quickly analyze her attraction to John. She liked the way he listened to her with rapt attention, as if what she were saying was the most important thing he'd heard all day. She enjoyed the way his face glowed with almost childish pleasure when they came up with an idea that worked, and the way his eyes set off a chain reaction of facial movements that erupted into a smile which could only be described as sunshine personified. Did she find John physically appealing? Absolutely.

Mentally stimulating? Without a doubt. Melanie found pleasure in his conversation, genius in his work, and eager anticipation preceding every meeting with him. But was she *sexually* attracted to him? Mel genuinely didn't know.

"Maybe. I'm not sure," she said honestly.

"I rest my case. Even if you're not sure, the fact that there's even a question means that *something* is there to keep you and your 'colleague' from being 'just friends.' Sexual desire and friendship do not mix. That's like dipping ants in chocolate."

"Listen, counselor, have you ever once considered the fact that you can just delight in being attracted to someone without having to end up in bed together? That it's okay to simply feel and enjoy sexual energy without *doing* anything with it?"

"But why *not* do something if the attraction is there?"

"Because it's not always the right thing to do. Sometimes acting on it just complicates the situation more than necessary."

"Well, that's you, girlie. If the spark is there, I'd rather light the fire than wonder what I'm missing," Candace declared as the two crossed the salon headed for the pedicure tubs.

"And speaking of sparks, you and Griffin have been spending a lot of time together. What's going on?" Mel asked, dipping her toes into the tub. Melanie felt herself relax the moment her feet slipped into that warm soapy water.

"Nothing," Candace replied coyly, avoiding Melanie's eyes.

Mel noted with interest the glaring lack of detail provided by her friend. That, in combination with the soft coo of her voice and sanguine grin that threatened to erupt from her lips, confirmed Melanie's suspicions. Mutual interest was definitely blowing in the crosswinds between Griff and Candace. Was Candy actually falling for a man whose essence outweighed his wallet?

"So has he heard anything about the movie?"

"They hired Joe Brandon."

"Well, he still has the play. How's that going?"

"Good. Griff's playing the lead."

*Was that pride lurking behind her words?* Mel wondered. "That's great. Griffin is really on his way."

"Come on, Melo. He might be working, but we're not talking August Wilson on the Great White Way here," Candy said, snapping back to the wickedly sarcastic, openly judgmental girlfriend Mel knew and loved. "This is a show written by some unknown playwright, being performed in some tiny hole-in-the-wall theater situated in a dark alley somewhere south of where-the-hell-are-we. He'll be lucky if anybody besides us and the rest of the cast's families show up."

"Plenty of great careers got started off-Broadway."

"We're talking so off-Broadway it's practically New Jersey. Translation: He ain't getting paid. But he still seems excited. Go figure."

"He should be excited. And you should be for him. Don't be so hard."

"I like hard. Especially when it comes to Griffin," Candace replied, sticking out her tongue.

"So he's just your boy-toy for when Frank's not around? Nobody you could get serious with?" Mel asked as Candace merely rolled her eyes in response. "Look at him, Candy. Sure, he's not rich, but he's fine, smart, funny, and thoughtful. He's got it all."

*He's got it all and still has nothing,* Candace screamed in her head with unspoken frustration.

She knew that Melo found her high standards to be unreasonable and unfair. But how could Melanie possibly understand? She grew up on D.C.'s gold coast, high among the branches of a family tree that bloomed generation after generation with doctors, lawyers, professors, and entrepreneurs. Candace, raised by a single mother who never married the selfish bastard who impregnated her, clung to feeble boughs of a Charlie Brown-esque pine tree, dropping to the ground weary kinfolk who never learned the fine distinction between living life and letting life live them.

Melanie took for granted all the wonderful, beautiful *things* that growing up with pedigree and disposable income could buy. *Things* that made her a member of the elite black bourgeois. *Things* that screamed to the world that she belonged.

Where Melo belonged, Candace simply associated. Candy grew up in Dayton, Ohio, and like her best friend, spent time socializing with the exclusive cliques of groups like Jack and Jill and the Links, but with a gaping difference in their connection. While Melo attended as a member, Candace frequented these functions as a visitor. Candy had swum in the warm sapphire-blue waters of the Caribbean, got up close and personal with Mickey Mouse, trekked the Mayan ruins of Mexico, and stayed in the luxurious surroundings of five-star hotels on family vacations, but always with someone else's family—never her own.

Candace's youth was spent making guest appearances in the good life. She had long determined that her adult years would be markedly different. She and her husband would plant their own strong, distinguished family tree—one that replicated the timbers she'd been temporarily nesting in all her life. Candace was smart enough to realize that the luxury cars, diamond jewelry, designer clothes, and world travel wouldn't make her happy. They would, however, place her squarely within a class of people who looked down instead of being looked down upon; folks who walked into the room like they owned it, not like they cleaned it. Candace wanted money not to buy happiness, but to purchase legitimacy and all the lovely acceptance it brought with it.

How could she make Melanie understand that Griffin Bell just didn't fit into her future? Griff was all those wonderful things that Mel had mentioned and more. But it would be years, if ever, before he could afford her the prestige and lifestyle she desperately craved. She had sacrificed a lot these past years, concentrating solely on building her own professional reputation, which is why exclusively dating married men had worked so well. But now that she was ready to settle down with a man of her own, Candace had neither the time nor the interest in backsliding into an one-day-we'll-have-it-all relationship. As far as Candy was concerned, that one day was already here.

"Look, Griff is a genuinely nice brother and has skills, both on- and offstage. But unfortunately, talent is all he has to offer. I need more," Candy explained with a hint of resignation in her tone.

"And Frank's got what you need?"

"Yeah. He does."

"Including a wife?"

Candace responded with a quick cut of her eyes in her friend's direction, letting Melanie know that she was trampling on dangerous ground. This time last year her days as his mistress seemed numbered, but now, with Frank's public profile quickly rising, his marriage appeared to be on a steady course toward reconciliation. And all this newfound marital bliss was reeking havoc on Candy's quest to become the next Mrs. Franklin Warren.

"Well, I think you really do like Griffin," Mel said quickly, jumping to safer conversational ground. "Much more than you're 'fessing up to."

"I do like him. We're buddies," Candace replied, unwilling to concede any further information on her feelings for Griffin.

"Didn't you just tell me that men and women can't be friends?"

"You have your kind of buddies and I have mine."

"Oh," Melanie said as it dawned on her what Candace meant. "You and Griffin are fuck-buddies."

"Exactly. And he exceeds all standards in that category."

"Spare me the details. You're talking to a woman who's been celibate for nearly a year. And you know what? Sex is like a postage stamp. It's not important unless you need one," Melanie groaned.

"A year? But you and Will have only been broken up for six months. Wait, are you serious? You and Will never did it?"

"No. We were waiting until our wedding night."

"How could you agree to marry him without a test drive? That's like buying shoes from a catalog. How do you know they'll fit? And how can you go this long without sex? Don't you miss all that delicious pokin' and strokin'?"

"Yes, I do, so can we change the subject now? Talking about it just makes me more frustrated."

"Weren't you just telling me that it was a good thing to simply feel and enjoy your sexual energy but not do anything with it?"

"Shut up, ho," Melanie retorted, making them both laugh. "Don't you know that chastity is a virtue?"

"Yeah, chastity is a virtue, and celibacy will have you biting your nails, thus ruining a perfectly good manicure," Candy said, waving her newly wrapped nails for emphasis. "Either way, you still wind up mad and horny."

\* \* \*

Will sat absentmindedly in front of the television, staring at the kaleidoscope of colors and images flashing before his eyes. He took another long sip of his scotch and soda, attempting to drown the pangs of his rising depression. He dropped his head and hands between his knees and looked down at the carpet beneath him. The floor was littered with the images of the woman he loved. Why he had chosen to torture himself by going through old photos of Melanie could only be explained by his desperate need to find some sign in the past that they still had a future.

Candace's e-mail had rocked his world and shaken his confidence. In all of their past communications she'd assured him that Melanie was still unattached, still uninterested in dating, and still working hard to forget him. Each report had given him cause to stay hopeful. And then, with today's news, hope quickly came tumbling down like a line of dominoes. Will's eyes scoured the floor, searching for the crumpled remains of Candace's disheartening communiqué. He found it lying ironically on top of a smiling photograph of Mel on the snowy day they'd met. Will picked up the photo and the printout and read for the hundredth time Candace's gentle warning tucked within the words of an invitation.

Subj: Griff's preview
From: LOLLIEPOP
To: STILLWILL


Hey Willi,


What's shaking down in D.C.? I'm sure you've already heard from Griffin that he's got the lead in a new play. I'm going to the preview on December 11th. The boy is actually nervous, which has to be a first for him, so I know he would appreciate seeing you in the audience. And yes, to answer your question, Melanie is going too.

A little friendly advice: You *really* should try to come up. Melo and I had a little girl-to-girl at the spa yesterday and apparently she's met someone. She says they're simply friends and at this point I believe her, but there's no reason to take chances. I have no idea who the brother is, but I really think you should make the effort to join us. We'll keep it on the down-low from Melo so she can't cop out at the last minute.

I do know that she is not bringing him to the preview, so the seat next to hers is yours. I expect to see you in it. You need to talk to Melanie and Griffin needs all of our support. It's a win-win for all of us.

Candace

Will finished reading and looked down at the photo of Melanie's smiling face. That smile had the power of magic. It was the door to his heart and the thought of losing her to another man devastated him. He had given Mel the requested time and space and not a damned thing had changed. And now this? Friend or otherwise, the time for sitting and waiting was over.

*Candace is right. There's no point in taking chances,* he thought as he reached for the phone. It didn't occur to Will until after he'd booked his flight and hotel that Candace's attitude toward Griffin had done a complete turnabout. Somehow that tidbit of insight bolstered his optimism. Without warning, Will found himself laughing out loud. If Candy and Griff, whose views on the world were as compatible as the liberals' and conservatives', could discover a middle ground on which to dwell, he and Melanie certainly could find their way back to each other.

# Chapter 10

Griffin paced backstage, praying to the theater gods for a successful performance. Even though this was a small production, intuitively he knew that this could be an important step up his career ladder. *Race for the Race* was a powerful vehicle that not only showcased his dramatic and comedic talents, but was also so emotionally potent that no observer would leave the place untouched.

Griff parted the drapes slightly and peeked out into the theater. With less than thirty minutes until the curtain went up, the seats were nearly full. Thanks to the efforts of the cast and crew to paper the house, enough free tickets had been distributed to friends and family to ensure a plentiful and appreciative audience. More importantly, Dirk, the playwright and director, had tugged all the strings available to get *New York Times* critic Frank Rich to review the play. One positive scribble from his pen and Griff's career would be off and running.

Griffin searched the room seat by seat, looking for the one face he earnestly wanted to behold. His smile broadened when he saw Melanie seated third row center and quickly faded when he noticed that she was sitting alone, surrounded by an empty seat on either side. Neither Will nor Candace were anywhere in sight.

Will's plan he knew, but where was Candace? It was almost show time. She'd promised to come, but with Candace promises made could become promises broken without thought or explanation. Griffin walked back to his dressing room disbelieving the depth of his disappointment. He shook his head in an attempt to dislodge the disruptive emotion from his psyche and clear his head for his upcoming performance.

He opened the door to a small dressing area and stepped onto a path of red-, pink-, and salmon-colored rose petals. Griff looked up to find Candace waiting—her long, sexy legs propped up on his makeup table. Golden stars dusted the tabletop and a bottle of champagne was chilling in a plastic bucket at her feet. Candy sat gently plucking the petals from a bright red American Beauty rose and dropping them into the pile on her lap while Griffin stood in shocked awe, motionless but for the slight jump in the crotch of his pants.

"I've been waiting for you. I wanted to give you these," she said as she stood and threw up a sprinkle of scented confetti into the air. Griffin watched the petals slowly rain down, several clinging to Candace's hair and exposed cleavage. "I also wanted to deliver this," she said, stepping toward him and bestowing a deep, soulful kiss on his lips. "Break a leg, baby. I'll see you after the show," she added with a promising drawl. She winked at a still-speechless Griffin and lightly brushed his genitals as she walked past him and out the door.

Griff chuckled out loud at this show of vintage Candace— impulsive, unpredictable, always sexy, and when you least expect it, surprisingly thoughtful. In between their rounds of erotic pillow talk these past nine weeks, Griffin had seen glimpses of emotion that urged him to search further for the true woman within. What he'd discovered behind her judgmental and opinionated banter was a strong core of warmth and compassion that Candace kept hidden from most of the world. Griffin sat down at the mirror to touch up his makeup and it suddenly occurred to him that his heart, not to mention his dick, was frantically waving the white flag. Staring back at his own surprise, Griff also realized, with the joy and apprehension that came with such a huge admission, that escape was not an option.

Candace hurried down the center aisle. She was nearly at her assigned row when a woman stepped out in front of her.

"Excuse me," the woman said, looking straight into Candace's face. Candy felt herself flinch. Standing behind the woman was Frank Warren.

"Frank, how are you? Candace Bennett—Margent, Katz, Crawford and Thames," she said in a totally professional tone that didn't match the wicked gleam in her eyes.

"Ah, yes, very good law firm," Frank responded, feeling his palms begin to perspire. He could only hope she didn't create a scene of some sort. With Candy he could never tell. "This is my wife, Regina."

"Hello," Regina said, extending her hand. Candace immediately noticed her David Yurman ring, which was the exact replica of the one Frank had given her.

"Beautiful ring," Candace said slyly as she revealed her own and then laughed, adding that they both had great taste in jewelry.

"Thank you, but actually my husband is the one with the great taste."

"So Frank, what brings you here?" Candace asked, turning her attention back to her nervous lover.

"Regina sits on the board of this theater company."

"Yes, and I'm really looking forward to the performance," Regina said, continuing to make small talk while suspecting nothing.

"Me too. My boyfriend is playing the lead," Candace said, looking directly at Frank. She was pleased to see his eyebrows converge in a subtle show of jealous displeasure. Let him think that Griff was her man. Shit, fair is fair, and if Frank was going to continue to play games, she was going to make sure that the field they played on was level.

"The show is starting soon, so if you'll excuse us," Frank interrupted. "Candace, it was nice running into you."

"You too. Enjoy the show."

*Asshole. How dare he buy his wife and me the same jewelry?* Candy fumed as she joined Melanie in the audience. *You're going to be sorry for that one, you dick-for-brains.*

The two sat quietly in their seats, taking in the excited preshow buzz. Whether the famous Booth Theatre on Broadway or this small thespian lab in the East Village, the ambience was exactly the same—excited anticipation.

"*Race for the Race* is about a black cyclist, right?" Melanie asked as she flipped through the program. "It says here that Major Taylor was the first black athlete to establish world records and to be part of an integrated pro team in *any* sport."

"He was the man *way* before Lance Armstrong came on the scene," Candace said, recapping Griffin's explanation. "The really messed-up thing is that even though Major was breaking all these world records around Europe, he had to fight here in America just to compete."

"Some folks just can't seem to handle a black man who excels in areas *outside* the stereotypical arenas," Mel commented. "Even today, seventy years later, Tiger Woods gets death threats."

"It's not just limited to black men. Serena and Venus have their share of player haters."

Melanie turned her attention back to the program while Candy amused herself by people-watching, careful not to let her eyes fall in Frank's direction. As the lights began to flicker, signaling the imminent start of the play, Candace stood up from her seat and canvassed the crowd.

"Who are you looking for?" Melanie asked, pulling off her jacket and placing it on the empty seat next to her.

"The critic from the *Times*," Candace fibbed. Where the hell was Will? Had he changed his mind about coming? Just as she considered heading back into the lobby to search for him, Candy saw his tall, imposing form step through the back doors and head down the side aisle. She glanced back at Melanie, who was busy rummaging through her purse, totally unaware of the jolt about to hit her. Candy crossed her fingers and smiled. Will had played it just right. By claiming his seat at the last possible moment, he would deprive Melanie of any opportunity to dash away.

With the grace of an ex-athlete, Will politely slipped past the others, offering a polite and apologetic "Excuse me" as he headed toward his seat. Melanie heard the friendly voice but before she could look up from her purse, the familiar and aromatic scent of Creed cologne swirled under her nose.

*It can't be*, Melanie thought, disbelieving each sweet inhale.

After six months of trying to ignore Will Freedman, he was once again back at her side.

"I think this belongs to you," he said, smiling as he handed Mel her jacket.

"Thanks," Mel said as her mind reeled. *Why is he here? Why wouldn't he be here? Griffin is his best friend. But why didn't Griff or Candace warn me? If they had, I wouldn't be sitting here feeling like an idiot and I certainly would have worn a better outfit.*

"Will Freedman, is that you?" Candace leaned over to ask in mock surprise.

"Candace."

New York Times *critic my ass,* Mel's eyes screamed in her friend's direction. As the house lights dimmed and darkness descended over the room, Melanie lightly dug her nails into Candy's arm in silent protest.

"Ouch," Candace replied in feigned distress, trying not to laugh aloud. Truth be told, she found pleasure in duping her friend. Candy was certain that while Melo might be uncomfortable now, she'd be thanking her later.

Any further exchange was halted by applause as the curtain went up and Griffin, transformed into Marshall W. (Major) Taylor, lay dying in a hospital bed, recounting his amazing life. Griff's performance kept Melanie mesmerized, as did this true story of yet another black hero whose life story and historical accomplishments stayed hidden, buried under a coat of racist dust and myopic exposure.

Mel managed to keep her thoughts focused on events unfolding onstage until a quiet lull in the dialogue tempted her to sneak a quick sideways peek. Apparently Will had the same urge and his broad, slightly gapped smile briefly met Mel's shy, tight-lipped grin before evaporating into the darkness. Melanie felt her chest rise and fall in a nervous exhale of breath as she turned forward, Will's face sticking in her mind like a black and white negative.

*He looks good,* she conceded before forcing herself to stay focused on the drama playing out on the stage and not in the seats.

The first act ended to rousing applause. When the house lights came on, Candace abruptly excused herself, wanting to give Will and Melo a chance to talk. She hurried up the center aisle toward the lobby, attempting to pass Frank and his wife without acknowledgment, but was stopped by Regina.

"Candace. Your boyfriend is extremely talented. I'm looking forward to the second act."

"Thank you. He is talented in so many ways . . . he also writes poetry and is a great lover . . . of the arts." Candace's words were directed toward Regina, though her strategically placed pauses clearly made her point to Frank. "I'm on my way to see him now, so if you'll excuse me . . ."

*Chew on that, motherfucker.* Candy sashayed up the rest of the aisle, sure that Frank's eyes were watching every to-and-fro movement of her swaying behind. She headed into the lobby, not knowing whether to laugh or cry, but absolutely certain that she needed a drink.

Revenge on Candace for deserting her, not drinking, was on Melanie's mind. The theater was clearing for intermission, but Mel felt trapped in the third row—guilty dread making her want to leave, civility and curiosity forcing her to stay.

"Pardon us," a voice requested. Melanie quickly stood to let them move past and inadvertently dumped the contents of her lap onto the floor. Two other couples waited as Will retrieved everything and then moved along, leaving him and Melanie alone in the row.

"Here you go," Will said, handing Mel her purse, program, and scarf while resisting the urge to bury his nose into the fabric to inhale her signature scent.

Melanie accepted her belongings in pin-dropping silence. Uneasiness plucked the words from her mouth and carried them away like crows pilfering a cornfield. She felt her eyes grow large as she bit her lower lip and sat back down.

"You do that whenever you're nervous," Will said, recalling one of the million of little quirks and habits he remembered and loved about her.

"Do what?"

"Bite your lip," he said, deciding not to reveal how this simple but very sexy gesture made him melt like a Florida snowman.

"Some habits are hard to break."

"So I guess that means you're still addicted to Red Vines licorice," Will said with a broad grin.

"Well, at least I don't eat mustard-and-tomato sandwiches," Mel countered, causing them to both break out into laughter.

"How are you, Melanie? You look good."

"Thank you. You do too."

"Thanks. Look, I'm sorry about just showing up like this, but we thought if you knew that I was coming, you might not, and that wouldn't be fair to Griffin."

"We? So Candace did know about this. Griff knew too?"

"Yes, but don't blame them. This was all my idea," Will fibbed, not wanting to get his friends in trouble. "I figured this would be a great opportunity for us to finally talk."

"Griff is doing a great job, isn't he?" Melanie said, purposely avoiding Will's intended topic of conversation.

"He is and we'll discuss his performance at length later, but right now I want to say something to you," Will said, reaching for her hand. "Melanie, this ongoing silence between us is crazy. Whatever we might have been, I'd like to think we're still friends. I've respected your need for space, but now I need you to respect mine for clarity."

Melanie nodded in contrite agreement. She had avoided him and their situation long enough. It was only fair that they finally have the conversation they should have had months ago.

"When can you get together?"

"How about tomorrow evening?" Will suggested while the photoplay of a romantic candlelight dinner strutted through in his head.

"Can't. I have a late meeting."

"You have to work on a Friday night?" Will asked, sounding much more possessive than he intended.

"It's crunch time on a big project I'm doing in Miami. It's so wonderful, Will. I'd love to tell you about it."

"So, why don't we have breakfast together on Saturday? You can fill me in on everything you've been up to."

"I'm sorry, but this weekend is impossible. I have to leave Sunday for South Beach and between now and then I still have a mountain of work to get done."

"You can't keep avoiding me, Mel. We have to talk. Let's get everything out on the table—all the whys and the why nots, the do's and the don'ts. I need answers. It's the only way for me to move on. I think you owe me that much, don't you?"

"I'm honestly not trying to put you off again. This just isn't a good time."

"It seems that there's never a good time with you," Will retorted in frustration. "First you needed space, now it's work. I don't intend to go on indefinitely not understanding how or why my life fell apart."

"I promise, as soon as I return from Miami, I'll give you a call and we'll talk."

"Fine," Will answered stiffly. He could not keep the frustration and disappointment from seeping through. Other than these few moments here in the theater, his time with Melanie was not going as planned. He had expected this to be a reunion of sorts, not simply another emotional extension for Melanie.

"Will, I *promise*, we'll talk soon," Melanie said, covering his hand with hers for emphasis.

Candace reclaimed her seat just as the lights began to flicker. "You two okay?" she asked.

"Everything is copacetic," Will offered lamely.

"It's all good," Mel chimed in, "though you and I *will* be chatting later."

Darkness once again filled the theater, leaving Melanie alone with her thoughts. Will was right—he was long overdue for an explanation of her past actions. She would keep her promise and call upon her return. As long as he only pressed her about the past, she'd be okay. Because as far as the present or the future was concerned, Melanie Hitts was fresh out of answers.

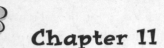

# Chapter 11

The funky hit song "Havin' It" blasted through the Carlson kitchen, breaking the characteristic calm. The infectious groove percolating underneath the sultry vocals made it impossible for Amanda to stand still. Taking a break from packing up the last of the holiday cookies for the children's hospital, she started gyrating behind the counter, using the soulful rhythms to dance away the confusion that was clogging her head.

Initially she'd declined Sharon's invitation to spend this day off from school making cookies, but on second thought, the idea of spending time together appealed to her. It still boggled her mind that in such a short span of time she'd come to look upon Sharon as the mother Catherine never tried to be. And with everything that was going on in her life, Mandy felt the strong need for some motherly advice.

She was grateful to have someone to talk to who was more experienced with boys and sex than her best friend Quincy and her other friends. Amanda had a huge decision to make. When she and Kevin talked last week, he'd made it clear that he still cared for her, but if they were to be a couple again sex would have to become a regular part of their relationship. He professed to be a young man with needs—needs that could no longer be met by unconsummated make-out sessions. And since they'd already done it once, there was no point in turning back.

"The most important thing is to go with your own instinct," Sharon had told her as they iced the sugar cookies. "Don't let anyone else's argument sway you into doing anything you aren't ready to do. No matter how convincing it sounds, or how much you want to please them."

Too bad Sharon's advice came too late. Amanda was savvy enough to know that Kevin was feeding her the classic line, "You would if you loved me," but she did love him, so why shouldn't they continue to have sex? She also knew that Kevin's mouth and hands made her body react in the most delightful manner, leaving her floating for hours in a pool of new and pleasurable sensations. But after surrendering her body as well as her heart to him, she'd felt guilty and confused. Not the emotions she'd expected to feel after making love for the first time. So how could she be sure if now was the right time and Kevin the right boy?

*Never force anything. If it's right and is supposed to happen, it will in a relaxed and natural way.* Sharon's advice ran through Amanda's head. And while her words made complete sense, Amanda was still confused.

Amanda sang along, about riches coming from love, waving her arms in the air to the loud music as she continued to dance around the kitchen. So caught up in the beat and her thoughts, the teenager didn't realize that John had entered the room until the music abruptly ceased.

"Who are you? What the hell are you doing? Where's Sharon?" John fired off his questions, giving Amanda no time to respond in between.

Amanda recognized Sharon's husband from numerous pictures around the house. Startled to find John home so early on a Friday afternoon, Amanda quickly spun around and inadvertently knocked a glass of soda off the table. It crashed to the tile, spewing broken glass around the floor and spraying Coca-Cola onto the cuff of John's khaki pants.

His eyes traveled slowly from the floor to his pants leg to Amanda's face. He peered suspiciously at this stranger whose saggy clothes and tangle of miniature braids, combined with her pale skin and WASPy features, left her looking like a quirky amalgamation of Britney Spears and rapper Missy Elliot.

"Sharon went to the store to get more ribbon. She'll be right back," she explained quickly. "I'm Amanda Weiss. I'm helping her package cookies for the hospital."

"Well, Amanda, can you keep the music down? You're not at some rave. This is my home," John demanded gruffly, his irritation obvious.

"I'm sorry. I didn't know you were here," Amanda said, a sprinkle of animosity creeping into her voice.

"Well, I am, and I'm trying to get some work done," he said as he turned and headed back to his study. It was times like this that John was glad they'd never had children. What was Sharon thinking, to leave some wayward teenager she'd admitted to meeting when the girl was shoplifting lurking around their home unsupervised? He and his wife were going to have to have a talk. He was not running some halfway house for delinquent youth.

Amanda, embarrassment still clinging to her cheeks, cleaned up the spill, making sure to retrieve every sliver of glass and each drop of soda. Satisfied with her work, she sat down to quietly await Sharon's return.

* * *

Sharon drove toward the house on automatic pilot. Her earlier conversation with Mandy still resounded in her ears. When to become sexually active was a difficult decision to make and one that could only be decided by the individual. Still, Sharon wanted Mandy to wait until there was no question in her mind that making love was the right thing *for her* to do. Her instincts told her that Amanda wasn't ready and Sharon hoped her advice to wait and not give in to Kevin's pressure was heard and followed.

*Though you regularly give in to John's demands,* she thought as she pulled into the driveway and witnessed the Christmas decorations tastefully adorning the house.

*It's ironic,* Sharon thought, *right now at this very moment my house contains everything I've ever wanted—a husband I adore and a child waiting for my return. But it's all an illusion,* she reminded herself. John seemed more distant and distracted. The child waiting for her wasn't her own and the house wouldn't be much longer. The apartment was well on its way toward completion and with the FOR SALE sign up, Sharon knew it was only a short matter of time before she would have to permanently vacate her home.

Sharon pushed the anger and resentment deep back into its emotional repository and turned her thoughts to Amanda. Thinking about someone else's problems seemed to relieve some of her own stress and discontent.

She parked and hurried toward the house, pleased with the idea that had popped in her head. She knew that Amanda was not only upset about Kevin, but about having to spend Christmas abroad. And while she could totally understand the girl's parents wanting their daughter to join them in Bali for the holidays, it seemed unfair that their insistence came with little regard for Amanda's feelings. Perhaps she had the answer.

"Amanda, I have a great idea," Sharon said as she burst through the door. "Why don't we ask your parents if you can join us for Christmas? John and I would love to have you."

"Absolutely not," John said hours later as he passed the bowl to his wife. "That girl should spend Christmas with her family."

"That girl's name is Amanda and she doesn't want to go to Bali," Sharon argued, angrily slapping a spoonful of wild rice on her plate.

"Not my problem. She needs to work that out with her parents."

"Sometimes you have to make other people's problems your own. Otherwise one becomes selfish and egotistical." *Like you can be,* she elected not to add. "Why are you being so negative about this?"

"I simply do not want her joining us." John was in no mood to explain his real reasons to Sharon.

"Amanda Weiss is a lost young girl whose parents abandon her every chance they get—" Sharon said, stubbornly refusing to drop the issue.

"She isn't you and her parents aren't yours," John interrupted.

"Maybe not, but I know how she feels. For some reason our paths crossed, and I refuse to let her ruin her life just because she's lonely and neglected."

"They have professionals who get paid to do that. You certainly can't save every sad and confused teenager you come across, Sharon."

"No, but maybe I can save this one." Helping Amanda meant more to Sharon than she could even begin to explain to her husband. Increasingly this needy young girl had begun to fill the cracks in her heart and in such a brief time had managed to bring a soulful satisfaction and purpose back into Sharon's life. John had no right to deny her.

"John Carlson, this will be the last Christmas I will ever spend in this house. And I intend to enjoy it surrounded by the people whom I love and cherish—all of them. So if her parents agree, Amanda Weiss *will* be spending Christmas with us and you have thirteen days to get used to the idea," Sharon stated defiantly.

John looked up from his dinner with surprise. Was his wife finally developing a backbone after all these years? And if indeed she was, how was he going to like it?

He certainly liked it on Melanie. She was young, full of energy, promise, and bravado. Melanie represented all the attributes of the popular clichés—grace under fire, poise under pressure. John recalled the first time he'd seen her. She had stood there, basically thrown to the wolves by her bosses, and dealt with his insolent remarks and irritable mood with great aplomb. John greatly admired courage, and found himself intrigued and impressed by Melanie's boldness. So why did he find Sharon's sudden audacity so unnerving?

His wife was definitely changing and John saw her relationship with Amanda as the unwelcome force driving this transformation. Ever since she'd taken this confused teenager under her wing, Sharon had become increasingly willing to defy his wishes and stand her ground on any issue that revolved around Amanda. These changes would be easier for him to accept if he could chalk it up to delayed personal growth, but it wasn't that innocent.

Amanda Weiss had awakened Sharon's long-dormant maternal instinct, and that made her dangerous to his marriage. It had taken him years to gently snuff his wife's desire for a child and he had no intention of letting that genie out of the bottle.

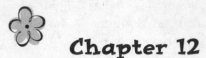

# Chapter 12

John could not recall when he'd enjoyed working on a Saturday morning so much. He lowered his head slightly so he could better see over the reading glasses perched on his nose. Ignoring the paperwork in his lap, he quietly studied Melanie as she sat at his drafting table intently sorting fabric and color swatches. His eyes watched her delicate hands come together and move toward her face. As Mel thoughtfully tapped them against her full mouth, John recalled the pleasurable touch of those sweet lips on his face.

"What are you over there pondering so intently?" he asked, suddenly desiring to hear her melodious voice.

"I think we need to add some high-quality color copies of the artwork on the presentation boards," Melanie answered. "They are the highlights of the entire hotel, so they really should be included."

"Sounds like a good idea."

"I have an even better one."

"You always do," John said, still charmed by her unending enthusiasm.

"Okay, but let me finish before you react. I know the building renderings are complete, but yesterday I got a fabulous idea. Instead of the rooftop sculpture garden, why don't we move the restaurant upstairs and make the ceiling retractable? We could call it the Starlight Gallery. I can't think of anything more romantic than dining under the stars."

"It's not possible at this point, Jax. As you said, the plans are finished and ready to go."

Melanie listened as John gave her several more reasons why the Starlight Gallery wasn't economically feasible at this stage of the project. She was disappointed that he hadn't viewed the concept through his artistic eyes, but instead stayed focused only on the balance sheet. Still, she refused to let the subject die until he gave his honest *creative* opinion.

"So you don't think it's affordable at this point, but do you think it's a good idea?"

"It's a great idea. I wish you'd thought of it sooner."

"So let's run it past the owners and let them decide," Mel said, still stubbornly pushing.

"Absolutely not. Today is our last opportunity to finish the Casa de Arte presentation before Monday's meeting. There's no time for such a huge change."

Before Melanie could suggest postponing the meeting for a week, the intercom buzzed and a voice informed them that it was one-thirty and that their lunch was on its way up.

John excused himself to go to the men's room and soon after, a waiter from the executive dining room rolled in a table set with porcelain place settings for two, crystal highball glasses, a variety of soft drinks, and several containers of Chinese takeout.

"Shall I serve?" he asked.

"No, thank you," Melanie said, surprised that the waitstaff was working on the weekend. She stood viewing the setup, which was formal enough for a date at Le Bernardin, but totally unnecessary for a friendly working meal at the office. She quickly set about moving plates, a pair of chopsticks for both of them, two diet Cokes, and the takeout containers to the coffee table in front of the couch. Mel removed the pillows from the sofa and threw them to the floor on either side of the table. She stepped back and admired her work and smiled. *Now, that's how you're supposed to eat Chinese takeout,* Mel congratulated herself as she sat down on the pillow and waited for John to reappear.

"I hope you're hungry," she announced as he stepped back into the room and smiled at the sight of her. The look on his face immediately informed Melanie that her attempt to diffuse any illusion of a date had failed miserably. Instead, she had unwittingly created an even more intimate setting.

John eased his tall body down onto one of the cushions and tried to get situated. First he tried tucking his long legs underneath him, yoga-style. He stayed in that uncomfortable position only briefly before stretching them out under the table, nearly kicking Mel in the process.

"Sorry, I forget that everyone isn't built as close to the ground as I am. Would you prefer to sit at the table?"

"No, I like this. It's relaxed and . . . cozy."

Melanie smiled shyly and picked up her chopsticks. "Let's see what we have here . . . sesame noodles, moo goo gai pan, shrimp with lobster sauce, and Hunan beef. Mmmm, a virtual smorgasbord of Asian delights," she said as she served both their plates.

"We're only missing one thing. Forks," John added.

"Don't tell me that a world traveler like yourself doesn't know how to eat with chopsticks."

"We all have our shortcomings. One of mine is that I am totally utensil-dependent."

"Well, then, it's time to learn. First, pick up one chopstick, holding it in your right hand as you would a pencil," Melanie explained. "Then place the second on top, using your middle finger to keep the sticks slightly separated. Like this," she said, illustrating her directions with action.

"Now use your index finger to move the top stick up and down and grasp your food," Mel said, expertly lifting a shrimp from her plate and gently placing it between her lips. "It's that easy."

*God, I want to kiss that mouth,* John thought, mesmerized by the innocent seduction of her action. *Does she know how damn sexy she is? Or is that why she's so appealing, because she's totally unaware of the absolute power she has to render me helpless?*

"Go on, now. You try," she prompted.

John picked up his chopsticks, holding them the way he'd been shown. After a few clumsy and failed attempts, he managed to extract a broccoli floret from his plate and carry it slowly to his mouth. Just as he was about to claim success, it slipped through his chopsticks and plopped onto his chest, leaving a large brown spot on his white cotton shirt.

Melanie grimaced playfully as she laid her forehead onto her open hands and shook with laughter. "And you were so close," she said as she got up and grabbed a bottle of club soda from the table. "Another half an inch and you were in there." She doused her napkin with water and proceeded to gently blot the stain on his chest.

Even through the layers of cotton separating her hand from his skin, John could feel the heat of her caress. It seemed so appropriate that she would pat him there, a physical reenactment of the way she had already touched his heart with her mind and spirit. Acting on sheer reflex, John covered her hand with his and squeezed it gently before bringing it to his lips for a light kiss.

"Maybe you should use a fork," Melanie suggested, gently pulling her hand away to diffuse the escalating tension.

"Never let it be said that I'm a quitter. No matter how many shirts I have to ruin, I will finish my meal with these blasted sticks," John vowed. He let the moment pass, knowing that he would replay it countless times until it was replaced by the next magic flash between them.

"Okay, but how about we do this?" Mel said as she tucked her napkin under her chin and watched as John repeated the action on himself.

They resumed eating and soon the two found themselves once again chatting amicably. Conversation was often interrupted with laughter as John's foibles with his chopsticks left his makeshift bib covered in splotches of soy sauce. The longer they sat, the less their discourse held any semblance to a business meeting, but instead more of a man and a woman determined to mine the rich recesses of the person they were greatly interested in. Slowly they began to reveal the safe inner parts of their lives, building on the intimacy they'd established while scouring the flea market. John revealed how this job had begun to rekindle the passion for his work. Melanie divulged how the success of this project meant everything to her because if the Casa de Arte was a triumph, she would then know that the personal sacrifices she'd made had been worthwhile. They enjoyed a meaningful pause, and with silence serenading them like a perfectly orchestrated song, they communicated their confusing and inexplicable feelings with the depth and clarity that only the language of soulful eye contact can properly convey.

John reached out for her hand, needing to touch the woman to assure himself that this was not a mirage. Melanie allowed the contact, needing the man to translate verbatim what his eyes had expressed.

"John, what exactly do you see happening between us?"

"I wish I could tell you, but I really haven't a clue. All I know is that you're like a bottle of extra-potent vitamins. When I'm around you I feel younger and lighter and freer. And I like it," he told her, looking deep in her eyes.

"What do you want from me?"

"At this point, I simply want to spend time with you. I want us to continue sharing ideas on work and the world and be together when we can. You are the reason that I wake up excited about going to work because I know at some point in the day I'm going to speak with you."

"But you're . . . married."

"I know I am, and believe me, I love Sharon dearly, but this has nothing to do with her. Whatever I'm feeling for you comes from a totally separate place, far and apart from my marriage. I am drawn to you in a way I can't seem to explain, no matter how hard I try," he said, amazed by his very revealing admission.

"Melanie, I no womanizer. I have never cheated on my wife and I've never been interested in some tawdry affair—"

"Is that what you see happening between us—an affair?"

*Affair.* The noun stuck in John's head. On one hand, it was a word that connoted a large and frivolous occasion—like opening night at the opera or a charity ball. On the other, it held the sleazy insinuation of an immoral liaison. What did either of these definitions have to do with the incredible fondness he felt toward this lovely young woman?

"I don't date married men."

"I know you don't, and I certainly haven't had a date in nearly twenty-five years. But Melanie, there's something here between us that I've never experienced before. And I refuse to simply shut it down until I know what it is." John paused, waiting for Mel to respond. Instead, she silently pushed the food around her plate.

"I know you feel it too," he said softly.

"And just how do you know this?" Melanie could see John trying to read her expression, searching for clues that either confirmed or denied his assertion, but she remained poker-faced, unwilling to reveal her disparate emotions.

"I just know," John said with a wink, as he reached over and wrapped a springy bronze curl around his finger.

"So what do we do now?"

"Just let things naturally unfold, I guess." Instinctively he could tell that now was not the time to push forward with this subject. Neither of them had any explanation that made any sense at this point. "And in the meantime, we should decide who gets the last water chestnut," John declared.

"I believe that has *my* name on it," Mel responded, grateful for his diversion.

With the expertise that comes with any defining stand-and-deliver moment, John adroitly picked up the slippery water chestnut with his chopsticks and slowly moved it toward her. "We'll take this nice and easy," he said as he proudly delivered the chestnut to Melanie's waiting mouth. "That way we won't make a mess."

After leaving John in his office, Melanie spent the rest of Saturday at hers trying to complete her work on the Casa de Arte.

What should have taken only a couple of hours took nearly four. She'd mixed up several copies of artwork, erroneously attaching them on the wrong boards. Detaching the swatches and photocopies had proven to be a messy affair, necessitating the complete redo of several displays. It was nearly eight o'clock when she put the final touches on her presentation boards, packed them up, and headed home.

Melanie knew the exact reason for her lapse of concentration. Her mind kept drifting back to John, replaying each encounter they'd had, from their caustic first meeting in September to today's emotional revelation. And each storyboard scene of their relationship seemed to indicate that an inexplicable and potent force was steadily drawing them together.

It was a dynamism that felt natural and safe, exciting and salient, but also confusing and uncertain. It was a force that was slowly pulling them across lines drawn in the societal sand by moralists of all colors, steadfast in their conservative beliefs about love and appropriate coupling. John Carlson had all the right stuff in the wrong package. He was talented, intelligent, sexy, and successful. He was also married, white, eighteen years her senior, as well as her teacher and partner. His age and race were serious considerations, but much less than the married colleague issue. Both huge no-no's in Melanie's personal code of ethics.

Mel walked into the apartment to the sounds of a ringing phone. Candace sat on the couch, filing her nails and ignoring the noise. Melanie glanced over at her friend in wonder as she picked up the handset.

"Good evening, Melanie," Frank said in a deep and very proper voice. "Is Candace there? We were supposed to meet at nine o'clock and she's nearly half an hour late."

"Hi, Frank," Mel answered, glancing over at her roommate for instructions. She watched as Candy shook her head no.

"She's right here. Hold on a sec," Mel said, deliberately ignoring Candace. Rolling her eyes and sucking her teeth, Candy snatched the phone.

"Frank."

"Where are you?"

"Sorry, but I lost track of time."

"Or maybe your *boyfriend* was a little slow getting up and out for work tonight?"

Candace laughed coyly, letting Frank stew in his own erroneous conclusions. She hadn't seen Griffin since last night, as he was in rehearsals all day with an understudy for tonight's performance. "Look, I'm walking out the door. Wait for me," she said, hanging up and plopping down on the couch.

"Didn't you just tell Frank you were leaving?" Melanie questioned as she hung up her coat.

"He can wait a little longer. Maybe the Mrs. jumps when he hollers, but I am nobody's beck-and-call woman. Besides, he'll wait. He's trying hard to make up for the other night."

"Candy, why do you even bother playing these games with Frank?"

"Do you know where he's taking me? First to dinner at the Palm and then to the Niche. I've been trying to get into that club for months."

"What about Griff?"

"Like he could afford either one, let alone both. But I'll hook him up later."

"So you want a benefactor, not a mate."

"There's absolutely no reason why I can't have both," Candy

replied, dismissing Melanie's statement. "You can lose that high-and-mighty look. Don't tell me you've never double-dipped, Melo. Every single girl should have a mate and a date. Men do it all the time. Girl, life is too short. Live a little. Now, if Griffin calls, tell him I'm having drinks with the partners." Candace turned to leave, unwilling to divulge to her friend that she wanted and needed Frank Warren not only for the things he represented, but because having him in her life helped maintain the distance between her and Griff.

Melanie shook her head in double disbelief as her roommate departed. She hoped that Griffin never called. She didn't want to be in the position of lying to one friend in order to cover up the deceit of another. This situation was becoming increasingly uncomfortable. It was one thing witnessing all of Candace's Machiavellian escapades, but it was quite another to be forced into being her accomplice—particularly when Candy's victim was someone Melanie liked and admired very much. Where did loyalty to others end and devotion to one's personal values begin?

*Why is life always so damn confusing?* Mel wondered. Just when she thought she'd come to terms with her feelings toward Will, just when her career was taking off in ways she'd only dreamed of, and just when she thought she'd found a mentor and friend she could learn from—BAM—complications abounded, leaving her feeling emotionally dazed and morally confused.

Melanie decided that the only remedy for what ailed her was a hot, sudsy tub. She headed first to the kitchen, grabbed an open bottle of red wine and a glass, and then crossed the hall to the bathroom, where she proceeded to draw herself a bubble bath. She lit several candles and turned on the radio before stripping down and easing into the warm jasmine-scented water.

Her body parts seemed to sigh in unison as she sat down. Mel sank deep into the bubbles, letting the soapy suds coddle her skin while she waited for the magic combination of water, music, and wine to relax her and shake loose all of her questions and frustrations.

Melanie felt the heat of the bath float over her naked body and instead of feeling mellow, a new agitation took over. After nearly a year without a man's touch, her untreated lust was begging to be satiated. Mel could feel her earlier confusion completely dissipate. Rising up in its place was a defiant cry from a body demanding immediate sexual gratification.

As R&B singer Joe's sexy voice sang about doing all the things her man wouldn't, Melanie stretched out into the warm liquid and let the bubbles caress her nakedness. But soapy effervescence was a poor substitute for the soft contact of gentle hands stroking her skin. Mel closed her eyes and let her mind wander into the enticing realm of fantasy seduction, pulling from her vivid imagination a sexy, faceless lover. She pictured him soothing her body with his silken touch, liberating the sexual tension built up from months of restraint.

She drew her hands through her hair in a long lazy stretch. Imagining her hands to be his, she parted her lips and gently sucked her fingertips, experiencing the erotic pull in her fingers and in areas below. Tilting her face to the ceiling, she slowly ran her hands down her neck, shoulders, and breasts, cupping them and gently squeezing them together.

Melanie reached for the Neutrogena body oil from atop the radiator, tipped the bottle over her chest, and watched as the golden liquid pooled in the valley between her bosom. As the light sesame scent traveled up to her nostrils, Melanie slowly began massaging the warm oil into her skin, gently kneading and stroking her breasts until they began to swell under the slippery smoothness of her oiled fingers. She could feel her nipples grow longer and harder as they strained against the moist air in search of his mouth.

Her fantasy lover seduced Melanie into higher levels of arousal, leaving her begging for instant relief. She slipped her hand into the sudsy water and began to stroke herself as Joe's naughty-and-oh-so-nice lyrics fondled her mind. Melanie massaged her clitoris in a soft circular motion, causing her to wriggle as she felt it grow deliciously tighter and tighter. Soft groans escaped her mouth and mingled with the sounds of water gently splashing the sides of the tub.

Melanie penetrated herself with two fingers and continued to pet her clitoris, her rational mind lost in the fantasy of him making love to her. The thought of his hardness penetrating her and gloriously gliding in and out of her body pushed Mel closer and closer to the verge of orgasmic delight.

"Oh, John," Mel moaned as her inner muscles exploded around her fingers into contractions that were both pleasurable and powerful. She sank deeper into the tub, enjoying the drunken aftermath of her self-love experience. She lay there for several moments, savoring the delicious sensations, before the realization of her utterance settled in. Melanie bolted upright, splashing water over the sides and onto the bathroom floor.

She'd known all along that she was intellectually and creatively drawn to John Carlson—two important components to a sound personal and professional *friendship*. But she now had the answer to the question Candace had asked a couple weeks back. Yes, she was definitely sexually attracted to the man.

Mel sat back into the now-tepid water, abruptly seized by yet another unsettling truth. While her orgasm had momentarily taken the edge off of her pent-up desire, it was merely a hors d'oeuvre to what she really craved—a full-course gourmet meal of sensual pleasure. Melanie was sexually ravenous and tomorrow she would be on a plane headed for one of the most popular sin cities in North America with a man she found wildly desirable and totally untouchable.

Could things get any more complicated?

# Chapter 13

As they strolled across busy Collins Avenue, Melanie lagged behind, ignored by both her partner and client. While the two men chatted amicably, Melanie took in the sunshine and seductive sights of South Beach and played a round of the good news, bad news game. The good news: Containing her attraction to John was obviously not going to be a problem.

On the flight down, John had been too preoccupied with some unexplained issue to say more than a few words to her. Immediately after checking into the five-star, Royal Palm Hotel, he canceled their scheduled dinner and disappeared into his suite. Melanie ate alone in her room, hoping that John's troubled mood would dissipate before their meeting. His disposition hadn't brightened this morning and they silently shared a taxi to survey the site where, if all went well these next two days, the Casa de Arte would stand.

Melanie sidestepped an enthusiastic shopper laden with bags from the many nearby designer stores as she stood considering the bad news. The charming man of flea market confessions and cozy office dinners was gone and in his stead was the cave dweller she'd first met and detested. Mel was totally confused by his sudden reversal of behavior. Since shaking hands this morning with Roberto Alvarez, a wealthy Cuban real estate developer, he had morphed into John Carlson—arrogant, world-class architect.

All morning, both he and Roberto sought her opinion only on minor questions, which were more about polite conversation than sincere professional counsel. Roberto she could almost excuse. It was obvious that he was enamored of John's prestigious reputation, just as she'd been in the beginning. But for John there was no exoneration. Instead of treating Melanie as his respected partner who had conceived and helped develop the concept, John behaved as if she were his humble assistant. Gone was his penchant for soliciting her approval and crediting her ideas, replaced instead by an insulting authoritarian attitude that Melanie neither appreciated nor understood.

Despite her disappointment and anger, Melanie was determined not to let John's attitude dampen her enthusiasm. While John and Roberto walked back to inspect the existing façade, Melanie decided to take in the view from across the street. She was struck by the wonderful location of her first major project. South Beach was a virtual mosaic of sensuous hues, sounds, and scents. As she watched the colorful characters zipping by on bikes, in-line skates, high heels, or flip-flopped feet, Melanie was reassured that their decision to create an inviting option for those who preferred more unique accommodations was dead on target.

Melanie closed her eyes and raised her face to the sun before releasing a frustrated exhale. She lifted her lids and looked up into the azure sky, clear but for a few wispy strokes of white cloud.

*This is beautiful. Too exquisite to be covered by plaster,* she thought. Melanie knew that the Starlight Gallery Restaurant must be included. It would be the hotel's pièce de résistance, its calling card for locals and tourists alike. But John had been absolute in his opposition to presenting the idea to Roberto and, given his current temperament, would not be conducive to any last-minute discussion. Still, Mel was sure that its addition would make all the difference between the Casa de Arte staying a good hotel or becoming a great one.

Melanie looked back across the street and saw John waving her over. She strolled over to the crosswalk and as she waited for the light to change, a flyer tacked to the street sign caught her attention. It was an announcement for the upcoming Art Miami Festival in late January. *Perfect timing,* Mel thought as she removed the notice and tucked it into her pocket.

Sitting in the Blue Door Restaurant in the famed Delano Hotel, John proceeded to bask in Roberto's unadulterated hero worship, while Melanie continued to go over every design detail with a keen eye. When it opened, the hotel made the front page of every style magazine in the country for its funky, whimsical, and sophisticated décor. Melanie glanced around the room from their secluded corner table. There was something to suit every taste in this hotel—from the eclectic furniture groupings to the heavily used billiard table to the stream of "beautiful people" parading through the lobby on their way to the Alice-in-Wonderlandesque patio deck.

The conversation abruptly concluded when Felipe Martinez, Roberto's partner and main investor, joined the group. After brief introductions, the business meeting began.

"So, Melanie, John tells me that it was your idea to change the name of the hotel," Roberto remarked with an accent that, prior to deeming him a chauvinistic asshole, she would have found charming.

*At last, some credit.* "I thought it fit the concept and at the same time retained the exclusive connotation that the original name held," Melanie replied adeptly.

"I agree. I like it. In fact, I like the entire artistic theme very much. I find the approach to be refreshingly luxe, particularly in this city of sparse and desperately hip accommodations," Roberto continued.

"That is our plan, Señor Alvarez, to use luxurious textures inside and out, as a compliment to the sensual nature of the art-work. Isn't that right, John?" Melanie asked smartly.

"Yes, it is."

"I too like very much the art theme, but I do have a problem with the exterior of the building," Felipe Martinez spoke up, turning to John for clarification. "Our hotel will be built in the middle of the famous Art Deco District. I'm concerned that such understatement might get lost among the more colorful and elaborate architecture."

"I'm sure a man of John's obvious experience and success has considered this," Roberto commented with complete deference.

"Of course I have, and I am absolutely confident that my design is strong enough to compete with any other building," John said with indignant authority.

"But we are here on the same block as the Delano, the Raleigh, and the Marlin Hotels—all bright, trendy-looking celebrity magnets. What about the look of our hotel is strong enough to pull away the likes of Michael Douglas and Catherine Zeta Jones and bring them here?"

"A beautiful environment, an effective marketing campaign, and a reputation for intimate and fine service, Señor Martinez. Creating the environment is my job, letting the public know about it and building a superb reputation is yours," John countered.

*His job?* Melanie thought. *How about* our *job? Or has he totally forgotten who was responsible for most of the design ideas going into this hotel?* Melanie felt herself teetering on the verge of full-fledged fury. To avoid a potentially embarrassing outburst, she silently recited the alphabet before mentally rejoining the conversation.

"I was also under the impression, gentlemen, that I was to have full control from concept to finish on this project. Has something changed that I need to know?"

"No, absolutely not, John. We trust your judgment completely."

"Yes, Roberto, but surely thirty million buys us *some* say," Felipe said, his temper now flared.

Suddenly a bomb of XY chromosomes dropped, releasing over the table an uneasy silence fat with male ego. This meeting, and perhaps project, was headed straight for the toilet, and Melanie refused to let this important opportunity become career sewage because of some silly testosterone-induced terrorism.

"Señor Martinez, maybe I can explain," Melanie offered with a subtle touch of feminine wiles.

"Please. Perhaps a woman's voice of reason is just what this meeting requires," Felipe replied.

"When John and I discussed the external look of the Casa de Arte, like you, we wanted it to be different and stand out on this crowded street of flashy exteriors. So we based its design on the same appeal a classy and elegant woman has for a discerning gentleman. Like any great beauty, the sexiest part of the Casa de Arte allure will be her mystery. Her exterior may be wrapped in understated sophistication, but once the doors are open, she comes alive with color and sensuality." Melanie completed her statement and then looked at each man. Felipe appeared charmed and placated; Roberto, amazed that she had a brain; and John's face remained expressionless. Was he grateful for her positive interference or angry with her for speaking up? Melanie had no clue.

"Ms. Hitts, you make your point well. As the interior designer, what other thoughts do you have about our project?"

"If you wouldn't mind, Señor Martinez—"

"Felipe."

"Felipe. I do have a couple of thoughts," Melanie went on. To hell with John Carlson. For all intents and purposes, he had deserted her and Melanie was on her own, fighting for her professional integrity. For the first time since arriving in this sun-drenched city, someone attached to this project was asking for her opinion, and she was going to deliver. She purposely avoided looking John's way, but took their clients' nods as a positive sign of their interest.

"As we were surveying the hotel site this morning, I happened to notice a flyer announcing the Art Miami Festival. It occurred to me that this might be the perfect time to announce the coming of Miami's newest and most fabulous art repository. I know the turnaround is short, a little over a month, but I'm sure it could be done, and done well."

"That is a clever idea, Ms. Hitts. One we will get our people on immediately. You are a surprising wealth of creativity."

*Finally, a man in this crowd who recognizes that fact and is willing to acknowledge it,* Melanie thought.

"Thank you, and please, call me Melanie," she said with a smile sprinkled with her natural allure. "While I am totally behind our design thematic, both exterior and interior, I do understand your concern, Felipe. Sometimes, less needs just a tad more. And it is true that every 'woman' needs some special accessory to make her more memorable," Mel remarked, fingering the amber clasp of her vintage garnet necklace for emphasis. "So, I have an idea. One that I think will bring you all the recognition and *star* pull you desire."

"I've come to learn that Ms. Hitts is an unending source of inspiration," John added, his voice perfectly pitched between sarcasm and sincerity. He knew exactly what idea she was referring to and he had no intention of opening up that can of Spam, not with everything else that had just crashed onto his plate. "But it might be best to share any new concepts *after* we've gone over the original plans in greater detail." There was tempered admonition in his tone, suggesting to Melanie that she rethink her decision.

Mel, fed up with John ignoring her contributions while dictating every phase of this meeting, heard the warning and refused to heed it. "No, John. I think now is as good a time as any."

Melanie defiantly proceeded to share her idea for the Starlight Gallery Restaurant, emphasizing the unique charm and atmosphere its retracting roof would provide. She didn't dare risk a look John's way, but the growing enthusiasm overtaking Roberto and Felipe fueled her courage.

Not wanting to appear out of control of his project, John joined in the conversation. "I would suggest a slightly domed ceiling, much like a large skylight," he said, drawing a quick sketch on a cocktail napkin. John continued to offer suggestions for other potential designs, cautioning that such an extensive change would be a costly augmentation. Despite his seemingly enthusiastic behavior, Melanie could tell that he was furious with her for defying his wishes.

Roberto and Felipe were completely sold, dismissing the extra expense into the you-must-spend-money-to-make-money category. So enamored with both the idea of starlit dining and

Melanie, they ordered a bottle of Tattinger's premiere curvée, Comtes de Champagne, to toast the deal. By the time the last delicious drops had passed their lips, the decision had been made—the Starlight, or Luz de la Estrella, was to become the top marketing tool of the Casa de Arte. Felipe also decided that if they were to announce this incredible gem by the Art Miami Festival on January twenty-fifth, a new budget and updated drawings had to been done immediately. Their afternoon appointment was canceled and rescheduled for late the next day.

John bade his good-byes at the table and took care of the bill while Melanie walked their clients through the billowy white linen curtains on the Delano's front porch. Before returning indoors, she sat down on the porch sofa, nestled her body into the large white pillows, and allowed herself a moment to revel in her professional coup. Her instinct to let the client decide on the change had been correct. More importantly, they were entirely on board, now trusting John *and* Melanie with both their vision and their millions.

Melanie stood and once again raised her face to the sunshine. She soaked in the extra energy in preparation for the wrath of John she was sure to encounter upon her return. Despite her clients' joy, her partner was no doubt livid. Whatever had put him in this foul and funky mood was now compounded by her perceived act of insubordination.

Mel's glee over her personal accomplishment began to pale as momentary uncertainty over her bold behavior surfaced. Still, as she stepped back into the cool darkness of the lobby, her anger over John's behavior came rushing back. Moving down the center corridor with a calm and confident stride, she could feel her contrition completely dissolve. In her soul Mel knew she'd done nothing wrong. In fact, from her vantage point, she had actually saved the project from an early demolition. John Carlson had hired her for her design expertise and whether he liked it or not, that was exactly what he was going to get.

Melanie walked onto the balcony of John's suite, leaving him to make his calls. She could hear him talking to his employees in New York, angrily demanding numbers crunched, phone calls returned, and faxes sent posthaste. When she heard him slam the receiver back into the cradle she reentered the room, ready to skirmish. This fifty-year-old man was behaving like a two-year-old child and she'd had just about enough.

"John, can we please talk?"

"I have a lot of pressing business to take care of, Melanie. Now is not the time."

"I think it is. We need to work through this if we're to put on a united front tomorrow."

"Fine. Let's start with, what the hell were you thinking?" John lambasted her. "Didn't I specifically tell you not to mention the retractable roof?"

"Yes, you did, and I'm sorry, but it was a great idea. You even said so yourself. I thought it should at least be heard."

"I told you it was too much, too late."

"But if the client likes it and is willing to pay for it, what does it matter? So what if we have to draw new plans and work up a new budget? In the end it will be well worth the effort."

"That's not the point," John sniped as he walked to the mini bar and poured himself a drink.

"Then what is?"

"You were told not to bring it up and you ignored my orders."

"Your orders?" Mel snapped back, totally losing her temper. "You're upset because you think that I challenged your authority? My mistake. I thought this was a partnership. Or is this how you treat all of your partners? Equality exists only if you dare not defy the *great* John Carlson?"

"Your behavior at the meeting made us look unorganized and unprofessional."

"What behavior? I barely had an opportunity to speak. *You* made damn sure of that," Melanie added sarcastically.

"You were flirting with Felipe Alvarez. Comparing our building to a sexy, mysterious woman. Smiling coyly, fingering your jewelry. All very manipulative and not at all businesslike."

"Flirting with him?" Mel asked, angrily continuing to repeat every asinine charge he threw at her. "I was not flirting with him, and how dare you suggest otherwise. But even if one word or action of mine could be construed as flirtation, it got us much further than your display of outdated and unnecessary machismo."

"Men doing business," John stated simply.

"Don't give me that boys-will-be-boys baloney. Do you know what I think is *really* bothering you? I think it's the fact that it wasn't your idea that they loved the most, but mine."

John blew a deep breath—a sure sign of deep frustration. Whether she knew it or not, Melanie had hit a chord—one that reverberated long and deep in John's fragile ego.

"You are the interior designer on this project. Curtains, couches, carpets, those are the items under your domain. The structure, from top to bottom, is mine," he stated with a iron force that left Melanie temporarily speechless.

The residue from their angry words pollinated the room, dropping weeds of disillusionment among the flowers that had recently sprouted between them.

"I will remember that," Mel said as she walked toward the door. "I learned a lot about you today, John. Who would have known that your reputation as the all-seeing, all-knowing architect from Oz was earned by taking credit for other people's hard work?"

"Where are you going? We have work to do," John said, feeling the sharp, uncomfortable sting of her disappointment.

"No. *You* have work to do. My domain is complete. These changes are about structure. You don't need me," Melanie retorted before walking out the door. Out in the hall, she took several deep breaths before walking back into the room with one final thought.

"You know, less than seventy-two hours ago, we were sitting in your office making revelations about our feelings for each other. But ever since we've been in Miami, you have revealed yourself to be nothing but a major jackass. I'm so glad I learned the truth before I did anything stupid."

The door slammed behind her, and regardless of her harsh words, John found himself smiling, impressed by her constant show of spunk. But as quickly as it surfaced, his grin died.

*Did you see the look on her face? She's totally disappointed in you. And she's right. You are a jackass,* a stern voice from inside reminded him.

Melanie had every reason to be angry with him. Hell, he was incensed with himself. Everything about this trip from the beginning had gone wrong. What he had hoped would be a wonderful professional and personal trip for the two of them had disintegrated into an unqualified mess and he was the only one to blame.

The vibration of his cell phone interrupted his self-repudiation. It was Austin Riley with more bad news about the Vogue Belize Resort. "How many?" he asked. "Damn. Call me when you know for sure," John said, and hung up. Twenty more men had walked off the job and there was suspicion of sabotage by disgruntled workers who wanted more money. Construction on the resort has slowed considerably and all signs were pointing to a complete work stoppage. He now dreaded answering his phone because with each report the situation got worse. A job he thought was in the simmer stage, allowing him to concentrate on this, his pet project, was now back on the front burner and about to boil over.

John pushed aside the Vogue's problems as he walked over to the desk and pulled out the Casa de Arte blueprints. He unfurled them across the bed and let his eyes run over the plans while his brain unraveled the disappointing string of events that had put him in this uncomfortable place with Melanie.

Austin had initially delivered the bad news yesterday as John sat in LaGuardia Airport waiting to board the flight to Miami. By the time Melanie had arrived, the full impact of what this delay would cost all parties involved had set in. On the flight down he had been much too consumed with trying to figure out a way to contain the damage to have any meaningful conversation with her. Once in Miami, he retired into his room to make calls and put out fires, emerging this morning with his irritation still intact. The worst part—John hadn't explained any of this to Melanie. It was no wonder she was perplexed and angered by his mood.

He'd mishandled so many things these past twenty-four hours, like being so concerned about receiving credit for the project that he'd allowed Roberto to shut Melanie out of the meeting. John knew he was wrong, but how could he make her realize that after months of feeling washed up and out of step, Roberto Alvarez's admiration and obvious confidence in his abilities made him feel on top again? And how could John possibly explain that his reluctance to give Melanie her well-deserved credit came not from ego but fear? Would she understand his panic that these clients, who were putting millions of dollars behind *his* expertise and vision, would see right through him? See that he'd lost his creative edge? Felipe Martinez certainly had.

He too had questions about the exterior, but ultimately felt his approach worked the best. In the past, John would have a well-thought-out rationale for his decisions, but today, in a slip of confidence, he hadn't felt adequately prepared to defend his choice. Melanie had stepped in and done a spectacular job of deflecting the investor's concerns. And how had he shown his gratitude? By accusing her of being unprofessional, when in truth he was childishly trying to hide his jealousy.

As the swell of John's bloated ego subsided, he realized that Melanie had been correct to mention the new roof. Looking over the blueprints, it was clear to him that the Luz de la Estrella's addition had made a great concept even better. But John had known that at the time she'd first presented the idea. Yet instead of acknowledging it for what it was—another superb inspiration— he'd simply dismissed it, unwilling to add another tally to Melanie's already long list of conceptual milestones.

Melanie had spoken the truth about so many issues. But she was wrong about one very important thing—he did need her. It was as if a part of him was broken and she held the repair kit. In just three months, this incredible young woman had captured his essence—flaws and all—and made him feel good about being who he was as no other person had ever managed to do. She understood him better than those he'd been acquainted with for most of his existence. Melanie Hitts had fast become one of the good things in his life, and John couldn't bear the thought of her thinking that he was some arrogant, idea-stealing tyrant.

He sat down at his desk and began to sketch with new determination. In less than an hour he had finished his renderings for the retractable roof and faxed them up to New York to be properly drawn and sent overnight with the new budget for tomorrow's meeting. With that task complete, he picked up the hotel phone and called the concierge. Just as Mel had so aptly pointed out, he had work to do.

# Chapter 14

**M**elanie had just finished writing her monthly letter to the Hawkins family and was trying to figure out what to do for dinner when the bell to her suite rang. She looked through the peephole and saw a hotel employee holding an impressive floral bouquet. She smiled broadly before opening the door to accept the delivery. Her smile turned into laughter as she inspected the flowers. Someone had sent her Stargazer lilies.

Still chuckling, she examined the attached card. On the outside of the envelope, written in handwriting she didn't recognize, it said, "Thank you." Mel quickly unsealed the flap, sure that the flowers were a token of appreciation from her clients, and read the card.

*Great ideas are meant to be shared. Only idiots try to block them.*

*John*

Melanie buried her nose into the blooms and sighed. She wanted to give in to her feelings of appreciation for John's effort, but she still had doubts. Yes, his note implied contrition for trying to silence her ideas, but what about everything else? What about him calling her unprofessional and manipulative? Plus, he hadn't even bothered to use the words "I'm sorry." So was he really regretful or was he simply trying to smooth things over in order to get through the remainder of this project?

*John Carlson, what am I going to do with you?*

Before she could even think of an answer, Melanie's thoughts were interrupted by the telephone.

"Did you like the flowers?" John asked, his voice soft and tentative.

"Yes. Interesting choice. They're beautiful. Thank you."

"I thought they were a rather apropos icebreaker. Melanie, I've made such a mess of this trip," he admitted. "I'd like to take you to dinner and explain everything," he told her.

Melanie's silence spoke volumes. Afraid he'd alienated her friendship, John continued to gently push and cajole her into saying yes.

"Okay, give me ten minutes to get ready," Melanie said, amused by his persistence.

"Thank you. I'll wait in the lobby. Dress casually, and it might be best to leave your high heels in the room tonight," he cautioned with a laugh. Already his heart felt lighter. Thank goodness she'd agreed to see him.

Fifteen minutes later, Melanie stepped out of the elevator, looking every bit as cool, regal, and confident as the mystical girl from Ipanema. Dressed in a chic linen shirt and slacks and low-heeled sandals, to John's eyes she was the personification of everything she'd described this afternoon—a classy and elegant woman wrapped in understated sophistication, but alive with color and sensuality. Judging by the admiring looks of the males populating the hotel lobby, he wasn't alone in his thinking.

"You look beautiful," he said, speaking for them all. Instinctively John took Melanie's arm and, with pride for a prize he did not rightfully possess, escorted her though the lobby, secretly reveling in the stares of admiration, curiosity, and envy their appearance as a couple generated.

"Where are we going?" she asked as the car sped away.

"On a cruise to nowhere. I thought we'd do a little stargazing," he answered, locking eyes with her. Eight minutes later the sedan pulled up at the Miami Beach Marina. They exited the car and the driver handed John a small package from the front seat. Melanie could hear the gentle lapping of water against wood as they walked the length of the dock toward the last slip. Docked there was a luxurious 115-foot private yacht, with the name *Sun-Fire* emblazoned on its stern.

"Yours?" Melanie asked in wide-eyed amazement as they climbed aboard.

"A friend's."

"Impressive."

"I understand that short of the soon-to-be-built Casa de Arte, this is the best venue around for bathing in starlight. And as someone once told me, there isn't a more romantic place to have dinner than under the stars," John said with a wink.

The idea of spending a romantic night under the stars sent a swift, apprehensive chill through her body. Quickly Melanie tried to analyze her emotions. Immediately she ascertained that the shiver was not caused by fear, but more by the delicious agitation that came with entering unknown and forbidden territory. Additionally, a large cause of her anxiety was firmly rooted in the fact that ever since she was a child, Melanie got violently seasick at the mere thought of stepping onto a boat.

"Where's the restroom?" Mel asked, hoping like hell that such a remarkable marine vessel would have a well-stocked medicine cabinet. John directed her downstairs before slipping up to the pilothouse to talk with the captain.

Melanie strolled past the four other cabins and entered what looked to be the master stateroom. She stepped into what could be mistaken for the finest suite in any plush five-star hotel. The design schematic was impeccable, combining the utility of built-in teak cabinetry with a tasteful tone-on-tone cream color palette. Mel quickly entered the full bath, amazed that even on the high seas one did not have to give up the luxury of a hot shower or deep whirlpool bath. She opened the medicine cabinet, which was fully stocked with various personal sundries. She rummaged around and quickly struck gold—a package of motion-sickness pills. She studied the box, dismayed to find that these were not the nondrowsy formula.

She quickly swallowed two tablets when she heard the motor revving. Deciding that it was better to be sleepy than nauseous, she hurried back up on deck. John joined her at the bow as the yacht gracefully exited the slip and headed out into the Atlantic Ocean. She took a refreshing breath as she witnessed the beauty of Miami at night. The sun had set over an hour ago in a glory of red, pink, and orange streaks. In its place was left a dark slate packed with bright stars to compete with the artificial twinkle of the city lights. A crescent moon dangled in the sky, its silvery light rippling across the ocean waves. It was an awe-inspiring setting—one that fueled the imagination with fairy-tale fantasies. Mel unconsciously wrapped her arms around her body as if donning a layer of protective armor.

"I think, in the sight of something so magnificent," John said as he turned to face the lovely woman beside him, "any and all mis-demeanors should be forgiven, don't you?" As he went on to explain the impetus behind his mood and actions from the Vogue Belize to the Luz de la Estrella, Mel's earlier anger quickly turned into sincere concern. She listened as he admitted his feelings of professional insecurity and jealousy, of admiration for her talent and remorse for his actions, and with each divulgence Melanie's heart grew more full.

"You know, all of this—the yacht, dinner—is really unneces-sary," Mel told him. "All I really wanted to hear was that you were sorry. You'd be amazed how effective those simple little words, when delivered with sincerity, can be."

John paused as he looked deep into her eyes. "I am sorry. Will you please accept my apology?" he asked contritely, using words he hadn't uttered in years. After sharing his innermost emotions with Melanie, John was spent and at the same time exuberant. It felt so liberating to release the burden of his pent-up feelings. What about this woman brought out a tender, vulnerable side to him that even his wife couldn't?

"Yes, on one condition."

"Anything."

"Don't shut me out like that again. We're partners on this proj-ect. If something is bothering you, talk to me. I will understand, but don't leave me to play guessing games."

"I'll never do that to you again, I promise," John said tenderly.

"Don't do it to *anyone* you love." The words slipped out of her mouth before Melanie could silence them. She hadn't meant to infer that John loved her, but that was exactly what her comment sounded like, and, to be bluntly honest, what his actions felt like.

"I, uh . . . mean . . . you know, your wife, friends, whoever, it's not fair to shut out anyone who cares about you."

"Mr. Carlson. Ms. Hitts. Your dinner is ready," the chef announced, allowing Melanie to gracefully exit the uncomfortable verbal hole she'd fallen into.

"Thank you." John led Melanie back to the *SunFire*'s aft, where tucked away in the corner stood an impressively set table for two, replete with soft flickering candlelight, safely encased in a glass hurricane lamp.

"How many people are onboard with us?" Mel inquired, realizing that they had dropped anchor at some point during their conversation.

"Just two—the captain and chef. I didn't think we'd need a full staff."

"No, two is just enough." Melanie had to stop herself from letting out a huge "whew" as she accepted a glass of red wine. Since stepping aboard, she could feel her morning game of good news/bad news turning all bad. But with crew members along as unofficial chaperones on this romantic ride, Melanie felt much more confident that she could keep her lustful desires in check.

"I hope you're hungry. I asked the chef to prepare a very special meal—roasted crow." John laughed.

Melanie met John's laughter with her own, which to his ears sounded like a refreshing gentle breeze blowing through perfectly tuned wind chimes. The chef appeared again, this time with a tray teeming with a variety of culinary bliss. After refilling her wineglass, John politely dismissed him, unwilling to share his guest one moment longer than necessary.

"A toast," he proposed, raising his wine. "To gratefully accepting things we do not understand." The two touched glasses and Melanie, looking for relief from her nervous state, gratefully sipped from her goblet.

Mel took a savory bite of her brandy-and-herb-soaked quail and quipped, "Crow tastes remarkably like chicken." Easy laughter erupted between them, wiping out the stain of their earlier conflict. Conversation during dinner flowed smoothly and easily. They talked of John's love of the game of golf, his trip last year to Scotland, and his unwavering loyalty to the New York Yankees. Mel filled him in on her secret desire to loosen up the stodgy interior of 1600 Pennsylvania Avenue with a funky mix of aristocratic pomp and trendy cultural pop. It was only after dessert that the how-do-we-continue-to-avoid-the-unavoidable silence descended.

"Come with me. Let's take a little walk," John suggested, breaking the heavy hush and reaching for her hand. They strolled along the rail, quietly taking in the splendor of this magnificent Miami night. John led her to the mid-deck lounge and they both sat down on the black-and-white-striped sofa carved into the front of the aft cabin house.

"I have something for you," John declared, breaking the quiet and handing her the small package she'd seen the driver hand him.

"The flowers, dinner, that's apology enough."

"This is not part of my apology. It's an early Christmas present."

"John, this isn't necessary," she said, gently fingering the purple silk wrapping.

"Which is the only time one receives real pleasure in giving. Now open it."

With curiosity and pleasure compelling her to rip off the material like a kid on Christmas morning, Melanie maintained dignified control by deliberately separating the box from its casing. Slowly she lifted the box top and pulled back the gold tissue paper to reveal the same antique handbag she'd admired last month.

"My purse!" Mel shrieked in excitement. "But when? Why?"

"I bought it that same day. I saw how much you wanted it and it didn't seem fair that two such beautiful things should be separated." John hoped she wouldn't be put off by his flattery, but tonight his thoughts and words seemed to bypass the censor in his brain and flow directly from a place deep within.

"Thank you, but . . ." she began in a soft voice, unsure if she should accept such an expensive gift.

"Open it. There's something else inside."

Melanie tucked her bottom lip under her two front teeth as she opened the beaded bag and pulled out a velvet jewelry pouch. "John, I can't accept this. It's all too much."

"Before you say no, open it up and take a look. If you still think it's too much, you can return it with no hard feelings. Okay?"

Mel smiled before gently loosening the drawstring and pouring the contents into her lap. Her grin erupted into laughter as a colorful array of dimestore jacks and a small, multicolored rubber ball bounced out. John smiled at her delight, realizing this simple gift was so much more pleasing than the ruby pin he'd briefly considered.

"This is obviously a challenge. Clear the decks, Mr. Carlson, I'm about to take you to school."

With sheer childish pleasure, John and Melanie threw cushions onto the deck, got down on their knees, and played a rousing game. He gave her first roll and despite the slight pitching of the boat and playful taunts, Melanie went all the way from onesies through tens without John even getting a turn.

"Come on, best two out of three. I'll let you go first this time," she dared him, her competitive streak blazing.

"I think it's best that I concede. I mean, you are the jacks champion of Page Elementary School," he said, helping her off the floor and back onto the couch.

"You remember that?"

"I remember everything you tell me," John said with a much more serious tone. "Like how you've always felt out of place in the world of other people's expectations, and how you love vintage jewelry because every piece has a history, and how if something makes your heart sing you go after it."

"Wow, you do listen."

John smiled tenderly as he reached out and cupped Melanie's left cheek in his hand. "Yes, I do. And I must tell you, Miss Jacks Champion of Page Elementary School, my heart has been making all kinds of beautiful music since I've met you," he said as he gently traced the outline of her face with his fingers. John's compliment came with a string of hesitation attached. He had promised Melanie to go slow and not make a mess of things, but each time he looked in those gorgeous expressive eyes or he spoke her name or heard her infectious laugh, he wanted to tell her that he was falling in love.

"You are so exquisite. I love the way your hair dances around that lovely face of yours and how your lips always provide the perfect punctuation for whatever your mood." John wanted to tell Melanie how he'd never realized the incredible beauty of black women until now, when he was up close and personal with one of the finest. How he was intrigued by her flawless brown skin—like lush, milk-chocolate-colored velvet—and how much he wanted to treat his hand to the pleasure of it's touch and his eyes to the intriguing sight of his white skin mingled with hers. John wanted to tell Mel these things, but was fearful that they would sound disrespectful or, even worse, racist, so he simply spoke another truth. "It's your eyes I love the most."

Melanie gaped at John in pleasant disbelief. Her full, kissable lips, tight behind, and shapely legs had often been cited as the prime points of interest on the Melanie Hitts hot spots tour, but no man had ever mentioned her basic brown eyes.

"I love the way they make me feel when you look at me—like I'm someone special and worthwhile," John explained as Melanie felt her last vestige of reserve melt away.

Immediately her head began screaming out a litany of warnings: INAPPROPRIATE! MARRIED! COMPLICATED! while her heart responded with ideas of its own: DESIRABLE! INEVITABLE! DESTINY!

With her head and heart tied up in battle, Melanie had no response other than to return John's smile. As their eyes met, her mind and willpower surrendered and Mel's desire marched ahead with her heart, prompting her to simply live out this moment and let it take her wherever she was meant to go.

"You are special and I feel connected to you in more ways than I am probably willing to admit," Melanie told him. "At first I thought it was because of our mutual interest in design and architecture, but then I found myself discussing things with you that I've never talked to anyone about. I feel safe with you and . . ." She paused.

"And . . . go on. Don't be afraid to tell me anything."

"And I'm very attracted to you," she admitted, the dual effect of wine and medication making her feel slightly drunk and uninhibited. *Attracted, enamored, captivated, bewitched.* The list of her feelings for John Carlson was growing longer and more confusing by the day.

"And I to you in so many more ways than the obvious."

Melanie whispered his name softly, caressing John with the sound. Her voice ran over him like feathers on naked skin, making him ache to finally touch the woman he'd spent hours dreaming about.

His resistance depleted, John took Mel into his arms and kissed her, formally at first, but more naturally as she accepted his gesture. His kiss was warm and loving as his tongue gently explored the sweet recesses of her mouth. He lightly ran his hands up and down Mel's arms, neck, and shoulders, marveling at the smooth, velvety touch of her skin, while Melanie threaded her hands languidly through his hair, experiencing the erotic tingle of each silky strand as it passed through her fingers. The intensity of their feelings pushed them back onto the couch until they were both lying under the stars, and for minutes that seemed like hours, they each got lost in the soft sensuality of the moment—everything and everyone else forgotten.

John grazed her face with his lips, reverently paying homage to each exquisite feature. The two snuggled closer, arms wrapped around each other like a warm and cozy security blanket. Nestled in their seafaring cradle, they lay there in tranquil stillness, gently rocking in the sway of the ocean waves, serenaded by the calming lullaby of the sea.

"I don't know what's happening here," he whispered. "I have never felt like this before," he said, inhaling Melanie's fragrant scent.

"I love you," he said, his voice barely audible, before kissing the top of her head. The words floated out of his mouth, sounding as true and natural as they felt. Hearing no response, he looked down to find that Melanie, succumbing to the gentle rocking of the yacht, had drifted off. John smiled down upon his beautiful Jax, the nickname he'd bestowed on her, and felt a wide, wondrous smile break out on his face. It really didn't matter if she'd heard his admission, John knew his heart would sing those words to her many times again.

There would be no lovemaking tonight, but that really didn't disappoint him. The physical attraction between them was strong and palatable but, on the other hand, really not of premiere importance. Would he like to make love to this extraordinary creature? Without a doubt—his current erection stood as firm testimony. But no orgasm could compete with the sheer emotional pleasure he had just received from their kiss—one that lingered deliciously and dangerously to remind him that his life would never be the same from this moment forward.

Enjoying the sensation of this woman he adored sleeping in his arms, John took a moment to ponder this emotional quandary. For the first time this evening, he allowed thoughts of Sharon to surface. Despite all of the inherently good things about her and their life together, something was missing. What that something was, John wasn't sure, but as soon as his lips had touched hers, it also became brilliantly clear that Melanie touched a part of him that had lain dormant for a lifetime.

With the skill of an archaeologist, she had gently unearthed in him new emotions that he now constantly craved. Jax had brushed away the suffocating silt of his ennui and made him feel light-hearted and young and productive again. In the moments they spent together she allowed him to relive the splendor of simply being John Carlson sans all of the titles and burdensome responsibilities they brought with them.

*You've made me love you, Jax,* he acknowledged to himself. *But just as sweet, you've made me love the man I am when I'm with you.*

"Good morning," John's cheerful voice greeted her.

"Good morning," Melanie whispered into the phone. She lay back onto her pillows, grateful for last night's snowfall. She loved the hushed stillness of snow days, which she believed to be God-given gifts, perfect for serious cocooning.

"I can't talk long. I simply wanted to hear your voice and tell you again how much I enjoyed our time together in Miami," John said.

"Miami was very special for me too."

"I'm glad to hear you feel that way. I wasn't sure. I mean, here I thought we were having this fairy-tale evening, but instead of my kiss waking you up, it put you to sleep. So what does that say for my powers as a legitimate Prince Charming?" John teased.

"I'm so sorry," Melanie said with a self-consciousness chuckle. How could she have fallen asleep at such an endearing instance? That episode would surely go down in her infamous file of life's most embarrassing moments.

"My untimely bout of narcolepsy makes no editorial statement on your Prince Charming status, but should definitely stand as a public warning against combining Dramamine and alcohol. Believe me, you weren't the tiniest bit boring," she said, touching her fingers to her lips and remembering his kiss.

"I've never had a woman fall asleep while I'm baring my heart, but then again, it's been a very long time. I'm probably very rusty."

John's statement caused Mel to sit up. *Oh, my God. What else did he say to me?*

"Melanie, don't worry. I'm as confused as you are," he responded as if reading her mind. "We'll just muddle our way through this. I won't let either one of us get hurt, I promise. Okay?"

"Okay."

"Look, I have to go to Belize. Things are getting worse down there. I'm flying out the twenty-eighth."

"How long will you be away?"

"I'm not sure. A week at least, maybe more. I'd like to see you before I go. Do you think we could get together on Monday?"

"I'll be out of town. . . ."

"Oh," John said, his disappointment obvious.

"But I won't be far, just down in D.C. I'm sure I can come back a day early," Mel said, surprised at her unwillingness to pass up a chance to see him.

"Great. I'll see you soon. Why don't we meet at the company apartment?"

"I guess so," Melanie replied, caution permeating her voice.

"Don't worry, you're safe with me. I just want to go someplace where we can talk freely," John assured her.

"Okay, then. See you on Monday. Have a Merry Christmas."

"You too, lovely. I'll be in touch."

Melanie hung up the phone, wishing she could stay in bed with a hot carafe of French vanilla coffee and engage in some seriously deep self-reflection. But with only five days until Christmas, and over three thousand things left to do before leaving for D.C., there was no time for such luxury.

She pushed back the covers and, with them, all thoughts of

John Carlson. Mel slipped on her warm and comfy chenille robe and padded out to the living room, where the delicious aroma of freshly brewed coffee and the angry sound of Candace's rage welcomed her. She walked into the kitchen to find her friend dressed and yelling into her cell phone.

"Fuck you and your goddamn wife. You and your precious fucking marriage can go to hell," she screamed before hanging up.

Melanie poured herself a cup of coffee without comment, knowing it was best to let Candy simmer down before trying to talk. Melanie was sure that Frank was canceling Christmas Eve plans with her, just as he'd done on the Fourth of July and his birthday. It continued to boggle Melanie's mind that even after Candace's numerous affairs with married men, she still didn't understand that holidays and important family events always belonged to the wife. It disturbed Mel even more that Candy, despite her constant disappointment, seemed to revel in her role as the other woman.

"I can't believe that asshole said he wants to take a break. He says he ought to give his marriage another try, that the bottom line is, divorce is too expensive and he's too old to start over. Well, if Frank Warren thinks I'm going to sit around waiting for his tired ass, he's as fucking crazy as that bad-weave-havin', ruin-a-good-Versace-outfit-wearin' bitch he's married to. Fuck him," she said, tears hiding behind her anger.

"Why do you keep putting yourself through this?" Mel asked.

"Not now, Melo. I've heard it all before."

"At the risk of pissing you off, maybe you need to keep on hearing it until you start listening. You should have been out of this affair long ago. *You* are the *other* woman, Candy, not Regina. You must have realized at some point that this is how it's always going to be, no matter what promises Frank makes to you."

"How can I possibly know that?"

Melanie stared at Candace in total bewilderment. How could she *not* know? Turn on any talk show, pick up any magazine, log on to any relationship message board, and you'll hear mistress after mistress admitting that when given the ultimatum, a man will rarely leave his wife. The truth Candace refused to acknowledge was that she was in a no-win, going-nowhere-fast relationship with a married man—a man who viewed her as his personal amusement park of sexual thrills where the cost of admission was well worth the exhilaration of the ride.

"Don't knock it till you've tried it," Candace retorted. Melanie let the comment slide, unwilling to examine the ironic circumstances of her own budding relationship with Sharon Carlson's husband. "Let me give you the short but sweet list of why it's good being the other woman," Candace continued.

"First of all, there is no commitment, which means I can live life on my own terms, which is a damn good thing. Plus the sex is phenomenal because it never becomes routine or boring."

Mel listened as Candace explained how the time she and Frank spent together was always quality because they weren't mired down in the realities of living a real life together. Or how getting stood up on occasion was a small price to pay for the great gifts given to relieve her anger and assuage Frank's guilt.

Melanie had to admit that if she listened without fully investigating the other side, Candace's arguments sounded good. On the surface she appeared to have it all—great sex, companionship, and the ability to live on her terms without all the personal sacrifice that comes from sharing one's life.

But for each "pro" Candace espoused, two more "cons" popped up in Melanie's head. Didn't Candace recognize that Frank's trinkets weren't expressions of love, but rather payola for services rendered? Or that by constantly engaging in these one-sided, make-love-but-not-a-life-together alliances, Candace would never learn to deal with the pressures or share the joys of a complete, sunshine-and-rain, splendor-and-pain union? Couldn't Candace see that it wasn't the ease of having a man without the maintenance that drove her to relationships with married men, but rather the fear of true intimacy? And what "perks" could ever be enough to keep her sidelined and mateless on this one-way, dead-end street?

"In other words, the wife does all the shit work and I get all the benefits," Candace concluded, pulling Melanie away from her thoughts and back into the conversation.

"Don't you feel any guilt at all?" Melanie asked as she followed Candace out of the kitchen and into the living area. Candy angrily plopped down onto the couch as Melanie headed for the dining room table piled high with boxes, gift wrap, ribbon, and various other holiday supplies.

"Guilty for what? I'm single. I'm not the one cheating."

"What about karma? Aren't you afraid that all of this is going to come back around on you?"

"No, because I know how to meet my man's needs. If Regina made Frank happy, he wouldn't be with me. She obviously isn't taking care of business, and I am."

"Then why he's taking a break from *you*, not her?"

"Thanks for the pep talk, Melo. With friends like you . . ." Candace said, rising to make her exit.

Mel jumped at the sound of the door slamming behind Candace. As Melanie began wrapping Christmas gifts, she couldn't help feeling struck by the hypocrisy of her argument. Here she was, ragging on Candace for her indiscretions with Frank, and all the while she herself was teetering on the perimeter of becoming a marital interloper.

Mel was forced to reexamine the reasons—not the excuses—why she had hopped out of her relationship with Will. Was it because she was afraid of the exact same things her friend was trying to avoid? And if so, perhaps this skip she was taking in John Carlson's direction had less to do with feelings of love and more about safety. Because John was a married white man, and therefore technically off-limits, was she merely looking to him to fulfill her emotional and physical needs without having to jump into a real relationship?

Melanie's thoughts swirled around her head as she tied a ribbon around a gift box and picked up a silk poinsettia. As she reached for her glue gun to attach the flower, she noticed the message light blinking. She clicked on the speakerphone to retrieve her messages and soon Will's voice filled the room.

"Hey, Mel. It's Will. Just calling to see if you'd gotten back to town. Give me a call before you head this way. I'm looking forward to hearing your voice. 'Bye, now."

Melanie disengaged the line and began dialing Will's number. Two touches short of completion, she paused to ponder her action. Was she really ready to talk with him? Hadn't she had enough emotional upheaval for one week?

*A promise is a promise,* the dutiful sister/daughter/friend inside of her sang out. *But confusion is king,* her befuddled ex-fiancée/premistress neighbor chimed in. *Forget it,* Mel decided and hung up the phone. She'd call him after the holidays. She'd quietly slip into town, drink a little eggnog, sing a few carols, and bask in the crazy chaos of a Hitts family Christmas. Perhaps a little Yuletide cheer was just what she needed to blow away the confusion and put her head back on straight.

"But Mommy, Santa Claus is not a brown," Eva insisted as she stared at the papier-mâché rendering of St. Nick, dressed in a Hawaiian shirt and shorts, checking his naughty and nice list.

"Honey, Santa *is* brown, but because there are so many children in the world, he has lots of helpers who are all different colors," Francesca explained to her daughter.

"Melme, is Santa Claus a brown?" Eva asked Mel, apparently not sure who or what to believe. Melanie heard Eva's endearing mispronunciation of her name and smiled at her sweet, precocious niece, surprised that even at the tender age of five, race was already an issue.

"What color do you think Santa is?" Mel asked.

"Red and white," Eva proclaimed.

"You are so right," Melanie answered, laughing and drawing her niece into a loud, demonstrative bear hug. Eva wasn't concerned with Santa's skin color, only that his uniform was not in order.

*Out of the mouths of babes truly comes the wisdom of the world,* Melanie thought. *If only we grown-ups would listen.*

"Eva the Diva, come over here and let me tell you the story about Leroy the gold-toothed reindeer and his very shiny car," Xavier said.

"No, Daddy, that's not how it goes," Eva insisted, while

Francesca and Mel burst into laughter. "PopPop, you tell the story. Daddy doesn't know it right."

Lawrence Hitts gladly obliged his granddaughter, sitting her in his lap to share the story of Rudolph. Xavier sat on the floor and quietly coaxed Jena over using a red satin ribbon, succeeding in bringing both baby and mother to his side. Melanie stood near the front window and let her eyes canvass the room, first taking in the twinkling tree packed with sentimental ornaments, and then examining the black nativity scene gracing the coffee table, an artistic rendition of the true meaning of the season. Lastly she moved on to the hand-stitched stockings hanging from the staircase. They were stretched and worn from years of excited hands dipping into their overstuffed innards, but to Mel's eyes they were still icons of childhood pleasure.

Melanie inhaled the delicious and inviting scent of her mother's sweet potato pies baking in the oven mingling with the crisp, tart aroma of cinnamon-spiked apple cider warming on the stove. She stood observing the tender scene with mixed sentiments. She was so grateful to be part of a loving family with such meaningful traditions, but the same scene made her question if she'd ever be ready to create these precious Kodak moments with her own husband and children.

A loud thud from upstairs interrupted both the storytelling and Mel's personal contemplation. "What's Mom doing up there?" she asked. "Chopping wood?"

"She's wrapping gifts," Franti explained, her voice distinct with that teasing I-know-something-you-don't-know tone left over from childhood.

Suddenly the festive tinkling of sleigh bells sounded from

above. Immediately Eva jumped from her grandfather's lap and ran toward the foyer. "That's not Grandma, that's Santa Claus," she announced, clapping her hands.

From the top of the stairs, they all heard the hearty and cheerful sounds of Santa's laughter, followed by the heavy thud of boots on wood. They all watched as red velvet legs tucked in black, fur-topped galoshes descended the stairs. "Ho, ho, ho. Merry Christmas," Santa's familiar voice called out. The hearty sound of his greeting sent baby Jena scurrying to the safety of her mother's arms, while a wide-eyed Eva stood frozen by the staircase with Melanie, watching this Yuletide hero appear before her very eyes.

"I told you, Melme, Santa is red and white," she whispered to her aunt.

*Red and white and Will Freedman all over*, Melanie thought as she lightly tugged Eva's braids. What was wrong with everyone around here? First Candace and now Francesca trying to sandbag her every step by inviting Will any- and everywhere. These folks had some major payback coming.

"Where's Eva Gabrielle?" Santa asked, brightening the room with Will's joyous, gapped smile.

"I'm Eva."

"Well, come let's see what special something Santa has in his bag for you." As Eva followed Mr. Claus to the armchair near the fireplace, Francesca, chuckling into her hand, slid over next to Melanie.

"And what's so damn funny?" Mel whispered.

"You. You'd have thought you'd seen the real St. Nick, the way your face looked when Will came bouncing down the stairs."

"Was this your idea of a joke?"

"My idea, yes. Joke, no."

"Why?" Mel whispered, trying to be discreet when she really felt like pinching her sister.

"Because we like him, Melanie. He still feels like family. You may have broken up with him, but does that mean the rest of us have to?"

A new wave of remorse washed over her. She was the one responsible for not only taking away Will's marriage, but the only family he had left in the world. How could she not help make his holidays bright? Melanie looked over and watched the dear, tender way Will was responding to Eva and her unending list of Christmas desires. After reminding the child that only very good girls received such elaborate gifts, he kissed her on the top of her forehead, pulled out a box, suspiciously the same size as WNBA Barbie, and sent Eva happily on her way.

"Now, where is Melanie Lorraine?" Santa inquired.

Francesca indiscreetly shoved Mel forward in Will's direction. "Here she is, Santa."

Melanie moved with trepidation as the adults silently chuckled to themselves. There wasn't one person in this room, other than Melanie, who didn't think that these two belonged together and, whether forced or voluntary, found pleasure in seeing them together.

"Sit on Santa's lap so we can get a picture," Francesca insisted, skillfully avoiding the optical daggers being slung in her direction.

Melanie reluctantly sat down on Will's lap, both embarrassed and amused. She had to admit that he did look awfully cute all dressed up like the Claus man. This was definitely one for the scrapbooks.

"Have you been naughty or nice, little girl?" Will inquired, playing his role to perfection.

"I guess that depends on whom you ask, Santa," Mel answered, feeling the uncomfortable rush of remorse seep from her guilty conscious.

"Well, Santa still brought you a very special present." Will leaned over and handed Melanie a large box from his velvet sack.

"Open it, Melme," Eva prompted. "I'll help." Eva rushed over to help her aunt strip the gold wrapping paper from the box. Quickly she pulled off the top and Melanie's laughter filled the room as she lifted out a huge tub of Red Vines licorice. Her discomfort was melted away by the appropriateness of Will's choice—sweet, inexpensive, and yet highly personal.

"Thank you, Santa. This was on the tip-top of my list," Mel said as she opened the container and handed him a fat red licorice whip. This simple action flashed her back to the very first time she'd shared her favorite sweet with Will.

They had met shortly after Melanie returned to D.C. following her father's heart attack. After weeks of nursing her dad, Mel had gratefully allowed Candace to drag her to the Black Enterprise Ski Challenge in Vail, Colorado, for some much-needed R&R. Following her lesson on their last morning in Vail, Melanie was feeling confident enough to take a run down the novice trail. She started off well, snowplowing her way back and forth down the mountain, but when she tried to escape the path of a renegade snowboarder, Mel found herself flying downhill fast and furious. Panicked by her failed attempts to slow down, she slid out of control into a group of skiers stopped on the side of the trail. She rammed directly into Will, and, despite her petite build, managed to knock him over.

Luckily, neither was injured and they decided to retire to the lodge for a drink. As a feeble attempt toward reparation, Melanie offered Will a whip of licorice. This action turned out to be a yummy icebreaker, leading them into a friendly debate over the taste of Twizzlers vs. Red Vines. After exhausting that tasty subject, the two continued to talk for hours. Mel, naturally curious and genuinely interested, was full of questions about the man and his livelihood. Will spoke excitedly of his job at America Online and his ideas on the vast untapped opportunities available for African-Americans in cyberspace.

His promise to contact her when they both returned to Washington, D.C., was fulfilled the moment he hit his front door. Will persevered after Melanie with tenacious gusto, letting nothing impede his pursuit of her. When she had plans for Super Bowl Sunday, he promptly convinced her to cancel her date and attend another party with him. There he was attentive and gallant, making a yeoman effort to assure that she was comfortable and having a good time.

Their first official date had to be canceled when Lawrence Hitts had another heart scare while Mel's mother was down South visiting her relatives. Will canceled their planned visit to the Corcoran Museum to view the Gordon Parks exhibit, and instead packed a romantic picnic dinner and brought it over to the house with a coffee table book of Parks's photography and a package of licorice. His thoughtfulness warmed her heart and placed Will Freedman at the top of her short list of favorite people. Once again there was no lack of conversation, but this time Will's were the questions asked and answered. By night's end, after sharing their first kiss, both knew that the other was someone special.

In the weeks following, Will and Melanie were nearly inseparable, and quickly became an official couple. By Easter, he was certain that she was the one. Will surprised her at a Hitts family dinner a couple weeks later with an engagement ring tucked inside a beautiful egg-shaped music box. Full of love and appreciation for this special man, Melanie agreed to marry him without hesitation.

So much had happened between them since those happy times. And now, after months of Mel trying to deny his existence, he was here, rekindling feelings and memories that made a mockery out of her vow to get over him and move on with her life.

While Nat King Cole sang about chestnuts roasting, Melanie and Will sat on the floor in front of the fire playing a friendly game of poker. The Hitts family's traditional Christmas Eve dinner of Louisiana gumbo had been heartily consumed, and with appetites satiated and dishes done, the group disbanded to various areas of the house. Xavier and Francesca were upstairs with screwdrivers and batteries, playing Santa's elves after tucking their exhausted daughters into bed. Lawrence and Elizabeth had long retired to their bedroom, leaving the ex-couple alone in the glowing warmth of the living room.

Mel watched closely as Will studied his cards. He triumphantly threw a pair of kings into the middle pile, winning the hand and the game. "Victory is mine!" he exclaimed as he brushed the pile of pistachio nuts over to his side.

"It was never you," Mel told him, dismissing his jubilation. Her out-of-left-field comment pushed away the joviality of their friendly card game and spun the evening around into an entirely different direction. "I left you because I didn't want to be in the way. I didn't want to keep you from finding the kind of love you deserve."

"Don't you understand that by leaving you didn't remove an obstacle? You created a hole."

"I'm sorry."

"And what made you think that *you* couldn't give me the kind of love I need?"

"Well, for starters—the house."

"Why would me buying us a house run you away?"

"Because it told me that you didn't know me as well as I thought. Otherwise, how can you explain making a purchase that major without telling me? How did you know that I even wanted to live in D.C.?"

"This is where I work. Your family is here. I just assumed that this is where we'd continue to live."

"Exactly. You assumed. You didn't know. But I'm not blaming you. We were so busy planning a wedding, we didn't take the time to plan our life. We didn't talk about where we'd live, when or if we'd have children, or what we wanted out of life as individuals or a couple. We didn't discuss any of those things. I mean, on the surface, maybe, but not in any great depth. How could we get married when there were so many things we didn't know about each other?"

Will stood to stretch his legs and search his heart. It was true that they didn't know each other as well as many couples who'd spent years dating before marriage, but that didn't make his feelings for her any less true. The important basics were in place between them—loyalty, strong values, and similar morals. The other things were simply icing on what he believed to be an already splendid chocolate cake.

He stretched out his arms and drew Melanie to her feet, then placed his hands on her shoulders and looked deep into her eyes. "I want you to look past all of your confusion and answer me from here," Will said lightly, pounding his chest with his fist. "Do you still love me?"

Tears began to form in Melanie's eyes. "Yes," she answered. Will wrapped her up in his arms and hugged her tight. He could feel his own tears begin to fall as Melanie confirmed what he'd always known. As long as she still was in love with him, he was confident that things would be all right. He bent down and touched her lips tenderly with his. His kiss was brief yet powerful and communicated all the things his heart was feeling but his mouth was afraid to say.

A sense of déjà vu ran through Melanie's body. Just a week ago, John had done the exact same thing and summoned forth similar emotions—tenderness, warmth, arousal. The feelings were comparable in that they both evoked desire, but they were also very different, as one stemmed from present experience, the other from past memories.

A tremor of confusion followed. Never had two such different men, while occupying the same slice of her life, brought forth such equally potent feelings. Deep inside, Mel knew that she still loved Will Freedman, but at the same time she felt apprehensive, not understanding what was truly happening between her and John Carlson. On that yacht in Miami both delightful and disquieting feelings for John had gripped her imagination and left her pondering what, if any, possibilities lay ahead for them. Yet, standing here wrapped in the protective shell of Will's embrace, she was convinced that their relationship deserved one more chance.

Will stepped back and lightly wiped the tears from her cheeks and gingerly offered a smile. "Melanie, you just said you love me, and I love you. Nothing has changed. I still want you to have my babies. I still want to grow old with you. How can we let a silly house keep us from being together?"

"It's not just the house," Melanie snapped, pulling away in frustration. "Didn't you hear a word I said? You want all those things, but how do you know what I want? Like I said, we don't know each other well enough to be married."

Will pulled her back into a hug, unwilling to lose any further ground. "Baby, I heard you. And I do believe you're jumping the gun a bit. I don't recall having asked you to marry me again," Will joked, teasing her back into good humor.

"I understand what you're saying to me, Mel. But it would be criminal not to try again. All I'm asking is that we take the time get to know each other better. Then we make a decision about where we go from there."

"How do we do that?" Melanie inquired. "How do we go from being engaged to being just friends?"

"We start at the beginning," he said, extending his hand. "Hello, Melanie Hitts. My name is William Gregory Freedman and I've been waiting all of my life to meet you."

Melanie looked down at her hand safely encased in his and finally realized the truth in her mother's statement that a man's hands revealed a lot about his character. Will's well-groomed hands were strong and powerful. The scars on his knuckles from years of playing football spoke the truth of a man who had worked and played hard all of his life. On the flip side, his palms, despite a few weightlifting calluses, were smooth and supple, the flesh as soft and giving as his heart.

"Nice to meet you, Will Freedman."

"So we're starting fresh?"

"Yes, but promise me, no expectations. No pressure," Melanie insisted.

"I promise not to pressure you if you promise to communicate openly and honestly."

"I promise. Cross my heart," Mel said, pantomiming her words and already feeling like a liar. Could she tell the truth to Will about *everything*? Would he understand her relationship with John? Especially when she didn't?

"Would it be pressuring you to ask you to spend New Year's Eve with me?" Will asked, hope shining in his eyes. He was praying like hell that she hadn't already made a date with her "friend."

Mel took a moment to consider Will's invitation. She and Candy had talked about hanging out together, and now that she and Frank were on the outs, Griffin would most likely be her date. It might be fun for the four of them to ring in the new year together.

"I do have plans already," Mel began. Will felt his spirits drop and rebound as she went on to explain with whom. "But with that cast of characters, it could get a bit crazy."

"Crazy sounds perfect," Will replied, locking his gaze onto hers. He lifted Mel's hand to his lips and tenderly kissed her knuckles. The simple touch of his mouth on her skin sent powerful and familiar sensations throughout her body. Again, their smiles met, but this time without the trepidation that had peppered them earlier. These smiles communicated the remnant intimacies shared between two people whose life paths had once poignantly intersected.

Melanie had no choice but to place her relationships with both

Will and John into God's hands and see where things went. After all, wasn't that where faith came in? Allowing God and the Universe to guide you when yelling "Timber" in the forest did absolutely nothing to clear the trees.

# Chapter 15

Amanda sat quietly studying the faces around the Carlsons' dinner table as they chatted over dessert and coffee. The festive scene around her left Mandy feeling even more connected with her mentor. Just as Amanda had begun to do with Quincy and her crew, Sharon had created a makeshift family of good friends. Gwendolyn and Bob Robinson with their sons, Nicholas and Ryan, had obviously adopted Sharon, and thanks to them, she was able to experience the extended love that came with being part of a large family.

Mandy surveyed the scene, her feelings alternating between joy and trepidation. She was particularly grateful to her parents for allowing her to stay in the States and celebrate a family Christmas, even if it wasn't with her own. Throughout the evening, Sharon and her friends included Amanda in all of their traditions—the singing, joke-telling, and gift exchange—trying to make her feel part of the celebration. And despite their rocky start on the Bloomingdale's sales floor, even Gwen had warmed up to her, presenting her with a pink suede journal and funky roller-ball pen.

Sharon's husband was a vastly different story. No matter what she had to say about any subject, John reacted with negative disdain. His distant and disapproving air made her feel nervous and unwelcome. Perhaps that was why her stomach had started to feel queasy again.

"Amanda and her friends are going to help out at the nursing home for a few months," Sharon announced, once again trying to draw Mandy into the conversation.

"Is this some sort of community service project?" Gwen asked.

"Sort of," Amanda responded, not volunteering any additional information.

"What are you, a Girl Scout or something?" Ryan asked.

"No," Amanda snapped. She was horrified, as any hip fifteen-year-old would be, that Ryan would dare suggest such a disgustingly infantile thing. "I got arrested and have to do fifteen hours of community service."

All activity around the table ceased. Forks were suspended in midair, mouths agape at the news. John immediately shot his wife an I-told-you-so look, though Sharon, Bob, and the boys were both flabbergasted and intrigued. Gwen, like John, seemed not surprised in the least.

"You were arrested?" Nicholas asked. "That's deep."

"Yeah, but the charges were dismissed."

"What were you charged with?" Bob Robinson asked in his authentic lawyer's voice.

"Disorderly conduct," she answered, picking at her pound cake and ignoring Sharon's imploring eyes. Amanda was sorry she'd let the news slip. She'd told Sharon only that she had to complete a community service project. Sharon had naturally assumed it was for school and had asked no further questions.

"What exactly did you do?" Gwen asked.

"Nothing."

"It had to be something," John remarked sharply.

"It was a couple weeks after this kid at school got caught with a gun, and a bunch of us got together to demonstrate against violence in schools. We were minding our own business and the police started hassling us. This one cop kept yelling for us to move along and we kept telling him that we had the right to be there."

"Did you have a permit?" Bob asked.

"Well, no, but we really thought we had the right, you know, free speech, the right to assemble, and all. It turns out we did need a permit, but we didn't know and he didn't have to be so nasty. He pulled out his nightstick and said that if we didn't go, he'd arrest us, and my friend told him to go ahead. The cop got rough with him, grabbed him by the arm, threw him on the ground, and handcuffed him. A group of us started yelling at the cop and tried to pull Max away, and he arrested us all."

"And that's it?" John asked. "It doesn't sound plausible that the officer would react so strongly, unless you and your friends were baiting him."

"We didn't bait him. We were yelling at him to leave Max alone because we were afraid."

"I think you're leaving something out," John insisted.

Amanda shot up from the table and sprinted toward the bathroom. She could no longer fight the nausea and didn't want to further embarrass herself.

"John, you've upset her," Sharon said as she pushed her chair back from the table, ready to follow and console Amanda.

"Sit down, Sharon," her husband instructed.

"Maybe it would be best to give her a little time alone," Gwen suggested, trying to protect both her friend and the young girl.

"Why were you so hard on her?" Sharon implored reluctantly, returning to her seat.

"That girl is nothing but trouble," John said.

"She said she did nothing wrong and I believe her. Apparently so did the judge. And you've been rude to her all night, even before you found out about the arrest."

"I told you that it was inappropriate for her to join us in the first place. She has her own family, for chrissake. But you totally ignored what I had to say and invited her anyway."

"I'm sorry. I didn't realize it was *your* job to determine who was appropriate for me to invite into *my* home," Sharon replied sarcastically and with uncustomary defiance.

John could well gauge his wife's anger by her uncharacteristic willingness to ignore the presence of their friends as she waged this battle. Out of the corner of his eye, he could see Bob and the boys trying to disappear into their chairs, while Gwen suppressed an I-am-woman smile, pleased that Sharon was standing up to him.

"This is not the time, Sharon. We have company," John stated, dismissing the subject.

"Gwen and Bob are family, not guests. And they already know how dictatorial you can be."

The words left an eerie echo in John's ears. Melanie had said something similar while they were in Miami. She too had accused him of being controlling and unyielding, though he'd always thought of himself as taking charge. And wasn't that the way Sharon expected him to be? For their entire marriage she had looked to him for his decisive leadership, just as the employees of Carlson and Tuck and his clients around the world did. Was this not the role in which he'd been cast? But had he begun to take it all too seriously? Had he become, as Melanie and now his wife suggested, an arrogant tyrant?

"I'm sorry. I don't mean to be imperious and I apologize if I have been rude to Amanda. Why don't you go see how she's doing?" John suggested to the surprise of them all. It was not his usual habit to publicly apologize for his actions.

Sharon left her seat and walked to the guest bathroom in the hallway. She put her ear to the door, expecting to hear sobs, but instead it was the sound of Amanda's retching that greeted her. Concern enveloped her as she knocked on the door. "Mandy, are you all right? May I come in?"

After several seconds, an ashen-faced Amanda opened the door. "Are you feeling sick?" Sharon asked.

"A little. My stomach has been kind of upset the last couple of days."

"It must be that flu bug that's going around," Sharon said as she laid her hand across Amanda's forehead to check for fever. "You don't seem warm, but would you like to lay down for a while?"

"Maybe I should go home. I can call a car to come pick me up," Amanda suggested.

"Nonsense. You're spending the night, just as we planned."

"But Mr. Carlson—"

"John asked me to apologize for his behavior," Sharon told her, stretching the truth a tad, but for good reason. She could not bear the thought of Mandy spending her Christmas with the maid. It was terribly sad that her parents seemed all too happy to let strangers look after their child. "He's been under a lot of strain lately at work, and he's taking it out on everyone. You're always welcome in our home," Sharon said, giving her a hug.

It was well after midnight when John and Sharon said good-bye to their guests and went up to bed. Mandy had retired to the guest room shortly after eleven, pleading a sour stomach. In truth, her stomach was fine, but she still felt uncomfortable around John and was reluctant to place Sharon in the middle of their mutual dislike.

Sharon changed into her pale pink silk nightgown and sat down at the vanity to brush her hair. John approached carrying a shimmering gold bag with tissue paper speckled with confetti peeking from the top. He took a moment to view their reflection in the mirror before gently removing the brush from his wife's hands and laying it on the table. Slowly John pulled Sharon to her feet and turned her body into his.

"I'm sincerely sorry if I said or did anything to spoil your evening," he said softly. He marveled at the ease with which those words slipped through his lips. He could tell by the surprised but pleased look on Sharon's face that Melanie was right—a sincere apology meant a lot and carried much more weight than any expensive gift ever could.

"She really is a good girl. If you just took the time to get to know her, you'd see."

John let her comment slide without response. He still had his apprehensions about Amanda Weiss, but he was done with that topic for the evening. "Merry Christmas. This is for you," he said, handing her the bag.

Sharon rummaged inside and pulled out the mother-of-pearl purse John had found at the flea market. She pulled open the elaborate turquoise clasp with curious admiration. The clutch was lovely but it certainly wasn't new.

"It's vintage. I picked it out myself," he told her.

"Thank you, honey. It's beautiful." *When did John start shopping at thrift shops?* The notion crossed Sharon's mind but she promptly dismissed it, caring only that he'd taken the time to choose this gift himself instead of relying on his secretary or jeweler as he usually did. She was truly touched and she couldn't help wondering what had gotten into her husband.

# Chapter 16

"**H**i," Melanie mouthed as she motioned John to come in. She held the phone between her ear and shoulder as she took his coat and gestured for him to take a seat.

John sat down and glanced around the apartment, admiring the way the soft feminine colors of sage and peach pleasantly combined with the heavy wooden African art. He was happy that Melanie called to say she was expecting some important phone calls and asked to change their meeting from the company apartment to her place. It gave him the opportunity to see her domestic side.

He made himself comfortable on the sofa and while he waited for Melanie to conclude her phone call, he picked up *Soul*, a tome of photos by French fashion photographer Thierry Le Gouès, from the coffee table. John flipped through the pages and became engrossed in the sensual and evocative collection of nudes and portraits of some of the world's top models of African descent. Though the entire body of each woman was coated from forehead to foot with gleaming black paint, he recognized supermodels Naomi Campbell, Iman, and Alek, each in stunning, sexy, and highly erotic poses. Every page depicted the statuesque mystery, seductive elegance, and allure of black women from around the globe.

"But we're talking about eight people. Surely you can free up two rooms," he heard Melanie implore. Her voice stole his attention away from the artistic fantasy in his hands to the beauty standing across the room. He'd honestly never really appreciated the fetching nature of black women before becoming involved with Melanie. But the realization struck him that the standard features of women of color—from their full, luscious lips and round bottoms to their hairstyles and fashion statements—had steadily infiltrated the mainstream view of traditional European beauty.

"Sorry about that," Melanie said, concern and frustration coloring her apology.

"Everything okay?"

"Not really." Things had taken a downward slide following her Yuletide détente with Will. Besides lightly spraining her ankle while trying out her Kristi Yamaguchi moves with her sister and niece, she'd just received the bad news that the Hawkins family had lost their home in a Christmas Eve fire. Mel took a moment to explain how nearly everything was destroyed due to the smoke and water damage, but luckily the entire family, while homeless, was safe.

The news hit Melanie hard. Mamie Hawkins and her kids were like her extended family after all these years. In the past, Mel had sent them whatever she could—from essentials to extravagances—and last year Candace and some of her other friends had chipped in to buy them a washing machine. But this went way beyond their reach. How could she possibly help them put a roof back over their heads?

"I'm trying to make a deal with the motel manager in Greenville, Mississippi, to house them for at least a week until we can figure out something more permanent," she explained.

"You do all this for them and you're not even related?" John asked.

"If I don't, who will? I mean, it's not like it takes a lot of time or effort on my part to help just one family. And it honestly feels good on both sides of the giving."

John looked at her with new esteem for her generosity of spirit toward people she'd never met and seemed to have nothing in common with. Her statement made him rethink his recent conversation with Sharon about Amanda Weiss.

"My wife was saying the same thing about saving one person. She's taken this teenager whose life seems full of issues under her wing. The girl is a handful and I'm still not sure why Sharon wants to be bothered."

"When someone touches your heart like that, it ceases to become something you *want* to do. It becomes something you *need* to do because you realize what's really important in this world."

"And that is?" John asked.

"Love." Melanie spoke the word with quiet reverence. They sat in silence for a moment, both digesting the enormity of her statement.

"Love is such a tricky thing, isn't it? It's the one thing that we all want to find but are too afraid to accept when it appears."

Instinctively Mel knew that John was not referring to the universal love between all human beings but the very personal kind between a man and a woman. "You're right. Love presents itself to us in all kinds of ways but too many times we turn it away because it doesn't come in the right package—sex, color, tax bracket."

"Or marital status?" John blurted out.

"Yes."

"What was wrong with Will's package?" John asked, curious about the unsatisfactory traits of the man who was unable to capture the heart of this dazzling woman.

Melanie's first reaction was to avoid the subject as she'd successfully done for months, but just having spent the holiday with Will, it was a topic she needed to explore further if she was to sort out all these questions in her mind. Once she began her story, she found herself speaking candidly about the situation, grateful for John's nonjudgmental ears. It felt good to be able to release all the stored-up emotion and guilt without condemnation.

"To be honest," she concluded, "I'm not sure I *ever* want to get married. I'm not willing to sacrifice the things I want in life. Pretty selfish, huh?" she said, admitting to John what she hadn't dared to reveal to anyone else.

"There is a huge difference between self*ish* and self*ness*, Melanie."

"But isn't a successful marriage one where you put the needs of your spouse above your own? At least that's what my mother always told me, and she and my father have been married for forty-two years."

"Of course *some* self-sacrifice is essential, but if you don't value your own needs, how can you value your partner's? In almost twenty-four years, I've learned that marriage is an unrelenting tug-of-war. How can it not be when the people involved are constantly changing?"

"So if you're both constantly changing, how do you know that who you marry today is the right partner for the person you will become tomorrow?" Mel asked with a confused sigh.

"You don't. That's why you just have to keep making it up as you go along. There's no one right way to be married, Melanie. What matters most is that the couple fit *comfortably* into a marriage of their *own* making—whatever form it takes and regardless of who does or doesn't approve."

Melanie got up and went to the kitchen, using the pause in the conversation to digest John's ideas. His explanations made great sense to her as she weighed them against the more conventional life lessons she'd been taught.

"May I ask you something personal?" Melanie inquired, returning with a tray of coffee and two slices of her mother's sweet potato pie.

"Sure."

"Why don't you and Sharon have any children?"

Melanie's query caught John off guard. It had been years since anyone had asked that question, and he had to take a moment to think before answering. John quickly sorted through the usual excuses why he and Sharon were childless, but as with most of his deep and most personal emotions, he found himself telling Melanie the truth.

"We did try to get pregnant for several years. Eventually we found out that I was sterile and I took it as a sign that I was not meant to be a parent."

"Why would you think that?" she asked as she poured the coffee.

"Because I don't know how to love like that. You have to know a father's love in order to be able to give it," John said. The bitter sadness that accompanied his statement caused Melanie to close the gap between them and take his hands in hers.

"I've never wanted to make a child feel as worthless as my father made me feel, so I decided that I'd never take the chance," he told her. He clung to Melanie's hand, finding strength and solace in her touch.

"But don't you want to leave more to this world than a legacy of concrete and steel?"

"I never really thought about it like that, though I suppose Sharon must have. She's wanted to adopt for years. In fact, we had a baby all lined up but at the last minute I said no, insisting that she and I were family enough. I thought it was better to hurt her and love her through the pain than raise a child who didn't understand why his father couldn't love him. To this day Sharon thinks that I simply don't like children."

"Why don't you just tell her how you really feel?"

"As much as I know she loves me, there's a lot about me she just doesn't understand," John told her.

"You can't expect her to understand you if you don't share yourself," Melanie said gently. She hoped John could not see the duplicity she felt as she spoke. She was sitting here telling him not to do the very same thing she had done to Will—lock him out of her heart without sharing the real reasons why.

"Maybe. But she's not like you," John admitted before raising her hands to his lips. "I feel safe with you. You don't expect me to be anyone other than who I am."

It was true. Melanie was the first woman he'd ever met with whom he wanted to be totally naked, *without* removing one stitch of clothing. There was an emotional closeness between them that ran deeper than any relationship he'd shared with anyone, from birth to this precious moment in time. Sitting together with their bodies close and hearts open, John was fully conscious of how much he wanted to make love to Melanie while at the same time increasingly aware of how unnecessary it was to cross that boundary. In fact, but for their stolen kiss on the *SunFire*, they had not again shared such an ardent kiss. And yet the passion between them was deeper than ever.

Theirs was a loving connection that revolved around heart-to-heart talks—intimacy built through words, private revelations, and exposed frailties. This affectionate bond was a sensual treat, tightly packaged in a cellophane wrap of romantic sexual tension. Each knowing look, each gentle touch, was like a finger prick trying to penetrate the taut clingy barrier and get to the delicious creamy middle. There was something enormously stimulating about their sexless interludes, a high that stayed with John and kept him going when his love and lust got bogged down in the minutiae of marriage. And in the back of his mind, John was also aware that his sexual restraint was an attempt to stay separate and above his adulterous father's destructive behavior.

Melanie and John melted comfortably into their hug, not feeling the need to talk, only to be together. They both recognized the depth of their emotions, but were unwilling and unable to determine if they were appropriate, for to measure their relationship against what society said was wrong or right was to deny themselves the beauty of the truth. A lifetime seemed to pass between them before John spoke again.

"I guess it's time for me to go. I have to stop by the apartment and pick up my bags before I head out to the airport. I'm not sure how long I'll be in Belize, but I'll be in touch and you can reach me by e-mail as well."

Melanie retrieved and helped John on with his coat, taking the time to close each button. They hugged one last time before he opened the door.

"This is for you. I suggest you read it and then toss it. Just to be on the safe side," Melanie told him as she retrieved an envelope from the entry console. She gave him the letter and then lightly kissed his mouth.

John took several steps down the hall before turning around. "I love you, Jax."

"I love you too." Their eyes locked, acknowledging the pleasure and uncertainty that their mutual declaration brought.

John sat in his first-class seat and pulled Melanie's letter from his breast pocket. Happy to be alone in his row, he reclined his seat slightly, making himself comfortable as he prepared to devour Melanie's words. He'd waited until now for this uninterrupted moment when he could savor her note. He held the envelope to his nose, inhaling the scent of her perfume before slowly unsealing the envelope and pulling out the celery-colored stationery. He took a moment to enjoy the artistry of her script, amused by the flowery flow of her handwriting. There was nothing about Jax that didn't reek of womanliness.

> *Dear John,*
>
> *It feels strange to begin a letter expressing my adoration with the phrase usually used to end a relationship; especially when I find myself constantly thanking God for bringing you into my life.*
>
> *I can't tell you how many times I have relived our Miami trip together. From our angry words to our evening spent under the stars, every moment seemed part of a greater plan to bring us closer. You called our trip on the* SunFire *a cruise to nowhere. I*

*think that's such a misnomer. For me it was a trip to Shangri-la—
a picnic for my soul packed with delicious memories that I'll savor
and cherish forever.*

*Thank you so much for the beautiful purse. It was such a won-
derful and thoughtful surprise. But it was nothing compared to
the gift of your unwavering belief in me. You've given me a confidence that I've never known before. Since you've come into my
life, I feel like I can do anything, be anyone. You make me feel talented, intelligent, and beautiful. With your guidance and support
I am ready to take on this world.*

*You, dear John, have become my mentor, my friend, my soul-
mate. Who knows what will become of us, but I believe these feelings will last throughout this lifetime and into the next. Thank
you so very much.*

*Love Always,*
*Jax*

John reread the letter twice before placing it back into the envelope. How much he wanted to shout to the world that he loved
and was loved in return by Melanie, but the circumstances surrounding their affection for each other left his options few. He
once again lifted the note back to his nose and the sweet smell
sparked his imagination. He reached for the in-flight phone to call
his office and smiled as he swiped his credit card. He was determined to express to Melanie his joyful gratitude and two ideas
came to mind. One he could take care of immediately, the other
would take a little time, but both had the potential of adding
much-sought-after satisfaction to his personal *and* professional
life.

Subj: Thank You
From: VINTAGEJEWEL@AOL.COM
To: JCARLSON@CARLSONTUCK.COM

John, you sweet, sweet man. Thank you so much for your generosity towards Mamie Hawkins and her children. It was so unbelievably remarkable of you to go through the effort of finding the family, providing them temporary housing, and hiring a construction crew to repair their home. I do so love you for doing this. When she called to thank me, I was floored. It was as much a surprise to me as it was to her. She said her prayers had been answered and that I was her guardian angel. She's so wrong. You are the angel and I feel so blessed.

Love you,<br>
Jax

Subj: Re: Thank You
From: JCARLSON@CARLSONTUCK.COM
To: VINTAGEJEWEL@AOL.COM

Dear Jax,

Thanks are not necessary. I did nothing but make a few phone calls. The repairs on the house should be complete in three to four weeks and I've arranged for it to be totally refurbished as well. Carlson and Tuck will pick up the motel tab and construction costs. It was my pleasure to help, mainly because I knew that helping Mrs. Hawkins would not only make you happy, but also allow you to rest easier. And the truth be told, the whole thing made me feel pretty damn good too.

I've only been here in Belize for a couple of days, but things are not looking good. One of the drawbacks of working internationally is having to deal with local politics. I will get through this, but it would be much easier if you could be here with me. I need to hear your laugh. There is something about the sound of your laughter that warms my soul and makes me smile from the inside out. Be well, my sweet.

Love,
John

Subj: Happy New Year
From: VINTAGEJEWEL@AOL.COM
To: JCARLSON@CARLSONTUCK.COM

Hi. How are you? I'm sorry to hear that the situation in Belize is difficult. I'm sure with you now in the mix, things will get resolved quickly and fairly. Please take care of yourself.

I'm sitting here making a list of my New Year's resolutions. First on the list is to begin a gratitude journal, where I'm sure your name will pop up throughout! I've also decided to begin a yoga class and to cut back my dependence on caffeine and new shoes. The last will be the toughest!

I hate the idea of you spending New Year's alone in a strange country. I will be at home with several of my friends, but know that my thoughts are with you.

Love you,
J.

Subj: Re: Happy New Year
From: JCARLSON@CARLSONTUCK.COM
To: VINTAGEJEWEL@AOL.COM

Hello Lovely. Your resolutions sound honorable enough. Though if I can add my two cents, I'd say keep the shoe fetish. There's something about those sexy little feet of yours adorned in high heels that makes my heart race!

I've decided on a few resolutions of my own. Besides the usual diet and exercise promises, I've decided to start painting again. In fact, I've already bought a set of watercolors and have been spending my free time (what little I have) reproducing some of the incredible scenery around here. See what a positive influence you have on me! I haven't felt this free in a very long time. When I return we'll have to get together so you can critique my work.

Don't worry about me being alone for New Year's Eve. Sharon flew down to join me. So you have fun with your pals and know that I am but a whisper away.

Love Always,
John

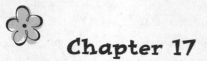

# Chapter 17

"**M**elo, what are you doing in there? It's after seven."

"I'll be out in a sec, Candace." Melanie quickly shut down her computer while John's latest message still happily buzzed around her head. She was surprised by how much she looked forward to getting his daily e-mail.

She pulled on her toffee-colored suede pants and a soft silk turtleneck of the same color. She primped in the mirror, checking herself out from all sides. *Melo, you're looking good, girl.* More importantly she felt good. *I guess that's what love will do for you,* she thought, grateful for the abundant flow that had recently engulfed her.

"Let's get a move on," Candace called out again. "Griffin and Will are going to be here in half an hour."

"Okay. Okay," Mel said as she pulled on her leopardskin ankle boots. *Will's going to be here soon,* sang out an excited little voice in her head.

Love certainly was a tricky thing. She'd spent the past five days totally caught up in her feelings for John Carlson, but standing here anticipating Will's arrival, Melanie could honestly say that she was eagerly looking forward to her evening with him. *Is it really possible to love two people?* she wondered. Mel decided to leave that question to future meditation and stepped into the bathroom to put on her makeup.

While Melo finished getting dressed, Candace sat on the sofa steeped in true Geminian confusion. One astrological twin was not a happy camper. Here she was, dressed like she was going to the movies, in the party capital of the world, on New Year's Eve. Instead of wearing a hot, sexy number to some fabu dance club or VIP's private party, she and Griff were planning to ring in the new year playing party games with Will and Melanie. This was exactly what she got for dating a man with no money and having friends who didn't care.

Yet, the other zodiac double was excited as hell about actually spending the evening as part of a twosome. Visits to official coupledom were rare for Candace and the idea was as appealing as the man who was her partner. Frank's abrupt departure from her life had hurt her terribly and Candace had neither the desire nor the fight left to continue blocking her feelings for Griffin Bell.

Candace was changing and the prospect frightened her. She'd spent a lot of time thinking about her recent argument with Melanie. Thanks to Melo's anything-but-subtle comments, she'd begun to wonder if maybe she was in a no-win, going-nowhere-fast relationship with Frank. But what really got her thinking was Melanie's question about karma. Candace had been quick to voice the reasons why her actions would not come back to bite her in the butt, but how much did she really believe them? Whether it was Regina Warren or any of the other wives whose husbands she'd shared over the years, in the back of her mind Candace always knew that she was treading on another woman's territory. But until now, she'd never let the thought come to the forefront.

Maybe it was time to change—time to get her own man and stop messing around with everyone else's.

Even the part of her argument that heralded the advantage of the mistress bounty was now in question. Take Christmas, for example. In years past with lovers gone by, Candy could always count on impressive gifts complete with highly coveted cache and exceptional value. Through the years she'd amassed a grand collection of fine jewelry, designer clothes and purses, even valuable artwork. Most of these presents had been delivered days before or after the actual holiday. Those few that had been received on the actual date were dropped off during some rushed exchange that ended abruptly when it was time for the giver to dash back to his family.

This year had been remarkably different. With Frank out of the picture, she'd utilized her fall-back position and spent the holiday with Griffin. Candace had given him the complete works of Langston Hughes, and instead of the usual material madness, Griff had created a book of poetry for her. From the paper to the original poems to the book's whipstitched binding, it was a true labor of love. His thoughtfulness touched Candy in such a way that she chose not to share his token of affection with even her best friend. She chose instead to secretly luxuriate in this priceless gift, which gave her extreme pleasure each time she turned a page. Unlike a ring or watch that Candace would usually share with thousands of other consumers having similar taste, Griffin's poems were penned specifically for and about her, and they pirouetted around her imagination day and night.

"With you as my canvas . . . I paint my name . . . on the bottom of your feet . . . with brushstrokes from my tongue . . . so that if you ever become lost . . . you'll find your way back . . . to me." Candace softly recited her favorite poem from the book as she moved around the apartment lighting candles and putting the finishing touches on their party details.

"What are you looking all dreamy-eyed about?" Melanie asked as she entered the living room.

"Just looking forward to getting out of this tired-ass year and seeing what the new one has in store. Next year has got to beat the hell out of this one," Candy said as she began mixing up cocktails.

The heavy knock of knuckles on wood put an end to their dialogue.

Melanie answered the door, giving both men warm hugs and kisses on their cheeks before taking their coats.

"Melo, you're looking fly as ever," Griffin commented, receiving an appreciative grin in return.

"Griffin speaks the truth. You look great, baby." Will smiled warmly, handing her a bundle of salmon-colored tulips tied with matching satin ribbon. Mel looked sharp as ever in her fashion-forward ensemble. She also had a new happy glow about her that enhanced her natural beauty. And best of all, she seemed genuinely pleased to see him.

"Thank you," she said, accepting the flowers. "You both look terrific as well. This is a great color on you, Will," she said affectionately, rubbing the soft cashmere sleeve of his ocean-blue sweater.

Her compliment and touch gave Will an internal meltdown. The remnants of his week spent marinating in sweet anticipation were beginning to simmer, replaced by a giddy gratitude for the opportunity to share Melanie's company on such an important date night. New Year's Eve. Valentine's Day. Birthdays. These were the lovers' holidays that meant something. In Will's mind, the fact that he was here this evening spoke volumes about their future together.

Candace surried up behind Mel and handed each of them a chilled martini. Once the drinks were served, she reached up and gave Griff an erotic kiss laced with lusty promises for the night to come. Will and Melanie walked into the living room, leaving the couple to privately complete their sexy hello.

Predinner cocktail chatter flowed easily among the four. By the time they all sat around the large oval coffee table to dine on a sumptuous meal of surf and turf, double-baked potatoes, and blanched string beans, they were laughing and talking like old married couples who'd been sharing this tradition for years. Candace and Griff were rarely out of physical touch, sitting on the floor thigh to thigh, arms and hands brushing each other as they picked from each other's plates with companionable ease.

Melanie and Will, while physically maintaining their company manners, had little trouble falling back into their old habit of sharp, witty conversation, playful teasing, and steady, comfortable laughter.

By ten o'clock, the early evening composed of food and a rousing game of Charades that even Candace enjoyed had given way to some booty-shakin' New Year's madness. Griffin had brought his collection of seventies music and the four of them were getting their dance on, doin' the bump to Parliament's catchy funk classic, "Flashlight." By eleven-thirty the foursome was pleasantly inebriated and eagerly anticipating the arrival of the next year.

At 11:55, Candace turned on the television to Dick Clark's *Rockin' New Year's Eve* show. Melanie distributed the requisite hats, noisemakers, and champagne flutes, while Candy followed behind, pouring a spot of the bubbly into everyone's glass.

"Ten, nine, eight, seven, six . . ." The four of them counted down aloud and watched the glowing ball descend from the skies of Times Square. "Five, four, three, two . . . Happy New Year!" They blew horns, toasted joyfully, and hugged each other before coupling off for the traditional New Year's kiss as the familiar strains of "Auld Lang Syne" played in the background.

"Happy New Year, Melanie," Will said before bringing his mouth to hers. His tongue sensuously parted her lips and tenderly explored the softness of her mouth. His kiss was slow and delicate, plainly telling her that there was no other place he'd rather be.

Melanie allowed herself to revel in the glow of this bright moment. The words and actions of the previous days had slipped from her mind, replaced by the joyful love she felt for this man. It felt not only good, but right to be back in Will's arms again. She felt protected and safe and his kiss simultaneously closed the curtain on Act One of their relationship and left both of them anticipating the uncertain promise of Act Two.

"Time for a change of pace," Griffin, the evening's self-appointed deejay, announced. He put on the B-side of the Isley Brothers' album *The Heat Is On.* Griff knew, as did every brother who spent any time in the basement under the blue lights, that the combination of "For the Love of You," "Sensuality," and "Make Me Say It Again, Girl" provided nearly twenty minutes of unadulterated sexy, soulful, slow-drag seduction.

Will and Melanie came together, and Mel wrapped her arms around his waist and rested her head lightly on his chest. After several stanzas, Will took a step back, partly out of deference, but mostly because he was embarrassed by the enormous erection he felt coming on. The combination of Ron Isley's low, lusty wails and the warm, taut body of the woman he loved in such close proximity left him helpless to control the blood rushing from his head to his groin.

Melanie too was hearing the frantic pleas of a body desperately seeking sex. She felt a delightful nagging sensation in her pleasure zone, like a juicy ripe plum ready to burst. By the start of "Make Me Say It Again, Girl," the cotton strip of her panties was wet and Melanie found herself uncontrollably pushing her hips into Will's. They rocked together, lightly grinding their pelvises into each other, enjoying the flood of sensations fluttering through their bodies.

Will burrowed his face into her neck, kissing the hot spot behind her ears that caused her body and resolve to melt like chocolate in the midday sun. Slowly his lips made their way to her mouth, but not before kissing every delectable speck of skin in between. Their bodies continued to slowly drag to the lusty beat of the music while their tongues danced a lazy, seductive tango. Will's hand slipped to her behind, lightly caressing her buttocks. Melanie could feel his erection through his jeans, and was both appreciative and regretful for the cloth boundary that obstructed their individual sexual treasures.

The music stopped and several sensational moments passed before Melanie pulled herself away. Griffin and Candace were nowhere to be found, having retired into Candy's bedroom sometime during the second song.

Will and Melanie sat back on the couch, staring at each other, their chests heaving as they tried to settle their breath, shortened by unconsummated desire. Melanie felt like she was back in high school—making out on the living room couch while her parents watched television upstairs. There was something magically delicious about turning up the heat with stolen kisses and secret touches, feeling safe in the knowledge that things could progress only so far.

While one couple sat on the sofa trying to cool their desires, the second romped in the bed, lustily bringing each other to roaring orgasm.

"Happy New Year," Candace said as she watched the exquisite contortions of her lover's face as he came.

"Same to you," Griffin said as he brushed the bangs from her eyes. "I love you."

Candace let out a low chuckle as she happily snuggled closer. "I love you too. So, how many women have you charmed with those words?"

"Only one. Until now, she was the love of my life."

"What happened?" Candace inquired, feeling strangely jealous of a woman she didn't know and would never meet.

Griffin was silent, making it obvious that his memories were painful. "Let's just say it would have never worked out, so I had to cut her loose."

"Why?" Candace asked, though the look in his eye made her wonder if she really wanted to find out.

"She cheated on me and, as the Wayans brothers say, 'Homey don't play that.'"

"So whatcha got cookin'? Something smells good in there," Candace said, walking into the kitchen.

"Fried chicken, waffles, eggs, and grits," Melanie replied.

"Go 'head, Ms. Sylvia," Candace said, referring to the proprietress of Harlem's famous soul food restaurant. "I see Big Willie spent the night. So did you two finally get busy?"

"No. We slept together, but nothing happened."

"But when we left, you were grinding up a storm on the dance floor. I just knew you were going finally break down and give him some."

"We're taking things slow, but girl, let me tell you, I wanted to—*bad*. Damn, that boy can kiss."

"Then what the hell are you waiting for? Give some. Get some. Everybody's happy."

"All in due time," Melanie answered.

"When are you going to figure it out that he is the one?"

"What about you?" Mel asked, ignoring her question. "You're looking mighty chipper this morning. Maybe you've finally figured out that Griff's the one."

"Maybe," Candace admitted with an actual blush to her cheeks. She stood pouring two cups of coffee, while skillfully avoiding Melanie's eyes.

Maybe was as good as a yes when it came to Candy, and her admission shocked Melanie. Lord, it really must be a new year if Candace Bennett was cracking!

"Melo, I told Griffin that I loved him last night," Candace divulged with a girlish giggle.

"Did you mean it?" Melanie certainly hoped she did, because it was obvious, just by looking at Griff, that he was head over heels.

"I think I did. I mean, I woke up this morning with no regret."

"If you want to love him, just love him and don't ask why," Mel advised, speaking to herself as well as her roommate. "Would you and Griffin care to join us for brunch, or will you be having breakfast in bed?"

"No and no. Griff is taking me out. He wants to show me something."

"I'm really happy for you, Candy. This could be the start of something big for you."

"You too," Candy replied with a wink as Will entered the room. Candace walked back to her bedroom, carrying two cups of steaming coffee—one for her and one for her man.

"It smells good in here," Will declared as he approached Melanie and kissed her good morning. "You definitely know the shortcut to my heart."

"That must explain the unusual joy you find in setting the dinner table."

"As my father used to say, an empty plate is merely a prelude to a heapin' spoonful of homemade love."

"Coffee's ready," Mel said in an easy tone that to Will's wishful ears sounded distinctly wifely. "I hope you're hungry. I cooked for four, but it looks like Candy and Griff won't be joining us.

*Hungry? More like ravenous,* he thought. *Ravenous for you, your body, your love. Ravenous for the opportunity to relive this scene every morning of my life.*

Will poured himself a cup of coffee while watching Melanie hover over the waffle iron. He loved the look and feel of this wonderfully simple domestic scene and couldn't help feeling mournful for their thwarted marriage.

*But hey, it's a brand-new year and you're here starting it together. If that isn't a great omen for the future, then John Coltrane ain't the baddest saxophonist to ever live.*

Melanie looked up from her cooking and caught Will's eye. They both smiled, silently expressing their pleasure in being in each other's company.

*Get used to having me around, Ms. Hitts. Now that I'm back, I'm not letting you go again.*

\* \* \*

Hand in hand, Griff and Candace strolled up Broadway through Times Square. The street crews were busy finishing the cleanup from the previous night's world party. Tourists clogged the sidewalks and street, headed for whatever satisfied their fancy, served up only as New York can.

There was an icy chill to the air and Candy snuggled closer to Griff, enjoying the warmth of his body. Together they took in the offbeat combination of holiday decorations and multimedia missives flashing around them. From the ticker tape boards to the latest in trendy underwear and television programs, this was the advertising playground where consumers and marketers happily converged.

"I don't care what anyone says, this is the best street in New York City," Griffin said with all the respect and awe reserved for the few true rarities that have the power to fuel one's dream. "There is more life energy in one square foot of this place than the entire stretch of Madison Avenue." As one who heartily believed in this true wonder of the shopping world, Candace silently disagreed.

Griffin turned onto Forty-eighth Street and stopped in front of the Walter Kerr Theatre. "This is where it all started," he told her. "I saw *The Piano Lesson*, starring Charles Dutton, here. It was my first Broadway play and I was totally blown away. I was twenty-three years old, and before the end of the first act, I knew that acting was what I wanted to do with my life. Nothing I'd experienced up until then left an impression nearly as deep as those two hours sitting in the dark of this theater. I felt like I was home for the first time in my life."

"What do you mean?" Candace asked.

"I grew up moving around a lot and I was always the new kid. I never felt like I had roots, only wings, taking me to the next situation. That's how I thought about each new army post. Not that I was going to a new home, but moving on to the latest situation. I really hated it and eventually, as a way to cope, I became a different person for each new circumstance. Sitting here in the audience ten years ago, I realized that I had been acting all my life.

"Now every time I step onstage it's like I'm alive for the first time. All the rejection and frustration, all the putting off having a steady job, love, money—it's all worth it for those few moments under the lights."

Candace listened and watched closely as Griffin revealed himself. He looked much younger, almost like a little boy, when he talked about his dreams. And she'd never heard anyone, even people much more successful than Griff, speak with such passion, love, and dedication. His fire overwhelmed her and she impulsively threw her arms around him.

"I know it's going to happen. Lately I have the sweet taste of success in my mouth," he said, abruptly extricating himself from her arms and pounding his hands against the box office window. "One day soon, I am going to own Broadway!"

"But what about movies? Don't you make more money doing films?" Candace asked instinctively. She could understand his love of acting, but why not in a medium that certainly paid better?

"Yes, eventually I guess you do, but it's not about the money. It's about making real art, not commercial hits. That's why Charles Dutton has been my inspiration and hero ever since I first saw him work. When you look at his body of work, you realize he knows that the stage is the only real place to make art as an actor."

"But he does a lot of film and television too," Candace pointed out.

"True, and I'll do my share of film and TV as well, but the greats always come back to the theater. And when they return, I'm going to be here ready to work with them. God, I want this *so* bad," Griff said, choking on the ambitious hunger building in the back of his throat. "And, baby, I want you to be a part of it too. Look, Candace, I've dropped women or been dropped in the past because my lifestyle was too tough for anything serious to develop, but I can't do it this time. I love you, and I want you to be the one with me at the beginning of the big time. I know you're high-maintenance, but that's okay, you deserve the best and I want to give it to you. But the reality is that it will be rough for a while. I don't have a lot of money. Hell, I don't have *any* money. But I believe in me, baby. And I want you to believe in me too."

"Aren't you Griffin Bell? The actor from *Race for the Race?*" Candace and Griff's conversation was interrupted by one of two attractive black women who looked to be in their twenties. They approached Griff, one bold and outspoken, the other quiet, obviously suffering from the adoration and hero worship typically reserved for sports legends and musicians.

"We saw you onstage and in the *Village Voice*. You are one awesome brother," the bold, pretty one purred.

"And fine too," her shy friend said under her breath but loud enough for Candy's territorial ears.

"Can I get your autograph?" the first girl asked.

"Sure." Griffin watched with complete ego gratification as the girl slipped her coat off her shoulders, lifted up her sweater, and offered him a fresh white T-shirt to sign. Candace eyed the pushy woman with a "bitch, is you crazy?" glare.

"Maybe I should sign on the back," he said, pulling a pen from his pocket and moving behind her.

"I'm an acting student at NYU. I'd love to sit down with you and pick your brain. Maybe you could jot down your phone number as well?" the girl asked with a suggestive twirl of her hair.

*What, bitch? Am I invisible? I guess you don't see me standing here about to pop your silly ass upside the head?* "I'm afraid not," Candy interrupted, possessively taking hold of Griff's arm.

She led her man off with a triumphant smirk and did some quick reasoning. He owned nothing to speak of, and that was bad. But he also had great potential to make money, and lots of it. And though she'd never been a huge fan of potential, this time it might be different. This time the man she loved was willing to love her full-time, not only when it was convenient for his schedule. And how could she throw Griff away into a crowd of hungry heifers who would happily eat him up like a vat of Italian gelato? He was her man, damn it. Piss-poor as he might be, Griffin Bell still belonged to her.

"Candace, baby, are you jealous?" he asked, smiling.

"Of those tired ho cakes? Be for real. But about what you were saying before missy did her sidewalk striptease, I do believe in you and I love you too. And I think that you should move in with me."

Griffin stopped in the middle of Broadway and turned to face his woman. "Are you serious? You know my situation. I mean, I'll help out whenever I can, but . . ."

"It doesn't matter. I can handle it. You just concentrate on becoming a star," she said before giving him a sloppy kiss, well aware of the envious eyes of his two fans following behind.

# Chapter 18

Amanda watched as Ilah Rogers's blue-veined, milky-white hands trembled. Slowly and deliberately, the eighty-eight-year-old filled the small plastic scoop with potting soil and deposited it into the ceramic pot. Before arriving, Amanda was sure that she was going to hate working with these senior citizens, but now, after completing six of her fifteen hours, she found that she was pleasantly surprised. Apart from the old-lady smells of violet toilet water and mothballs that made her feel slightly nauseous, she found she actually liked being here.

"Here are some lovely crocus bulbs and ivy," Sharon said as she stopped by the table with a carton full of plants.

"Ooh, do you have yellow and purple ones? Those are Mrs. Cramer's favorite colors," Amanda's friend Quincy announced. She took the time to select the marked bulbs and choose the freshest ivy from Sharon's box, wanting the best for her senior chum.

"I guess we'll take the tulips, freesia, and ivy," Amanda decided. "Is that cool with you, Miss Ilah?" Ilah agreed and Amanda placed their choice next to the elderly woman. Amanda removed the ivy plants from their small pots and arranged them and the bulbs in the larger container. Together she and Ilah pressed them down into the soil, Mandy adding a few more scoops of dirt along the way.

Sharon watched as Amanda and her friend respectfully interacted with their adult charges. She realized that in many ways, from her dress to her choice of music to her use of urban slang, Mandy had adopted the cultural cues of her best friend. Quincy appeared to be a perfectly nice young lady, but Sharon could not help wondering why Amanda didn't have any girlfriends from her own race.

"Ms. Ilah, you're a mess." Amanda laughed as she reached over and tenderly brushed potting soil from the old woman's left cheek.

Sharon watched Amanda clean Ilah's face, and a sad and frightening reality began to haunt her. There would be no children or grandchildren to visit and care for her when her useful days were gone. Instead she'd be stuck in a place like this, receiving doses of pity and friendship from people sentenced to do so by either the law or their bored and guilty conscience. The thought depressed her thoroughly and she excused herself to the ladies' room, not wanting to upset the teenagers or their elderly companions.


"Miss Ilah was pretty cool. I had a good time," Amanda said as they pulled off the highway. "Oh, this is my jam. Mind if I turn this up?"

"Go ahead," Sharon said, once again struck by Amanda's musical preference. Sharon listened as Mandy sang the words proclaiming the total unacceptability of ignoring opportunity's knock. "May I ask you a question?" she inquired as Eminem's song segued into a medley of annoying commercials.

"Yeah?"

"I see that you and Quincy are really close."

"Yeah, she's my girl."

"She seems very nice, but I was wondering: Do you have any friends who are . . . you know, who are . . ."

"What? White?"

"Well, yes."

"Yeah, of course I do. I hang with all types of people. Why?"

"I was just curious why you seem to be drawn more to Quincy's culture than your own."

"You're beginning to sound like Catherine and Nelson. Why do you all have such a problem?" Amanda said defensively. "Don't you have any black friends?"

Amanda's pointed question took Sharon by surprise. She was certainly "friendly" with several people who were African-American, but she'd be exaggerating to actually call them friends. It's not like she avoided such relationships. Her life simply did not cross paths with many people of color—at least not in any substantial way. No black families lived in their immediate neighborhood or belonged to their country club. And other than the Pulleys, a couple she and John often chatted with during First Sundays at their church, and Claudia Johnson, the director of the local literacy program, Sharon had no regular conversations with any black women. And even their talks revolved around fundraising and current world affairs. Never anything personal or confidential. Until now she'd never even considered the lack of color in her friendships. Certainly she wasn't racist, but why did Amanda's query make her feel so guilty?

"Don't get upset, honey. I'm only asking because I'm trying to understand you better. I'm not judging you or your friend," Sharon said, ignoring the question.

"I like Quincy because she's cool and we like the same things. She just happens to be black, that's all. I like black people because they aren't afraid to be themselves. They aren't worried about what other folks think. If they want to put their baseball cap on backwards, they do. If they want to wear clothes that are big and baggie or skin-tight, even, they do. And if they think that kids going around shooting other kids is wack, they'll stand up and say so, even if it means getting arrested. The kids Catherine knows and wants me to be friends with would never do any of those things. They're afraid of being themselves because they're afraid of being different. I'm not down with that. My black friends are just more expressive, and I like that. But if Quince was white, that would be cool too. It just so happens that she's not."

"Understood," Sharon replied, secretly satisfied that Amanda's circle of friends was more inclusive than she originally suspected. It may not be true in her life, but she did feel it was important that Mandy have a balanced cultural experience.

*Is this what mothering a teenager is like?* she wondered as she turned into the train station to drop off Amanda. It was harder than it looked, but better than she could ever imagine.

"I think that couple that came by last week is going to make a serious offer," Sharon said in a wobbly voice later that evening. She'd saved this important but most distressing bit of information for last as she filled John in on the events that had taken place while he was away.

"We've been here a long time, it's tough for me to say good-bye too," he said, covering her hand with his. "But this isn't just the end of an era, it's the beginning of a great new one for us. I promise you, you'll come to love your life in the city just as much as you've loved this one."

"I keep telling myself that, but it seems harder leaving a home that I love just because we *can*. Maybe if we *had* to it would feel different."

"I know, sweetheart, and I have an idea to take your mind off of things. Why don't we throw a party at the apartment?" John suggested.

"A housewarming?"

"No. February fourteenth is right around the corner, or have you forgotten?" he asked, teasing her.

"Have I ever forgotten our anniversary? But why a party? Why don't we go away somewhere?"

"Honey, I know you don't like large shindigs, but I think this would be fun."

Huge celebrations were not Sharon's style. She'd much prefer a small intimate dinner with close friends than a big bash with a room full of people she didn't know. "Will you have the time?" she asked, grasping for any excuse.

Sharon's question was on point. He really was too busy for some extravagant soiree, but the bigger picture took precedent over his tight schedule. An anniversary party would give Sharon something to concentrate on while he was traveling back and forth to Belize these next few weeks. John was also hoping that celebrating their marriage in the apartment might also help her to feel more connected to the place. Help her loosen the attachment she had to this house and the unfulfilled desires that haunted her.

It was his greatest hope that in this new environment, Sharon would find the peace of soul and the same renewed enthusiasm for life that he had recently discovered. And for reasons still unclear, John greatly desired a public celebration to mark his twenty-fourth wedding anniversary.

*Maybe to make up for your private feelings for Jax?* John refused to confirm or deny his intuitive thought, and instead took his wife into his arms. "We can celebrate the beginning of our life together in our new home," he said softly in her ear. "And why don't you invite Amanda to join us?"

Sharon pulled back enough to examine the face that had uttered those shocking words. When it came to Amanda, John often behaved like a jealous sibling, so for him to make such an offer was the ultimate compromise. Knowing that the teenager would not be comfortable in such a setting, the invitation would never be extended, but Sharon was touched by her husband's thoughtfulness.

"It might be fun," she conceded.

"It will be. I promise."

"I love you, John."

"And I do love you, Sharon." John spoke the solemn truth as thoughts of Melanie Hitts breezed through his head.

# Chapter 19

"**M**y feet are absolutely screaming," Melanie announced as she threw her purse on the couch and followed with her body. "And for nothing. I don't believe they rented that apartment before I got there, especially after I called yesterday to tell them I'd be over with the deposit. Now it's back to square one."

"Let me take a look at those dogs," Will said as he slipped off her shoes and began massaging her tired feet.

"Hmm, this feels so good," Mel moaned as she laid back into the sofa and closed her eyes.

Will fought the urge to lean in and kiss her. Since New Year's, he'd successfully walked that fine line between being a love interest and becoming a nuisance, but keeping the scope of his intentions in check was definitely becoming a challenge. When Melanie had mentioned on the phone that she was going to spend the weekend apartment-hunting, he'd gladly volunteered to accompany her and was thrilled when she took him up on his offer. "I still can't believe that Dark Gable is living with Candace," he said, breaking the silence.

"Me either. And even though she said there was no hurry for me to leave, the way they are constantly on each other, three is definitely a crowd." Mel finished her comment slightly embarrassed by the suggestive context, as she and Will were still struggling to maintain their sexual distance. Will was living up to his promise to take it slow, while Mel was trying to resist making love with either John or Will until she was totally sure where her relationship with each of them was headed.

"My boy is totally whipped."

"Hold that thought," Mel said, reaching over to pick up the ringing phone.

"Hello there, Jax," John's voice boomed through the receiver.

"Hi. Where are you?" Mel asked as she immediately pulled her feet from Will's grasp and sat up. Her abrupt change in position put Will's ears, eyes, and male instinct on full alert.

"Back in Belize. It's good to hear your voice. How are you?"

Afraid Will might hear John's deep voice through the phone, Mel got up from the couch and walked over to the window. "Good. How are things down there? Have you gotten everything straightened out?" she asked, keeping the conversation chatty and friendly.

*Who's on the phone that she needs to walk all the way across the room to talk to?* Will wondered.

"The situation is better, but not solved. But I really don't want to waste our time talking about my problems here. Austin tells me that the press announcement at the Art Miami Festival went well. I'm not at all surprised."

"Folks seemed to be excited about the concept, though we were preaching to the choir. I mean, it was a room full of art lovers."

"Well, I'm sorry I couldn't be there with you. So how have you been doing aside from work?"

"Okay, I guess. I just got back from apartment-hunting. I have to be out of my place by month's end, but I'm having a little trouble finding something I like and can afford."

"Where are you looking?" John asked.

"At this point, anywhere."

"How does Tribeca sound to you?"

"Great, but way out of my price range."

"What if I could work something out? A friend of mine just finished renovating some terrific condos on Duane Street."

"Not 129 Duane?"

"You know it?"

"Not specifically, but a friend of mine has a client moving into that building. It's gorgeous."

"I know that a couple of the smaller units are still available and I could speak with him, if you're interested."

*Am I interested?* Suddenly visions of Will helping her move into a luxury apartment secured for her by John made Mel reluctantly acknowledge the traitorous thought that she was becoming more like Candace than she was comfortable with. A mate and a date. Weren't those Candace's ingredients for cooking up the perfect love life? One man to supply the goodies, another to enjoy them with? *But it's a very different set of circumstances*, she argued with herself. *He's only offering to help you find a place, not pay for it. And this is Tribeca. How can you pass up such a golden opportunity?*

"I'd appreciate it very much," she told him.

"Consider it done."

"It's really very nice of you."

"I would build you a castle if I could, but since I can't, making a phone call is the very least I can do."

"When are you coming back?" Mel asked.

"Why? Do you miss me?"

"Maybe," she said, while unconsciously running her hand through her hair.

*Definitely a man,* Will decided. *And a brother she's interested in. Her conversation may sound casual and friendly, but her body language is screaming out something totally different.*

"Well, just in case you do, I'm coming in sometime late next week. There's a serious bid on the house, so I need to be there to do the paperwork," John said.

"Word around the office is that the new apartment has turned out wonderfully."

"Jude did a great job. In fact, Sharon's having a Valentine's party there, so that's another reason I need to get home," he told her, reluctant to reveal that this was also his anniversary celebration. "But mainly I want to get back because I have something I want to show you. I thought we might be able to use it in the Casa de Arte, but I want to get the approval of my favorite art critic."

"Really?" Melanie asked with a tiny chuckle. She cut her eyes over at Will. He was casually flipping through one of her design magazines, trying hard to appear not to be eavesdropping. "Why don't you e-mail me and tell me all about it?" she said softly.

*Oh, no, she didn't just give him that sexy little half laugh of hers. And did she just lower her voice? This isn't friend talk. This is lover talk. Who is this motherfucker, and what does he want with my woman?*

"I'll see you soon, then."

"Looking forward to it." Melanie disconnected the call and took a few seconds before turning her attention back to Will. Hearing John's voice had brought to the surface all the warm feelings that being in Will's cherished presence had muffled. Her heart love for one man comingled with her soul love for the other, creating a potent emotional cocktail. Mel enjoyed the heady sentimental buzz, joyfully intoxicated by her true feelings for both.

"That was a friend of mine who is out of town on business. He was calling to check in," she told him, feeling compelled to explain.

*A friend. I don't think so.* Mel's casual use of the term, juxtaposed with her earlier body language, disturbed Will, hitting him in the face like a prizefighter's punch.

"Mel, remember at Christmas we promised to take things slow, but to be honest and open with each other?"

"Yes."

"Well, are you sleeping with someone?" Will blurted out the question much more abruptly than he'd intended.

Melanie debated whether to tell Will about John and vice versa. On one hand, she might feel less deceitful by doing so. On the other hand, why should she feel like she was cheating on both of them when neither was her lover? And how could she explain her relationship with John? Would Will really understand that they were romantic friends—in love but not lovers? Emotionally intimate but physically celibate? What she and John knew, but others could not comprehend, forced their relationship into the very back of their lives' secret drawer. And now that she was accustomed to her unique role in his life and his in hers, Melanie wanted to keep their relationship in this special place, dwelling somewhere between the shadows and the soul.

"No, I'm not sleeping with anyone," she answered honestly.

Will smiled. He believed her, but he also believed that he'd better hightail it to New York on a permanent basis, and soon, or the next time he asked that question, the reply would be much different.

\*   \*   \*

In the far-off distance, Melanie heard a buzzing sound. She slowly opened her eyes and looked at the clock, it read 6:06 P.M., which meant she'd been asleep for approximately an hour and a half. Feeling disoriented, she took a minute to retrace her recent steps. Soon after arriving home from BenAlex, she'd considered sending a Valentine's Day wish to John, but decided against it, feeling it was best that his wife be the only love on his mind on this special day. She'd tried to call Will to add a personal wish to the card she'd sent, but his answering machine had picked up. He'd wanted to come up and have dinner together, but was unable to get away because of a big meeting the next day. Mel had been disappointed, but relieved as well. She wasn't sure she could trust herself to contain her physical impulses, and while the flesh was more than willing, the mind was not. So, Valentineless, she'd sat down to meditate, but had obviously dozed off.

Another buzz from the intercom nudged her into complete coherence. Mel jumped up from the couch to answer the doorman's call, and was informed that a delivery person was on his way up. Moments later she heard a soft knock and, peering through the peephole, was surprised to find Will Freedman standing at her door, holding several grocery bags and a single red rose between his teeth.

"What are you doing here?" she asked after flinging open the door. "I thought you had a big meeting in the morning."

"I do," Will replied once Mel removed the flower from his mouth. "But after thinking it over, I decided it was stupid to let a meeting tomorrow keep me from spending time with you tonight."

"You came all the way to New York for just a couple of hours?"

"I think you're definitely worth it, don't you? Now step aside, I have very little time to create some major magic here."

"Well, then come on in," Mel said, touched by his thoughtfulness. She followed him into the kitchen but was promptly dismissed. While Will unpacked his groceries, she disappeared into her bedroom to freshen up and make herself more presentable. When she returned, he was waiting with a chilled glass of champagne. Silence descended as he gently secured a brightly colored scarf over her eyes, checking to make sure there was no way she could peek.

"I've never eaten dinner blindfolded before," she said before accepting a sip of champagne.

"That's because you've never experienced a Will Freedman sweetheart-of-a-meal. We specialize in sensual dining. So sit back, relax, and enjoy. This will be a dinner that you will never forget," Will said, delivering a quick kiss to her lips before traipsing off to the kitchen.

Melanie could hear him happily humming along to the sexy Latin tunes of Marc Anthony as he puttered around the kitchen. She smiled as well, a joyful confirmation that she was in the right place, with the right person.

"First course, coming up," Will announced as he reentered the room fifteen minutes later carrying a tray of various delicious edibles.

Will picked up a steamed asparagus, dipped the tip in maple mustard sauce, and brought it slowly near her mouth. Mel's nose twitched slightly as the sweet syrupy scent mixed with the sharp bite of Dijon wafted up her nostrils. He slowly parted her teeth with the vegetable and Melanie bit down on the tender crisp stem, releasing a spray of juice in her mouth. She chewed slowly, savoring the mélange of tastes.

The cold metallic taste of a spoon replaced the warmth before the sweet shock of lemon sorbet exploded on her tongue, cleansing the vegetable from her palate and preparing her mouth for the next delectable onslaught.

Melanie smelled the briny odor of the shellfish as it approached her mouth. Will once again parted her lower lip, this time with a hard cold crustacean. With a little prompting, the raw oyster drenched in a spicy red wine cocktail sauce slid onto her tongue. Mel took several moments to enjoy its silky feel and savory taste as the peppery scent of Tabasco tingled her nose.

Dinner continued in silence, a healthy sexual tension crowding the necessity for conversation out of the room. Touch, smell, taste, and sounds other than talk were the preferred side dishes served with this sensual main course.

Will followed the oyster with several tender chunks of lobster dunked in warm drawn butter. Another cleansing dollop of sorbet ensued, but this time he purposely spread the cool frozen treat on Melanie's lips and watched as she slowly licked them clean.

"Time for dessert," he whispered huskily into her ear before disappearing once again into the kitchen.

Melanie sipped her champagne as she listened to the refrigerator door open and close, utensils clink and fall, followed by the distinctive tone of the microwave being pressed into service.

"Sweets for my Valentine," Will announced, reentering the room and leading her from the dining room to the sofa. "I trust that you will allow me to take certain liberties with the silverware."

"I won't tell Miss Manners if you don't," Melanie said, laughing over his unnecessary concern.

"Good," he said as he dipped into the dish and coated his finger with melted milk chocolate. The scent of the sweet rich confection caused Melanie to part her lips in anticipation. She immediately found pleasure in the guilty taste of warm chocolate. Feeling shameless, Mel gently sucked away the creamy cocoa, secretly enjoying the salty taste of Will's finger in her mouth and the arousing visions it produced in her head.

The seductive pull on his index finger made Will squirm in his seat. Maybe this wasn't such a good idea after all. This meal, designed to tempt and tantalize his love, was turning into pure hell. *But the torture is worth it,* Will reminded himself, *if it helps to weaken Melanie's resolve and keep me first and foremost in her mind.*

"Mmmm," Melanie moaned with both culinary and carnal pleasure. "Delicious." She sighed deeply and smiled with delight. Without her eyesight, all her other senses teamed together to produce the most erotic, all-encompassing dining experience she'd ever had. Never would she look at food or dinner the same again.

"Yes, you are," Will said quietly under his breath. He reached up and untied Mel's blindfold, before gently touching his mouth to hers. "You had a bit of chocolate on you lip," he announced slyly after their enticing kiss.

"I did, did I? I think there's still a speck left right above my chin."

"Ah, yes," Will murmured before his tongue gently parted her lips and began caressing the warm chocolate inside of her mouth. Both could feel the heat rising between them as they leaned deep into the couch. Will ran his hands over Melanie's back, arms, and breasts and she could feel Will's hardness press against her. Their kisses became more and more ardent and as their desire grew, Will silently cursed his bad luck. He was sure that after all these months of yearning, tonight he would finally touch the soul of the woman he so desperately adored. But the love he wanted to show

Melanie would take time—something he didn't have. According to the clock on the mantel, he would have to leave in twenty minutes if he was going to catch the last flight back to Washington. And as much as he wanted to stay the night, his breakfast meeting tomorrow was too important to miss. If all went as planned, he may well be joining Melanie in New York on a full-time basis.

"As much as I hate to break this up, baby, I have to go. The last shuttle leaves at nine-thirty."

"I never knew you to be so cruel, Mr. Freedman. You come up here and seduce me with a romantic, sexy dinner, kiss me until my toes curl, and then you just up and leave. Can't you stay longer? Please?" she asked, biting her bottom lip in a sexy, impossible-to-deny manner. This evening had succeeded in pulling down Melanie's defenses; she wanted and needed to answer her body's demands for loving sex.

"Baby, you know how much I'd like to stay, but I can't. I'm sorry. I have to get back."

"So, that's it?" she whined with playful indignation.

"Not exactly," Will said, reaching under the sofa and handing her the gift he'd hidden away earlier in the evening. "Happy Valentine's Day."

"How sweet," she said, accepting a package that smelled suspiciously like chocolate.

"Open it," Will prompted.

Melanie unwrapped the gift to reveal a small box of Godiva chocolates. She lifted the lid and found not only four pieces of gourmet candy but also her returned engagement ring. Mel paused as a whirlwind of emotion blew through her.

"Melanie Hitts, will you do me the honor of being my very

special friend?" he asked, slipping the diamond onto her right hand. "When I first gave this to you, it was to honor our love. Now I want to honor our friendship. I love you and that won't change, even if this ring never moves back onto the other hand."

Melanie smiled up at Will, totally engulfed in emotion. She'd known he was special the first time they met, but ever since New Year's Eve she'd felt touched by his unique brand of sensitive and potent love in a way she'd not experienced while they were engaged. It suddenly dawned on Melanie that Will wasn't any different, she was. He was still the same tender, romantic man he'd always been. It was she who had changed. Suddenly love didn't seem so suffocating or threatening.

"Yes, I accept your proposal of friendship and I certainly offer you the same with the intention of more to come. Will, tonight was very special. And I'll never forget it," she told him, wanting more than ever to take him to bed.

"Good. Then my work is done here. Well, almost. The rest will have to wait until another time, but I promise, you won't forget that either." He laughed, witnessing the lusty desire in her eyes. "Now come walk me to the door before I decide to stay and throw away my professional future." Despite the throbs of protests emanating from his pants, Will forced himself up and off the couch. He pulled Mel up into a hug, lifting her off her feet. "Happy Valentine's Day. I love you so much, baby."

"I love you too," Melanie said, feeling sincere adoration for this thoughtful man.

They shared a passionate farewell kiss, promising to talk the next day. Melanie closed the door behind him and stood in the entry basking in the aftermath of his thoughtful surprise and the lovely residual feelings he'd left with her.

Will chuckled with satisfaction as he walked down the hall toward the elevator. Thank goodness she'd accepted the ring. It was a huge step in his final push to win Mel back. Hopefully, she'd soon move the diamond back to her wedding finger, where it rightfully belonged. Until then it would certainly put any "friend" on notice that Big Willie was back and in a big, big way.

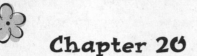

# Chapter 20

John smiled as he raised his arm to admire this unexpected gift. His smiled turned into a chuckle as he thought of the personal secret attached to her present. Melanie had given him sterling silver cuff links, shaped like jacks, as a thank-you for helping her to secure the apartment in Tribeca. And while he appreciated her thoughtfulness, in fact his help had been very limited. True, his phone call to Stan had helped open the door, but it was Melanie's foresight and gutsiness that put the key in her hand. Mel had adeptly bartered a winning arrangement in which she would decorate Stan's model apartments around the city for a greatly reduced monthly rent. John found her deal-making to be nothing less than brilliant. Not only could she now afford to live in this trendy upscale neighborhood, but her work would be showcased throughout Manhattan—a lucrative calling card for future business.

Quickly John mined his memory for the content of her accompanying note, which was now tucked safely away with the rest of her letters and e-mails in an old briefcase stowed in the back of his closet in Connecticut. Even though Melanie had suggested destroying all correspondence between them, her words were a guilty pleasure he could not seem to give up.

*Dearest John,*

*This is just a small token to say thank you for helping me find an apartment, but mostly for allowing me the joy and privilege of basking in the warmth of your sunshine.*

*Love Always,*
*Jax*

As usual her words warmed him and left John feeling awash in emotion. For a moment, he allowed himself to wonder with whom Melanie might be spending this lover's holiday. He tried not to concern himself with such thoughts, knowing that possessiveness in this matter was not only unfair but futile. Despite their feelings for each other, the fact was that he had a life that did not include her, and she was entitled and expected to pursue the same. Still, the thought of Melanie crossing the same romantic boundaries that he voluntarily avoided fueled his jealousy.

"Here you are," Sharon said as she entered the room. Her voice quickly caused John to put all musings of Melanie in the back of his mind. Tonight he vowed to concentrate solely on Sharon and their anniversary celebration.

"You look beautiful," he told her, smiling in admiration.

"You look pretty dapper yourself," she said, reaching up to straighten his tie. "Dapper but tired. Are you okay?"

"Just a little headache."

"Again? Your head's been hurting for the past few days."

"Nothing to worry about. I took a couple of aspirin. I'll be fine."

"You're really pushing yourself, John. Are you sure you have to return immediately to Belize?"

"Afraid so. Hopefully things there should be ironed out soon. But let's not talk about work or some nuisance of a headache. Tonight I simply want to concentrate on us," John told her, affectionately pushing a stray hair behind her ear.

"Are those new?" Sharon asked, admiring his cuff links. "Jacks? Don't tell me you're reverting back to grade school in your old age," she teased.

"I'm just trying to keep up with my young wife," John said as a slight twinge of discomfort pulled at his smile.

"Just don't let me find you in the bedroom shooting marbles," she said, laughing.

"What a beautiful sound. I always want to hear you laugh. It means you're happy."

The doorbell rang, interrupting their playful talk, and soon the cheerful cries of an unyielding rush of partygoers rang out. "I love you," he whispered in Sharon's ear as they walked out into their newly renovated living room to join their guests. Sharon squeezed his hand before leaving his side to relieve the rented butler and welcome their guests. John stood back, taking a moment to watch and marvel at his mate. She did look lovely in her red St. John knit dinner suit and understated jewelry. But appearances aside, he was struck by the fact that although Sharon absolutely abhorred such large gatherings, not an inkling of those feelings could be found in the friendliness of her demeanor, the graciousness of her smile, or the genuineness of her hospitality.

It didn't take long for the room to fill up, and enveloped within the welcoming décor of their new home, the jazzy piano music fought for airspace with the lively chatter of people enjoying themselves. The hours passed quickly, another telling sign of a successful party.

"Great party, John," Austin Riley remarked. "And by the way, we secured that parcel you wanted."

"How much?"

"Sixty-eight thousand, less than you'd budgeted."

"Great job, Austin. Gale has the blueprints. I want to get moving on this pronto. You're in charge until I get this Vogue mess straightened out. Keep me posted. Now find your girlfriend and enjoy the party." Austin's news excited him. In fact this entire idea of starting a new subsidiary company specializing in small boutique hotels had lit a blaze under him that was burning like a Texas bonfire. If things kept proceeding on pace, he could soon approach Melanie about coming on board to run the design department.

John left his employee and searched the room for Sharon. He located her in the dining room laughing with Joe Nunn and his wife Myrtle, Gwen Robinson, and Jude from the BenAlex Design Group.

"John, I was just telling your decorator what a great job he did on this apartment. It's magnificent. Very New York, but with enough of Sharon's homey country chic," Myrtle remarked.

"Well, you can take the girl out of Connecticut, but you can't take the Connecticut out of the girl," John quipped. "But you're right. Sharon and Jude did a wonderful job. I think we're going to be very happy living here." John pulled his wife to his side and kissed her temple.

"So when do you think you'll be moving in?" Myrtle asked.

"We accepted a bid on the house a couple of days ago, so pending any legal disasters, I'd say six weeks, eight tops," John said. "Unfortunately, that means my dear wife will be doing most of the packing."

"John," a gruff male voice called out before a large bald man joined the group.

"Ray, glad you could make it."

"I know this is a happy occasion and I don't want to tarnish it with business talk, but I just wanted to let you know that the reconstruction on that Mississippi house job is done. It turned out great. Mrs. Hawkins and her kids were real happy. The final invoices should be in your office sometime this month."

"Thanks, Ray. I appreciate your help." John noticed the inquiring look in his wife's eyes and felt the need to explain. "A woman's house caught on fire in Mississippi right before Christmas. I . . . we . . . the company helped rebuild it as a charity thing," he told the group.

Sharon stared at John in disbelief. Never had she heard him speak of any desire to perform a charitable act, let alone undertake such an action. Gwen shot her a surprised look, which Sharon acknowledged with a slight raise of her eyebrow.

"How did you get involved with a house all the way down in Mississippi?" Joe asked, to Sharon's silent gratitude. She too was curious, but was reluctant to reveal that this was her first time hearing of this uncommon deed.

"A colleague who was acquainted with the family asked if Carlson and Tuck could help and we did. Really it was no big deal.

"And now it's time I proposed a toast to my lovely wife," he announced, shifting the subject. On cue the waiters began passing out glasses of champagne, while in unison, Myrtle and Gwen struck the sides of their flutes with the backs of their heavy wedding rings, calling the room to order.

"If I can have your attention, everyone," he began. "We're here tonight to celebrate my incredible good fortune to have met and married this wonderful woman. She's been a loyal, loving, and generous partner these past twenty-four years. And I am well aware and forever grateful that whoever I am now, and whoever I become in the years ahead, it is all because of her. I love you, Sharon. Happy anniversary." Emotion clogged his airway, causing John to pause and clear his throat. A tear fell from his right eye and he quickly brushed it away.

Sharon immediately drew her husband into her arms, causing a sigh of appreciation from their guests. It was clear that John's feelings were strong and genuine, but only his wife understood the enormous change that this display represented. Though he'd expressed his love in many different ways throughout the years, never had John been brought to tears by his feelings, and never in such a public setting. Acts of charity. Public tears. He had the same face as her husband, but this was a different man. What had gotten into John and brought to the surface this soft tender side she'd never seen?

John left Sharon's embrace and once again cleared his throat. "Please join me in toasting my wife!" A chorus of cheers and best wishes circled the room as champagne glasses filled the air. John raised his glass and lightly tapped it against his wife's, noticing the silver gleam of his cuff links as they bounced off the light.

The flash of his jewelry brought Melanie to the forefront of his mind, and for the first time since the party began, John allowed himself to think of Jax. Melanie Hitts was everything that a man could desire in a woman. Yet, standing here, holding Sharon, he knew that she was everything he wanted in a spouse. It suddenly occurred to him that against all conventional wisdom, his love for Mel had in no way diminished his love or commitment to Sharon, but instead had only increased his capacity to love his wife. The concept boggled his mind, but put his heart at peace. Together these two women made him exquisitely happy and, if left up to him, he would love and need both of them for the rest of their lives.


Melanie and John sat side by side in the beige club chairs in the Continental Airlines President's Club. They were alone on this side of the room, except for an older woman wearing a red sweater, sitting solo in a nearby chair. The place was relatively empty, as it was 5:05 A.M. and John had less than a half an hour before he'd have to board his flight for Belize.

Their personal and work schedules had been so crazy the past few days that the two had not been able to synchronize their agendas to get together before this morning. When Mel suggested she meet him at the airport for a drink, she hadn't guessed that her chosen beverage would be strong black coffee. But John had been anxious to see her, so even if it meant getting up and out to JFK before daybreak, sharing a few sunrise moments with him at the airport was certainly better than not seeing him at all.

"The construction on the Casa de Arte is moving right along," John informed her, looking deep into her eyes, wanting to talk about so many things other than work.

"How much longer before they'll need me on site?"

"I'd say another three to four months at least. I'm looking forward to spending more time with you in South Beach," he told her, noticing the diamond ring as he reached for her hand. From the corner of his eye, John could see the woman sitting near them glaring. He wasn't sure if she was reacting to their age difference or to the contrast in their skin color, but he didn't care. In fact, her negative reaction made him feel all the more adventurous.

"Will?" John asked, lifting her right hand.

"Yes," Mel responded, not knowing if she was more uncomfortable because of the stranger's glower or the turn in their conversation. "I wanted to talk to you about it, but it just didn't seem . . . right."

"I know," John replied.

"It is a little strange, isn't it? It's like we both know there are other people in our lives, but it almost seems disrespectful to bring them up in conversation," Mel commented. The truth was that she and John could discuss for hours the issues and concerns surrounding their personal feelings and problems, but rarely did they talk in depth about their significant others.

"I wouldn't say disrespectful, just uncomfortable. To me, talking about them intrudes on our relationship, and I see us as very separate from them." John spoke but his mind was reeling with questions he would never ask. He knew that Mel was seeing Will again, and judging from the large diamond on her right hand, they had come to some sort of agreement about their relationship, though obviously not an official engagement. Would she choose to push aside this relationship in order to concentrate wholly on theirs? John had no right to expect her to do any less, but the idea worried him nonetheless.

"I just know that we have a very special . . . friendship that has had an amazing impact on my life," he said.

"Definitely," Melanie agreed. "It's like despite whoever else we love, I know our feelings are true and I just give in to the emotions and try not to anticipate the end."

"Our relationship is something I want to hold on to for the rest of my life."

*But can this realistically last forever?* Melanie wondered, thinking about her growing pull toward Will. "Let's not worry about forever, let's just enjoy this moment for as long as it lasts."

John nodded in agreement, feeling an uncomfortable tug of insecurity on his heart. This was the second time in this conversation that Mel had intimated that forever was not her agenda, and the thought of his life without her influence was unsettling.

Off in the distance they could hear his flight being called. John once again took her hands in his and looked deeply into Melanie's lovely brown eyes. "You often talk about learning lessons. Well, you've taught me that I have a lot more love inside than I've been willing to give. In fact, since meeting you, I'm in love with the whole damn world. I even love that old bat sitting over their clicking her dentures at us in disgust," he said, making them both laugh.

The couple embraced again for several moments. Before pulling away, John reached down and briefly kissed her on the lips before bringing his mouth to her ears. "As much as I enjoy kissing you," he whispered, "that one was for Miss Daisy over there."

Once again John's flight was announced over the PA system. "I've got to get going," he said, standing upright before pulling Mel up to him. "When I get back I want us to sit down and talk about some exciting business ideas I have for the two of us," he said. One way or another, he'd find a way to keep her in his life.

Melanie walked him out of the lounge and back into the terminal. She watched for a moment as John headed toward the gate, amazed by the effect their conversation had on her. It seemed that each time they talked, Mel learned something new about life, and her place in it.

In many ways, her relationship with John had begun to clarify and solidify her feelings for Will. The confusion that had been circling like a windmill in her mind was beginning to dissipate. Melanie looked down at her hands, mentally moving the diamond on her right ring finger to the same on her left, feeling that it was time to seriously consider the possibility of marriage. Her romantic and loving friendship with John was certainly unconventional and if she could love two men without guilt or regret and feel good and honest about herself in the process, she just might be able build a marriage *her way*.

"It's your turn," Francesca said hours later as she fanned out the deck of Heart-to-Heart conversation cards. "And this time you have to really answer the question. No half-stepping."

"Where did you get these things?" Mel asked, selecting a card from the right side of the deck. Their annual weekend together was dubbed a sisterly retreat, but for Francesca it was more of a temporary reprieve from the madness of motherhood.

"I picked them up for Valentine's Day. Xavier and I played them and had a ball. I thought it would be fun for us too. Now quit stalling and go."

" 'What's the most romantic night you've ever had?' " Melanie read. Immediately her mind went back to Will's amazing Valentine's dinner. She smiled as the memories of that night charged her head. Mel savored the vision for several moments before her head switched channels, replaying Miami and her starlight cruise with John on the *SunFire*. She found that she couldn't choose between the two occasions, as both were equally special.

"Forget this game. Here's a question for you: Do you think it's possible to love two people?"

"Yes and no. Differently, yes, but not equally," Francesca answered.

"How can you say that? I mean, you have two kids, you love them differently. You love Mom and Dad differently and in a different way than you love your husband. Are you saying that you love any one of them less than the other?"

"Well, no. I don't know. Maybe. What exactly are you asking me?"

"Is it possible for a woman to love two men with equal intensity, but in different ways?"

"Two men? What haven't you been telling me? I thought you and Will were trying to work things out. You haven't fallen in love with someone else, have you?" Her sister's silence no doubt confirmed Franti's suspicion.

"That is so unfair, Melanie. Why did you give Will any encouragement if you still wanted to date other men? And why did you take his ring back?"

"It's not like I was looking for this to happen. It just did."

"Who is he?" Francesca queried her sister.

"John Carlson."

"But he's white."

"I know. I've never really been attracted to white men, and I can't explain it except for the corny but true line: Love is colorblind," Melanie tried to explain.

"Mommy and Daddy will have a fit."

"Tell me about it. He's also married," Mel added, deciding to put the whole truth on the table.

"You're really tripping. How can you cheat on Will with a man who cheats on his wife, no less?"

"I hate that word—*cheat*. It describes nothing that has to do with the feelings involved here. I'm not trying to get over on anyone. And what constitutes cheating anyway? Let me ask you a question. Is it fair to 'cheat' myself out of experiencing this totally unsolicited gift of love that God has given me?" Melanie shot back.

"Are you so sure that this is a gift from God? I mean, the Lord is pretty clear on the subject: Thou shalt not commit adultery."

"But if all love comes from God, then how can my feelings for John not be a Divine gift?"

"Have you considered the option that this might simply be a test—a tempting present from the devil, wrapped up in shiny packaging?"

"If this was simply about lust, maybe I'd agree, but it's not. I haven't had sex with either one of them. My relationship with John is about a real and powerful love, but it's so gentle it doesn't interfere with my love or life with Will."

"Are you so sure it doesn't?"

"It's crazy, Franti, my heart stops each time I see Will and beats a hundred miles an hour when I'm with John."

"But he's married. How would you feel if he was your husband, or mine?" Francesca asked in hurt indignation.

"I know, and I'm not interested in breaking up his marriage. I don't want to be John's wife, I just want to be his . . ." *His what?* Her question stopped her mouth from uttering any further words.

"His lover?"

"No. Yes. I guess so, but not the way you think. It's more like we're lovers in mind and spirit, but not body."

"And how long can that last? How can you love someone and not want to have sex with him?" Franti asked.

"I don't know the answer to that question. I really don't. But I do know that I've had plenty of opportunity to do so, but haven't."

"Maybe because you know deep down inside that sleeping with a married man is wrong?"

"Maybe. I just know that I'm in love with both of them."

"I guess the question is then: What kind of love are you in?"

"I'm not exactly sure. That's the problem," Mel admitted softly.

"What is it that you love about John Carlson?"

"Many things. John has this uncanny ability to see depths of me that even Will can't see. He understands why I love what I do for a living and why the feeling of working your passion is enough to put the things Mom or society says I should want and have on hold. He's so talented and makes me feel confident in my abilities as a designer and woman. He feeds my creative, artistic side and loves me for who I am. He's taught me to appreciate the side of Melanie Hitts that nobody else seems to understand and made me see that I can love other people without compromising myself."

"And Will?"

"Will is so special. He loves me and when I'm with him I feel respected and revered. He's romantic and intelligent and ambitious. Will makes me laugh and is always full of surprises. I adore his gentleness and his desire to make sure that I always feel safe and protected. There is a real ease being together. Mom and Dad love him and I know that we could have a good future together, and he'd make a great husband and father."

"When you break it down like that, together you have the perfect man. John touches the artist in you, while Will touches the woman in you. All you have to do is figure out which is more important to you in the long run. It seems to me that when you look at the big picture, John Carlson is just one more flower in life's vase—beautiful while it lasts, but bound to lose its bloom. Will, on the other hand, is the strong oak tree that will be around forever."

"But why can't I marry Will and still have John in my life?"

"Because your husband is the one who is supposed to be your soulmate and most intimate friend. You're not supposed to go outside marriage for those things."

"Who says you're allowed only one soulmate per person? And how can one person be expected to meet your every emotional need for the rest of your life? People change too fast. And life changes even faster."

"But it's the honest thing to do," Francesca argued.

Melanie didn't know how to explain her beliefs to Franti, still a faithful worshiper. In the years since she'd stopped going to church and started her quest to find God *within* herself, she'd discovered that truth and honesty were two entirely different things. Being honest was about obeying rules and scenarios made up by men to justify their actions and reactions to others. Honesty wasn't necessarily about *real* truth. Individual truth. Universal truth. But how could she make her sister understand?

"Melanie, face it: The world just doesn't work that way. We are meant to love only one person at a time."

"Says who? All I can go by is what's true for *me*, Franti. I know that I love Will, and I also know that God has given me no choice but to love John as well."

"We always have choices. The question is: Are you prepared to live with the consequences?"

# Chapter 21

"**Y**our move, sexy," Griff prompted Candace.

She stared at the chessboard as if she were deeply considering her next move. In actuality, she was bored shitless. Spring had sprung and she was still stuck inside, sitting for the umpteenth time with a chessboard between her and the man she was trying her damnedest to support and continue to love. It was hard to believe that she and Griffin had already been living together under her roof for over three months. Sometimes it felt like three days, at other times—like now—more like thirty years.

She nonchalantly moved her knight one rank up and two files left and captured Griff's pawn. Her move prompted Griffin to move his bishop diagonally to the right and land in striking distance of her king.

"Check," he announced, the thrill of his impending kill gleaming in his eyes. She acted out the requisite dismay, took a long sip of her Cabernet Sauvignon, and continued to stare at the board while her mind raced ahead.

It was amazing how drastically different her social life had become. Instead of the usual club-hopping at the hippest, hottest spots in the city, or eating fine food at all the most expensive restaurants in town, she and Griffin had partied on the low-key. She'd been to poetry clubs to hear him read, house parties with his theater buddies, and had pulled into every Caribbean and Ethiopian restaurant within a subway ride distance.

Candy had to admit that despite her current boredom, in many ways playing house with Griff had been heavenly. There was a certain indescribable bliss associated with coming home every night to his waiting arms. Her current case was in full litigation, and realizing that at the end of a tough day Griffin would be home to massage her shoulders and sooth her jagged nerves was a pleasure she'd never known, but had quickly grown accustomed to. And although Candy enjoyed the idea of having her own man for a change, she was unable to shake the negative feelings about her irregular home life.

Perhaps she'd been a bit hasty in extending her invitation to Griffin to move in with her. Candace hadn't anticipated the irritation and humiliation that would come with assuming the role of primary breadwinner. They lived very well on her salary, and while she may bring home the bacon, Griffin was the one who fried it up in the pan. It had been Griffin's idea to save money by firing the cleaning lady. In fact, he did a better job of tidying the place than Sonia had. Griff kept the house running smoothly—toilet paper on the roll, pantry stocked at all times, and the laundry washed and folded to perfection. He took care of the cooking, cleaning, and lovemaking with a flawlessness that appeared effortless. All things considered, Griffin was the perfect wife. And that was the problem.

Candace just couldn't get with the concept of supporting a househusband. She knew that he was not some lowlife, trifling Negro using and abusing her, but despite that fact, their reversal of roles disturbed her. Years down the road Candy could picture him playing Mr. Mom to their kids while she went off to the office, and she found the vision appalling.

The irony of the entire situation was that she and Griffin enjoyed a good life together. They lived comfortably and amicably just like two people in love ought to. Candace had everything she thought she always wanted, and yet it was still not enough—not when she was the one responsible for bankrolling their paradise.

In all fairness, Griffin was trying to get his career going. The play had closed to rave reviews for his performance, and a flurry of phone calls ensued, none of which had yet turned into a full-time paying job. He'd done one minor appearance on *Law & Order,* and was constantly out on casting calls for various projects. His agent was furiously working on getting him auditions, but nothing had come to fruition. Through all this, Griffin remained positive about his future and concerned about his present. He had suggested taking a job as a waiter for his friend's catering business, but Candy's ego wasn't having it. How could she explain to her friends and business associates that her man was a will-work-for-tips snack jockey? Hell, no, she had her standards.

At the sound of Griffin's throaty prompt, Candace cleared her mind and tried to concentrate on the game. Defeated by her own inattention, she soon realized that she had no way to rescue her king. Immediately Griff swooped in, gleefully exclaiming, "Checkmate."

Glad to be done with this tedious exercise, she threw herself back on the couch and expelled a huge sigh.

"So out with it," Griffin said.

"Out with what?"

"What's wrong? You've been moody as hell lately. What's bothering you?"

*I want a man with his own money,* she screamed in silence. *I'm supposed to be the queen of the castle, the pampered housewife, just like Frank's wife.* Frank once again popped into her head, just as he did several times a day since they'd recently met for a drink. She'd been too curious and too eager to flaunt her new relationship in his face to say no, but now Candace could not get him or his invitation to accompany him to Palm Springs off her mind. Candace was aching to go on vacation, but they couldn't afford it. Correction, she could afford it, but Griff could not and his male ego would not allow her to pay his way. And honestly she didn't feel like shelling out another grand or so just to get him there and then have to spend even more for his food and recreation. She could not deny that she missed Frank and, in particular, the good times he provided.

"I'm just tired. Baby, I need to get away. This case is kicking my ass and I desperately need some R&R," she answered.

"That's all that's bothering you? There's an easy remedy for that. Go."

"But you said you wouldn't let me pay for you."

"No, I won't, but that shouldn't stop you from taking some well-deserved time off."

"You don't care if I go alone or with a friend?"

"Why should I? It's your money and your life."

"But what about you?"

"I'll be here doing my thing." Griffin started to tell her how one of the actors originally cast in Lexis Richards's film had backed out at last minute, and now the director was giving Griff a second look. Instead he stayed with his plan to wait and surprise her with the good news if and when the part came through. "Now let me get dinner on," he said, giving her a quick kiss on the forehead.

Candace sat back, confused by the uncomfortable tug-of-war taking place inside her body. She was feeling both appreciative and angry. Griff understood her need for independence and wasn't interested in standing in the way of her needs—professional or personal. At the same time, here she finally had a full-time man and she still had to go on vacation alone? Shit, she might as well go with Frank to Palm Springs. What was the goddamn point of being tied down to a brother who couldn't support her or her desired lifestyle? Especially when she had one who could.

*Maybe his wealth is measured in the way he loves and respects you,* an inner voice remarked. *So damn what?* she argued back, quickly muting the voice of compassionate reasoning. Griffin Bell may be a great guy and rich in all the ways she was poor, but instead of completing Candace, it pissed her the fuck off.

She angrily threw herself off the couch and walked into the kitchen, fully intending to replace her pent-up anger and frustration with some hot and nasty, spontaneous sex. *Thank God fucking is free,* she thought, *or we wouldn't have any fun.*

"Feelin' better?"

"Shut up," Candace commanded softly as she pulled Griffin away from the refrigerator and started to unbutton his pants.

As Candace began to ravish Griff's body, she suddenly saw the absolute necessity of having both men in her life. One to love her and one to spoil her. And until either Frank or Griffin could take care of *all* her needs, together they made her perfect man.

Melanie sat at the dining room table sorting fabric swatches and thinking about Will. The light from the chandelier caught the diamond on her hand, sending up a sparkly spray of light. She admired the fiery twinkle of her friendship ring, enjoying everything it represented at this time.

Her thoughts were halted by the sound of the door buzzer. It was the doorman informing her that there was a package for her at the front desk. Mel took the elevator down and returned to her apartment several moments later carrying a Federal Express box.

She yanked the tab on the container and pulled out a smaller gift-wrapped box. She stripped away the shiny green paper and tissue paper to find a letter nestled among gardenia-scented potpourri. She inhaled the fragrant scent of her favorite flower before unfolding the masculine gray-colored stationery covered top to bottom with Will's bold handwriting.

*Hi Baby,*

*I have been thinking about you in "that" way much more than I should admit. Thinking what it would be like to make love to you. Wondering how it must feel to have your naked body stretched next to mine. To feel my hands in your hair and see the desire in your eyes right before we give in to the inevitable.*

*There are so many things I want in life right now, Melanie. And at the top of that list is you. I want to whisper your sweet name in your ear before making a meal of your lobe. I want to memorize your face with my lips and introduce my tongue to every sensuous curve of your body. I want to feel your breasts crushed against my chest and hear that faint and exquisite rush of breath as I enter you.*

*I know that we decided not to make love until we were married (back then it seemed like a good idea) and now we're waiting to see what becomes of us. But each time our lips touch or I hold you, denying my needs becomes more difficult. Kissing you, baby, is like sipping from the Black Sea. The more I drink, the thirstier I become.*

*I will try to wait patiently for the right time between us. Until then, I want you to tell me your thoughts, your fantasies, your fears, so that when we do make love, I am loving every idea and desire that makes you so uniquely, so beautifully, so lusciously you.*

*I, Will, love you always*

Reading his sexy and amorous letter completed Mel's hormonal meltdown. His lovely declaration painted erotic pictures in her head, magnetically pulling her into a fantasy world. Her body wanted what he wanted, but until they could be together, she would have to take matters into her own hands.

"Hmmm," Melanie purred softly. *Will, can you imagine me . . . loving me . . . thinking of you?* she thought, employing mental telepathy to send her message. Melanie closed her eyes and, using his words and her hands, swiftly brought herself to climax.

Mel lay back, eyes closed, luxuriating in the wake of Will's words. As her breath resumed its normal pattern, she came to a pleasant revelation. Her smile got wider, eventually bursting open and releasing gales of happy laughter as her instinct confirmed her heart. The decision was finally made, and yet it felt like she'd known it all along.

She reached for the phone and quickly dialed Will's number. His hello, spoken in a smooth buttery timbre that was seductive and inviting, melted over her body, sugarcoating her resolve.

"I got your beautiful letter," Mel purred softly. "It was, shall I say, 'inspiring,' and the most beautiful gift I've ever received. I don't think I've ever felt more touched. Thank you."

"You're very welcome," Will replied, happy his gesture pleased her.

"I've been wanting to ask you something, but have been a bit reluctant because I didn't want you to think—"

"Baby, you can ask me anything. You know that."

"Well, it's about the ring," Mel began. "I'd rather do this in person, but I can't continue to wear this another day. . . ."

Will took a deep, silent breath of defeat, sure that Melanie wanted to return the diamond yet again.

"It's really too tight for my right hand, so I was wondering if you'd mind me wearing it on my left."

"Melanie, are you saying what I think you're saying?"

"If you think I'm saying that I want to marry you, then yes, I'm saying what you think I'm saying," she said with a happy giggle.

Will held the phone between his ear and shoulder as he pumped his hands in the air, a sign of both gratitude and glee. He felt breathless and full as sheer joy consumed his body. The marathon was over and he finally could claim his cherished trophy.

"Oh, baby, you don't know how long I have waited to hear those words."

"I do love you, Will. I always have, even though I've given you plenty of reason to doubt it."

"So when? Let's set a date right now. We'll do it however and whenever your heart desires."

Melanie paused. She hadn't thought that far ahead. The realization that she absolutely wanted to marry Will was still too new. She wasn't ready to go beyond that decision. She wanted to continue to take things slow and easy. She still had a lot to work out in her head. The most difficult being how this would impact her relationship with John. On one hand, she didn't really owe him a thing. On the other, she owed him everything. Her career. Her newly acquired sense of confidence and personal independence. Her willingness to commit to marriage. Until she sorted through and put their relationship into proper perspective, she was not comfortable setting a wedding date with Will.

"Baby, let's just be engaged for a while. We'll take this one step at a time. There's no need to rush into anything. In fact, can we keep this between you and me? I'm not ready to tell my parents yet. You know how my mother is. Okay?"

*No, it's not okay.* Will could feel that familiar sense of dread and uncertainty usurp his earlier feelings of delight. If Melanie was absolutely positive that she wanted to marry him, why was she so reluctant to set a date or share the news with her family? Who or what was holding her back from full commitment?

"Don't worry, I'm not going anywhere," Melanie said, as if reading his mind. "I just want to make sure we do it right this time. We have a lot of *life* decisions to make. Making wedding plans isn't that urgent—at least not now."

"Okay, we'll take our time. As long as we love each other and are both committed to making things work, we'll be fine," Will replied with more gusto than he felt. Even though her words made perfect sense, he couldn't help but feel uneasy. He'd been burned once. A second time would destroy him.

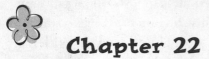

# Chapter 22

**S**haron slid the original version of *Sabrina* into the VCR, pushed PLAY, and sat back on the couch. John had just called from Belize, and Sharon was happily settling in for a marathon evening of classic romantic movies. She'd be elated, however, when the issues that were taking her husband away were settled and she and John could cozy up on the sofa together.

She truly missed him. There were changes in her husband that Sharon could only deem remarkable. Despite this latest business crisis in Belize, he seemed happier, more mellow and easygoing. He was even painting again, something he hadn't done in years. Their sex life had picked up and there was a new vitality to their lovemaking. He was talking about his feelings and confiding in her more. And even though he still had reservations about her relationship with Amanda, he'd stopped trying to forbid their interaction.

Sharon pinned the change on work. John's recent projects were turning out to be quite successful, and suddenly his entire life seemed revitalized. Whatever the catalyst, he was happier than he'd been in a long while and his happiness had rained down on their marriage.

Ignoring the multitude of previews and advertisements crossing the screen, Sharon's eyes panned the room, staring at the
empty spaces on the wall where paintings, now hanging in New
York, once hung. She had to start packing up her things soon and
eventually every area of her house would be dismantled. With the
New York apartment having been totally decorated with new fur-
nishings, only a few pieces from this house would be moved. The
rest was being donated to charity. This unpleasant thought was
certainly made more acceptable by the fact that she really did feel
as if she and John were beginning a new, exciting life together.

The opening credits pulled Sharon's attention away from her
own situation and drew her into the lives of the megarich
Larrabee brothers. She watched in rapt attention as the story progressed, pitting William Holden and Humphrey Bogart against
each other as they both fell under the spell of Audrey Hepburn's
many charms. Just as Sabrina realized she was falling for big
brother Linus, Sharon was forced to pause the story and answer
the door.

Expecting to see the Federal Express man with his usual delivery of blueprints and paperwork for John, Sharon was shocked to
find a very agitated Amanda on her front doorstep. She stood,
dressed in her favorite baggy overalls, her face bloated with previ-
ously cried tears.

"Amanda. Honey, this is a surprise. What are you doing here?
Are you okay?"

"I'm sorry to come without telling you, but I couldn't think of
anywhere else to go," the girl said as she tried to fight back the
tears.

"It's okay. Come in and tell me what's going on." Sharon
stepped aside to let Amanda in and then followed the teenager

into the house. "Let's go in here," she said, pointing her toward the family room.

"Is your husband here?"

"No. He's out of town. It's just us, so we can talk freely."

"Sharon, I don't know what to do."

"Do about what, Amanda?" Sharon asked, her concern growing.

"It only happened once . . . I didn't think . . ."

"Honey, slow down. Just tell me what's wrong."

"I'm pregnant," Amanda blurted out before breaking into tears.

Shock sent Sharon into temporary paralysis. Driven by the force of Amanda's wails, she forced her body to move and gathered Mandy up into her arms. Sharon rocked the young woman against her breast and allowed her to expel her tears. As Amanda sobbed wildly, Sharon, in a rush of maternal love, tried to sort out the situation in her head, wanting desperately to find a way to help the girl through this difficult situation.

As the intensity of Amanda's sobs began to subside, she asked, "How far along are you?" The memory of Amanda's nausea and vomiting at Christmas had Sharon counting the months.

"About seven months, I think. At least that's how many periods I've missed."

"Seven months? Amanda, why didn't you tell me about this sooner?" Sharon asked, mentally eliminating one option from her list of possible solutions. How had she missed the signs? Granted, Mandy was always wearing those baggy hip-hop clothes, but shouldn't she have noticed something?

"I didn't know. I didn't even suspect until after my fourth month. My periods have always been irregular."

"Is it Kevin's?"

"Yes," Amanda replied softly. "We only did it once, but . . ."

"If you don't use protection, once is all it takes to get pregnant and a lot worse. Does he know?"

"Yes. I told him yesterday."

"And?"

"And he doesn't want it."

"So he's willing to hang around long enough to make a baby, but not to father it?" Sharon asked, angrily anticipating the answer.

Woefully, Amanda proceeded to relay Kevin's thoughts on the subject. He had big plans for his future and none of them included her or a baby at this moment. His solution was for her to terminate the pregnancy, and when she told him that it was too late for that, he got angry and accused Amanda of trying to trick him into staying with her by getting pregnant.

"Did you get pregnant on purpose?" Sharon probed gently.

"*No!* I wouldn't do that. That's stupid."

"But you did have sex to try and keep him interested in you?"

"Yes." Amanda's soft admission brought on a fresh onslaught of tears. "But that was stupid too. Catherine is going to kill me. What am I going to do?" Amanda stared down at her stomach and she wiped the tears from her eyes with the back of her shirt-sleeve. She lifted up her head and looked directly into Sharon's eyes, searching for the love and advice she'd come to expect.

"Sharon, tell me what I should do," Amanda pleaded.

Immediately a solution came to mind, and just as immediately, Sharon dismissed it. Tears—both of compassion and frustration—began to fall. Could she adopt Amanda's baby? Her heart wanted to suggest the option, but how could she? What about the girl's parents? They had to be told, and the decision over the fate of their grandbaby was ultimately up to them. But even if the Sarbains could be persuaded, Sharon was sure that John could not. His unyielding dislike of youngsters had kept them childless for all of these years. How could she ever convince him to adopt the offspring of a child he despised? He'd never go for the idea. He'd find a way to make her choose between him and the baby, just as he did before.

*You win again, John,* she conceded.


The wail that emanated from Sharon's slight frame began in the deepest, most personal depths of her soul. Her mournful cry bounced off the study walls and echoed throughout each room of her expansive home. She felt both fiery hot and frosty cold as her stomach began to churn like a Cuisinart gone mad.

*How could I not have known that John was cheating on me?* she lamented as the realization of her husband's infidelity sucked the air from her chest. She stood staring at the papers in her hand until the tears welling up in her eyes spilled over, turning the treasonous words into a handwritten blur of feminine swirls. Her body began to shake as the sobs flowed uncontrollably. Gasping to catch her breath, Sharon released the handful of pear-scented stationery and watched the pages flutter to the floor in slow motion. Angrily she kicked aside John's long-retired leather attaché and added her crumpled body to the pile of old clothes and personal belongings she'd been packing up to give away.

Sharon wrapped herself in her arms in an attempt to ward off the cold, ugly truth: The man she had loved and adored for the over twenty-five years was in love with another woman. Like a metronome keeping time with her heartbeat, she began to rock back and forth, giving in to the agonizing anguish that consumed her.

*How could my husband be in love with another woman and I not notice? Didn't we just celebrate our anniversary?*

The memories rang in her head like the bells that had sounded years ago outside the quaint church in Carmel, California, where she and John were married. The memory of that day pulled her to her feet and toward the display of five-by-seven portraits sitting on top of the credenza across the room. She picked through the chronological display of her life's most treasured moments and selected the antique sterling silver frame, which represented, without a doubt, the happiest and most important day of her life.

Sharon studied the photo through a fresh onslaught of tears. The two of them looked so undeniably right together standing in front of the chapel doors. John so tall and handsome in his navy-blue suit, striped tie, and white shirt, accessorized with only a single white rose in his lapel and a huge smile that threatened to outshine the sun. She too radiated happiness as she stood by his side, glowing angelically in a simple white A-line dress, holding a bouquet of pink and white roses. Never had she felt so complete, so beautiful, and so very much in love than on the day she'd become Mrs. John Carlson.

How could she not have known that he was so unhappy being married to her?

Sharon involuntarily jumped, shocked from her thoughts by the shrill ring of the phone. She walked over to the desk and glanced down to see the house line lit up. After the third ring the machine answered, announcing in John's voice that they were unavailable. When Sharon heard her friend's perpetually cheerful and soothing voice over the speaker, she decided to pick up.

"Hi, Gwen," she said, trying to put a bit of life back in her voice, but failing miserably.

"I was about to hang up. You okay? You sound like you've been crying," Gwen remarked, concern coloring her voice.

For an instant Sharon considered divulging her heartbreaking discovery, but she was too embarrassed to share her devastation with anyone, particularly a woman who had the perfect marriage. She knew that Gwen would be loving and supportive, but this discovery was too new, too raw, and far too painful to share with even her closest friend.

"I'm fine. Just a case of the dust sniffles. I've been cleaning out closets all morning. I'm knee-high in old junk and memories."

"I think it's a bit more than that," Gwen said. "I think that this move is really bothering you more than you're willing to admit."

Grateful for any excuse to blame for her depressed mood, Sharon followed Gwen's train of thought. "The reality of moving is harder to take than I thought."

"Sharon, you know how much I love John. He's always been a good friend to me and a good husband to you, but honey, you're nearly forty-five years old now. If you don't want to move, you have every right to say so. Whatever you want, make him see your point of view. This is your life too."

"John is my life," Sharon said, feeling a new batch of tears coming on. "He always has been and always will be."

"Sharon, tell him how you feel. You've done everything he's always wanted you to do. Now it's your turn. Let him make a sacrifice for you for a change."

Gwen's word stung like a slap in the face. She was so right. Sharon had given up everything to give John the perfect life he craved, and all she expected in return was his love. And this was how he treated her? By cheating on her. In one powerful swoop, the pain and devastation she'd felt just minutes ago was replaced by an anger so palpable it demanded action.

"Gwen, I have to go. I forgot that I promised to fax something to John."

"He's still at the office? It's after ten o'clock."

"He's been working on a presentation for some new business venture since he got back from Belize. He's staying at the company apartment all week."

*Or so he says. Is that a lie too? Is he with her?* Sharon wondered.

"Okay, but after you send the fax, go take a hot bath and think about what I said. Be fair to yourself. Life is stressful enough, don't take on any more than necessary."

Sharon hung up the phone and glanced around at the jumbled mess surrounding her. This mess had become a metaphor for her once-tidy life. Thanks to John, the man she'd entrusted with her love . . . her happiness, her life was in a shambles just like this room.

First Amanda, now John. Was she sleepwalking through life, oblivious to the people around her? How could John have been with another woman and she not know? Was this the first time, or had he been a philandering womanizer their entire marriage?

Angrily she took herself behind the desk and turned on the computer. What she had to say couldn't wait. If he was at the office as he said he would be, he'd get the fax now. If he wasn't there, someone in the morning would find it. Let him suffer the embarrassment. She took her furor out on the keyboard and after several hours of composing and editing, she pushed the required buttons and, through the magic of Ma Bell, sent John a piece of her bewildered, hurt, and angry mind.

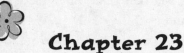

# Chapter 23

The three men, shirtsleeves rolled to their elbows, heads bowed, stood huddled around the conference table. Amid the empty takeout containers, Styrofoam coffee cups, and cans of cola sat the focus of their attention—a chipboard model of a new boutique hotel in the heart of Dallas, Texas. This was to be the first project of the recently incorporated subsidiary, Carlson Properties. The new company was inspired by John's work with Melanie on the Casa de Arte, and financed by investors he was preparing to meet in two days.

"The entry stairway looks off," John commented.

"We had to move it in order to accommodate the concierge's desk," Austin explained. His comment was punctuated by the distant ring of the fax machine located in the far corner near John's secretary's desk. Austin glanced at his watch. It was 1:47 A.M.

"At this hour, that's got to be Giuseppe from Carrera with the quote for the Italian marble," Trevor said. "I'll run over and get it so we can finish plugging in the numbers for the reception area."

"I'll get it," John volunteered. "I need to pick up the blueprints from my desk for the office areas."

He held back a yawn as he walked. His exhaustion was tempered by the excitement he felt about his new endeavor. It was like the early days when his body seemed to run on little more than adrenaline and creative juice. As excited as he was about his idea, he'd be glad to be done with the initial details. The birthing of this new enterprise, combined with his travel back and forth to Belize, had consumed all of his time and energy, making it difficult to spend time with either Sharon or Melanie. He'd looked forward to getting things into place so he could return to his incredible life.

While not a deeply religious man, John could not help but believe that God was truly good. He had been blessed with a wonderful wife, a sterling reputation, and a thriving career that had been revitalized thanks in great part to his beautiful friend and muse, Melanie. He was so grateful for the day Mel had walked into his office, leaving a sea of pearls in her wake. In many ways she was like a flashlight, shining light on the parts of him that he'd kept in the dark. His entire life had changed because of her. With her smile came the sunlight that had warmed his soul and made him truly believe in the wonder of love—both for self and others—for the very first time in his life. Even his relationship with his wife had changed because of her influence. His newfound willingness to share more honestly his feelings with Sharon had begun to add a new depth to their marriage.

The fax machine beeped, signaling the end of the transmission. John picked up papers and began reading, expecting a multitude of numbers, not the stunning words that dropped him limply into the nearest chair.

# FACSIMILE COVER PAGE

TO: John Remington Carlson          FROM: Sharon Carlson
TIME: 1:46 A.M.                     PAGES (including cover): 2

*John,*

*Since you're already accustomed to receiving personal and poten-
tially embarrassing messages from your lover, I didn't think
you'd care if you got one from your wife. If you do, that's too
damn bad.*

*Yes, I know about you and your friend Jax. I found several of
her e-mails and love letters you saved in that old attaché case of
yours. I guess if the Salvation Army wasn't coming by tomorrow,
I'd have never known that for twenty-four years I have been
married to such a lying, cheating bastard.*

*How could you do this to me? I gave up everything for you. I
left college to move east so you could further your career. I understood the need to scrimp and save while you poured our money
into your architectural firm. And when you became a big-time
architect (and even when you weren't) I understood the need for
you to be away so much, traveling all over the world to build up
your firm's reputation. Did you ever know how lonely I was,
John? Of course you didn't, because I never let my needs get in the
way of yours.*

*Most of all, didn't I understand when we learned that
because of you we couldn't have children? I even accepted your
rationale that we were a perfect team as we were, just the two*

*of us, and refused to saddle you with any guilt despite how cheated I felt.*

*Throughout our marriage I've done everything you asked me to do. Why wasn't that enough, John? Why wasn't I enough?*

*Call me crazy, but I thought that we'd actually become closer these past few months. But now I understand the source of the new kinder and gentler John Carlson. I now understand your recent benevolence towards the needy. Was it your guilt over living inside of two women that drove your new tenderness?*

*Were those cuff links a gift from your mistress or something you picked up to keep her ever present in your mind? And I suppose she was the one who sparked your curiosity in antique shopping. Do I have "Vintagejewel" to thank for my Christmas gift?*

*How could I have lived the last twenty-four years with you and not know that you had this incredible thirst for more—a thirst that I obviously could not quench? One that she obviously can. Is Jax the reason you want to move back to New York? How long ago did you stop loving me? Before or after you met her?*

*So what do we do now? Call in the lawyers? I know divorce is inevitable because how could I possibly trust you with my heart again? So tell me, how do we pack away the accumulated memories and the history that is our marriage? We're like one person— same house, same name—how do we begin to dismantle us? How, John? Goddamn it, tell me how.*

With each breath John took, panic seemed to rush in through his nostrils and race through his body, turning the dull ache in his head into a full-blown migraine. Why hadn't he thrown out those letters, as Melanie had requested? Now, thanks to his stupidity, his marvelous life, the one he'd just been gratefully giving homage to God for, was about to explode. He could only hope that the fall-out would not be too costly.

He held his head in his hands and squeezed, hoping to stop the throbbing. Finding no relief, he took a deep breath and dialed his number. As he listened to it ring, he prayed that Sharon would pick up the phone with her usual sense of fair play and compassion. But judging by her angry fax, a huge miracle was needed to get him through this miserable situation. After several moments, the machine came on. Determined, John hung up and dialed again. Still no answer. He tried a third time, his disappointment and anger at being ignored growing. Reluctantly he left a message.

"Sharon, it's me. It's two in the morning. I know you're home, so please answer the phone. Thank God no one else picked up your fax. Why the hell would you do something like that? Sharon? Sharon? PLEASE, DAMN IT. PICK UP THE PHONE.

"Look, I'm sorry. I don't mean to yell, it's just . . . we need to talk. Sharon? Okay, fine, if you won't talk, then at least listen to me. Look, whatever you're imagining might have happened, it's not what you think. I can explain everything and will, just as soon as I see you.

"I will try to call again later and I'll drive home first thing in the morning. We'll get this all straightened out when I—" John heard the end beep and slammed the phone down in frustration.

*I know about you and your friend Jax.* Sharon's declaration haunted him, adding concern for Melanie to his emotional gumbo. What if Sharon tried to contact Mel? He had to warn her. John picked up the phone once again and dialed the unlisted phone number. "Shit," he cursed after Mel's answering machine picked up. For a second time in less than fifteen minutes, John left a reluctant message for a woman he loved.

"It's me. I know it's late, and I'm sorry to have to tell you like this, but I have no other choice. Sharon found some of your letters and faxed me a rather desperate note here at the office.

"I don't want you to worry about this. We'll all get through this situation somehow, though at this very moment, I haven't a clue how. I'll try and call you tomorrow if I can. I . . ." *love you.* The words died in his throat. Though the sentiment was entirely true, it seemed inappropriate to express at this delicate time. "I'll talk to you soon. 'Bye."

After his unsatisfactory attempt to contact both Sharon and Melanie, John felt like a zombie. Fear, remorse, and uncertainty consumed his body, suffocating the brain cells he desperately needed right now in order to think straight.

He forced himself to concentrate as he tried to place himself in Sharon's position. He went over every line of Melanie's letters, long ago committed to memory. Usually her sweet and supportive words brought him joy, but tonight he mentally analyzed their content like a private detective looking for clues. At face value he had to admit that there was enough circumstantial evidence to convict him in the court of adulterous affairs. But the whole truth was that when taken out of context, the letters told only part of the story.

*Am I wrong for loving another human being just because she is a woman and I'm a married man?* John thought. He'd been forced to keep his friendship under wraps like some dirty secret, simply because the world believed that a penis and vagina could not coexist in a state of unconsummated friendship.

Yes, they had kissed. And yes, he had indeed entertained lustful thoughts about her, but had always respected the boundaries between them. Thoughts of sex and actually having sex were two totally different things to John. Hell, he didn't know a man alive—straight or gay—who never had sexy musings about someone other than his partner. For what other reason did the Halle Berrys, Pamela Andersons, and Lucy Lius of the world exist?

But John had learned a long time ago that how you see life is how you choose to look at it. He understood that his perspective and his wife's would be drastically different on this issue. To save his marriage he would either have to change her vision or be forced to acquiesce to her reality.

He reached into his desk drawer and pulled out a bottle of Tylenol. He swallowed three extra-strength painkillers before once again cradling his head in his hands, willing his headache and this uncomfortable situation to miraculously disappear. Instead his mind began to replay scenes from his youth—tearful, hysterical scenes starring his mother and father, acting and reacting to accusations of infidelity and blatant disrespect. *This is nothing like that*, John told himself. *I am not my father. I am nothing like that bastard.*

A light tapping on his office door interrupted John's mental reverie and announced Austin's presence. "Did you get the numbers from Italy?"

"No."

"Is everything all right?"

"Ah, yes," John replied, barely looking up. "I just have a monster headache. We're in pretty good shape here. I think we might as well knock off for tonight. Why don't you all head home?"

"Are you going to be okay?"

"Yes," John said, looking up and offering a weak smile. His eye caught the small pile of paperwork he promised Gale he'd sign and leave for her in the morning. "I'm going to jot down a few notes and then head back to the apartment myself."

"Okay. See you in the morning, then."

"Right." John waited for Austin to leave before pulling the stack of blueprints, contracts, and correspondence that required his signature. He had quickly worked through most of the pile when an idea struck him. He opened a drawer and pulled out several sheets of his personal stationery. He wrote his pain, earnestly purging both his love and contrition as he poured his feelings onto each page.

Forty minutes later, John placed the signed documents and reports into his out box for Gale to mail in the morning, packed up his briefcase, and wearily headed for the parking garage. A love note had gotten him into this mess. Hopefully the same would help get him out.

John woke up early Wednesday morning with the same excruciating headache he'd gone to bed with. Though he'd done so hundreds of times in past years, waking up alone in bed this morning frightened him. It sent an ominous chill through his body, a haunting suggestion of his possible future—a future he had no desire to live.

He got up and swallowed several more painkillers before getting dressed. Minutes after eight he called the office, leaving a message on his secretary's voice mail that he was leaving for Connecticut and would be unavailable all day. He dialed home to let Sharon know that he was on his way but hung up after once again getting the answering machine. He considered calling back, but decided to wait until he was on the road, just in case she'd gotten as little sleep as he had.

He pulled his Lexus out of the parking garage and onto the street, grateful for the long ride ahead of him. He hoped that the hour or so on the road would help clear his head and give him time to find the words needed to explain this very complicated and delicate situation to his wife.

As John maneuvered his way onto the West Side Highway, he continued to analyze the decisions and events that had led up to this day. Though he had mentioned Melanie's name to Sharon in connection with work, in all honesty he enjoyed his secret infatuation. She was a special part of his life that he had little desire to share. Still, pushing that selfish pleasure aside, if John had thought Sharon would understand, he might have told her about Melanie. But how could he explain to his wife, a woman whom he truly loved and respected, that he also loved and respected Melanie—but in an entirely different way? That while he didn't want to build his life around Melanie Hitts, he certainly wanted her to be part of it. Would Sharon have been able to hear those words without feeling threatened? Hell, no, which is exactly why his friendship had remained a secret.

John massaged his left temple, trying to rub away the pain while he cursed the unfairness of it all. Sharon and Gwen Robinson were the very best of friends. They shared their most intimate thoughts and details about their individual lives, talked at all hours of the day and night, vacationed together, and would cross the country at a moment's notice to come to each other's emotional rescue. But here

John felt the same about a woman and somehow it was an unacceptable relationship because he was male, straight, and married.

*But if this was about Sharon and a friendship with another man, would you so readily believe in its innocence?* John thought as he passed an off-duty ambulance and then merged into the far lane. He took a moment to ponder the question further before coming to the honest conclusion that prior to meeting Melanie Hitts the answer would have been a resounding no. He'd be just as hurt, angry, and suspicious as his wife was at this very moment.

As he inched up toward the exit ramp, his thoughts were abruptly interrupted by the ring of his cell phone. He picked up his Nokia from the passenger seat and said hello.

"John, it's Melanie. I got your message. How are you doing?"

"Don't ask."

"You sound funny. Are you okay?"

"I didn't get much sleep last night and I have this horrible headache I can't seem to shake."

"John, I'm so sorry if I did anything to hurt you or your marriage."

"Melanie, this is my fault. You told me to get rid of your letters and I didn't. Now I just have to deal with the fallout. I'm sorry to drag you into this."

"I . . . I don't know . . . what to say," Melanie stuttered. After all of their heartfelt conversation these past months she didn't know what to tell John. In less than twenty-four hours everything about their relationship had changed. Yesterday, their friendship felt good and nurturing and positive. But now, with Sharon knowing and suspecting who knows what, Melanie actually felt an uncomfortable and unfair sense of dishonesty about their association.

"You don't have to say anything. And I don't want you to feel guilty about anything. I'd hate that, Jax. I don't know what's going to happen to any of us now, but I'd like to think we could still find a way to be friends."

"Me too, but we have to be real about this. Other people just can't put their arms around a relationship like ours," Mel said, trying to imagine Will's reaction.

"I know."

Melanie considered for a brief moment telling him about her engagement, but quickly decided that now was not the time to break the news. "John, whatever happens, promise you won't forget me." Mel could feel the tears pooling behind her eyes. This felt so much like good-bye. And even if it wasn't, she knew that things between them would never be the same.

"That could never happen."

"Take care of yourself. Be happy."

"You do the same." John disconnected the call, his heart feeling as heavy and painful as his head. He decided to call home again, and dialed the number. He held the phone away from his ear, the ringing sound further irritating his headache. After four rings, Sharon picked up.

"Hi, it's me," John said with soft uncertainty. He could hear her breathing on the other end of the phone. "Sharon?" Immediately he heard a click, followed by the dial tone.

With the frustrating noise came a thought that sent dread rushing through his body. What if Sharon left him? He was not prepared for that possibility. Yes, he loved Melanie, but his life was with Sharon. There was never a question about that, never a choice to be made between the two. But what if Sharon made the choice for him?

*Sharon, I do love you,* he thought as the pounding and pain in his head became unbearable. He again put his hand to his head and closed his eyes for a millisecond. Somewhere in the distance he heard the screech of tires, the crunch of metal, and the hiss of air. And as his head bobbed against the airbag the blackness became silent.

*You've reached the Carlson residence. Please leave your name and number and we'll return your call promptly.*

"Mr. and Mrs. Carlson, Fern Greenberg from Prudential Real Estate. It's a little after eleven this morning. I need to speak with you at your earliest convenience. The sale on your buyer's home has fallen through. They've asked for a thirty-day extension on their contract. Please give me a call and let me know if you're agreeable to this change. Talk to you soon."

*You've reached the Carlson residence. Please leave your name and number and we'll return your call promptly.*

"Sharon, it's Gwen. Give me—"

"Hi. I'm here. I thought you might be John again."

"Screening your calls to avoid your husband?"

"Yes," Sharon admitted.

"Why? What's wrong?"

"He's cheating on me. I found . . . love letters and e-mail . . . from a woman . . . obviously his mistress. Gwen, how could I not have known? And how could he stand up at our anniversary party and say all those things if he . . ." Sharon's gush of words was halted by her need to take a breath.

"When did you find the letters?"

"Last night. Right before you called. I was packing and found them in the closet."

"Why didn't you say something then?"

"I was too devastated, but I've gone from depression to extreme anger overnight. I guess mood swings are to be expected when your entire life is falling apart."

"Have you talked to him?" Gwen asked.

"I faxed him at the office, telling him I know about his affair. He called but I wouldn't pick up the phone, so he just kept talking. Basically he told me that I didn't see what I thought I saw. How stupid does he think I am? I know what I read. He called again this morning but I hung up on him. This is probably him now," Sharon said, hearing the call-waiting signal.

"Do you want to get that?"

"No. He can leave a message."

"Sharon, are you afraid to speak with John?" Gwen probed tactfully.

"No . . . maybe. What if he wants to leave me?" Sharon asked with a sad whimper. Suddenly the anger that had punctuated their conversation dissipated.

"Don't jump to conclusions. You and John simply have to talk this out. I know things must look pretty bad right now, but they will get better. You *will* wake up from this nightmare and you and John *will* get through this, I promise."

"I wouldn't know how to live without John."

"I doubt it will come to that, but if it did, you'd find a way. You're a lot stronger than you think."

Sharon hung up with her friend and immediately released the latest assault of tears, anger, and unending questions invading her body. How could John destroy their lives like this? How could he fall in love with someone else?

"If you had to cheat, why couldn't you just have sex with her? Why did you have to fall in love?" Sharon screamed. "What am I going to do now? I don't know how to be divorced. I don't want to be alone," she cried, her shouts turning into sniffles.

"Gwen's right. You can't sit here and drive yourself crazy obsessing over this," she told herself sternly. Sharon made herself a cup of tea and tried to think about something else, but the only other issue on her mind was just as depressing.

Before discovering John's betrayal, Sharon had been consumed with Amanda's situation. They'd visited Sharon's gynecologist and learned that Amanda's pregnancy was proceeding normally and she was expected to deliver in early July—two days before Independence Day and five days after Amanda's parents were due to return from Japan. Despite Sharon's insistence, Amanda refused to tell her mother and stepfather anything during their weekly phone call. Sharon had reluctantly remained silent, promising to help her come to some decision, but now, with her own life falling apart, it was difficult to focus on Amanda and her pregnancy.

She thought about returning the real estate agent's call, but had no answer to give and no desire to chat about selling her house. Nothing on television interested her and every song on the radio further depressed her. As a last attempt to derail her morose thoughts, Sharon leaned over and sorted through the stack of magazines, picking up the latest copy of *More*.

Willing herself to concentrate on the issues at hand and not her head, she flipped through the pages until the title "Creating the Life You Want" teased her into perusing the article. Sharon read the piece and immediately decided to try the recommended exercise in the accompanying sidebar. The first task called for her to make a list of her unique talents and how she used them. Sharon sat stumped, realizing that she had no discernible talent. Not like John, who was a master architect and had serious artistic ability. Or Gwen, who used her wicked sense of humor to write greeting cards that provided levity for others.

*I have no talent,* she admitted to herself as she pushed aside the magazine, *and I have accomplished nothing. I have nothing to show for taking up space on this earth. No career. No children. And now, no husband. No wonder John has a mistress. He's fed up being tied to a useless bore.*

Sharon once again broke down crying, her attempt at diversion a horrible bust. When the phone rang again, she immediately picked up, tired of trying to avoid her husband. If he was planning to leave her, she needed to know.

"Mrs. John Carlson. This is the emergency room at St. Paul's Hospital. Your husband has been in a serious automobile accident."

"Is he . . ." Sharon could not push the dreadful words from her mouth.

"He is unconscious and his status is critical. It would be a good idea for you to get here as soon as possible."

Sharon sat by John's bed in the critical care unit, her heart breaking with each noisy breath he took. Hooked up to a ventilator and heart monitor, a feeding tube down his nose, and a myriad of IV tubes attached to his arm, he resembled some kind of crazy science experiment. Certainly not the vigorous and vital man he was before suffering a stroke and lapsing into a coma one week ago.

Every day she thanked God that an off-duty ambulance had been on the road when the accident occurred. Because they got him to the hospital so quickly, the blood loss to John's brain had been contained and hopefully his life spared. But even if he did live, at this point it was too early too tell how much, if any, damage had been done.

The sun was setting on this nightmare of a day, but the toxic combination of emotions produced by the last week continued to rise through her body. At this moment, it was damning guilt and paralyzing numbness that clung to Sharon, threatening to choke the sanity from her. The doctor explained that John's hemorrhagic stroke, due to a ruptured brain aneurysm, had caused him to black out at the wheel, but Sharon couldn't help feeling responsible. Why hadn't she paid more attention to his recent headaches and forced him to slow down and see the doctor? Or if she hadn't sent that fax or had talked to him when he called, maybe John's stress level and blood pressure wouldn't have risen to the level of rupture and caused him to lose control of the car.

*And if he hadn't been cheating on you, you wouldn't have done either,* an angry thought intruded. *Shut up,* she argued back. *Instead of worrying about the possible death of your husband, you're focused on the death of your marriage.*

The truth of her current emotional state emerged with such force that Sharon felt light-headed. She'd buried the anger and hurt that had preceded John's accident under strain, sleep deprivation, and worry. But sitting here, quietly standing guard over his seemingly lifeless body, Sharon was shocked by the harsh reality of her feelings. There was a part of her that had been sentenced to death by John's infidelity and was now being slowly executed by her residual feelings of betrayal and abandonment.

In the days since John's accident she questioned every offer of condolence by business associates, colleagues, and employees, wondering how many people in his life knew the truth. How many of their sympathetic looks were because she was the idiot wife who didn't know her husband had a mistress and not simply because he was in the hospital fighting for his life?

There was a huge part of Sharon that wanted to come face-to-face with John's mistress. Sharon needed to look into the eyes of the person who had snared her husband's love and attention so she could understand why she wasn't good enough. But did she really want to know? Would learning her identity cause Sharon to go crazy comparing herself to this woman? Maybe it would, but having no comparison was worse.

"Damn it, John. You cheated on me for God only knows how long and now you're cheating me again with this accident. Wake up and talk to me. I deserve to know the entire story. I deserve to know who this woman is and what your plans are. You owe me that much," she said as she angrily punched his inert shoulder and broke into tears.

Ashamed by her uncustomary behavior, Sharon left the room and slipped into a nearby stairwell. She sat and cried for several minutes, lamenting every aspect of her life right now. The ring of her cell phone interrupted her weeping. Not wanting to answer but afraid it might be John's doctor, she pressed SEND.

"Mrs. Carlson. Fern Greenberg again. I'm sorry to call after business hours, but hadn't heard from you regarding the house."

"Hi, Fern. I'm sorry I haven't returned your call. My husband was in a car accident and is in the hospital. Our lives are pretty much on hold right now. So please apologize to the Martins, but under the circumstances I can't make any decisions. I'll have to get back to you later on this."

Sharon pushed the disconnect button but couldn't keep the fear from penetrating her body. These were the kind of decisions John always made. He was the one who took care of the bills, the insurance, the investments, the taxes . . . the list went on and on. Now what was she going to do? If it came down to her living alone—whether through divorce or death—how was she ever going to survive?

# Chapter 24

"**W**hat are you doing in here?" Candace called out, bursting into her girlfriend's bedroom. Melanie was sitting quietly in the corner chair with her eyes closed, breathing deeply. "Girl, I've been hangin' out in your living room for twenty minutes. Are we going to the movies or not?"

"Yes," Mel said, opening her eyes.

"What's with you lately? Every time I call you or come by, you're lighting candles and meditating like a fiend. You're like a junkie waiting for her next fix when it comes to that mumbo-jumbo stuff. And knowing you the way I do, you only kick your mantra into overdrive when you're upset or worried about something."

"I wasn't really meditating. Just being quiet for a minute to find some answers."

"So why not come to the source?" Candace asked, playfully thumping her chest.

"Just because your big head is shaped like an eight-ball doesn't mean you're psychic," Melanie teased. "And how many times do I have to tell you that you have all the answers? You just have to be willing to be still, dig deep, and listen."

"Okay, enough of the swami salami stuff. Tell me what's got you in this pensive mood, and don't feed me any more BS," Candace said.

"You're right. I am worried about someone," Melanie volunteered.

"Friend or foe?"

"Friend."

"A he-friend or she-friend?"

"He-friend."

"Is this the guy you met through work?"

"Yes."

"Okay, Melo, we can continue to play twenty questions, which is not only time-consuming but boring as shit, or you can just come out and tell me what the hell is going on."

Melanie crossed the room to her dresser as she decided whether to confide in her friend. It was a very personal situation, but who better than Candace to give advice about married men and their scorned wives?

"This is strictly confidential."

"Understood and obeyed."

"My friend is married and his wife recently found some letters I'd written him."

"What kind of letters?" Candace asked, intrigued by the idea that Melo might be part of the same lovers' triangle she so vehemently disapproved of. "Are we talking *Penthouse Forum* or 'Dear Ann Landers'?"

"Just letters about our feelings and relationship. But taken out of context, they could give the wrong impression."

"Did the words *miss you, love you,* or *fuck you* show up anywhere?" Candace asked.

"Well, yes. At least two of the three."

"Then everything is in its correct context. What did the wife do?"

"Other than letting him know she knew about us, I have no idea. I talked to him when he was on his way home, but haven't heard anything since. Something's not right. It's been days. He said he'd call."

"He's probably too busy getting his ass waxed to pick up the phone. Believe me, there's nothing worse than a wife on the warpath. She'll have his butt in the doghouse for months. Good thing you have Will to keep you occupied until his sentence is up."

"Candy, it's not like that." Melanie went on to explain the scope of her relationship with John, forcefully emphasizing the absence of sex from their liaison.

"Don't start that bullshit again. You told him you loved him?"

"Yes."

"And he said he loved you?"

"Yes."

"Then you're more than friends. So who is this brother? Do I know him?" Candace asked, not for one minute believing that they had not been intimate.

"It's John Carlson."

"That white boy you work with? What about Will? Why do you continue to dog that man? How much more humiliation are you going to put him through?"

"Just a minute ago you had no problem with me having Will and a married man on the side. Now it's an issue because you find out it's John? Why?"

"Because white men don't love black women. They may be curious about us and our supposed wild and promiscuous ways, but they don't love us. To them we're an anomaly. A curiosity fuck. They simply want to take us to bed so they can earn their zebra stripes and brag to their friends. They screw us and leave because they don't think we're good enough for them to stay."

"Why do you hate white men so much?"

"Because they're nothing but heartless cowards, a lesson I learned firsthand during my freshman year at Hampton. The first time I fell in love it was with my English lit professor. I thought he was the finest man—black or white—I'd ever seen and I loved everything about him. He said he loved me too—enough to screw me every chance he had until I got pregnant. Then he pretended he didn't know my name." Candace paused and swallowed her rancid memories before continuing.

"What happened?"

"I had an abortion and he found himself another chocolate honey to fuck. I learned right there what gray boys really want from black women."

"Candy, that must have been horrible, but you can't compare the two. John's nothing like that."

"I'm really tired of this holier-than-thou attitude you've got going when it comes to men. It's always been that way. Your men are perfect and mine are fucking dogs."

"You have to admit that your track record, beginning with this professor and ending with Frank, says something about your choices."

"Bullshit. All men have some dog in them and you're one stupid bitch if you don't see it."

Melanie could not believe the angry verbiage being directed toward her. She was sorry she'd shared her secret relationship with Candace. She'd been searching for compassion and understanding from her friend, but found judgmental disdain instead.

"Why don't we just skip the movie?" Mel suggested, no longer interested in their girls' night out.

"Fine. I'll call you when I get back from Palm Springs. And now that we're obviously rowing the same boat, I trust that you'll still cover for me while I'm away. Remember, I'm in Nassau."

"I told you that I don't feel comfortable lying to Griffin."

"Even if it's to help out your *best* friend?"

"My *best* friend wouldn't ask me to lie."

"I'll remember that, Melo," Candace said as she turned her back and strolled out the door.


Melanie woke up thirty minutes before the alarm with John Carlson on her mind. This was the second dream she'd had about him this week, confirming her hunch that something was not right. She needed to reach out and learn what was going on between John and his wife, and how their situation was ultimately going to affect her.

She got up and showered, unable to wash away the feelings of sadness that things had turned into such an ugly, deceitful mess. *Another relationship on the injured reserve list. Mercury must be in retrograde*, Melanie thought.

Two of her three most important alliances were floundering right now. First John and now Candace. Melanie still wasn't sure what she'd done wrong to raise Candace's ire to such a fever pitch, but until her grudge-bearing friend decided it was time to make up, the chilly air between them would remain. Thank goodness she and Will were doing well. Melanie was looking forward to spending the upcoming weekend with her fiancé.

An hour later, Mel was in her office sorting through her mail. She finished reading a memo from Felipe Martinez in Miami regarding select pieces of art and made several notes before noticing a large manila envelope addressed to her in John's handwriting. She immediately ripped open the mailer and pulled out a series of sketches and a heavy envelope. Mel could feel some sort of object tucked inside. Curious, she tore the short edge away and turned the envelope over, causing the enclosed ruby pin to drop onto her desk.

Mel picked up the brooch and examined its features, impressed by its beauty and design. She momentarily placed it aside with the letter and took a moment to concentrate on the illustrations of what appeared to be a new hotel. She glanced through each sketch, once again overwhelmed by John's immense talent. A sigh escaped her mouth as she reached over and picked up the pin, comparing the set of stairs John had designed to its real-life example. Sketched from both above and below, the majestic double staircase radiated glamour and drama even on paper. With its bowed shape converging at the concierge's desk, which was positioned at the top to resemble a clasp, it reminded Melanie of a monumental necklace. As usual, John's work impressed and excited her. Wanting more details, she reached for the letter.

*My dearest Jax,*

*So, what do you think of The Jewel, Dallas' newest five-star boutique hotel? It's the first project birthed from the creative loins of Carlson Properties. And do you recognize the pin? I found it the day we went to the flea market together—the day that I regained my ability to see art and inspiration in everything. I want you to have it because that was also the same day I realized that you were going to be someone very special in my life.*

*These past months have been so revealing. Our relationship has taught me so much. Perhaps the most important thing I learned is that I'm capable of loving and being intimate in ways that I thought could only be expressed physically. Talking, feeling, sharing—these are all viable ways to make love. I understand this now.*

*I love you, Jax, and a part of me always will. But I also love my wife, and as I sit here writing you this letter, I am so scared that I might lose her. It's so unbelievable to me that if I had not met you, I might never have realized how much I love and need Sharon. I'm also sorry that I've cheated her out of the kind of love she deserves. All these years I've been her caretaker, instead of her husband, and I've forced her to pay for that care by selfishly dictating our life together. I've bent and molded our marriage to meet my needs, but have they met hers? No. I want to change all of that, if she'll let me. And if she does, we'll both have you to thank.*

*It's such a shame that the world isn't ready for our kind of love. I'd like to think that in time things might change, but right now I have to do what's best for Sharon and me. I know you understand, because it's also what's best for you and Will. Marry him, Jax. I know you love him and he's damn lucky to have you.*

*So, my sweet Melanie, we have to say good-bye, at least for now. I'd like you to think of The Jewel as a monument of sorts. I'm building it for you and me, for Sharon and Will. It is my tribute to love in all of its wonderful and varied incarnations.*

*Be well. And please know that even though you don't hear from me, you're always in my thoughts.*

*Love,*
*John*

Melanie felt the tears fall as she finished the letter. The season between them had turned, and though she knew intellectually that everything must change, emotionally it was still a painful reality to endure.

She worked nonstop the rest of the day, trying to keep her mind occupied, but every now and again, thoughts of John would slip into her head and yank at her heart. Her only regret was that the termination of their relationship was so abrupt and uncomfortable, particularly for him. It should have been smooth and natural, the way it began.

Mel returned home that evening emotionally drained. After dinner and an hour of television, she eagerly lit her meditation candle, sat back onto the couch, and began repeating her mantra. After breathing slowly and deeply for several moments, she could feel herself slipping into the comforting and familiar void.

As she sat in stillness, Melanie sensed herself falling deeper into the gap than usual. She could feel the sensation of being pulled lower and lower, as if she were riding a cosmic elevator down to the basement level of her soul. After several moments of blissful stillness, John's presence came to her. She didn't actually see him, but his spirit was as strong as if he were standing right in front of her.

Melanie felt her essence drawn to John's and the feeling of being cradled in his arms was real. She felt pressure on her lips and a warm and all-encompassing energy that enveloped her core from the inside out. Here in this wonderful, spiritual netherland they held each other and she and John made love in spirit, as they had never done in the flesh. Their union was intense and beautiful. This was not about physical pleasure, this was a soul-coupling—two spirits united in a powerful and otherworldly encounter that eclipsed anything she'd ever experienced in human form. The intensity of their joining brought on an onslaught of tears—not of joy or unhappiness, but simply pure, unadulterated emotion.

"I love you," she heard John say as he slowly slipped away.

Eyes closed, Melanie remained in her still and hushed state, savoring the multitude of feelings running through her. She felt peaceful, joyful, and overwhelmingly loved. Mel allowed herself several more moments to slowly recover from this remarkable encounter.

Eventually she opened her eyes and glanced around the room, silently greeting familiar objects—each proof that she was still of this earth. She blew out a deep breath. Besides being sexually intense, this had also been the most spiritually profound session she'd had since she'd begun mediating five years ago. It was also a moving and appropriate end to a beautiful relationship born in the heavens to forever change the way she lived and loved.

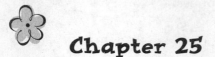

# Chapter 25

Griffin Bell stood in front of the mirror with the script in his hand, running his lines. He was due to begin rehearsals for *Local Color* in two weeks and he could tell by his initial read that this was going to be his much-anticipated career break. Unlike *Race for the Race,* this project would have an audience of hundreds of thousands. Griffin proudly ran his finger across his name listed in the credits. If he shined in this movie just half as much he knew he was capable of, Denzel, Wesley, and Samuel L. better watch their backs.

Griffin couldn't wait to share the good news with Candace. When his sexy baby returned five days from now, he had a big surprise waiting for her. His career was no longer sputtering in neutral, but zooming pedal to the metal ahead. He hoped that it would get her out of this major funk she'd been in for the past few weeks. Griffin was glad that she was in the Bahamas with her friends chilling and hopefully getting her attitude readjusted.

"Mirror, mirror on the wall, who's the talented, finest mack daddy of them all?" he said, giving his reflection a huge Hollywood grin. Before the mirror had a chance to respond, the phone rang. Griff quickly picked up, hoping to hear Candy's voice. Instead it was Kylle Summers, from Candace's law firm, asking for her phone number in Palm Springs.

*Palm Springs? Why is this paralegal asking about Palm Springs when Candace is in Nassau?* Griffin wondered.

"Sorry, Kylle, I know she left her itinerary around here someplace, but I can't put my hands on it right now," Griff lied. His ego wouldn't allow him to admit to a stranger that he was obviously getting played. There was no itinerary, no other number to call in Nassau or Palm Springs. Candace had been purposely vague on her contact information, claiming that her assistant had all the particulars and he could always reach her on her cell.

"When you find it, could you call me? She has a client with a bit of an emergency who really needs to talk with her and can't seem to get through on her cell phone."

"I'll get back to you." Griffin hung up the phone and felt the anger and suspicion fill his veins and travel to every inch of his body. What was Candace trying to pull? Why had she told him that she was going to the Caribbean, and her office that she was on a business trip in California?

Griffin spent the next ninety minutes tearing up the house looking for information on where and with whom Candy might be. On her desk he found no travel documents, only a pink message sheet from the office with the name Frank and a phone number written across it. Reaching into the desk drawer, he pulled out a stack of bills, including an invoice from AT&T Wireless. Griffin searched the statement looking for Frank's number, but did not find it listed among the calls. Another set of digits, however, kept popping up throughout the month. Griff punched the numbers into the phone and got a voice-mail message from Attorney Frank Warren, announcing that he was out of the office until next Wednesday. Still curious, Griffin dialed the operator and asked for the area code for Palm Springs. The answer came back 760—the same as on the pink sheet.

Griffin angrily slammed the receiver back into its cradle and took a minute to think. Sure it could be a big fat funky coincidence that they were both out of town at the same time, but how could he explain this phone call? After a few deep breaths, he began dialing again, this time calling Melanie Hitts. When she answered, raw skepticism caused him to dispense with all the proper formalities and Griff simply blurted out his question. "Who is Frank Warren?"

Melanie asked him to wait while she put her call with Will on hold. She paused before clicking back over, disbelieving her bad luck and furious with Candace for placing her in this tenuous position.

"He's a lawyer that Candy knows," Melanie answered, hoping he wouldn't ask any further questions.

"Are they working on a case together?"

"I don't know."

"Melanie, be straight with me. What's the story?" Griffin kept pressing, wanting confirmation on what he already knew.

Melanie crossed her fingers before opening her mouth. "They were together a while back, but they've been over for a long time," she said, failing at her resolve not to lie, but unwilling to be the one to hurt him with the truth.

"Then why is his phone number all over her bill this month? And why is he out of town the same time she is? And why did she lie about where she was going?"

"I don't know, Griff. You're going to have to ask Candace those questions." Melanie could not believe how sloppy Candace had been. The girl had just left town two days ago and already Griffin had managed to sniff out her trail. It was almost as if she wanted to be discovered.

Griffin disconnected the call, too crushed to say any more. Why did he seem to fall in love with women who wanted to be players, not partners? He'd known Candace Bennett was high-maintenance going into the relationship, and that by having no money of his own, he was at a distinct disadvantage. That was exactly the reason he'd busted his ass these past months to pull his weight around the house. Griffin always knew that this reversal of fortunes was only temporary, but apparently Candace couldn't wait. He had offered her all the love and respect he had to give, but it wasn't enough. *He* wasn't enough.

Griffin immediately shot down his mind's suggestion to at least give her the opportunity to explain. Better to cut his losses and move on. If Candace couldn't remain faithful in a live-in relationship of four months, how could she last the next fifty years? With a future full of location shoots and work-related separations looming ahead of them, how could he ever feel secure in her fidelity? No explanation she could utter was enough to make him risk his heart for a lifetime.

He may love Candace but Griffin had no intention of staying in a relationship with a woman he found untrustworthy. She had defaced his heart with emotional graffiti that could not be washed away with apologetic words. Anger fired up his imagination and inspiration came down hard as he quickly roved the apartment, packing his belongings. Griffin grabbed the AT&T bill and wrote his farewell message across it. He finished his scribblings, stuck the paper on her pillow, and took a last look at her picture on the bedside table. As a parting memento, Griff tossed the *Local Color* script onto the pile. He could get another, and it couldn't hurt to let her know that he wasn't half the chump she'd played him to be.

Griffin picked up his bags and took a last look at the bed he once thought of as heaven. It suddenly dawned on him that he'd been whipped into believing that Candace was the one. How wrong he'd been. He'd correctly sized her up the first time he'd met her. Behind the law degree and liberal lust, Candy was about bling bling and bullshit. How had he lost sight of that fact? Candace wanted a man whose love came attached to a platinum credit card with her name emblazoned on the front and his address on the bill. He was not that man.

With the timbre of a Shakespearean actor, Griffin recited his version of poetic justice as he walked through the front door and out of her life.

*"She was my everything and yet she was nothing.*
*She was the dream of a lifetime, but time had run out.*
*She always said the right things*
*but when I caught her with another*
*her words circled and spiraled into*
*nothingness*
*spraying meaningless graffiti on the*
*four walls of her own room.*
*Now when I see sprayed buildings, walls and billboards*
*on top of shops and malls*

*I know where she's been
and where not to go."*

Candace stepped into a quiet apartment, grateful for the gift of solitude Griffin's absence presented her. She tossed her bags into the entry and immediately threw her travel-weary body onto the couch. Thank God she'd been able to change her flight. It had been worth paying the penalty not to have to stay one more minute with that bastard Frank Warren. What a damn fool she'd been. Why did the grass always look greener on the other side until you strolled on over and stepped in a pile of shit?

Frank wasn't interested in getting serious about their relationship. That line had simply been the bait to get her out to the coast and into his bed. At first everything had been lovely. Frank picked her up at the airport in a limo and took her back to the hotel, where six dozen roses, a dozen for each night they would be spending together, awaited her. He wined and dined her, flirted with and fucked her all night and the following two days. Everything was fine until his wife called while he was in the shower. Candace only picked up the hotel phone because she thought it was the concierge desk with information about their dinner reservations. She was quick to let Regina know that she had the wrong room and when she called back, Frank's wet and dripping ass was out of the shower and answering the phone.

After diverting that possible crisis, a shaken Frank proceeded to break the news that he and his wife were moving to Chicago. Yes, he wanted Candace back, but not in any real way. He simply needed to know that Candace was available, whenever and however he desired, just as she'd always been.

Candy felt a tear squeeze from beneath her lids. How had she let herself get suckered into his tired rap yet again? She hated to admit it, but Melanie had been absolutely right. Thank God she still had Griffin. He may be broke but at least he was dependable and kept his drama onstage where it belonged. Candace picked herself up off the couch and headed toward the bedroom, reiterating the statement she'd made abundantly clear to Frank, "Never the fuck again."

Tired and ready for a nap in her own bed, she strolled into her room, noticing for the first time that the apartment looked particularly tidy. Griffin must have been on some sort of cleaning spree, she decided. She immediately saw the note left on the pillow, and his thoughtfulness brightened her mood considerably. She stripped down to her lingerie before climbing onto the bed and curling up with the pillows. Before reaching for the note, her eyes fell onto the script and she picked it up. She read the title page and then opened the cover and saw the credits, which listed Griffin T. Bell as Taj Kenmore. She quickly flipped through the text, her excitement growing as she realized just how large a part his was.

Candace threw the bound document into the air, cheering loudly for Griff and his accomplishment. "My baby is a movie star!" she shouted into the air while she pictured the two of them walking the red carpet in Cannes. Thank goodness she hadn't kicked him to the curb!

*When did this happen? And why didn't he tell me?* she wondered as her chest filled with pride. Immediately her hand reached for the note in anticipation of further information, but instead she received a dose of breath-stealing rejection.

She threw the poem on the bed and immediately went to the closet, followed by the dresser and then the office area. She saw the pink message sheet with Frank's hotel number in Palm Springs on the desktop, but all of Griff's books and writing materials were gone. He and his belongings had vanished from her apartment and, apparently, her life.

*How the hell did he find out?* The question kept twirling through her head as she dialed Melanie's number. She tapped her nails impatiently on the desk, her anger growing by the second. When Melanie finally answered, Candy's rage exploded into the phone, slapping Mel in the face with wicked outrage.

"You just couldn't keep your mouth shut, could you?"

"Hello to you too, Candace."

"Thanks to you, Griffin has moved out. I hope you're happy."

"Why would that make me happy? I'm sorry Griff moved out, but this isn't my fault," Mel insisted.

"Why did you tell him that I was with Frank?"

"I didn't tell him anything. He called asking a lot of questions about the two of you and the only thing I told him was that he needed to talk to you."

"Shit. That's just like admitting everything he was thinking was true. What the fuck is wrong with you?"

"Wrong with *me*? You might as well have left a trail of bread crumbs for him to follow," Mel shot back in angry self-defense. How dare Candace blame her for the mess she'd created. "Why the hell would you tell him you were going to Nassau and your office that you were in Palm Springs? I didn't have to tell him a thing. He figured out everything on his own, thanks to the loose ends you didn't bother to tie up before you left. I told you not to lie to him, Candy."

"Yeah, well, you should talk, judging by the bullshit you're feeding Will. How do you think he'd react if he knew that his on-again-off-again-on-again fiancée was not only in love with some-one else, but spending her days trying to figure out how she can have her cake and eat the *vanilla* icing too. After all the public humiliation you've already put him through, how do you think that bit of news is going to go over?"

Melanie sat silently in stunned disbelief. Was Candace issuing some sort of threat? What was going on between them? They had argued before, but this felt different. How had a friendship of over ten years disintegrated to this level?

"Will and I have a lot in common," Candace declared, mistak-ing Melo's silence for surrender. "We're both dumbass fools for trusting you."

Melanie hung up the phone without another word, knowing two things for certain. Her friendship with Candace Bennett was mortally wounded and if she didn't tell Will about John, Candy would.

Melanie raised her face to the blue sky laced with wisps of white clouds. She and Will sat in a small boat, holding hands as they slowly pedaled their way out into the middle of the Potomac River. She'd been in D.C. since Friday and thus far everything had been perfect. They'd spent the weekend doing couple things—eating out, walking through the trendy streets of Georgetown, listening to live jazz at Blues Alley, and discussing everything from politics to buttermilk pancakes. As the cherry on this perfect Sunday morning, Will had packed a picnic lunch and they'd driven to the tidal basin near East Potomac Park to tour the river in an old-fashioned paddleboat.

The only thing keeping Melanie from completely enjoying this fabulous weekend was the ominous task she knew lay before her. At some point she had to tell Will about her relationship with John before Candace had the opportunity to confuse him with her twisted and vengeful version of the truth. As she bought more time by trying to fortify her courage with sunlight, her fiancé brought Candace up in conversation.

"What's up with your girl? Why she have to do Griffin like that?"

"She's not exactly my girl anymore. And Candace plays by her own set of rules," Melanie replied.

"Wrong is wrong. You said that the man is married with kids. It wasn't right for her to interfere in someone's relationship like that, especially when she's got a man of her own—a man who loves, or should I say *loved*, her. I don't blame Griff for dumping her. I wouldn't play that BS either. Trust is everything."

Melanie felt suddenly warm and uncharacteristically guilty. Perhaps now was the time to tell Will about John, though she was not sure how he would take knowing that John too was married. Somehow she'd have to make him see that she and John were nothing like Candace and Frank. As she sat quietly searching for the words to begin, Will expelled his own revelation.

"I need to tell you something. I don't want you to think I've been sneaky or controlling, but I've been doing a little job-hunting in New York," he admitted. "I've been offered a position and before I decide what to do, I want to talk it over with you."

"New York? That's wonderful!"

"It's a great job—a VP slot," he explained, relieved that her reaction was positive.

"You're sure you want to live in Manhattan? I mean, you're not just doing this for me?"

"I know how important your career is to you and if you need to be in New York, then that's where we'll live. I'll do whatever I have to to make you happy."

"It's not *your* job to make me happy. That's *my* job. And it's yours to do the same for you. I ran away from you the first time because I was afraid of assuming that kind of responsibility. But if we're going to make it, we both have to be satisfied as *individuals*."

"You know, in a lot of ways our breakup was good for us," Will said. "It gave us the chance to get to know each other on an even deeper level. I can't speak for you, but it really made me look at myself and what I wanted out of life."

"Me too. And I finally know that you're the man I want to grow old and fat with," Melanie said, feeling grateful that their relationship had risen to such an awesome level. "But we've got to talk about something else."

"You're right. Kids. I know that you're not ready now, but I do want children at some point. At least two; I don't want to raise an only child, it's too lonely a life."

"Two sounds great—eventually. I don't want my legacy to be simply pretty rooms scattered around the world," she said, repeating the same thoughts she'd shared with John. "I want a couple of little knuckleheads running around making me proud, just like their father. Besides, it would be a crime to waste all that Santa Claus talent you've got going."

Will reached over and pulled Melanie to his heart. "God, I love you."

"Me too, baby," she said before getting lost in his kiss. Will pulled back with a satisfied sigh. He'd never felt so fortunate and content. The pain and turmoil of this past year had been worth the two hours they'd spent in this tiny little boat. As he sat there, bubbling over with anticipation and love, Will had never been more certain that Melanie was his true love and soulmate.

"You know what being on this water makes me think of? Venice. I can't think of a more romantic place to spend our honeymoon, can you?" he asked.

"Italy sounds perfect. I hear that there is nothing like a sunset over St. Mark's Square."

"Well, the sooner you make up your mind when you want to marry me, the sooner we can get there," Will teased.

Melanie reached into the river and let her hand trail along the water as she tried to once again broach the subject of John Carlson. She knew that until that issue was announced and whatever fallout settled, their wedding plans would have to remain on hold.

"Will . . ."

"Yes?" he said, running his finger tenderly down the side of her face. Melanie turned her eyes to the clouds, unwilling to look at Will's face.

"I have to tell you something . . . about someone I met while we were apart."

"I know all about the guy from work. He's the same one that called the day I went apartment-hunting with you. Look, I don't want to know the details. If the experience made you realize that I was the one for you, then I have nothing but thanks for the brother. We're together now and as long as I'm the only man you love, that's all that matters."

Melanie saw the unconditional love in his eyes and could not bring herself to break the spell. Maybe it wasn't necessary to tell him the whole truth. If Will was able to accept the *idea* of her relationship, perhaps the gritty details best remained undisclosed, particularly since she and John were over.

"Well, then," she said, "I hear Venice is lovely in October."

# Chapter 26

"Melanie, Austin Riley from Carlson and Tuck is on line two," the receptionist announced.

Melanie quickly picked up the phone, more anxious to uncover any information about John than to talk with Austin. Yes, their relationship was over, but Melanie certainly had not stopped caring about the man or what he might be going through.

"Mel, I just got the status report in on the Casa de Arte. Looks like they're ready for us to start on the interior, so I want to schedule a trip with you sometime in the next couple of weeks," Austin said.

"You'll be going down with me instead of John?"

"You haven't heard?" Austin's disclosure of John's accident and tentative condition caused her to fly out the door and into the first available cab.

Twenty minutes later, the taxi dropped her in front of St. Paul's Hospital. She hurried through the front door and stopped at the gift shop to buy flowers before heading up to the critical care unit. As she traveled up the elevator to the fifth floor, it suddenly occurred to her that Sharon Carlson would most probably be at her husband's bedside. Panic overtook her.

This was not the time or place for any type of scene and Melanie was in no frame of mind to properly defend herself and their relationship. But she needed to see how John was faring. What should she do? Neither fight nor flight seemed an acceptable option, so when the elevator doors opened, she steeled herself for whatever close encounter might occur and forged ahead.

She walked up to the nurses' station and while the RN on duty finished her phone call, Mel studied the large patient board on the far wall, noting John's name and room number. When the woman concluded her conversation, Melanie asked to see John, and was politely but adamantly informed that only family members were allowed to visit patients in the CCU. Obviously unable to pass for a sister or cousin, a disappointed Melanie turned away, her concern multiplied tenfold. She had to find a way to see him, instinctively knowing that this could well be her last time.

As she stepped back into the main corridor, she noticed the nurse leave the desk and disappear into another area. Melanie looked around and, seeing no other staff members, walked quickly down the hall to John's room. She took a quick peek through the glass window in the door to make sure that the room was empty before stepping inside.

Shock immediately sucked the air from her lungs when she saw the multitude of tubes and equipment hooked up to John's body. He appeared so lifeless and the idea of this talented, compassionate man being kept alive by machines deeply saddened her. She felt a tear slide down her face. She caught the salty drop on her tongue and commanded herself not to cry.

Melanie quickly glanced toward the door before reaching out to take John's limp hand in hers. She took a long look at him, noting how peaceful he looked and how his face—unadorned by his charming smile and curious eyes—looked remarkably older.

"Can you hear me?" she asked in a half whisper as she caressed the soft topside of his gifted hand. Melanie paused for a moment and looked toward the door to make sure that they were still alone.

"You have to get well, my sweet. There is so much we have to talk about. I want to tell you how fabulous The Jewel is. You are such an amazing artist.

"And there's something else I want to tell you. I'm officially engaged to Will. I'm finally ready to get married, and it's all because of you," she said, finding it difficult to keep her tears at bay.

Still clutching his hand, Melanie closed her eyes and sent both John and Sharon love and light before releasing a prayer up to God. She asked the Spirit to watch over her beloved friend, heal his body as he rested, and return him to his vigorous former self.

"John, fight hard to get better. There is a lot of love here waiting for you. I know things are kind of messy right now, but if you need me, I promise to help you through whatever is waiting for you when you return. So get well soon." Melanie finished speaking and gently squeezed his hand. Miraculously, she felt faint pressure being applied to hers.

Initially Mel wasn't sure if she'd simply imagined the squeeze, but before she had a chance to second-guess his action, John once again lightly pressed the pinky side of her hand.

"I'll take that as a yes," she said softly, smiling down on him. Melanie immediately sent up a grateful thank-you, brought her lips to John's forehead for a brief kiss, and turned to go. She looked up and saw a woman peering through the glass, wearing a stricken expression on her face. Their gazes locked for a brief moment and Melanie instantly recognized Sharon Carlson from the pictures in John's office. She also recognized the look in her eyes. It was indignant disbelief. Sharon turned and ran down the hall.

"Mrs. Carlson, wait, please," Melanie called out after her.

Sharon ignored the summons as she hurried down the hall and away from her husband's mistress. She slipped into the ladies' room and locked the door behind her before breaking down into hysterical sobs. Her thoughts came fast and furious. It was now clear that her marriage was over. The fact that John had picked someone so totally different was a blunt and direct admission that he no longer desired her.

For weeks she had tried to envision his lover. From blond waif to redhead temptress to raven-locked socialite, Sharon pictured her in a hundred variations of height and bust size, age and hair color, but never had it entered her mind . . . never would she have believed that John would betray her with a black woman.

The rush of feelings overwhelmed her. Surprise, outrage, defeat—the list was long and distressing. The news that John was having an affair had been devastating enough, but the fact that his mistress was African-American seemed to make it even worse. Somehow it made more sense that John would have an affair with a woman who was younger, richer, or prettier than her. Who couldn't understand a man losing his mind over a supermodel? But choosing Jax over her made Sharon feel like a big loser in this crazy game of three's a crowd.

Sharon had to admit that she was very pretty for a black woman—petite, well groomed, glowing brown skin, beautiful eyes and lips. There was a compelling exoticness about Jax that was in direct contrast to Sharon's WASPy whiteness. If that's what John desired in a woman, what could she do? She could make herself look younger, thinner, and even change her eye and hair color, but how could she change her race?

*What about this black girl is so unbelievable that he would risk his marriage?* Sharon wondered. And what could they possibly have in common? They were of two different ethnic groups, two different cultures, and apparently two different generations. Jay-Z and Billy Joel didn't go together. Nor did black-eyed peas and Beef Wellington. But they were obviously in love—her letters had made that point very clear.

Sharon did not want to acknowledge how much John's liaison with a woman of color shocked, disappointed, and embarrassed her. She revisited the scene she had just witnessed. Jax's dark hand holding John's pale one. The contrast of her brown face as she reached down to kiss his white skin. She never really examined her feelings about interracial dating because it had never impacted her life before. But *that* woman with *her* husband? The idea offended her.

*How could John fall in love with her?* she wondered as anger and humiliation stepped up to replace her confusion and dismay. Ugly questions, steeped in deeply buried racism, continued to nag Sharon's brain and worm their way into her heart. *Did he take her out in public? Do any of our friends know he has a black girlfriend?*

Sharon was ashamed to admit that there was a remote corner of her heart that almost wished John would die before he had the chance to dump her. In death, she'd be his widow instead of his humiliated ex-wife. She wouldn't be subject to the sad and sorry whispers of how he'd left her to be with a black woman. She wouldn't be the butt of jokes about her husband preferring his sugar brown.

Sharon stepped closer to the sink and took a long look at the woman in the mirror, disgusted by what she saw. The woman star-ing back was not only a weak and defective wife, but a racist as well. She had failed twice—once as a spouse, and then as a human being.

A knock on the door temporarily brought an end to Sharon's pity party. "Be just a minute," she said as she quickly blew her nose and fixed her face. She reached for the doorknob and froze. What if Jax was standing on the other side waiting for some sort of I-don't-care-if-you-are-his-wife-he's-mine confrontation?

"Sharon, are you in there?" Gwen Robinson's voice came through the door.

Sharon breathed a sigh of relief as she opened the door. She nearly knocked Gwen over as she rushed out of the bathroom and headed toward the elevator.

"Where are you going? Are you okay? What's wrong? Is it John?" The questions fell out of Gwen's mouth one after another, landing on deaf ears. "Sharon, what is the matter with you?"

"I saw her . . . Jax . . . she was in the room with John. She kissed him," Sharon said before bursting into tears.

"Honey, I'm sorry. What did she say?"

"Nothing. We just looked at each other. I ran away and she came after me, but I wouldn't stop. Gwen . . . she's . . ."

"She's what?"

"Black." Sharon looked at her best friend's face, unable to judge if Gwen's look of surprise was due to her news or to a politically incorrect reaction. "I know it shouldn't matter, but it does," she admitted.

Silence fell between them, neither knowing what to say. Gwen took her friend's arm and guided her into the stairwell to afford them some privacy.

"I hate him. I *hate* him," Sharon declared with mounting resolve. At this moment she despised her husband more than ever. Hated him for putting her in this uncomfortable position of questioning herself as a woman, a wife, and a person. For bringing her deep insecurities to the surface and making her confront feelings and issues of race she'd never before bothered to examine.

"Why? Because you think he picked a black woman over you?"

"*No!* Yes . . . maybe. I'm not prejudiced, but I can't help feeling like I've been slapped in the face. How could he love her over me?"

"If she were brunette and white, would you be saying the same thing?" Gwendolyn asked.

Sharon stood, playing with her wedding ring nervously while taking a moment to dredge up her true feelings. "I don't think so. Somehow that makes more sense to me, and is not so final. He obviously wants someone totally different than me. How can I compete with a black woman? I can't. So it's over."

"First of all, it isn't a competition. His choice has nothing to do with you or your self-worth, and second, we all have racist feelings and thoughts, and situations like this shock them to the surface. It's just unfortunate that you're having to deal with the cracks in your marriage at the same time."

"I've got to get out of here," Sharon decided, unwilling to explore her complicated feelings in public. The two walked back into the corridor and stood in silence as they waited for the elevator. The quiet continued as they rode down to the ground floor, neither woman knowing what to say in this confusing and complex situation.

Melanie sat in the lobby, her eyes directed toward the bank of elevators. She'd decided to wait, feeling she owed it to John to explain her presence and their relationship to his wife. It was apparent that John's accident could not have been more mis-timed. He'd obviously never had the opportunity to talk to Sharon, to tell her how much he loved her and wanted to work things out.

The doors on the far left opened and as the women advanced Melanie felt herself tensing, unable to take her eyes off of John's mate. Sharon looked different than she'd imagined. She was elegant but not glamorous and definitely not the society maven Mel had envisioned. She was dressed in expensive beige slacks, a baby blue cashmere sweater set, and comfortable Ferragamo loafers. Her blond hair was pulled back into a ponytail and her makeup was simple and natural. So natural, in fact, Mel could see the dark circles under her swollen and red eyes and other telling signs of stress and worry. Melanie felt compelled to reach out. She did not want today's visit to make the situation between Sharon and John any more tense than it must already be.

"Mrs. Carlson," Mel said as they come closer. "We've never met. I'm—"

"I know who you are," Sharon replied, cocking her head slightly to the left.

Her venomous tone sent an anxious chill through Melanie, freeze-drying her brain and, along with it, her ability to think. Should she apologize? If so, for what? Though sensitive to Sharon's pain, Mel could not bring herself to feel wrong about her feelings for the woman's husband.

"If you have a minute, I'd really like to talk with you."

"I have nothing to say to you. Haven't you done enough to ruin my life? Why are you stalking me?"

"I'm not stalking you. I came to see John."

"Why? You don't belong here, I don't care if you are his lover."

"But that's why we need to talk. You don't understand every-thing. I think I can help you—"

"I understand enough," Sharon said, angrily cutting her off. "I am not interested in anything you have to say and I certainly don't need any help from *you*. So stop flaunting your miserable existence in my face. And don't you dare show up at this hospital again or I'll call the police and have you charged with harassment." Sharon stormed away, leaving Melanie and Gwen in the lobby.

"John and I weren't having an affair," Melanie told the woman, steeling herself for another verbal assault.

"Sure didn't look that way by the letters you wrote or the kiss you just delivered," Gwen countered.

"It was a kiss on the forehead. I swear to you, John loves her. She's the only woman he wants and I have to let her know that."

"Now is not the time. Maybe later. She's dealing with a lot right now."

"I know. Please take this," Melanie said, handing Gwendolyn her business card. "Will you give it to her and tell her if she wants to talk to call me?"

Gwen accepted the card and slid it into her jacket pocket. "I have to say either you're the gutsiest girlfriend I've ever seen or you're telling the truth."

"I am telling the truth," Mel said, looking her directly in the eye. "And Sharon needs to know that before she says or does something she'll regret."

"You did *what*?" Francesca screamed. Melanie pulled the phone away from her ear and her sister's surprised and disapproving voice.

"After she saw me in John's room she was pretty upset, so I waited for her in the lobby."

"That was really a mean thing to do."

"How so? I just wanted to talk with her and explain the situation. She has it all wrong," Mel said as the frustration began to rise up her chest.

"Come on, Melanie. The poor woman finds out that her husband has been having an affair one day before he has an accident that puts him in a coma. Then she shows up at the hospital only to find the 'other woman' by his bedside, holding hands with her man. Stand in her pumps for a minute. How do you think she must feel?"

"You know what? I'm really sorry about all this, but does anyone give a damn about how I feel?" Melanie exploded with an anger she hadn't realized she was harboring. "She's allowed to grieve and her friends and family are rallying around her with all their love and sympathy. She doesn't have to make up excuses to explain why she's so concerned. She can pick up the phone and call any number of people and talk about John. What about me? People know me as his colleague. Not his confidante or close friend. I'm John Carlson's big secret. I turn to my family for support and all I get is a lecture about how I have no business being a part of his life. And for the last time, goddamn it, *we weren't having an affair*."

"Melanie, I know this is tough on you, but you have to know that seeing you hurt her. And you also have to know that you might be part of his *life*, but you aren't a part of his *family*. That is a huge and defining difference. And you've got to come out of this dream world and realize that it doesn't matter what *you* want to call it, to the rest of us who aren't living so lofty in the Universe, it looks like you *are* having an affair with the man. You said it yourself—you're his secret, which last I recall means something hidden or clandestine or concealed. So, if you two truly believed that you were just friends, why all the hiding?"

Melanie had no retort that would make sense to her sister or to Sharon Carlson. She could only concur with John's thoughts in his farewell letter. The world was not ready for a love like theirs. It was funny how far society had come and so sad how very far it still had to go. Thanks to the martyrs and heroes that had insisted on living life on *their* terms, interracial relationships, interfaith, and even gay marriages were now tolerated. But the idea of an intimate and loving bond between a man and a woman separate and apart from their spouses was still an objectionable blemish on the face of morality.

Melanie found no comfort in her conversation with Francesca, but she came to two important realizations. First, Franti was right: No matter how she and John labeled their relationship, the minds and hearts of most of the world were too small to see anything other than scandal. And second, based on Sharon's reaction, she could never tell Will about John Carlson.

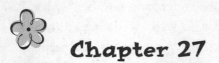

# Chapter 27

**S**haron walked through the guest bedroom, picking up Amanda's wet towels and dirty clothes. The girl had been staying with her since John's accident and in so many ways she behaved like a typical teenager. Messy room, music blaring, dirty dishes left all over the house. These were the things that, while vaguely annoying, also let Sharon know that Mandy was behaving like a normal teenager and not a young woman, who in less than five weeks was about to give birth.

Amanda's presence was also a blessing, helping to keep her mind off John and their situation. It had been forty-two days since the car crash, and he still had not regained consciousness and his prognosis remained uncertain. For Sharon it was like living a life sentence in purgatory. Since the day before his accident, her entire existence had become a wait-and-see proposition. While the world and all its inhabitants were spinning ahead, Sharon felt like she was standing still, glued to the exact spot where her life had begun to fall apart.

The base of this adulterous interracial triangle was an agonizing position. Since her encounter at the hospital with Jax, a.k.a. Melanie Hitts, as she learned from the business card the woman had the audacity to give Gwen, Sharon felt more depressed than ever. Their meeting had been an agonizing and disappointing personal exposé. She simply could not understand how her husband could fall in love with a woman who was 180 degrees different than him and his lifestyle. She tried to push the racial aspect out of the way and deal with the more important realities of the situation, but like a boulder blocking the road to her happiness, it refused to budge.

Sharon began to strip the bed and wondered about the last time she'd been happy. Really happy. She thought back through her childhood and teen years but no truly joyful memories jumped out. Oh, there were times when she felt pleased and mollified but never full of bliss. The day she married John perhaps came the closest, but none before and certainly none since. In truth, her melancholy attitude had been wrapped in a veneer of false pleasure for as long as she could remember.

As she snapped the top sheet into the air and watched it float toward the bed, Sharon realized that she was a master at faking happiness. She'd learned as a child to smile pretty, suck up disappointment, and expect nothing from anybody, especially the ones who were supposed to love her best. It was her grandparents who drilled into her head that self-sacrifice was admirable, self-gratification a sin. And as long as you went with the program—any program other than your own—the people you loved would continue to love you and keep coming back. But they didn't. Eventually they all left for good. Her parents had. Then her grandparents. And now John.

Like Chicken Little, Sharon felt like the sky was falling, raining down on her head all the personal revelations and pent-up anger that she'd spent years burying deep inside. She was angry at her parents, angry at John, and most of all angry at herself for being too weak to be her own woman. Living life through her husband meant that Sharon never had to summon the courage to identify and pursue her own desires. She'd spent a lifetime giving herself away in order to make others happy. And now she felt whittled down to nothing.

"Sharon, I'm ready if you are," Amanda called up the stairs, interrupting Sharon's painful introspection.

"I'll be right down." Sharon smoothed out the comforter and walked into the hallway, thinking about the young girl downstairs who had entered her life and opened her eyes. Even as a teenager, Amanda Weiss was practically fearless. She was not afraid to live life on her own terms, regardless of what her parents or anyone else thought. Most of all, she was not afraid to make blunders, endure the consequences, and move on. She knew at sixteen what Sharon was just learning at forty-five—that mistakes were not mistakes until you repeated them. Until then they were simply lessons to be learned.

Curiosity caused Sharon to step lightly and quickly down the stairs. She was keenly interested in what conclusion Amanda had come to concerning the future of her baby. They had talked for weeks about the various options available, and now, with the arrival of both her child and parents imminent, it was time to finalize her decision.

Amanda still didn't know that her folks had been aware of their daughter's pregnancy for some time now. Nor did she realize that she was living with Sharon with their permission. Despite Mandy's refusal to disclose her condition, Sharon hadn't felt right about keeping the Sarbains in the dark about such a monumental event in their young daughter's life. She'd been in periodic touch with Catherine since Christmas and found the woman rather frosty and unfeeling. It amazed Sharon that Amanda, such a bundle of empathetic warmth and worldly exhilaration, was the product of such a compassionless and self-centered woman.

Regardless of Catherine's attitude, Sharon was glad she'd followed her instincts and made the call. Amanda's mother had been livid about the pregnancy. She first tried to unsuccessfully blame Sharon for not convincing her child to have an abortion. Sharon was appalled that Catherine would relinquish such moral responsibility on a woman who'd known her child less than a year. Even after hearing the full story, Catherine placed all fault squarely on Amanda's shoulders. It never crossed her mind that if she was home being a mother instead of gallivanting all over the Orient with her third husband, this might have never happened.

Sharon had kept this information from Amanda, feeling it was better for her to believe that her parents still didn't know, rather than face the ugly reality that they didn't care. Amanda's mother seemed more worried about what the gossipmongers might think about *her* than about the crisis her daughter was going through.

"So you've decided what you'll tell your folks?" Sharon asked while making herself comfortable on the couch.

"The way I see it, I only have one choice. Keeping the baby is not an option. Catherine and Nelson would rather die first and I can't raise a baby now, it wouldn't be fair. So I've decided to give it up for adoption."

"That's a very loving thing for you to do," Sharon concurred. "Children really should have *two* parents who love them."

"Yeah, but how do I know that they won't treat my baby the way my folks treat me?" Amanda asked. Sharon was touched by the teenager's innate sense of maternal love while torn by her feelings of abandonment.

"For every crazy person who you see on the news accused of abusing their child, there are hundreds of thousands more who love their adopted children. We'll find a good home for your baby. You don't have to worry about that."

"I wouldn't worry at all if you adopted it," Amanda said, finally voicing what she'd been thinking for weeks.

Sharon listened intently to the sound of the words she'd heard so many times in her head but had never dared to utter aloud. For months she'd been living vicariously through the teenager's pregnancy—soaking up the experience through all the cravings, discoveries, and Lamaze techniques that come with expecting a child. And during it all, she had constantly turned that option over in her mind, studying it from every conceivable angle, only to determine it to be a solution riddled with impossibility. Still, hearing such a request from the closest facsimile to a daughter she could claim was cause for Sharon to yet again stop and ponder the possibility.

"You were meant to have kids. It's like you're wasting your talents by not having any," Amanda said with fervent sincerity.

Talent. There was that word again ringing in her head like a bell reminding Sharon of the how-to article she'd read about creating her own life. She thought about her volunteer work at both the children's hospital and the nursing home and the joy it brought her, as well as the pleasure she'd found befriending and mentoring Amanda. Maybe loving and caring about people was her special talent.

*But you still weren't skilled enough to keep your husband*, Sharon's wicked self-doubt reminded her. And with that doubt came the prompt dismissal of her adopting Amanda's baby. How could she take care of a child when she wasn't even certain she could take care of herself? And what would people think about her being a single mom?

"Amanda, I just can't make that kind of commitment right now. My life is in too much turmoil, with John in the hospital and . . ." *my marriage being over,* Sharon thought, but didn't verbalize. "I have to consider the entire situation."

"Are you? I mean, have you thought about the possibility that Mr. Carlson might never wake up? What if he stays in a coma, or worse? Then what?" Amanda asked, her gentle tone relaying her concern.

To be so young, this girl was very wise. Whether due to John's affair or his accident, any way Sharon looked at the situation, all bets on the future she'd once imagined for her and John were off. He could die, divorce her, or remain in a coma for the rest of his life. She could not continue to live in this suspended animation. Fate was forcing Sharon Carlson to take charge of her own life.

*If John can have his love on the side, why can't I?* she decided with defiance. *I'm tired of pretending that I don't mind not having children—because I do. And I'm tired of pretending that I'm happy when I'm not, or that I'm willing to move—when I don't want to. It's time I start taking responsibility for my own life and happiness.*

"Amanda, I'd love to help raise your child," Sharon announced, clearing the remnant fog of her epiphany with a smile. "I'm sure we can work something out so we can both play a role in your baby's life."

Mandy let go a happy holler and pushed her body into Sharon's for a hug. Just as quickly, she pulled away, grabbed Sharon's hand, and placed it over her stomach. Within moments, Sharon felt a swift kick against her hand. "I think the baby is happy about this too," Amanda announced. Her thrill over Sharon's decision was dampened only by the news she hadn't shared. Perhaps now was the time to tell her about Kevin.

*But what if she changes her mind once she finds out?* Amanda decided to wait. She'd tell Sharon later once everything had been worked out and there was less of a chance for her to reverse her decision.

As Sharon pulled the girl back into a hug, a thought popped into her head. *I don't want to raise this baby in New York.*

Before she could change her mind, Sharon got up and walked across the room. She picked up the phone and called the real estate agent, letting Fern know that she would not grant the extension and that the house was permanently off the market. Sharon hung up, amazed by her actions. In twenty-four years of marriage to John she had never made such a major decision without his approval. But she was not going to close the window on this sudden opportunity.

In a little more than a month, she was going to be a mother, she was going to raise her child in her own home, and John Carlson was in no position to stop her.

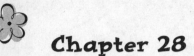

# Chapter 28

"If you do talk to him, will you tell him to give me a call?" Candace asked, frustration tingeing her voice. This was the fifth call she'd made to one of Griffin's actor friends, to no avail. Either they really didn't know where he was or the fraternal wall of silence was impenetrable. She wanted to explain to Griff why she lied, but he wouldn't give her the opportunity. Basically he'd tossed Candace out of his life without giving her a chance to make things right.

Candy checked her watch. She had to take a deposition at ten, which gave her another twenty-seven minutes to continue her missing-person investigation. On a whim she decided to take one last look through her e-mail. Hopefully Will had received her message and would come to her rescue with some information about Griff—anything to keep hope alive.

She clicked over to new mail and scrolled down through her mailbox, dismissing anything work-related. Candace felt her stomach jump with expectation when she came across a message from STILLWILL.

Subj: Re: SOS
From: STILLWILL
To: LOLLIPOP

Candace,

Sorry to hear about you and Griff, but you have to admit that what
you did was wrong. But I'm not here to judge, only to help out a
friend who was there for me when I needed one.

Griffin is in LA. He left shortly after he moved out of your place. The
studio put him up in a rented house in Laurel Canyon until they finish
shooting. I can't give you his address or telephone number because I
promised him I wouldn't, but I will personally deliver any message you
want to send. I have to be honest, though, he made it real clear to
both me and Mel that he's not interested in hearing from you.

I know this isn't great news, but hang in there. Who knows what
could happen once he's had a chance to cool down. I mean, look at
me. A year ago Mel and I were through and now we're making honeymoon plans for Italy!

Will

Candace read Will's hopeful words, but reality kept her from
believing them. If Griffin didn't want to hear from her now, he
never would. Sending a note or message via Will would be a
waste of time for all concerned. Griff had always been very clear
about how he felt about lying and cheating. Betrayal was non-
negotiable.

Why couldn't Griff be more like Will Freedman? She knew

Will well enough to know that his parting words about him and Melanie weren't meant as a gloat but as encouragement. Will was such a good man and friend. He was fine, in a teddy-bear kind of way, smart and had bank. Not only that, he was trusting and non-judgmental. Look how Will had let Melanie embarrass and hurt him, and still he took her back. There was a lot Griffin could learn from his friend—forgiveness, for starters.

What pissed off Candace most was the unfairness of this entire situation. While she was vilified for being such a conniving, two-timing cheat, Melanie was still flitting around wearing a halo and freshly starched angel wings. Melo was always so busy meditating and spouting off about truth and integrity, no one even suspected that she was just as deceitful and secretive as they all accused Candy of being.

*Well, I might be all of those things, but at least I'm a loyal friend,* Candace thought. *Which is far more than I can say for you, Melanie. Where does loyalty and allegiance fit into to all that spiritual goulash of yours?*

The hurt Candace felt over the demise of their relationship ran deep. Men came and went, but the bond between girlfriends should be ironclad. Sistafriends were the ones who always had your back, hooked you up when you were needy, shopped the hurt away when life came down hard. She had been Melanie's friend through her crisis, but when the stuff started to fly with Griffin, Mel had bailed without so much as a look back.

Candace didn't deserve that kind of betrayal and neither did Will. Funny how life turned out. The friendship she'd had with Melanie was over, but Will continued to be her friend and advocate, even though he was disappointed in her actions, which was more than she could say for his fiancée. Well, one loyal turn certainly deserved another. Will needed to know the truth. She hated to be the ant at his picnic, but it was better that he be hurt now than later after Melo married him under false pretenses.

"We can help each other pick up the pieces," she decided as she reached for her phone and dialed Will's number.


Will walked out of the Gold's Gym locker room and headed directly upstairs to the bag room. He pulled on his gloves and began pummeling the heavy bag, trying to beat out his anger and frustration over the latest descent in his up-and-down relationship with Melanie. With every blow he delivered, his fury mounted, and each exhale took the sound and form of the word *Why?*

*Why* had she agreed to marry him if she was in love with someone else? *Why* did she persist in yanking his chain and playing with his feelings? And *why,* after everything she'd put him through this past year, could he not get this woman out from under his skin?

He powerfully punched and pushed his leather opponent as if to prove his weakness for this woman was no reflection on his strength as a man. The sweat from his face mixed with his tears. His vision, blurred by the salty blend, seemed a symbolic view of his life. He could see nothing with clarity right now. Exhausted both emotionally and physically, he delivered one last blow and then wrapped his arms around the bag, his body collapsing against the rawhide before sliding onto the floor.

He sank down into the rubber mat, marveling how his life and that of his best friend were running parallel. Both men had been totally devastated by the women they genuinely believed to be their genie-granted wishes. How could they both have been so very wrong?

His relationship with Melanie was dead, and Will saw no chance of resurrection. He was tired of shadowboxing with her elusive sense of commitment. Was he second choice? Winner by default? If John Carlson weren't already married, would Melanie be making wedding plans with him?

She'd broken his heart twice now. A third break was not an option. His only chance for emotional survival was to rip a page from Melanie's manual on how to leave your lover. He would simply and immediately drop out of her life, just as she had done to him. The memories of that time had dulled with their recent reconnect, but they were still tender to the touch, an emotional bruise that hadn't quite healed. Her instantaneous departure had left him feeling as empty as a jack-o'-lantern—hollow inside, wearing a meaningless, frozen smile outside. At the time, he couldn't understand how she could be so cruel, but now the reasoning was as clear as that DeBeers isn't-she-worth-two-months'-salary diamond she was so brazenly wearing. To prolong the agony with talk and questions was masochistic. Leaving this way was quick and clean.

Will picked himself up off the floor and slowly treaded back toward the locker room. His head had finally accepted the fact that Melanie Hitts was never going to be his wife. Now if someone could convince his heart.

\* \* \*

Melanie sat in the dark, a single candle illuminating the printout of Will's short, parting e-mail. *I can't marry someone I can't trust.* Simple. Direct. Final.

What was happening? Just when she'd sorted out her feelings and put everything in its proper perspective, her personal life had become a gigantic mess. She was sadly incommunicado with the very people she'd come to depend on as her pillars of loving support. John was battling to get well. Candace and Will had apparently teamed up against her, both wrongfully accusing her of betrayal, each too hurt and angry to return her calls or listen to her explanations.

In hindsight, she was sorry she hadn't told Will everything about her relationship with John. Just as she'd feared, Candace had flung her vengeful tale, snaring Will in a net of half-truths and misinterpretations. What shocked her most was Will's readiness to believe Candy without so much as a question or confrontation. Didn't she at least deserve the chance to defend herself?

"What goes around comes around," Mel told herself, repeating the familiar karmic warning. In all fairness, she couldn't be angry with him. She could understand his confusion and pain. Will was working on the same unsettling level as Sharon Carlson, using assumptions to fill in the missing pieces of a puzzle, resulting in a painfully inaccurate picture. They both needed to know the truth, and with John in the hospital, she was the only one who could provide it. Melanie intended to find a way to make things right again.

John and Candace may be lost causes, but she refused to give up on Will. This year had come full circle and through the love of a good friend, she'd learned exactly how and with whom she wanted to live her life. There was no way that she was going to let William Gregory Freedman slip through her fingers for a second time. As soon as she returned from her business trip to South Beach, Melanie intended to do whatever it took to prove to Will that her love was true.

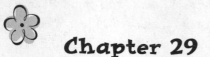

# Chapter 29

After sixty-two days without regaining consciousness, John's doctor recommended taking him off the respirator. Forty-eight hours later he was still comatose, but breathing on his own. The irony was not lost on Sharon that his CAT scan had detected increased brain activity following Melanie Hitts's visit. Apparently the woman had ways of stirring her husband that even a deep coma could not prevent.

It didn't matter what Gwen had revealed when she'd handed her Melanie Hitts's business card and delivered her message about the so-called reality of their relationship. What was she supposed to say, once she'd gotten caught trespassing in forbidden territory? John had briefly read from the same cue cards before his accident. "It's not what you think. I can explain everything." Sharon wasn't buying any of it. She'd seen the letters the woman had written—full of words declaring her love. And she'd witnessed the caring body language Melanie had exhibited at her husband's bedside.

*But what if they are telling the truth? What if John recuperates and decides he wants our marriage to continue?* she allowed herself to wonder. Between the bouts of anger came swells of hopefulness.

And with those swells the truth always buoyed to the top—she still loved John.

*He'll have to accept me, with the baby, and in this house,* Sharon decided as Amanda came downstairs dressed for their meeting with her mother. Sharon watched as she lumbered around the kitchen. The girl's face was marked with exhaustion and apprehension. Both were to be expected now that she was in the final stages of her pregnancy, but they were even more evident due to the anticipation of seeing her mother after such a long time and under such dubious circumstances.

"Here's the mail," Amanda said, handing Sharon a pile of envelopes and catalogs. Sharon tucked them into her tote bag to read later when she went to visit John.

An hour and forty minutes later, the two women stepped off the train at Grand Central Station and proceeded to flag down a cab to take them uptown to the Sarbains' Fifth Avenue apartment. Amanda continually shifted in her seat, her discomfort both emotional and physical. They rode in nervous silence, each mentally preparing themselves for the meeting about to take place. Both were steeling themselves for an icy tête-à-tête with Catherine Sarbain—Amanda consumed with the guilt of disappointing her mother in this most public manner, and Sharon feeling the need to protect Mandy from the woman who should be her ultimate source of comfort and unconditional love.

When the driver stopped behind a diplomat's double-parked limousine, Amanda turned to Sharon and cleared her throat. "I need to tell you something," she stated in a serious tone that immediately caused Sharon alarm.

"What is it, honey?"

"It's about Kevin."

"He hasn't changed his mind about the adoption, has he?" Sharon said, her panic increasing.

"No, but there is something about him I haven't told you. About his background."

Sharon closed her eyes as a myriad of possibilities ran through her head.

"He's African-American." That bombshell, accompanied by a painful moan, left Amanda's mouth. Sharon opened her eyes and focused on Amanda. Her eyebrows were knit together, framing a grimace of pain and confusion. Suddenly she closed her eyes and opened her mouth, the strain on her face screaming out in silent pain.

"Honey, what's wrong?" she asked as Amanda grabbed her stomach and released another small groan. Sharon was concerned, but also grateful for the distraction, as she had no idea how she felt about Amanda's revelation.

"I feel funny and I've got cramps."

"How long have you been having pains?"

"They started late last night."

"Why didn't you say something?" Sharon asked, trying not to sound as alarmed as she felt.

"They kept coming and going. I'm not due for another two weeks so I thought they were those Braxton Hicks things. Oh, God, I think I just peed on myself," Amanda whispered.

Sharon noticed the thighs of Amanda's maternity jeans were wet. "Driver, change of destination. Mount Sinai Hospital, please. And hurry," she requested, choosing the hospital nearest to the Sarbains'.

Amanda held tight to Sharon's hand as they rode the rest of the way in silence. Outwardly, as Sharon helped time the contrac-

tions, she appeared calm and reassuring. Inwardly, she was cracking like a crystal water goblet at a Jessye Norman recital. Was this
some kind of wacky practical joke the fates were playing on her?
Be careful what you wish for, you just might get it? Or was this a
we-are-the-world tutorial? God's artistic use of poetic justice to
teach her a lesson about the brotherhood of man?

Dazed, Sharon pinched herself, hoping the pain would wake
her up from this progressively bizarre nightmare. The small bruise
on her arm was proof enough that she was indeed awake, even if
she felt like she had fallen into the Twilight Zone. Suddenly a
decision that had felt so right now was being punched full of
holes by questions with answers that only created more questions.

Why hadn't Amanda revealed this information sooner? And
had she done so, would Sharon still have agreed to adopt this
baby? She had agreed to raise Amanda's child as a single parent,
knowing what a challenge that would be, but to raise a biracial
child into adulthood by herself? She was a white, middle-aged,
suburban housewife. What did she know about raising a child of
color? And what if it was a boy? She'd seen articles about African-
American men being called an endangered species. If this was
true, what expertise did she have to teach this child about surviv-
ing this world as a black man? That was veering off into
uncharted waters without so much as a compass. Particularly considering her recent revelations about her personal attitudes about
race.

*Am I capable of loving a child who is so different than me?* she
wondered. *Can I go through a lifetime of people staring at me and
this child? Whispering behind their backs, wondering how we could be
connected?*

She was forced to push all this to the side when they arrived at the hospital. Amanda's labor pains were ten minutes apart, Sharon informed the nurse after introducing herself as the labor coach. She left the girl in the capable hands of the medical staff in order to find the nearest pay phone and call Amanda's mother. When the maid told her that Mrs. Sarbain "was unavailable at the moment," Sharon left a hasty message asking her to meet them at the hospital and adding that Catherine's daughter urgently needed her. Sharon hung up, furious that the woman wasn't home, especially since she should be expecting them to arrive at any moment.

Sharon quickly dropped more money into the phone and punched in Gwen's number. She needed her own source of support as she readied herself to bring this child into the world. Gwendolyn had been her rock throughout all this turmoil and Sharon was forever grateful for their friendship. Once agreeing to the adoption, Gwen had helped her find a lawyer to make it a legal reality. Sharon was surprised to learn that it was all so easy. She alone could adopt the baby. As long as Amanda and Kevin gave their consent, the baby was hers and neither John nor Catherine Sarbain could stop her. Sharon didn't anticipate any resistance from any of the parties concerned, as she seemed to be the only one who earnestly wanted to keep and raise this baby. Or had, until half an hour ago. Now she wasn't so sure.

Gwen wasn't home either. Sharon left a message, leaving out Amanda's taxicab confession, and hung up. She took a moment to ask God to help them both get safely through this experience and then hurried back to Amanda, who had quickly progressed into active labor and had been taken to a labor/delivery room.

Sharon and Amanda worked together, breathing through each contraction just as they'd learned in Lamaze class. While Sharon coached her through each breath and massaged her lower back, she tried to keep her poisonous thoughts from derailing her concentration. She couldn't help thinking that this baby would be a cruel lifetime reminder of John and Melanie's dalliance. Did she really want to put herself through that? Sharon wished so much that she could freeze this moment and take some much-needed time to think about what she was really getting into.

An hour later, Amanda was close to being fully dilated and nearly ready to push. Sharon once again left the room to call the apartment and was told that Catherine had received the message. The maid offered no further information and Sharon, trying to keep her anger in check, hurried back to the labor/delivery room.

"Is my mom coming?" Amanda asked as Sharon wiped the girl's forehead.

"She's on her way," Sharon said, not knowing if it was true or not. No more talk was exchanged when Amanda let out a huge cry of pain.

"I think this baby is ready to make an appearance," the doctor said as he and the nurse prepared for the actual delivery. While they spread the sterile drapes and arranged their instruments, Sharon talked to Amanda, softly congratulating her on being so brave and wonderful, encouraging her to hang in there. Even though her labor had progressed quickly for a first-time pregnancy, Amanda was exhausted.

"Where's my mom?" Amanda asked again, squeezing Sharon's hand.

"She'll be here soon," Sharon promised, cursing Catherine Sarbain all the while.

Sharon stood at Amanda's side, positioned where she could both provide comfort and witness the actual birth. She watched in amazement as the baby's head began to crown. The doctor instructed Mandy to stop pushing as he helped ease the head out. Sharon observed in quiet awe as they suctioned the baby's nose and mouth before assisting the shoulders and torso. The rest of the body slid out easily, and immediately the room came alive with the thin cry of their newborn son.

"It's a boy!" Sharon told Amanda as she gave her a warm kiss. Mandy gazed with intense curiosity at her baby as the doctor placed him on her abdomen. He was a wrinkled, slightly scrawny, puffy-eyed bundle, not quite the little cherub she'd expected. His head was huge and slightly pointed and covered with a thatch of straight black hair. She tried to find herself and Kevin in his face, but the baby was still too smooshed from his journey through the birth canal to really tell.

Physically, she was tired and thirsty, relieved that this part of the ordeal was over. Emotionally, Amanda was a mishmash of feelings. She felt vaguely connected to this child, and yet strangely disengaged. More like a sister than a mother. Maybe it was the circumstances surrounding his conception and birth that prevented her from feeling particularly maternal. Or maybe she was just like Catherine—a depressing thought that made her glad she had decided to give the baby to Sharon. Amanda reached out and lightly brushed the baby's wet head. Even though she didn't want to raise this child, she was glad that Sharon did, so she could still maintain some contact.

"Would you like to cut the umbilical cord?" the doctor asked Sharon. She nervously snipped the cord right above the clamp and the nurse immediately whisked the newborn away to the warming table to clean him up and evaluate his condition. Once he was declared healthy and fit, the nurse swaddled the infant and presented him to Amanda.

"Why don't you give him to his mother?" Amanda suggested as her true emotions emerged. Mandy smiled as she watched the woman she viewed as her best friend fall in love with her baby, just like a *real* parent would. Seeing them together, Amanda realized that the reason she didn't feel like a mom was because all along she'd considered herself a surrogate for Sharon. She was so happy that the news about Kevin had not dissuaded Sharon from wanting her baby.

Sharon accepted the newborn and examined every aspect of his angelic face. His skin was light, with undertones more yellow than pink. The rims of his little ears were darker, revealing that his true skin color would deepen. Sharon peered into this child's open eyes and touched his tiny hands, counting every wonderful finger. Her earlier apprehensions about Melanie and John, about race and color and her ability to love past them tried to barge their way into this tender moment, but the realization that she already adored this tiny little creature blocked their advance.

"Happy birthday, baby boy," she whispered as she cuddled him closer. Sharon reached over to hold Amanda's hand, overwhelmed with emotion for both her baby and his birth mother. This was such an amazing and sacred exchange between them. A mutual gift, wrapped in unqualified love and blind trust.

"What are you going to name him?" Amanda asked.

"I don't know. I haven't really decided," Sharon admitted before the nurse gently took him from her arms and carried him off to the nursery.

"I like Craig Arthur Carlson," Amanda weighed in.

"Amanda Rose, are you in here?" an affected voice interrupted, before the poster child for New York's social register burst through the door. "Oh, my God. You've already delivered," Catherine Sarbain gasped. She surveyed the scene with a critical eye before going to her daughter and delivering a perfunctory kiss.

"Hi, Mommy," Amanda said, sounding like the young girl she still was. "I had a boy."

"Are you all right?" Catherine inquired, completely ignoring the reference to her newborn grandson.

"Yes. This is Sharon Carlson. I'm sorry you had to find out this way, but I didn't know how to tell you," Amanda said before breaking into tears. Sharon's heart broke for her as she watched Mandy drowning in self-recrimination while looking desperately toward her mother to toss her a forgiving lifeline.

"I already knew, darling. Sharon told me months ago," Catherine admitted, pushing a stray hair from the girl's face. Amanda looked up at Sharon, her eyes full of confusion. Sharon knew exactly what she was thinking, and after all the girl had been through, Sharon couldn't bear the thought of Amanda being hurt this way.

"I'm sorry, Amanda, but I thought it was best that your mother knew what was going on, so I called her in Tokyo. She wanted to come right away, but I finally convinced her to wait until you were closer to delivering," Sharon said as she looked first at Amanda and then at Catherine. "But we hadn't anticipated cutting it quite this close," she said, trying to add a bit of levity.

"Yes, dear. It was Sharon's idea that I wait or you know I would have come immediately," Catherine lied, suddenly feeling embarrassed by her delay not only in returning to the States, but getting to the hospital. She didn't reveal that she'd been sitting in the lobby for twenty minutes trying to figure out how to deal with the situation. How could this have happened? Yes, she knew of at least three of her friends whose daughters had found themselves in this unfortunate predicament, but they didn't have the child. If only Amanda had come to her she would have taken care of it quickly and quietly before anyone was the wiser. But not only had Amanda carried the baby to term, she had actually given birth in New York. They'd agreed that Sharon would arrange for the birth to take place in a Connecticut hospital, not in Catherine's own backyard.

"Mommy, Sharon is going to adopt the baby and she's going to let me see him whenever I want," Amanda said, unable to contain her yawn.

"Really. That is very nice of her, isn't it?" Catherine said, arching her right eyebrow in surprise. "You're tired, dear. I've arranged for a private room, so while they move you and you get a little rest, Sharon and I need to have a little chat."

"How could you promise her that?" Catherine barked once they had settled into a niche off the corridor. "I agreed to this arrangement because I thought you would be taking this baby away and Amanda could get back to her normal life."

"This is the way Amanda wants it."

"I don't care what she wants. I am her mother."

*Then why don't you act like one?* Sharon wanted to scream at the woman. "Catherine, I've spent a lot of time with Amanda recently. I think she needs this connection to her child, and I have no problem with it."

"Is this about money? Well, you can forget about it. We will not pay you one cent."

"I don't *need* your money," Sharon said, appalled at the suggestion. "This is about your daughter and grandchild." Sharon could see the discomfort rising up under Catherine's perfectly made-up face.

"Well, it's really a moot point, because as soon as she has recovered, Amanda Rose will be going off to boarding school in England," Catherine said, once again refusing to acknowledge the baby.

"Don't do that to her," Sharon protested strongly. "Amanda is a wonderful girl. Sending her away like that will suffocate the life out of her."

"I don't think I need *you* to tell me what's best for my own child."

"I think you do, because you have no idea who Amanda is and how much she loves and needs you." *Despite the awful way you ignore her,* Sharon thought but didn't speak. "Do you know how I met your daughter? She was trying to steal a pair of jeans from Bloomingdale's."

"That's ridiculous! She has a very substantial allowance. Amanda does not need to steal anything."

"She didn't even want the jeans. She wanted to get caught so you would stay here with her, instead of going to Japan with your husband. Amanda didn't want to get pregnant. She didn't even want to have sex—not really. What she did want was for the boy she loved to love her back. Maybe if she felt loved at home, she wouldn't have had to look elsewhere for it."

"She told you all of this?" Catherine asked. The harsh impact of the truth caused her voice to crumble along with her haughty demeanor.

"Yes. We talk quite a bit. And she'd talk to you too if you'd only pay attention to her and act like you're interested in who she *really* is—not who you want her to be. Catherine, Amanda is a remarkable young woman. She has given me back a part of myself I didn't even know I'd lost. Don't cheat yourself out of experiencing her love. And don't cheat her out of yours."

"I do love her. I do," Catherine insisted, finally revealing some tenderness. "It's just that she's so different from me. We don't like the same things or people. I don't understand her."

"She's a teenager. You're not supposed to like the same things."

"And my life . . . well, it's so complicated."

"That's definitely something we have in common."

"I just got married again and this time it has to work. I refuse to be divorced a third time. Nelson travels so much. I'm afraid if I'm not with him, I'll lose him."

"Trying to keep a marriage together is hard, but what kind of man makes you choose between him and your child?" Sharon asked.

"Nelson likes Amanda. He wanted her to come with us to Tokyo, but she said no, and I agreed because we'd just gotten married. Amanda is very stubborn and independent. I thought she'd be okay. . . ." Catherine's voice trailed off as she too heard the frailty of her excuses.

"Spend some time with your daughter. Talk with her. You'll find out that she needs her mother. In fact, she asked for you several times today."

"Really? She never acts like she needs anything. Sharon, I owe you an apology. And, it appears, a huge debt of gratitude."

"You owe me nothing. Your daughter gave me the one thing I've always wanted, and I want to repay her by helping her get back the only thing she really wants—you."

"Maybe I'd better get back to her now," Catherine said.

"I'm going to stop by the nursery. Why don't you come with me?"

The two women walked back toward the glass room that housed the city's newest tenants. Several people, some alone, others in small family clusters, gathered around the windows, all trying to take a peek at their own little arrivals. Fifteen feet from the nursery, Catherine stopped and turned to Sharon.

"No. I can't," she said softly, as she turned and walked back down the hall to join her daughter.

Sharon continued to the nursery and pressed her face up against the window. She scanned the rows of isolettes in front of her, looking for baby Weiss, soon to be Carlson, among all the pink and blue bundles. She couldn't find him in the group in front of her so she turned the corner and peered through the second glass wall. There he was, asleep in the second row, surrounded by a virtual rainbow of colorful faces, all peeking out from tiny knit caps. She watched as the nurses went about their duties—feeding, changing, soothing—doing whatever was needed to make the newborns' welcome to the world less traumatic.

Sharon stood for several moments, staring in wonder at all the little babies. They came into this world the same way, each exotic seedling waiting for the care and nurturing he or she needed to blossom. And no matter what variation of bloom, they all required the same the thing—loving attention. At that moment Sharon realized that even if she didn't know everything about the flower in her care, there were plenty of experts to help grow her little bud into adulthood.

She watched with wonder each breath he took, before breaking into laughter. John was never going to believe how much they now had in common.

Sharon arrived at St. Paul's shortly after five o'clock. John's doctors were in the middle of an examination, so Sharon decided to go down to the cafeteria and grab a cup of coffee until they finished.

She settled into her seat and pulled out the mail. She put aside the catalogs and began sorting through the letters, separating the junk mail into one pile, bills in another and personal correspondence in a third. She opened a note from Betsy at the club, who was writing to extend her warm wishes for John's full recovery, followed by an invitation to a thousand-dollar-a-plate political fundraiser, before she got to an envelope addressed to her in a cruelly familiar script. Sharon immediately recognized it from the letters she'd found in John's old briefcase a lifetime ago.

Her immediate reflex was to tear the letter in two. She had no desire to read anything this woman had to say, but curiosity gnawed away her disdain and she ripped open the seal and pulled out two sheets of paper.

"'Mrs. Carlson,'" she began reading in a low voice shaky with emotion. "'I thought you should see this. I hope it will answer some of your questions and help you understand that John loves you. And as soon as he's able, I know he'll tell you just how much. Melanie Hitts.'"

Sharon took a deep breath and slowly moved the second sheet to the forefront, and was greeted by a photocopy of John's last letter to Melanie. Once again she dropped her hands to her lap. Did she really want to put herself through this? As much as she ranted to Gwen about wanting to know the details of John's relationship with this woman, would ignorance prove to be more blissful at this point? No, she decided, and began to read.

By the second paragraph, Sharon was in tears, caught up in a truth that both thrilled and upset her. She felt sad and envious because though it was now clear that Melanie and John had never been physical lovers, they had certainly shared an intimacy that in twenty-four years she and her husband had never achieved. Both of them had told the truth when they stated, "It's not what you think." They were right. Their relationship was so much less, but still so much more.

But even this realization could not squelch the joyful news that John's letter delivered. It was she who he truly loved and desired. And not only did he love her, he wanted to start their marriage anew, which was her exact wish. Sharon realized that they had no choice but to begin afresh because nothing was the same. She was a different person and John had obviously been altered by this experience as well. And now they had a child to think about because John would have to accept her with the baby, if he truly wanted her back.

Sharon realized that despite their common wishes, they still had a lot to work out and success was not assured. Trust was going to be a crucial issue for her—both trusting John and her new sense of self. But they still had intact a solid base of mutual love and, most importantly, hope. And after living so long with John, she knew what every successful architect did—a strong foundation was the key to building a lasting structure.

Sharon quickly gathered her things and practically skipped back to John's room. In the corridor she ran into the doctor, who reported that John was making steady progress and was continuing to respond to stimulation. The news only compounded the authentic happiness that had been building since this morning. First the birth of a son, Amanda's reconciliation with her mother, Melanie Hitts's special delivery gift, and now John was showing signs of regaining consciousness.

She hurried to John's bedside and kissed his lips for only the second time since he'd been admitted. "I love you too," she said, and laid her head on his chest, wanting so badly to be close to him again. It had been so long. Too long. A lifetime of pain and progress had passed between them since they'd last spoken.

Sharon wiped her tears and made herself comfortable in the chair by his bed. She quickly filled him in on everything that had transpired since his accident, from her self-revelations to her decision not to sell the house and culminating with the news of the birth of their biracial son.

"At first I didn't think I'd be able to love a baby who wasn't . . . well, like me, but once I looked into his sweet little face I couldn't feel anything but love," she told him. "It really is simple, isn't it? You just have to close your eyes to the meaningless outer costume, open your heart, and just allow yourself to love. But I guess you learned the same thing with Melanie, which is actually a good thing if we're going to be that little guy's parents," Sharon said, aware of an uncomfortable tingle of jealousy the mention of Melanie Hitts's name caused. It was obvious that Sharon had a lot of unresolved feelings to work through, and it was going to take time before she could get over the idea that her husband loved another woman.

As expected, John had no response, but Sharon continued to talk on excitedly.

"The only thing is I still don't know what to call him," she said, pulling from her bag a copy of the *World's Best Baby Names*. "I thought about naming him after my father, but he's going to have enough to deal with without being stuck with a name like Ernest. I was considering Craig Arthur, which Amanda really likes, but now that I see him, I don't think he looks like a Craig."

Sharon opened the book and silently searched through possible names, every now and then calling out a moniker she thought might work. She'd gotten through most of the *G*'s when she thought she heard John stir. Sharon looked up, but nothing had changed, so she went back to her book and resumed her search.

"Parker," John's weak voice wobbled across the bed. Hearing her maiden name, Sharon shot up and rushed to his side. "Parker John Carlson," he whispered as she joyfully collapsed on his chest. Sharon had her husband, her child, and a whole new attitude. And for the first time in her life, she felt genuine happiness radiate through her body like sunshine and plant flowers in her heart.

# Chapter 30

**W**ill was fifteen minutes late for his noon lunch with Griffin. The restaurant's cool artificial air rushed in to rescue his grateful skin, overheated by the blistering Las Vegas heat. Apparently Griffin was running behind schedule as well, so Will allowed himself to be seated and ordered a glass of iced tea for the wait.

He felt indebted to his friend for planning this weekend getaway. With three days off from work, Griffin suggested that they get together to do a little gambling, play a little golf, and drown their respective sorrows. Will was only too happy to oblige, hoping this change of scenery would allow him at least one day without thoughts of Melanie running through his head. Trying to keep Mel out of his mind had become a full-time job. He'd held true to his promise to avoid her, which hadn't been easy, knowing how the same treatment had affected him. It hurt him to hurt her, regardless of the grief she'd inflicted.

Will glanced at his watch again. It was twelve-thirty and still no Griff. Perhaps his flight from LA was late. He finished his drink and, still thirsty, turned around to find his waiter. On cue, the man approached carrying another drink, and a plate covered with a silver dome.

"Thanks, man, but I didn't order anything yet."

"It's on the house, sir," the waiter explained as he left the plate and walked away, smiling.

Will lifted the cover and found plenty to whet his appetite. In bronze-colored lipstick he'd wiped from his lips many times were words that caused his heart to jump and his stomach to clog with bustling butterflies: WILL YOU MARRY ME? He took a moment to digest this romantic appetizer before standing up to search the room for the face he loved.

"You once told me that an empty plate was a prelude to a heapin' spoonful of homemade love," a known voice stated. Will turned to find Melanie standing on the other side of the table. She looked incredibly refreshing in a white matte jersey dress that breezed her body with reverent allure. Her silky brown skin glistened under the light, and her trademark spray of bronze curls were pushed off her lovely face by a white crystal headband. She couldn't have looked more like a bride had she been wearing a veil and carrying a bouquet of flowers.

Will sat back down in his chair, his gaze never leaving hers. Melanie's eyes searched his for some clue to his emotions. Gratefully she saw what she needed in order to continue—behind the shock and desperate vulnerability, love still shone.

"So I take it Griffin isn't coming," Will commented, his voice as unsteady as his nerves.

"No. Actually, he helped me set all of this up. We figured if you knew that I was coming, you wouldn't."

"That has a sneaky and familiar ring to it," Will said, remembering how he had ambushed her at Griffin's play.

"It should."

"Why are you here?"

"I thought that was obvious," Melanie said, gesturing to the dish in front of him.

"And I thought I'd said everything I had to in my last e-mail," Will said tersely, trying to maintain a hard-line attitude in order to protect his fragile emotions.

"Will you please just listen to me?" Melanie would not be deterred by Will's understandable resistance.

"There's nothing you can say to change the fact that if you love this John Carlson you can't possibly love me, at least not the way a wife should love her husband."

"I do love John, but I'm not *in* love with him. Not the way I'm so deeply in love with you. He's my friend, but you're my life." Will sat in stony silence as Melanie took the time to calmly explain the relationship she and John shared, both before Sharon's discovery and in its present state. She was very clear and honest about her feelings for the man and his for her, not wanting there to be anything left for Will to misinterpret.

"When we were in the boat on the Potomac, you said that you had nothing but thanks for John if he made me realize that it's you I wanted. Well, if it wasn't for him, I wouldn't be here right now begging you to marry me.

"Baby, so much of what happened before was because I was afraid that I couldn't be married and still be myself. I don't feel like that anymore. I'm confident now that I can be a world-class interior designer, astronaut, professional skier, pop singer, *and* your loving wife," Melanie said, smiling, as she tried to replace some of the heaviness with a little playful banter.

"I don't know about that professional skier thing," Will said, feeling his resolve threatening to melt under the warmth of her infectious smile. Melanie continued, her courage bolstered by Will's momentary thaw.

"I love you, William Gregory Freedman," she said, her tone once again turning serious. Melanie reached for Will's hand and intertwined her fingers with his, her eyes begging for understanding and forgiveness.

Will wanted so much to give in to those intriguing brown eyes and accept her proposal, but how could he be sure that this was not simply another prelude to some new issue that would pop up to crush him once again?

"Melanie, you have to know how much I love hearing this, but it's too late," he told her, trying to ignore the unbounded love in her eyes.

Will's refusal squeezed the air out of her body, and she felt her heart compress itself into a construction-paper cutout. The couple sat in sticky, uncomfortable silence, neither knowing what to say, nor understanding how such a great love had come to this very sad conclusion.

"Okay, then I guess this is good-bye," she said as the screech of her chair across the tile echoed through the room. Mel looked into his eyes one last time, her tears falling with every blink. She leaned over and kissed his lips before turning away to leave. Will watched her pause and quickly return to the table to once again hand over her engagement ring.

"I just want you to ask yourself one question," she told him. "What did I do that was wrong? I didn't cheat on you. I simply allowed myself to get close to a man who made me understand how to value and honor my desires to create a life *I* want—a life that revolves around *you*. What was so awful about that?"

"It should have been *me* who taught you that. *I'm* supposed to be the one."

"Oh, Will, what does it matter who does the teaching, as long as the lesson is learned?" Melanie asked with soft exasperation before she turned and hurried toward the ladies' room.

Will sat at the table stunned, asking himself the question she'd posed. What had Melanie really done wrong? Was his ego so fragile that he couldn't make room for other people in her life? He definitely didn't understand this wild tangle of emotions and he still had problems with the idea that Mel loved another man, but the one true thing he was certain of was that despite everything, he could not imagine his future without her.

*What am I doing? Here I am in the gambling capital of the world. Don't be a punk. Why not roll the dice and take a chance?*

Will glanced down at the plate sitting before him and suddenly felt very lucky. Melanie had not come out of the ladies' room, so if he acted fast, there might be time to catch her. Out of his peripheral vision movement caught his eye. He looked over at the table next to him and noticed a woman putting on lipstick. He reached into his pocket, pulled out a twenty-dollar bill, and offered to buy the tube. Thirty seconds later, he dropped another five on the table to pay for his iced tea, picked up the plate, and hurried after his woman.

He positioned himself outside the bathroom so that Melanie would see him when she turned the corner. He stood for several moments, holding his breath, when he heard the door open and the click of high heels on the bare tile floors. Melanie looked up to see a hopeful Will holding the dinner plate with a bright orange YES! scripted under her proposal. Their eyes met and their broad smiles connected.

"Well, then, let's go," she said, her demeanor brightening considerably as she gulped down a breath of relief and sent a thank-you up to the heavens.

"Right now?"

"Absolutely. I'm not letting you get away from me again. I've wasted enough time being a Hitts when I could have been your Mrs.," she said.

"Is there something I need to know?"

"Well, expecting good things, I reserved the Candlelight Wedding Chapel, located in the heart of the famous Las Vegas strip." Melanie laughed as she quoted the brochure. "Our wedding is at three, so we have to leave immediately to get a license."

After a quick trip to the marriage license bureau to flash their ID, pay the required fee, and sign some papers, they arrived at the chapel shortly before 2:35. Griffin was waiting for them with Will's suit, as was Mel's sister Francesca. While Will quickly changed and the minister lit the candles, Franti helped her sister touch up her makeup before handing Mclanie the red rose bouquet that came as part of their wedding package.

"Mom may get over this, but I don't know if Eva will ever forgive you for cheating her out of being a flower girl," Francesca teased as the two stood at the back of the chapel. "I'm so happy for you, Melanie. This is such the right thing for you."

Promptly at three, Pachelbel's Canon floated through the speakers hidden between the cascading silk ivy planted in the ceiling rafters. Melanie followed Francesca up the aisle, barely noticing the two large sprays of artificial flowers standing sentinel on either side of the altar. Her eyes were fixated on the handsome man who in minutes was to become her life companion. Any wedding jitters that had consumed her at their engagement party were gone, replaced by the solid knowledge that everything that had happened this past year had led her to *this* particular place at *this* particular time.

As Will watched his bride approach, tears of joy streamed freely down his cheeks. A wonderful peacefulness had replaced his earlier apprehensions. Thank God his love had overruled his ego, because only in this woman's eyes did he find home.

Melanie stopped next to a pedestal topped with a lit candelabra and stood happily by her man. Bathed in the buttery glow of candlelight, they pledged to forsake all others and love and honor each other until death do them part. In less than ten minutes, they had exchanged the matching platinum bands selected by Melanie and delivered by their witnesses, were proclaimed "man and wife," and Will gleefully kissed his bride.

Following the ceremony, the couple posed with their witnesses for wedding photos and Griffin substituted the traditional champagne toast with a short and sweet romantic poem, happy that love had worked out for his friends at least. The wonder of his words filled the ears of his small audience with melodic fantasies, and the silent consensus was that this was a wedding that had been sanctioned from above.

"Well, my darling husband. We have to scoot," Melanie said, positively glowing as she wiped a bit of wedding cake frosting from his chin.

"Already the Mrs. is ordering me around," Will said, teasing her. "So where exactly are you taking me now?"

"We have a honeymoon to get to," she said, biting her bottom lip and winking with erotic promise.

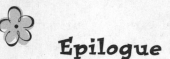

# Epilogue

**M**elanie pushed the button near the bed and watched the sunlight slowly spill into the room of their hotel suite. She glanced over at Will, grateful that the mechanical grind of the rising wooden shutter did not wake him. She pulled on the thick white terry-cloth robe emblazoned on the chest pocket with HOTEL DANIELI, and slipped through the terrace doors and out into yet another fabulous Venetian morning.

She took in a deep breath and hugged herself as she took in the view. No matter how many times she'd seen this same slice of heaven these past four days, at morning's first glimpse the sight still took her breath away. She looked directly out across the Grand Canal at the white domed roof of the Palladian church of Santa Maria della Salute and the terra-cotta tile rooftops of the surrounding buildings. Water taxis and gondolas lined the liquid boulevard, their drivers chatting in expressive Italian while the number 82 *vaporetto,* the Venetian equivalent of a city bus, pulled into its floating stop. Down below, vendors were setting up shop, preparing for the thousands of international visitors who would buy their cheap glass trinkets, papier-mâché masks, and other souvenirs. Dispersed in between the merchants were street artists whose similarly beautiful renditions of the city's numerous canals, churches, bridges, and gondolas made it nearly impossible to choose.

Melanie loved the quiet serenity of early morning and had made a point of starting each day with a few solitary moments in quiet gratitude. Standing witness to such magnificence, both man-made and Divine, she felt radiantly happy and thoroughly blessed. Venice was definitely a city for lovers and Melanie felt right at home.

She turned away from the window to gaze upon her new husband. She was finally married to the man she adored, and in so many ways she had John Carlson to thank. Still, arriving at this state of bliss had not come without pain. The strong feelings she and John shared for each other had hurt the two people they both loved more than anything in this world and she was genuinely sorry about that, but theirs was a relationship she would cherish forever. John's love and insight had saved her from making the biggest mistake of her life.

Mel turned back to the splendor of Venice as her thoughts shifted to the future. Would she allow herself to give and receive love from another man now that she was a wife? Or even more importantly, how would she react if Will happened upon another emotionally intimate soulmate? Would she be understanding and accepting of their friendship or would she find herself threatened? Mel genuinely hoped that after her experience true love, and not the fear of loss or insecurity that dictated most marriages, would rule her heart and relationship, but she truly had no idea how she would react.

"A bridge to cross at some other time," she whispered under her breath as she dismissed the could-be's and maybe's from her mind. The ups and downs of the recent past quickly dissipated into the cool Italian air, replaced by the excitement of the pure potentiality of her future. She certainly hoped that John and Sharon would find their way back to each other and view their years ahead with the same kind of magical anticipation. And maybe, once tempers cooled and grudges melted, she and Candace could eventually get their friendship back on track.

Melanie walked back into the room and woke Will with a sweet sprinkle of kisses. "Wake up, sleepyhead. Venice awaits."

"It's waited this long. It can wait a while longer," Will declared as he hungrily pulled his wife back between the sheets.

If you'd like to learn more about the Box Project or are interested in becoming a mentor contact the following organizations:

**The Box Project Inc.**
P.O. Box 435
87 East Street
Plainville, CT 06062
1-800-268-9928
www.boxproject.org

**America's Promise—The Alliance for Youth**
909 N. Washington Street
Suite 400
Alexandria, VA 22314
703-684-4500
www.americaspromise.org

**Big Brothers Big Sisters of America**
To find a local chapter near you visit their website at www.bbbsa.org.

# Fiction with Attitude...

The best new African-American writers from 🜂AVON TRADE.

*because every great bag deserves a great book!*

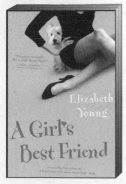